DENISE
ROBERTSON

The Bad Sister

This edition published in the United Kingdom in 2005 by Little Books Ltd,
48 Catherine Place, London SW1E 6HL

A CIP catalogue record for this book is available from
the British Library.

ISBN: 1 904435 42 4

Cover painting by Nguyen Thanh Binh,
courtesy of Durlacher Fine Art, London.

Printed and bound in Great Britain by Bookmarque Ltd, Croydon

Known to millions as the agony aunt from ITV's *This Morning* programme, Denise Robertson has worked extensively on television and radio and as a national newspaper journalist. Beginning with *The Land of Lost Content* in 1984, which won the Constable Trophy for Fiction, she has published eighteen successful novels. She lives near Sunderland with her husband and an assortment of dogs.

Also by Denise Robertson
The Beloved People trilogy:

The Beloved People
Strength for the Morning
Towards Jerusalem

BOOK ONE

Ard-na-shiel
1991

1

August 1991

I could smell her in the room: soap and something a little antiseptic. That was my sister, Sara's, smell and yet there was a huge bottle of Patou's 'Joy' on the dressing-table. I lifted it and sprayed myself liberally. If she hadn't the sense to use it, I had!

Her suede jacket was at the back of the wardrobe and I pulled it from the hanger. I'd made my first raid last night, when she was on duty, so the best was already gone and on my back. Still, no sense in missing a last chance. Even at eight in the morning her bed was already made, neat with hospital corners. For a moment I contemplated tearing it apart until it resembled the rat's nest I had left behind, but what was the point? She'd only smile one of her saintly smiles and make it up again in seconds. That was the trouble with Sara: she would never, ever retaliate.

I stood for a moment, the familiar guilt sweeping over me, then I hung the jacket back in the wardrobe. I waited on the landing until Nella, my mother, began to howl for me to come down. I always kept them waiting, to let them know I was my own boss. Just as they always ganged up on me, more like sisters than the mother and daughter they actually were. That was how it had always been. Nella and Sara, heads together, making plans, taking decisions, laughing together and, worst of all, exchanging glances that established total communion between them and shut me out.

I was two when I noticed it, five when I began to mind. There were only years between us but it might as well have been a century. From time to time I'd plan Sara's death; nothing lingering or painful – just terminal. And there were other times when all I wanted was to be near her, to have her like me. Like the times when Nella's latest would threaten to leave and I'd think it was the end of the world. Sara would let me share her bed then and tell me everything would be alright in the morning, which it usually was. And I would go to sleep cuddled into her and feel safe and warm and loved.

They were standing beside the car when I reached the street. It was a big black Jag and the man standing beside it was vaguely familiar.

'This is Giles,' Nella said. 'You remember Giles? It's so kind of him to offer you a lift.'

I grunted a kind of thank you without looking in his direction and turned my head away when Nella tried to kiss me goodbye. That didn't stop her. She kissed the air above my left cheek, and did it again on my right.

'You'll adore the journey! Scotland is ravishing! And a Jag – you lucky girl!'

Nella always talked in exclamation marks. She still does.

Sara moved in on me then and I flopped into the passenger seat to avoid her. Normally, I'd have allowed her a peck on the cheek, but I wasn't going to give an inch today so she contented herself with saying 'Take care of the dresses' and slamming the car door. I wanted her to know I was huffed with her. Besides, I had her best shirt on under my jacket, and her thin gold chain – the one she got when she was confirmed – around my neck so it was best not to come too close.

Not that she wore either of them much. All the same, we didn't want a scene on the doorstep – not in front of a stranger. Except that, with Sara, there wouldn't be a scene. She would wince a little at the sight of yet another possession purloined and then she would smile that lovely, tolerant smile that made me long to get my fingers round her throat! I turned my face resolutely away from her and concentrated on not telling the driver to get his finger out and move! After all, he wasn't to blame for anything, poor sod. Don't get me wrong; I'd endure the rack for my mother and my sister – family and all that. But that doesn't mean I have to *like* them, does it?

Normally, with such a posh car, I'd have given the neighbours the full works, even a royal wave. Today, however, I held my jacket closed and stared rigidly ahead as Nella poured gratitude over Giles, who couldn't take his eyes off her face as he put in the clutch and moved out into the traffic. I didn't need to look back to know my mother and my sister would be standing there, arm in arm, waving goodbye to me, the fly in the ointment, before they scampered back into the house.

'Fuck you,' I said under my breath, and then repeated it just for good measure. It was such a forbidden word that it soothed me and I settled into my seat.

'Right,' Giles said as we moved out of Ladbroke Grove and headed towards the Edgware Road. 'We'll push on as far as we can before lunch, Alexandra, but yell if you want to stop for anything. A drink, anything. You know the drill.'

Nice but dim, I thought. *Ex-public school and the Guards and afraid of naming bodily functions.* Most of Nella's boyfriends fitted that mould, except for the times she went mad and took up with gangsters or bullfighters or movie moguls who chewed cigars. This one wore cavalry twills and a Pringle sweater and his shoes were old but handmade. Actually, his clothes were better than his profile, which was entirely Chinless Wonder.

I murmured thanks and snuggled down in my seat to contemplate the awfulness of my situation. I didn't tell him that I preferred to be called Lexy, because after today I would probably never see him again and I didn't intend to have much to do with him on the way to the Highlands. If it hadn't been for him and his bloody Jag, I might have been able to stay in Notting Hill.

I'd been through two of Nella's nuptials so I knew exactly what the run-up to a wedding entailed. Excitement, excitement, excitement, and lashings of G&Ts. Instead, I was being sent up to the wilds of Scotland to be marooned in the castle of the bride-groom-to-be, deserted except for cattle and ancient retainers, no doubt. And I didn't even care much for Jamie. It was bloody unfair but it was also the way things were usually done in my family: Nella and Sara twined round each other and me banished as though I didn't belong.

My mother is Prunella Morgan. Unless you're a movie buff that won't mean much, but she was once a starlet and lost a role as a Bond girl by the skin of her teeth. She's been married four times: once to Sara's father, who was a famous gynaecologist but is now a drunk; once to a rich American who mysteriously became poor when the word 'alimony' was mentioned. Afterwards, she married my father, who might have been a fine actor, so they tell me, if he hadn't gone to Hollywood. He'd played her boyfriend in a Hammer horror movie; it was 1975 and they were both sure they were on their way to fame and fortune. It didn't turn out like that. Lastly, she wed good old George. God bless good old George – the only man who ever kept his promises.

Nella called the house we lived in 'quaint', but it was quite grotty, really, and full of the smell of spices from the curry house around the corner. Sara, who was always a swot, was a houseman at Bart's – or at least she would be until her marriage to Jamie Munro, who was fabulously rich and lorded it over half of Scotland if you believed everything Nella told anyone within earshot, which I did not.

'Why does she boast so much?' I once asked Sara.

She sighed and wrinkled her nose. 'She's had a lot of ups

and downs. I suppose it's insecurity. Anyway, it's best not to take any notice.'

That was Sara, always reasonable, always making excuses for people. Which only made me hate her more, because she was so good she made me realize how bad – how utterly vile and inadequate – I was. I suppose the nub of the problem was really that Sara was born beautiful and I was not. Also, she was a perfect size ten and I – well, one of Nella's friends once called me 'pleasantly plump', which is about as yucky as you can get. Also I have a big nose. It's a nice shape but it is definitely large. Sara's nose is Grace Kelly; so is the rest of her face, so you can see what I was up against. Neither of us had much in the way of wardrobe; Nella is to money what chancellors are to tax rebates. But Sara could throw on a shirt and sweater and look straight out of *Vogue*. It's a gift, that ability to look good no matter what. And I don't have it.

If Nella was short of money she was never short of admirers. At fifty-one she was still blonde, beautiful and could slip into a size eight without undoing zips. Sara is not only beautiful; she's noble, especially in her white coat with a stethoscope hanging from her neck. I expect that's why Jamie fell in love with her, when he was whisked into casualty with a dislocated kneecap and there she was, all cool fingers and coal-tar soap. Me, I like a good old squirt of Nella's 'Femme' if she leaves it lying around, but Sara is not into pampering, which made her landing a very rich man positively obscene and a dreadful waste.

The first time I saw Jamie I took him for a merchant banker or a Harley Street consultant. Saville Row suit, divine handmade shoes and a grave expression. Of course he was only trying to make an impression on his soon-to-be in-laws. I could tell that because his Adam's apple was bobbing all over the place! In fact he was a Scottish landowner who once trekked halfway across the tundra for charity. Which seems bizarre to me because he was rich enough to write a cheque and stay comfortably at home, which is what I'd do, given the chance. He *was* handsome, I have to admit that, but a bit too correct for my taste. I like at least a hint of wildness about the eyes – that or a facial scar somewhere. An unexplained scar... that is seriously cool.

I didn't begrudge Sara the money. Or Jamie, for that matter, because he was enormously intellectual and deeply into poetry and serious music. When I got married, I wanted a man who collected Harley Davidsons and hired jets on a whim – not someone who took care of his tenants and was descended from an ancient Scottish king, which may have thrilled Nella but did nothing for me.

All in all, I wasn't looking forward to a week with Jamie in a house above a loch. Nella kept calling it a 'castle', but Sara said it was just a very nice, stone-built house with breathtaking views of Loch Linnhe. I had warned them that I might easily go mad with boredom and throw myself from a turret but they were adamant. The wedding dress could not be risked on the train, a man called Giles had offered to transport it in his Jag as he went up to Fort William, and I must go with it to 'keep it safe'.

'Besides,' my mother had said in her 'Let's be practical' voice. 'It costs the earth to get up there by train. I'd go up with Giles myself if I could be spared, just to save money.'

I had offered to travel in standard class, stowaway in the guard's van, even run behind if I could wait and come up with them, but here I was in the Bentley with a whole week of boredom ahead of me. I am not a country-lover. I am a city woman to my fingertips and could easily end up climbing the walls at Ard-na-Shiel – but did they care?

Once she was married, Sara would be five hundred miles away from Nella but I would be away, too: back at school in North

Yorkshire, trying to study for A-levels in subjects that didn't interest me in the slightest. So, one way or another, I had little to be glad about that day we set out for Scotland – not even the rare prospect of a brand-new dress because I had no intention of being seen anywhere outside a church in white watered silk. As for the tartan sash, it didn't bear contemplation. I shrank down in my seat, closed my eyes and tried not to think of London fading away behind me.

At first I was bored. I know the suburbs of London by heart. We had lived in most of them, as Nella carted us from one house to another. But once the city was left behind, I began to enjoy the harvested fields with their golden stubble, the green meadows speckled with cows or sheep and the occasional glimpse of village spires. England is a pretty good place, or so it seemed to me that day.

We ate lunch near Carlisle, a very good lunch in a raftered pub Giles obviously knew well. He allowed me as much wine as I wanted and reminisced about Nella in her heyday. All I had to do was widen my eyes in appreciation as I ate my way through three courses, coffee and mints. 'So she danced every dance with you – *only* you! Amazing!' 'She let you keep her race card? Fancy that!' I kept on nodding amazement until he stopped for breath.

After lunch we drove on, but after a mile or two the engine began to cough. 'Hell's teeth,' Giles said and limped the car into the next garage. It was something called the solenoid, which would take ages to replace. Yet Giles was not wearing a Guard's tie for nothing; within minutes he had organized a battered Ford to whisk us off to a hotel, and we spent the afternoon drinking gin and tonics and swopping stories of the bloodiness of life. I decided I had misjudged Giles and kissed his cheek when word came that the Jag was repaired.

'Steady on, old girl,' he said, but he was pleased. I could hear it in his voice.

Once back in the car, I pretended to fall asleep – except that I felt a bit woozy with drink and somewhere around the border there was no more need to pretend. When I woke, it was dark and we were in the Highlands. I could see the tops of mountains against the night sky, and, as the road twisted and turned, the feathered outlines of fir trees swayed in the wind. The moon was a pale orb straddled with thin bands of clouds. It lent an eerie blue edge to the mountains until a cloud obscured it and a chill passed over me – even though it was warm in the car and the sound of the wind fell only faintly on my ear. At that moment I felt a tiny quiver of excitement. Perhaps a week in a Highland fortress wouldn't be so bad, after all. This was different ground: dangerous territory where anyone and anything could be hiding.

We drove over a moonlit moor that might have been haunted and entered a dark valley. 'Glencoe,' Giles said, in tones of doom. I knew the legend of Glencoe: the peaceful villagers wiped out by the treachery of the wicked Campbells. In the darkness it seemed perfectly possible that they might descend the slopes to massacre innocents once more. There were rocks here and there that might have been crouching Highlanders, and they cast long shadows that changed shape as we drove past. And then a cluster of lights dispelled the darkness and we rattled across a bridge.

'Ballachulish,' Giles offered. 'We're almost there. If your mama got it right, it's two miles on.'

I could see the loch gleaming on my left. To the right was a wooded slope, dark and forbidding. And all of a sudden I remembered drama lessons at school. 'Here be witches,' I murmured under my breath as Giles changed gear and the car slowed. The moon went behind a cloud then and I shivered. 'It should be about here,' I heard Giles say, and the next moment we had passed through massive stone pillars and the roadway was climbing, marked by white stones that caught the headlights and drew us on. We travelled for what seemed an age, then suddenly the moon came out again and there, ahead of me, was Ard-na-Shiel. Light reflected from a thousand windows, and the roof, silhouetted against the night sky, was studded with turrets and towers.

'Well,' Giles said, as he drew up at the dark portico. 'I might have known, with your mother, it would be straight out of the Brothers Grimm.'

As if on cue, the massive door opened and Jamie emerged, holding back a young black Labrador. Behind him waddled an elderly grey-and-black spaniel. I wound down the window and called 'Hello!' causing the young dog to go into a frenzy of greeting.

'You're here,' Jamie said, in what sounded like relieved tones. 'You've had a long journey.'

He was moving to the driver's side, still holding on to the dog, and I saw that he was wearing the kilt. I had only seen him in London, sober-suited or dressed for sport. Now, with the wind sighing in the treetops and the car's headlights carving a path through the darkness, he looked younger and much more romantic. His face was dark, almost hawk-like, but the mouth and eyes were kind. He looked Iranian or Italian... something dishy. And the set of the kilt as he swung around to lead me in was positively thrilling. I felt a strange sensation in my mouth, a dryness and a shortage of breath, and then Jamie was handing me out of the car as though I were visiting royalty.

'You'll come in for a dram?' he asked, but Giles shook his head and muttered about the car breaking down and the need to press on to Fort William. He was obviously relieved to be seeing the back of me and the dresses and the various boxes and bags with which his precious car was crammed.

An elderly retainer appeared and puffed in and out with the baggage as I held out my hand to Giles and said my prettiest thank you. I hadn't exactly been a sparkling travelling companion but I'd been charm itself at Carlisle, so he needn't have looked quite so pleased to be rid of me. I gave him the look of pure reproach I had often seen Nella use to great effect, but he just said 'Cheerio' and folded himself back into the car.

We stood as it crunched over the gravel, turned and began to descend towards the road.

'Now,' Jamie said, turning as the car was lost to view, 'Let's get you inside. What do you want first, board or bed?'

What I wanted was to explore this house from stem to stern, so I opted for food, although I wasn't hungry. Time enough for bed later.

We moved through a hall hung with mournful deer and even more mournful ancestors and into a room where a fire crackled, flanked by worn armchairs. That's the thing about having money: you can afford to be shabby. When you're poor you have to keep up appearances. Nella was forever fretting over something threadbare; 'new money' minds terribly.

'Sara's fine,' I said as we settled ourselves. 'She sends her love.'

'I know. We've just spoken on the telephone.'

He said it mildly enough but I felt a familiar rage stir within me. Whatever I did, whatever I said, she was there ahead of me. So she'd rung him or he'd rung her. No doubt they'd have discussed me and she would have commiserated with him about having to put up with me, and he'd have agreed it was a chore but he'd put up with anything if she asked him. I felt the devil within me and, as usual, it had to get out.

'I didn't want to come,' I said in my loftiest tone. 'Still, what I want doesn't count.' I expected him to huff a bit, but he just smiled and stirred the fire with the toe of his brogue. His knees were huge and bony but brown between kilt and knee-socks and I felt a little shiver as a log fell, sending up sparks.

'I'm sorry you didn't want to come,' he said at last. 'The wedding will be a whirl and then we'll be off for the honeymoon and I really wanted to show you some of the Highlands before all that. They say when you've seen them you have to come back, and I want you to do that.'

'Because Sara will be lonely, I suppose.'

I said it as ungraciously as I could because I didn't want him to see I was pleased.

'No.' Again his reply came after an interval for thought. 'I rather like you and I'd like you to like Ard-na-Shiel and feel at home here.'

'It should have been Sara who came first,' I said, as belligerently as I could. 'But she'll be being pampered, I expect, having face-lifts and things.'

He laughed out loud then, throwing back his head to roar. His throat was brown and smooth but muscly under the skin and his teeth were white and even. Why had I never realized before that he was so gorgeous?

'It's not funny!' I said huffily and at once he was contrite.

'It's not,' he said, 'but the idea of your sister wanting – or *needing* – a face-lift... A facial, perhaps.'

Of course I'd meant facials, but he needn't have rubbed it in.

I was glad that the aged retainer appeared with the food then because I wasn't sure what to say next. Cold salmon, tomatoes, crusty bread, wonderful salty butter and a pot of homemade mayonnaise. I rediscovered my appetite and ate like a pig, especially as Jamie had produced an excellent bottle of wine and two unbelievably heavy and interesting glasses to drink it with.

'Do you?' he asked, holding the bottle aloft.

'Of course,' I said. 'I got completely stoned when we were

held up in Carlisle.' I knew it was the wrong thing to say – silly, childish, boasting – but to my relief he only smiled as he held out my glass. I sipped, found it good and took a huge gulp.

'How old is this house?'

My voice sounded strange as I asked the question, and for a wild moment I wondered if the wine had been drugged and this was all part of a plan to be rid of me once and for all.

'Three hundred years old,' Jamie said. 'Built in sixteen-ninety-two but some of it is even more ancient, back to the fifteen-hundreds.'

I tried to nod wisely, but the wine was taking its toll. I had become fascinated with his knees: his large, brown knees which seemed to glow in the firelight.

'I'll show you around tomorrow. There's a priest-hole in the east turret and a walled garden and some fairly spectacular views. Oh, and one of the turrets has a ghost: a long dead Anderson who threw herself from the ramparts for love of a Munro.'

I could feel my eyelids drooping as he spoke and I closed them momentarily on a picture of a maiden dying for love. The romance was spoiled by a sudden vision of Sara in a Persil-white coat advancing on the corpse and ordering it to rise and walk. She would not tolerate a ghost, but I could and would, given half a chance.

'Why are you getting married here?' I asked, feeling foolish because I knew the answer: Nella was broke and a wedding up here would be cheaper than in London. Again Jamie took an age to answer and I liked him for it. Usually people answered my questions with a swift put-down. This man treated them with respect.

'I think Sara knows how much Ard-na-Shiel means to me. And a Highland wedding is quite an event – pipers and all!'

'*A hundred pipers an' a*', I suppose?'

I was definitely tipsy now. The fire was a rosy haze and the man opposite me a composite of Patrick Swayze and Tom Cruise.

'Not a hundred.' He was smiling but not an indulgent, humouring smile. This was a confiding smile, drawing me in. 'Three, maybe. But they'll make a mighty noise.'

Suddenly I wanted to tell him everything. How unfair life was. How Sara was always before me and everyone preferred her and I couldn't even hate her because she was seriously nice. How her father was really quite ugly but she had turned out beautiful, while my father looked like Robert Redford and I was as plain as a pikestaff. I could feel the words bubbling to the surface and I knew it would be dire if I uttered them. Knew, too, that I could no more stop them than stop time in its tracks.

Again it was Jamie who saved me.

'You're tired,' he said. 'And we've a full day ahead.'

He stood above me, holding out a hand. When I extended mine he hauled me gently to my feet and tucked my arm through his.

'Come on,' he said. 'We need you fresh for the morrow morn.'

He said it in a heavy Scots accent, completely unlike his usual public school English and I smiled my appreciation as we mounted the wide staircase together, dogs behind, past the dead lords of Ard-na-Shiel and their partners. Their eyes followed us as we paused on the landing to look down into the hall below.

'There was a gathering here to support the Young Pretender,' Jamie said, 'brave men but foolish. Few of them lived to tell the tale. That's my father, there: the portrait at the foot of the stairs. He died when I was three, on a climbing expedition in the Himalayas.'

I thought that, too, was a foolish waste of a life but I kept my mouth shut.

And then we were in a room filled with the scent of beeswax and lavender. My bags stood on the top of an ottoman at the foot of the bed and the hated bridesmaid dress, shrouded in cellophane, hung on the wardrobe door. It looked quite reasonable, just hanging there. Once on, it made me look like a choirboy – a Puritan choirboy. Sara's dress was the same. Nella called it 'sleek'. I called it boring.

'I've put some books by your bed, and a radio,' Jamie said. 'The bathroom is across the corridor. Shout if you need something.'

I smiled up at him and glanced longingly at the high bed to cover my confusion. How did you say goodnight to a future brother-in-law?

As if he read my thoughts he put his hands on my shoulders and bent to kiss my brow. 'Goodnight, Lexy. Sleep well. We're going to be great friends, you and I.' And then he was gone, closing the door behind him.

I stood for a moment, a foolish smile on my face, the place where he had kissed me feeling at once ticklish and exalted. A moment ago all I had wanted was to lie down and close my eyes. Now I didn't know *what* I wanted. And why had he smiled so much of the time, almost as though he was trying not to give way to laughter?

I moved towards a window, hidden behind heavy brocade curtains. I tugged at them for a full minute before I realized they were operated by tasselled cords that hung either side. I pulled and they glided apart to reveal Loch Linnhe in all its splendour.

Lights gleamed on the other shore but they were outshone by the glory of the moon on the water. I leaned my forehead against the glass and peered down into the darkness below. I could see nothing at first, and then things slowly became visible. A high wall and a wrought-iron gate. The walled garden? There was a tree ablaze with some kind of blossom. Or was it silver-leaved? I gave up wondering and turned for bed.

I had five whole days to explore Ard-na-Shiel before Sara arrived to take it from me.

Tomorrow would be time enough.

2

I woke, or rather I surfaced, from a dream in which a man was making love to me although the enthusiasm was all mine. I was clinging, my mouth seeking his, our bodies merging and melting so that we were whirled as though in an eddy and rose and sank only to rise again, gasping for air. And in that moment of release I saw his face.

It was Jamie.

I lay still for a moment, at first relishing the dream and then squirming with embarrassment. Why should I dream about Jamie, the almost-married man and Sara's possession into the bargain? And then I remembered his face last night, lit by the firelight: lean and dark and infinitely desirable. And the knees: smooth and rounded and brown when they had entwined with mine as we made love. Except that that had been a dream, which made it all the more weird that I felt so strange now. Was this what sex did to you? Even in dreams? We talked about sex non-stop at school, but no one had mentioned dreams.

I was liberated from delicious if slightly uncomfortable speculation by the sound of a dog barking. I leapt from the bed and crossed to the window-seat. The Labrador was there below, leaping and bounding around Jamie as he set off towards the loch. Grey mist lingered on the surrounding hills, but there was blue sky above and I could see the loch in all its glory, a soft tide seeming to flow left to right, seabirds bobbing amid the waves, white houses scattered across the opposite shore, the mountains rising behind them, dark and heather-clad. The whole scene filled me with a longing to be out there, in the sunshine. I hurried to the bathroom Jamie had told me was mine and set about getting ready.

The bath was white and ancient and set on clawed feet. I turned on the hot tap but nothing happened. The cold tap gushed as soon as I touched it. I turned it off, contemplating which would be worse, a cold bath or body odour, when suddenly there was a loud noise and the hot tap began to shudder. It went on shuddering as the noise grew louder and a thin trickle of brown water came forth, accompanied by a small cloud of steam.

Five minutes later I was soaking up to my neck in red-hot water that smelled deliciously of pine from the crystals I had found by the soap dish. There was pine soap, too, and a velvety face-cloth, a real loofah and a neat little rubber cushion on which to rest your head. Life at Ard-na-Shiel was getting better by the minute – until I remembered that soon all this would be Sara's and the pleasure dwindled.

Over the years I had perfected several methods of killing my sister. Which was strange, really, because I liked it a lot when she made a fuss of me. Still, it wasn't fair that she was so far ahead of me. So capable, so perfect and always, always *there!* Pushing her into a loch had not occurred to me, but it did now. Perhaps there was a secret room in Ard-na-Shiel into which I could lure her. Soundproof, preferably, so that they could search for days and never find her while she starved to death. Jamie had mentioned a priest-hole; that would do. I resolved to search the house as soon as I got the chance and then tried to forget that I was doomed forever to be the other sister, just like Princess Margaret, who had never quite got over it. After all, I was here at Ard-na-Shiel with Jamie and Sara was not. Not yet.

In my fairer moments I could understand why Sara and Nella were so close. My mother had been twenty when she married Sara's father, who was twenty-five years her senior. Five years later, when she could no longer stand his drunken rages, she filed for divorce and discovered she was pregnant on the same day. When Sara arrived, Nella was down to her last penny and her by-now ex-husband was drying out in Cheltenham.

I suppose they survived on hand-outs and the odd acting job Nella could get if she had someone to look after Sara. I asked her about it once and she raised her eyebrows to indicate anguish. Nella has wonderful eyebrows: straight and thick and several shades darker than her hair, which is blonde like Sara's. Mine is brown and my eyebrows resemble small stoats – or they did until Sara showed me how to pluck them.

Anyway, I suppose they had to cling together, mother and child, until Erwin Chambers III came along. He was a cutlery king and generous with his cash. He sent Sara to expensive schools and lavished expensive presents on Nella – which was a good job because she had to flog them one by one when Erwin went off with a Las Vegas showgirl.

So Sara and my mother were on their own again. Sara was nine by then. I've seen a picture of her, solemn-faced and anxious as my mother married my father. I was born in the Portland Clinic on May 8, 1975, and my father went off to Hollywood to prepare for the rest of the family coming over.

Unknown English actors are ten a penny in Hollywood. We never made it to America, and the bill from the Portland joined the other bills behind the George IV carriage clock on the mantelpiece. It was only paid when Nella married for the fourth time. Like Elizabeth Taylor, she believed in serial monogamy.

George Gibbs was a kind-hearted Lancastrian who sent Sara to medical school and died on the day she became M.B.B.S. By that time we had spent most of his money, which wasn't as much as we'd thought, anyway. We all cried at his funeral and not just because we were back to bread and water. He was alright, was old George.

Somehow, thinking about money (or the lack of it) took the

charm out of the deepest bath in the western world. How would we manage once Sara went? There would be no sponging off Jamie, that was sure. Nella's code wasn't strictly kosher, but she had one. I dried myself on a bath towel the size of the Isle of Wight and resolved not to think about money until the wedding was over – pipers and all.

When I got back to my room, an elderly woman was hovering over a loaded tray.

'Now, thank goodness you've come,' she said. 'Dinna let your eggs go cold.'

Eggs in the plural! I smiled her out of the room and lifted the covers. Eggs, bacon, mushrooms, crisp fried bread, a huge sausage, orange juice, toast, jam in a silver dish and an Indian tree teapot in a knitted cosy. I carried it to the high bed, deciding that I'd died and gone to heaven!

Half an hour later, the tray was practically empty and I was too full for comfort. I dragged myself upright and went to my case, only to find it empty. Everything in it had been hung up and deposited in drawers that smelled of summer. I put on my best jeans (Sara's originally and now mine) and my one really luxurious possession: an Emmanuel shirt that was straight out of Byron.

'This is a dream,' I said aloud as I looked in the mirror. 'I only hope it lasts!'

Because I looked *good*. Ugly me with the square jaw and the bad hairline looked suddenly wide-eyed and almost beautiful. Was it a magic mirror or had coming to Ard-na-Shiel worked a miracle?

'At last!' Jamie said when I descended the stairs. By day the hall was less gloomy, the portraits less intimidating. Jamie wore jeans, too, and a faded denim shirt. He was jangling a set of car keys, the dogs sitting to attention, waiting his next move. 'I hope you slept well?'

I wanted to be chilly and live up to my reputation for being a problem child, but the truth would out. 'Like a log,' I said. 'And the breakfast was evil. I can hardly move.'

He was turning for the door. 'Just as well I brought the car round.'

The car was a dark-blue Merc. I'm knowledgeable about cars and this one had cost a bomb. Lucky Sara! I thought of her in the future, skimming the road to Glasgow or Edinburgh with a wallet full of plastic. It wasn't fair – but beyond the door the sun was shining. I couldn't be jealous today.

'Where are we going?' I asked, and fell in behind man and dogs.

Jamie gave me three choices. We could go north to Mallaig or south to Oban or anywhere else I might choose. 'We can eat somewhere,' he added. 'Or picnic. They've packed something just in case.'

In my whole life I had only picnicked three times and one of those was at Ascot, which doesn't count as a real picnic because you're too dressed up.

'A picnic, please. Somewhere – anywhere. You choose and can we take the dogs?'

'Dogs it is,' he said and handed me into the car.

We drove through hedgerows edged with rosebay willow-herb and a yellow flower I hadn't seen before.

'Common ragwort,' Jamie told me. 'We Scots call it "Stinking Billy", after the Duke of Cumberland. He defeated us at the Battle of Culloden.'

'So it smells?'

'Only if you crush it. You have to be careful to keep it out of the fields, though. If it's cut and dried with hay and fed to stock it's poisonous. Rots their livers.'

I had never thought of Jamie as anything other than rich and idle. Now he was talking like a farmer, someone who understood nature and the land. I peeped sideways at him. He was a bit like Sean Connery, and his hands, where they gripped the wheel, were brown and strong: the hands of a worker. But they had been gentle last night, when they held and caressed me.

I tried to remind myself that it had only been a dream but strange things were happening deep in my gut – odd things but not unwelcome. I closed my eyes, imagining it again. His mouth on mine, warm and sweet, opening, our tongues touching, exploring... I had snogged before but never made love with anyone, although I'd heard it described often enough – my school wasn't big on virgins. Now I felt so strange I had to clench my fists until my nails dug into my palms. He was already taken. Trust Sara to pick someone well-nigh perfect.

I turned back to the scenery then, anxious to take it all in while I had the chance, for I would never come back to Ard-na-Shiel – not to see Sara ensconced in splendour. I wouldn't give her that satisfaction.

We were passing through Glencoe, the mountains towering either side, bleak and scarred with fissures in the rock, and once more I thought of the legend of Glencoe, the Campbells sneaking down on the peaceful villagers and wiping them out for no greater sin than being MacDonalds.

'It happened at night,' Jamie said as though he read my thoughts. 'That's what was so shameful: that they murdered women and children in their beds. And after accepting MacDonald hospitality.'

His voice was doom-laden, as though the massacre had happened yesterday, and it was a relief to emerge onto Rannoch Moor and drive between lakes of bright water.

Jamie rattled off their names: Loch Ba, Lochan-na-Stainge, Loch Tulla. We sped through a village called Bridge of Orchy and turned onto a minor road.

'I'm taking you to my favourite place,' Jamie said. As if they'd heard him, the dogs rose from the back seat, Toby, the Labrador, resting a warm head on my shoulder. 'He knows we're almost there,' Jamie smiled, and there was something in his voice that said this was a special and familiar place. We drove along a single track edged with passing places until at last we could pull off the road and spill out of the car.

We picnicked by the Falls of Orchy, the sound of tumbling water around us. There were layers of rock to sit on or use as a table: rock warmed by the sun and seamed with heather and tiny rock-plants. The falls were deep in a basin of cliff and fir trees and there was no one passing on the road nearby. I closed my eyes as Jamie set out the food, hearing the drone of a bee somewhere, smelling the scents of grass and heather.

When I opened my eyes Jamie stood above me, holding a finger to his lips. He gestured down towards the water. It was a beautiful scene and I was about to say so when he shook his head and again gestured for silence. I looked at him, narrowing my eyes in question until he gently pulled me to my feet and turned me to my left.

'There,' he whispered in my ear. 'There, on the rock.'

I saw it then, alert and motionless on a ledge above the shallows, a long-legged, long-necked bird, its white head topped with a dark crest.

'It's a heron.'

Jamie's breath was warm on my ear and his hands stayed on my forearms. We stood together as the bird suddenly stabbed the water with its bill, threw something into the air and swallowed it. Then, with huge flapping wings, it took flight and disappeared above the tree tops.

'You won't see that too often,' Jamie said, releasing me. My arms had been warm under his hands; now they felt lonely. We sat down either side of the rug, but all I could think of was the bird's flight and the moment Jamie had turned me so as not to miss the sight. His hands on my bare arms, my breasts suddenly engorged till my nipples pressed against the fabric of my shirt. I had never felt like that before.

'Eat up,' he said and gestured towards the food.

There were thick slices of ham, crusty bread and salty butter with a green salad. We had apple pie to follow, washed down with Chablis and then black coffee from a flask. I hardly heard the sound of the falls now and a delicious tiredness was overcoming me. I looked up to see Jamie smiling at me.

'I was going to suggest a walk,' he said, 'but you look half-asleep.'

He left me there, my head in a clump of heather, the rock warm beneath me. 'When I come back we'll go down to the water,' he said. 'The dogs like a dip before they go.'

I closed my eyes but the sun's image remained on my closed lids, bedazzling me.

I wanted this moment to go on. I wanted to stay here without thought of school or Sara or the bills behind the clock, to think of nothing except the heather and the heron and the sound of bees collecting nectar...

I must have slept then. When I woke, the sun had disappeared behind a white cloud. I raised myself on my elbows and looked down towards the heron rock. The dogs were there, in the shallows, and Jamie was climbing the bank towards me. He grinned up at me and I felt an odd sensation in my chest, a pressure so great that I had to press my hands against it. It did no good. The pressure spread, consuming me, penetrating my limbs, filling my mouth so that my lips parted in a small sigh. I had never felt anything like it before but I knew what it was. I was *in love* – in love with a man who, six days from today, would marry my sister.

3

The rest of that week was a mixture of agony and ecstasy. The ecstasy of those hours I spent with Jamie, the agony of knowing that time was ticking away. Soon, Sara would come to take this away from me as she had taken everything else – not deliberately, of course, so I couldn't even take refuge in hating her. But now she was perpetrating the greatest theft of all.

The day after the picnic I told myself I still had five days: five days of heaven and the slim chance of a miracle. Not that I wanted anything dreadful to happen to Sara – just enough trauma to keep her from ever crossing the Ballachulish bridge.

I eventually settled for some glamorous South American (she was partial to swarthy complexions) collapsing outside Bart's. After mouth-to-mouth resuscitation, he would recover and whisk Sara away to the darkest part of the rainforest, where she could tend all the underprivileged peons and live happily ever after. It was a lovely dream. I would get Jamie and make him happy. Nella would still get a landowner in the family. A happy ending for everyone. Except in my heart I knew it could never be. Sara was born to be the fairy princess. I was meant to be the outcast waiting at the gate.

On the way home from Glen Orchy, Jamie had outlined the plans for the rest of the week. On Wednesday, there was a shooting party forty miles away, where I would be welcome if I wanted to attend. 'Yes,' I'd said fervently. If Jamie had been about to descend a coalmine I'd've been there. On Thursday he had shopping to do in Glasgow and he'd be grateful for my assistance. Friday he had estate business, but I could come along. Saturday and Sunday we'd have time to explore the land around Ard-na-Shiel and get ready for the wedding.

'There's a party for the estate workers on Tuesday,' Jamie told me. 'It's a family tradition before weddings: a Highland ball. You'll enjoy it.'

I smiled agreement, but my mind was racing through the contents of my suitcases. A shooting party, a shopping expedition, a ball and, hopefully, more picnics. What would I wear?

It was as if Jamie and I shared the same wavelength. As soon as I posed myself a problem he came up with a solution.

'You'll need warm clothes tomorrow,' he said. 'If you haven't brought any, why not raid Sara's room? I'm sure she wouldn't mind.'

I said thank you for a good idea but jealousy was almost choking me. *Sara's room!* As usual she had been here before me, making Ard-na-Shiel her kingdom. As for her clothes, I'd been wearing her cast-offs all my life. Of course she wouldn't mind!

That night, after dinner at the grand table, the two of us seated side by side sharing wine and good plain Scots fare, Jamie took me up the grand staircase and showed me Sara's room.

'I'll leave you to it,' he said and pushed wide the door.

I walked into the room, seeing odd possessions I recognized scattered here and there. Her navy-blue dressing gown draped over the ottoman at the foot of the bed; Nella's silver ring tree on the dressing table; a worn teddy, the one thing she had never let me touch, propped against the headboard of the bed. And, worst of all, a man's robe hanging on the back of the door Jamie had just closed behind him.

In vain I tried to tell myself that Sara had simply borrowed it, yet I knew, in my heart, that when Sara was here they shared this room. I knew it and I couldn't bear it. I spent the next five minutes at the window, looking out at the loch, bathed now in evening sunlight, wishing I could be out there, in its dark and impenetrable depths.

In the end, though, crazy optimism conquered reason. I still had four days remaining – four days in which anything could happen. I left the window and opened the wardrobes.

Sara had never been a clothes-aholic like Nella, but she had obviously plundered our mother's vast wardrobe and there was plenty here to choose from for all the outdoor activities. The ball was another matter. Only one dress was grand enough to be called a ball-gown: a dark-red velvet, off the shoulder and a skirt cut on the bias. I slipped into it, praying my 36B-cup breasts would do it justice. Everywhere else I was lumpy. My boobs were flatter than Norfolk.

The dress fitted like a glove, a very tight-fitting glove, but when I twirled, the skirt lapped around my legs in a way that made me feel a star. I hung it back in the wardrobe, and resolved to fight Sara for it tooth and nail if she hadn't brought an alternative.

I opened the drawers, idly checking the contents. There was a packet of contraceptive pills in the bedside cabinet and an unopened, gift-wrapped bottle of Chanel in the centre drawer of the dressing-table. I contemplated taking it, but instead I opened it and gave myself a liberal sprinkling before I went back downstairs for the nightcap Jamie had promised me. We sat either side of the fire, not saying much, occasionally laughing as logs fell and sent up sparks.

Wild thoughts were going through my mind, ways in which I could make him come to me, comfort me. I could tell him I was suffering from an incurable disease... except that then he would treat me like porcelain. I wanted rougher treatment.

Perhaps I should say that Giles had taken advantage of me while we were held up in Carlisle. I would cry and bury my face in his shoulder and he would cup my face in his hands and tell me nothing would ever hurt me again. And I would say I was afraid of men and he would make love to me, tenderly, to show me everything would be OK.

By the time we were ready to mount the stairs I was drunk on wine and fantasy but not so drunk that I didn't lean against him on the stairs so that he would get the full force of the stolen Chanel. He sniffed once or twice but I think it was just a tickling sensation in his nose.

I used the perfume again the next morning, before we set off in a Range Rover for the moor where the shooting party was to assemble. I was wearing a green tweed jacket, a tan suede riding skirt and a pair of brogues that looked like gin traps but felt like slippers.

As he drove, Jamie explained what lay ahead. The members of the shoot would have paid through the nose to be there. 'Once upon a time you invited your friends. Nowadays, a shoot has to pay its way. There's a social cachet to it – that's what they pay for.'

When we arrived at the first drive I saw what he meant. In spite of summer weather, the women wore tweeds in muted greens and browns, here an occasional heather or blue. They were well-worn but they had been cut by a genius and must have cost nearly as much as the diamonds that adorned their fingers. The men wore cord or moleskin plus-fours and jackets that shrieked Saville Row, and although their faces were weathered, their hands were soft and white. Jamie introduced me to his friends, our hosts, and they in turn introduced the rest of the party. They all welcomed me in a friendly enough fashion, but their eyes were already looking for a kill.

There was mist resting on the treetops and a wonderful scent of heather and damp earth. The men, and some of the women, moved forward to their allotted places, or 'pegs', as Jamie called them, and suddenly the peace of the day was gone – vanished in a frenzy of noise as birds fell out of the sky. I felt a small victory each time one flapped its way on and up, out of danger, but a terrible number fell to earth, to be retrieved by the dogs that dashed, workmanlike, about the scene.

It would have been sickening if it had not been so precise. As it was, the rising tide of dead birds mounted, feathers ruffling softly in the breeze. 'They're all for Sainsbury's,' our hostess said sadly, pushing her fists further down into the pockets of her Musto coat. Jamie had told me that each gun would only take home a brace, no matter how many he shot, so at the rate we were going the hosts were going to do well for themselves.

I tried to tell myself it was alright – that they were being shot for food and not for pleasure. But it was hard to remember that when you looked at the triumphant faces of the shooters.

At eleven o'clock we stopped for 'bullshots': tiny metal cups of a liquid that seared the throat but spread like fire through my limbs.

'What is it?' I whispered to Jamie.

He grinned. 'Celia's special brew. Bouillon laced with sherry. The trick is that the sherry's been laced with chilli.'

I pulled a face but I drained my cup.

'Not much longer now,' Jamie said. 'We break for lunch after the next drive.'

Lunch was nursery food: stew and mash, steamed pudding and custard, washed down with wine. And then it was back to the slaughter. In the end I turned my eyes away, looking only at Jamie, clinical in his sightings, clean in his shots, breaking to reload and firing again in one fluid movement but never, ever, looking as though this was anything other than a necessary part of rural life. I felt a surge of pride at his behaviour and then I thought ahead to the journey home and the dinner we would share back at Ard-na-Shiel and I felt a flutter in my chest. Three more days. Three more days that no one could spoil – not even Sara because she was too far away.

The dinner was as wonderful as I had imagined, but I should have remembered that Sara's power to spoil things for me was far-reaching. I flirted with Jamie through the meal and he responded gallantly until I was awash with triumph and desire.

He liked me. I could tell he liked me.

And then, just as I was about to make a move, he uttered the dreaded words: 'Tell me about Sara, when you were growing up together. I want to know as much about her as I possibly can.'

I managed to keep on smiling as I told him of childhood exploits and I kept my tears for later, when I was safe upstairs and could let my humiliation show. *Fool,* I thought. Fool, fool, fool to think I could take anything of Sara's. When would I ever learn?

The following day we went to Glasgow, speeding through Ballachulish, the peaks stark against a blue sky, on to where the road divided, one branch to Kinlochleven and the other to Crianlarrich. It took an hour to reach the outskirts of Glasgow, but the time seemed to fly by as I watched Jamie's hands on the wheel, lean and brown, dark hairs on the wrists and a white band peeping from beneath his watch.

Occasionally I narrowed my eyes, ready to feign sleep, and peeped at his profile, trying to analyze what I was feeling. That it was sexual I had no doubt, but it could not be lust because it was too tender. Except that I had never known real lust, so who was I to judge? All I knew was that I wanted to be within those arms, stretched out now to the wheel, wanted to put my lips against the brown throat that showed in his shirt neck – wanted, above all, to blot out the image of him with Sara.

It isn't fair! I said to myself, and put my hand to my mouth for fear I had spoken aloud.

We went to two men's outfitters in Glasgow, and took one of Jamie's guns, a Purdey, to a gunsmith's to be overhauled. The next stop was a jeweller's, a dark and wondrous place with very little on display, which meant its prices were probably horrendous. The woman behind the counter smiled at Jamie and vanished into the back shop. When she re-emerged she was accompanied by a man carrying three leather boxes.

The first contained a brooch delicately wrought in silver to resemble a snowdrop, its petals made of pearls, its calyx a dark green stone that might have been jade.

'That's for your mother,' Jamie said. 'And this is for Sara.'

The second box contained a fine gold chain, the single diamond hanging from it the size of a pea.

'It's lovely,' I said, with more enthusiasm than I felt. I knew the third box would be for me, but that wasn't the point. The diamond drop was for his bride, and that was Sara.

He pocketed the third case without opening it.

'That's for later,' he said and smiled at me.

He was the first person to smile at me without indulgence or sarcasm. It was the smile of an equal. I felt my resentment melt away.

Two more days, I thought. *At least I have two more days.*

We took the dogs out as soon as we got home, letting them run ahead of us towards the loch. We were moving through woodland, dead branches crackling beneath our feet, the dogs sniffing wildly at piles of leaf-mould and the gnarled roots of trees. When emerged from the wood, the loch lay before us, water constantly moving, shimmering in the late sun. There was the road, quiet now in the late afternoon.

I glanced to my left and saw a cliff of stone and shrub, above it Ard-na-Shiel perched like a magic tower.

'It's steep,' Jamie said, following my gaze. 'It's steep, but it can be climbed. I did it often when I was a boy and didn't mind the odd scratch.'

On the other side of the loch the slopes were wooded, only a thin strip of shoreline separating trees from water. The tops of the hills were bare and craggy and devoid of sheep, and there was a curious band of light around the highest peaks.

'There's a storm coming,' Jamie said, pointing to a dark cloud just visible behind the trees.

And come it did, sweeping over the loch, whipping the surface of the water to a frenzy. We retreated to the trees but after a while the dripping from the leaves became worse than the downpour.

'Let's make a run for it,' Jamie said, and took my hand.

By the time we reached the house, we were soaked to the skin and I knew my hair had betrayed me and shrunk into terrible ringlets all over my head.

'You're soaked,' Jamie said as we stood in the porch, shaking ourselves like dogs to get rid of surplus water. 'You look like a mermaid.'

He put up a hand to move wet hair from my brow, smiling as he did so. I wanted to move forward then and plant my face against the wet shirt that clung to his chest. Instead I stood there, smiling foolishly, until he had stroked the last wisp away and turned to open the door.

'Come down to the library when you've changed. I'll light the fire.' He called up the dogs and crossed the hall while I willed legs that had suddenly grown weak to mount the stairs.

He was waiting in the library when I came down. I had blown my hair to smoothness once again and given myself a generous dash of Chanel. Jamie had changed into an Argyle sweater, its sleeves pushed up to the elbow, and his cords were faded to a pale yellow.

'We could do with some of Celia's bullshots,' he said, 'but we'll have to make do with a good malt.'

The whisky was curiously thick and cloudy but velvet on the tongue. I rolled it around my mouth, trying not to betray that its strength was robbing me of breath.

Jamie smiled. 'Strictly speaking, we shouldn't drink the grain before nightfall but I can't have my bridesmaid dying of a fever.'

Why did he have to mention the wedding? I smiled my appreciation of the very adult drink, glad that neither Nella or Sara were here to raise warning eyebrows. *Two more days.* Why hadn't I come sooner, grown up quicker? I was more of a mate for Jamie than Sara would ever be. But for once I found the grace not to whinge my complaint or say something outrageous just to get attention. Instead, I smiled my sweetest smile and said, 'What are we going to do tomorrow?'

What we did was take to the road on bicycles, gleaming monsters with a multiplicity of gears. It only took a few minutes around the courtyard for me to get the hang of it and then we were away, the only cloud on the horizon the fact that it was Sara's bike I was riding and every byroad and track we took he must have ridden with her on one of her visits to Ard-na-Shiel.

We rode through Onich and into North Ballachulish, rolling across the bridge and on, through South Ballachulish towards Glencoe. There was no traffic on the road and we rode abreast of one another, sometimes throwing remarks across, at others laughing when a cycle wobbled and we threatened to collide. I felt exultant, lifting my face to the sun, glorying in the space and freedom and this feeling that had grown up inside me – a kind of knowledge of being alive and being in love.

Jamie was enjoying my company. I knew that from his smile and the occasional childish gesture that said *We're having fun, aren't we?* He would never have free-wheeled down slopes with cautious, sensible Sara, never joined in a chorus of *Guantanamera* and collapsed with laughter at the inappropriateness of such a song on a bleak Highland moor. By the time we turned for home, I was in heaven. Someone had laid out lunch in the library: cold chicken and salad and thick chunks of egg custard liberally anointed with nutmeg, all covered over with a lace-edged cloth.

'What now?' Jamie said when we'd finished eating and carried our coffee to the window-seat overlooking the loch. 'Tomorrow I've things to do on the estate as I won't be here for the next week or two, but today I'm a free man. Make your choice.'

I shut out the thought of his being on honeymoon for three weeks and concentrated on now. 'Let's go back to Glen Orchy,' I said. I wanted to recapture that moment when I had opened my eyes to see him climbing towards me and felt my whole body respond to the sight.

We took the dogs with us in the Land Rover, the Labrador's head resting on my shoulder, his gaze never leaving the road ahead. I refrained from glancing at Jamie. Instead, I closed my eyes and I pictured myself lying on the warm rock, heather scratching gently at my skin, the buzz of bees all around me and Jamie coming closer, except that this time I would sit up and hold out my arms and he would come to me and take the virginity everyone at school had been dying to lose and which had never meant much to me until now. I *must* make love with Jamie, even if it was only once, even if I could never look Sara in the eye again.

I suddenly felt ashamed. Why was I doing this? Did I really want him or did I simply want to take what was Sara's and have it for myself? But I couldn't do it at Ard-na-Shiel, in a bed they had shared. It had to be here, in the open air, in the place where I first realized it was meant to be.

Except that it wasn't, of course. The moment he pulled off the road and the dogs grew mad at the prospect of freedom, the heavens opened.

'Too bad,' Jamie said and turned for home.

We scampered into the house and made for the library. The log fire had been re-laid and he put a match to it and watched as the flames wavered, almost died and then took hold. I sat down in a worn leather chair so deep that the sides almost enveloped me and stretched out my legs in contentment. My disappointment at being driven from Glen Orchy was fast receding. There was a stillness about this room, lined as it was with leather-bound books and mellowed panelling, that made it seem supremely private and safe. What better place could there be for that first, unforgettable act of love – the act I had heard described in gory details so many times in whispered, giggling conversations at school by girls anxious to boast that at last it was done? It was painful at first and then sensational, that's what everyone said. Well, I would never tell anyone about today. It was too precious, too important to share. Tease as they might, they would never hear of it from me.

But if seduction was on my mind, Jamie had other plans. He moved to one of the towering book stacks and gestured.

'What do you fancy?'

For a moment the truth trembled on my lips, but how would he react if I told him I wanted him stripped and bathed and delivered to my tent?

'Have you anything about Glencoe?'

It was said on the spur of the moment but it hit the spot. His eyes crinkled with pleasure and he moved to another section, walking in a lithe way that had me clenching muscles of whose existence I had hitherto been unaware. So this was *it* – the mysterious thing called lust.

And I *liked* it.

He took down a brown, leather-clad book embossed in gold and another, smaller volume. 'There's the true story,' he said, handing me the larger book, 'and here's Scott's version.'

'I know the story,' I said. 'At least I think I do. The Campbells crept down the mountain and murdered the MacDonalds in their beds.'

'Worse than that.'

Jamie perched himself on the wide fender beside my chair, his hands – his lean, desirable hands – still holding Sir Walter Scott's book.

'The Campbells came to the MacDonalds as friends,' he said. 'They accepted their hospitality, they dandled the MacDonald children on their knees and then, at a given moment, they turned on their hosts and slaughtered them: men, women, even the very children they had nursed a moment before. And then they burned the village to the ground.'

He opened the book, needing to turn only a page or two to find a well-remembered place, and began to read, his voice suddenly more Scottish and more thrilling for that.

> *The hand that mingled in the meal,*
> *At midnight drew the felon steel,*
> *And gave the host's kind breast to feel*
> *Meed for his hospitality.*

I wanted to say 'Don't stop!' as he closed the book and handed it to me, but I stayed silent.

'Your bedtime reading,' he said and smiled. 'Unless you detest Scottish poets.'

'I love poetry.' I omitted to mention that I had loathed it until the moment he opened his mouth.

'Any favourites?' he said, getting to his feet.

I shook my head. 'I like them all – well, most of them. Not that we do anything at school that's remotely…' I was waffling and any moment now he would know it. 'Who's your favourite?' I said.

He was reaching for a slim suede-backed volume, its cover faded to a dull rose and well-thumbed. 'Dowson,' he said. 'Ernest Dowson,' and began to read aloud.

> *They are not long, the days of wine and roses, love*
> *and desire and hate.*
> *I think they have no portion in us after we pass*
> *the gate.*
> *They are not long, the weeping and the laughter.*
> *As from a misty dream our path emerges for a while*
> *then closes, within a dream.*

I smiled, afraid to speak in case he closed the book, wanting only for him to continue reading about love and desire and hate. When I had come to Ard-na-Shiel, I had only known how to hate; now I felt as though I knew everything.

That night I lay in the wide bed and went over and over the poem, shakily at first but then instinctively knowing what the missing words would be. *They are not long, the days of wine and roses, love and desire and hate.* We had not made love in the library, but what had happened there had almost been more important.

I had been at Ard-na-Shiel for such a short time; now I had just one day left, but I wouldn't have swopped this time for the whole of the rest of my life.

I think they have no portion in us after we pass the gate. What was the gate? Being old enough to run your own life? But surely that was when love and desire began? Hate was always there. I could remember feeling it in my high chair. But I wasn't going to think of Sara now. I turned on my side, closed my eyes and went on reciting under my breath.

When at last I slept it was to dream of some faceless man who came to my bed and loved me as I wanted to be loved. When I woke I could still feel his lips at my mouth, my neck, my breasts, his hands gentle as they parted my thighs. I had read of the act of love a thousand times, discussed it in a hundred giggling conversations, but nothing had prepared me for how it would feel, even in the half-reality of dreams.

I lay awake long after, remembering, only this time it was Jamie Munro who took me, Jamie Munro, Lord of Ard-na-Shiel, the only man I would ever love and the man I would lose forever a few short hours from now.

4

It was a relief when daylight penetrated the curtains and I could get up and run a bath. I came to the breakfast table in a cloud of Chanel, hoping the guilt of my night-time exploits did not show on my face. Jamie greeted me pleasantly enough, but I could see he was preoccupied.

'You're going to be busy today?' I said.

He looked up from his bacon and eggs. 'You can come with me if you want to. Otherwise, I'll get someone to drive you into Oban or Mallaig.'

'I'll come with you,' I said and buried my whoop of joy in my kedgeree.

Half an hour later we were seated in the Land Rover, the dogs in attendance behind, making for the first of the tenant farms we were to visit that day. I tried to look interested while Jamie talked crops and machinery with the various farmers, but there was an easy intimacy between tenant and landowner that shut outsiders out. I wondered if Jamie was really what they called a 'laird', but didn't ask for fear of looking foolish. The expression on my face was revealing enough! I caught a glimpse of myself in a cracked mirror in a farm kitchen, flushed and grinning like a proud parent at a speech day. How much more perfect could this man be, and how much more foolish could I get? I tried to think of Sara's wedding dress, hanging in the flowery bedroom, and when that didn't work I made myself think of them on the wedding night, when the celebrations were over and they would be alone.

I had seen Sara naked often enough. I could imagine Jamie, brown and lithe, his limbs entwining with hers, gently at first and then thrusting, thrusting. 'Oh God,' I said, and realized I had spoken aloud. Two surprised faces confronted me: Jamie and the farmer. 'Sorry,' I said. 'I just remembered something I meant to do.'

We went to visit the sheep then, black-faced creatures that shied away when I spoke to them and were then driven forward by curiosity until their breath came warm and sweet on my outstretched hand. We all agreed they were fine beasts and left them staring after us, looking incredibly wise and ancient and superior and not at all as I had imagined sheep to be.

The third farm we visited was a story-book white building, set far back from the road. The woman who came to the door was heavily pregnant, but her eyes lit up at the sight of Jamie.

'He's away to the barn,' she said. 'The Jersey's due and he canna take his eyes off her. Will you be taking tea?'

She was looking at me with open curiosity as Jamie introduced us. 'Mrs McKechnie, may I present Alexandra Gallagher, soon to be my sister-in-law.'

'The wee bridesmaid,' Mrs McKechnie said archly and held out a work-reddened hand. I smiled sweetly while wishing labour pains from hell upon her. I didn't want to be reminded that I was the 'wee bridesmaid' – I was trying to forget it! We thanked her politely for her offer of tea but declined.

'I've a lot to do before the wedding, Mrs McKechnie,' Jamie said, and she grinned in reply, patting her swollen belly as she did so.

'Aye, it's no' long now, Mr Jamie. I'll be there to see it if this wee'un bides.'

From the look of her, she'd be lucky to last the night, but who was I to judge the progress of a pregnancy? We went 'out bye' to the barn, as she advised, and found her man leaning on the wall of a byre. Inside, a mournful cow, looking straight out of Disney, was chewing the cud and fluttering its amazing eyelashes at its owner.

'Not long now,' Jamie said.

'Aye.' Mr McKechnie shifted his feet.

'She looks good,' Jamie offered.

'Aye,' said McKechnie.

Jamie tried again. 'Is she going to the hospital in Oban?'

McKechnie straightened up. 'Hospital?'

'Mrs McKechnie,' Jamie said.

'Ah,' the farmer nodded his comprehension. 'I was thinking you were meaning the beast. She was due yesterday.'

Jamie leaned to pat the smooth but woefully distended belly. 'She's fine. They often keep you waiting the first time. I should get the vet, though, if you haven't seen action by tomorrow.'

I tried to work out who the vet was for, the wife or the cow, but gave up in the end.

We again refused the offer of tea or a wee dram and returned to the Land Rover. 'Fish farm next,' Jamie said and waved goodbye to the McKechnies as they stood together at their gate.

'How will she get to hospital?' I asked as we rejoined the main track. Around us there was only isolation, not a dwelling in sight.

'McKechnie will ring for an ambulance.' Jamie turned to grin at me and my heart lurched at the sight. 'It's not deepest Africa, you know. We do have telephones. Now, if we manage to get done by seven, how would you fancy a meal out in Tyndrum?'

'Lovely,' I said. 'As long as you have the time.'

I imagined the return journey through the blackness of Glencoe. The front wheel of the Land Rover would hit a rock dropped in the road by some kind-hearted god, we would lurch off the track and spend the rest of the night curled up together for warmth. Lovely stuff! By the time we got back to Ard-na-Shiel I was drunk with daydreams.

We dined in a small hotel with a flickering candle on the table between us, while he spun me tales of the wild Highlands of yore and the waiters kept a respectable distance. There was no mishap on the road home but it was bliss simply to be there beside him in the dark, both of us enveloped in the aura of Chanel. Once or twice, before we left the house, I saw his nostrils twitch and wondered if I had overdone it, but now it had evaporated or he had adjusted to it because he seemed perfectly happy.

As we walked from the Land Rover to the house, he put a companionable arm around my shoulders. 'Only one day left,' he said. 'We must think up something special.'

I drifted upstairs on a cloud. So he, too, was counting the days. My head suggested he might be counting the days to Sara's arrival. My heart knew better.

When I had undressed I curled up on the window-seat to look out on the moonlit loch and think about tomorrow when there would surely be some miracle that would allow Jamie and me to be together forever. Perhaps Sara would decide her career came first. That would be perfect because it involved no guilt for anyone.

When at last I left my perch and climbed into bed, I knew everything was going to be alright. For the first time in my life, I was going to *win*. And if a shiver of doubt overtook me as my head hit the pillow, I drove it away.

If ever anything was meant to be, it was this!

5

I woke to the sound of rain drumming on the windows, and when I looked out, it was thrashing the surface of the loch. Lights burned in windows on the opposite shore, although it was eight in the morning and daylight. I stood for a moment watching rain flurries sweep, bird-like, across the water, exulting in the thought that the weather would keep Jamie and me locked within Ard-na-Shiel. It might even bring trains to a halt and keep Nella and Sara at bay. I scurried to the bathroom, all sorts of wild and wonderful ideas teeming around my brain.

I came downstairs half an hour later to find Jamie had already breakfasted and was in the library, reading the morning papers. He looked up and smiled as I came in. 'The Scottish air agrees with you, Lexy. You must have slept well.'

Lexy! He had used my pet name. I tried to be cool and content myself with what was meant to be a smile, but was more like the opening of the Dartford Tunnel. 'I'll only be a few minutes over breakfast. What shall we do today?'

He was laying out the possibilities when the phone rang. As he listened I saw his face change, his brow furrow. Guilt swept over me as I imagined a train thundering north, a line washed away by floods, Nella and Sara trapped in the wreckage. Had I ill-wished them?

But it was not my mother and sister who were in trouble; it was the McKechnies. 'He's fallen in the byre. She thinks his leg's broken. There's an ambulance on its way but she can't move him.' He was halfway out of the door as he spoke but I was hot on his heels, all thought of breakfast forgotten.

'I can help,' I said when he tried to dissuade me. 'She'll need someone – a woman.'

His hesitation was momentary. 'Wrap up then,' he said. 'And wear something sensible on your feet. It'll be a quagmire up there.'

The windscreen wipers could scarcely deal with the rain as we crawled towards the croft. Jamie's hands were tense on the wheel, his body hunched forward as he tried to make out the twists and turns of the road. 'Will the ambulance get through?' I asked.

'They always get through, but it'll take time. How's your first aid?'

My knowledge of things medical was culled from hospital dramas on television but I tried to sound confident. 'I know a bit.'

The thought that he might quite properly wish it was Sara beside him now instead of me was like ashes on my tongue. She was even ahead of me professionally: a qualified doctor when I had difficulty opening Elastoplast. For one sweet moment I let myself think of the derailed train and all that could be seen of Big Sister: one capable but decidedly limp hand sticking out from the wreckage. But with my luck, Sara would right the fallen train, turn off the rain and restore the whole countryside to order.

We passed through the stone gateposts of the farm and slid down a path that resembled a river. Mrs McKechnie stood in the doorway of the byre, one hand on her distended belly, the other wiping rain from her forehead as she peered out at the Land Rover.

'In here!' she called. 'Thank God, you've come.'

I could hear a cow bellowing and a general chorus of distress from the other cows. McKechnie lay against a wall, one leg twisted under him, his upper body covered by a motley pile of sacks and old coats. His face was wet – with tears or sweat, I couldn't make out which – and his lips were drawn back from his teeth in a grimace of pain.

'OK?' Jamie said. And then: 'Silly question. Still, we'll have you out of here soon.'

The man's eyes turned towards his wife.

'Get her out of here. It's not good... get her out bye. And the beasts – they're not milked and the heifer is breeching, I think.'

Jamie let out a long breath, his tongue touched his upper lip briefly and then he turned to me. 'Take her up to the house, Alexandra. No arguments – just go. Make tea, plenty of sugar, then bring two mugs here. She stays in the kitchen till the ambulance comes, then they both go. She can't stay here alone in that state.'

I didn't argue. As I half-dragged Mrs McKechnie out of the byre, he was already rolling up his sleeves. We both had work to do.

I held her arm tightly as we negotiated the yard. The drum of rain was almost an assault and the wind was driving it straight at us. It was a relief to reach the calm of the kitchen – until I looked at her face: chalk-white with eyes that seemed sunken in pits of navy-blue.

'Sit down.' I barked it like a command and she accepted it as one, sinking onto a bentwood chair and putting both hands on her belly.

'Will he be alright?' Her eyes were anxious and I nodded.

''Course he will. It's only a broken leg. Now, where's the kettle?'

I put on the kettle and set about looking for tea and sugar.

She looked at the clock. 'It's two hours,' she said. 'They should've been here by now.'

I was glad that the kettle boiled then and I could busy myself with brewing the tea. Pointless to tell her that the region was probably littered with similar accidents and ambulances in short supply.

I gave her a mug of tea laced with sugar and milk and then set three more on a tray. 'I'm taking them some tea. Don't move and listen for the ambulance – it'll be here any moment. Send them down to the byre but don't come with them; you'd only be in the way. When he's safely on board they'll come for you.'

Dim memories of childbirth in books and on TV surfaced. 'Have you got a bag packed?'

I fetched the bag from the back room, a shadowy place that smelled of polish, and set it at her feet. 'OK. Stay there. I'll be back in a moment if they're not here before me.'

Mercifully, the wind was on my back as I went back to the barn carrying the tray but it was still a perilous journey. The yard was a sea of mud now, as earth was washed from the edges and carried across the concrete. As I neared the barn I could hear the heifer, its cries more piteous, almost drowning the noise of the other cows.

'Good girl,' Jamie said as I entered the byre. He was seated beside a cow, fitting metal cups to its teats. 'Give him a drink. Any sign of the ambulance?'

I shook my head. In the far stall the cries of the cow in labour were fainter. 'Is she alright?' I asked. It was McKechnie who replied.

'If it's a breech she's better off dead. The vet'll no make it now.' His voice was flat and undramatic and it made his words all the more poignant. His beloved heifer was doomed and there was nothing he could do about it.

I found myself moving towards the noise. At least I could pat its head and be there for it. Jamie rose to his feet and switched on the milking machine. He stood for a second, watching my doubtful progress, and then suddenly he was moving towards the door of the byre. 'In here,' he said and stood aside as two ambulance men entered, bearing a stretcher.

'We'll take the wife,' one of them said as they lifted the injured shepherd. 'You'll see to the herd.' It was half entreaty, half command.

'I'll see to everything,' Jamie said, laying a hand briefly on McKechnie's shoulder before he was taken away. Then he turned back into the byre. 'What do you know about midwifery?' he asked me ruefully.

The heifer had ceased to bellow and was panting now, its head down. A bag of what looked like blood and water hung from its backside. 'I'll give it a try,' Jamie said. 'And if I can't…' His eyes flicked back towards the open door and the house, beyond. I knew what he meant. There were guns in a cupboard on the wall there.

'Please,' I said under my breath. 'Please, God, let it come.'

Jamie had taken off his jacket. Now he rolled shirtsleeves back from strong hairy arms. His fingers looked white and suddenly thin as he plunged them into a bucket of water, plunged them again and then shook them dry.

'It's not exactly antisepsis,' he said, 'but it's the best I can do.'

I stood as he inserted a hand into the cow's bloodied and gaping vagina. 'I know you can turn them,' he said. 'I'm just not sure how.' He plunged further, his cheek against the heaving flank. 'Oh God, Lexy,' he said. 'I hope I'm not making things worse.'

There was a sudden bellow, sharper than the rest, and blood gushing. I squeezed my eyes shut, afraid to look, opening them again in time to see two tiny hooves emerging, ballerina like, and then a steaming body unbelievably long and thin, arched like a bow, wrapped in a greyish filament. The heifer's head was turning, seeking its baby.

'You have to clean the mouth out,' I said and goggled at this knowledge I had not known I possessed.

A few moments later the calf was clear of the coil and bleating like a lamb. A second later it tried to rise, fell to its knees, tried again and stood upright on still-wobbly legs.

'You've done it, Jamie! You've done it!'

I don't know who moved first. I only know I was in his arms, his cheek wet against mine, each of us exultant, holding on, unable to believe our miracle. 'I love you,' I said and felt him stiffen. 'I love you, too,' he said, but his voice told me the spell was broken. 'I think you rub them down with hay,' he said. 'I seem to remember that comes next.'

Two neighbours arrived then, swathed in oilskins and looking capable. They admired the calf, declared it a grand wee beastie and decided the mother would come to no harm once the vet had paid her a visit.

We did not speak on the way back to Ard-na-Shiel except to express our longing for warmth and food and the luxury of a bath. I ran upstairs as soon as we reached the house, unwilling to meet Jamie's eye. If only I hadn't spoken! What magic might have happened then...

In the bath, I began to cheer up. After, all he had reciprocated. *I love you, too,* he had said – in brotherly tones, no doubt, but that could change. I towel-dried my hair, pulled on sweater and jeans and hurried onto the landing to repair the damage my foolish outburst had caused.

I was on the first stair when I saw them in the centre of the hall, locked in one another's arms, oblivious of any watcher. 'Oh Sara,' I heard him say. 'I've been longing for this.' Behind them the door was open to the rain-washed courtyard, Nella must be outside, seeing to the luggage.

I stood for what seemed an age, one foot poised to descend, and then I quietly withdrew, tiptoeing along the landing although I could have clog-danced without disturbing the lovers below.

And that was when I knew I could no more stand up for my sister at her wedding to Jamie than fly to the moon. When at last I went down to face them, my plans for escape were complete down to the tiniest detail.

'Lexy!' Sara said my name with utter delight, as though the one thing in the world she wanted was to see me. I let her fold me in her arms, feeling the old, familiar comfort as I gave way to her embrace, longing to be held forever and wishing with all my heart that I could pay her back for ruining my life.

6

I could hardly meet Nella's eyes when she entered the room. 'I hear you've had a wonderful time,' she said. 'I told you you would.' Beside her, Jamie and Sara stood, arms linked now in the casual way of lovers.

'Yes,' I said. 'It's been an amazing week. We weren't expecting you until tomorrow.'

I sounded flat, but they didn't seem to notice. They were full of themselves, their journey, their plans, their bloody good intentions. Little Sister had had her week of special attention. Now she must return to the back seat where she belonged.

I hardly spoke over dinner. It didn't matter. Everyone else was full of plans and expectations, tiny details and broad expanses. We discussed flowers and cars, orders of service, timings and – worst of all – the honeymoon plans. Or rather *they* discussed and I listened. I might have been on Mars for all they cared. Even Jamie, who had seemed so much on my wavelength, had forgotten my existence, although he did praise me for my help at the McKechnies.

'She was grand,' he said. 'I couldn't have managed without her.' He smiled at me then, but it didn't really mean anything. One look into Sara's eyes and he was hooked. Even Nella – *my* mother, too, although you'd never guess – looked moonstruck. *They're happy,* I thought. *All of them happy and I am dying.* To salve my wounds I went over and over my plans.

I would get away as soon as I could – straight after dinner, if possible. The night was fine now. Through the window I could see stars coming out in the evening sky, but the trees were visible and the mountains beyond. When it was really dark and the house was sleeping, I would make my escape. One of the mountain bikes would take me as far as Crianlarich. It was signposted from the bridge at Ballachulish so there was no fear of getting lost. Jamie had called Crianlarich the hub of the universe. 'Every road in Scotland comes through here,' he'd said. It was probably an exaggeration but I could be sure of getting a lift there to Stirling or Edinburgh – anywhere, as long as it was away from here.

I had eleven pounds seventy-five in my wallet and sixty-two pounds in my Girobank. When that was gone I would work at something. As we ate apple charlotte, I tried to imagine myself with a job and a place of my own, but when the vision extended to a boyfriend I felt my eyes fill. There would never be any other man for me. Not now.

I pleaded a headache after coffee, kissed everyone goodnight and made for the stairs.

'I'll pop in and see you when I come up,' Nella said, and for a moment I weakened. She was looking at me in a puzzled way, as though she knew something was wrong but wasn't sure what. For a crazy moment I almost said 'Yes, please,' thinking I could tell her the truth and she would get me out of it. Except that I knew she wouldn't. She would talk about girlish crushes and family loyalty and a host of other useless things.

'Don't bother, Mum,' I said. 'I'm awfully tired after all the drama at the barn. I'll be asleep before my head touches the pillow.'

I paused on the stairs and looked back through the open door. Jamie was leaning back in his chair, a glass in one hand, the other behind his head. He was smiling at Sara and listening intently.

I love you, Jamie, I said, but I said it to myself.

I contemplated keeping my clothes on until I left, but there was always the chance of Nella looking in on me so I put on my nightie and sat down to wait. But when the knock came at the door, it wasn't Nella. It was Sara.

'Can I come in?' she said and, a little unwillingly, I nodded my head. She moved towards me.

'Lexy?' Her eyes were questioning but I had no answers. She reached out and brushed the hair from my forehead. 'I'm glad you're here. That you'll be there for me on Saturday. I'm quite scared, you know. But you being there… and Mum – that'll make all the difference.'

I nodded but all the while I was fighting the urge to move into her arms and hug her and be comforted. 'Make it come right,' I used to say when I was little and Sara would always oblige. But I was grown up now, and there was nothing she could do for me.

She reached to kiss me. 'Good night' she said. 'Sweet dreams.'

And I smiled a Judas smile. 'You too,' I said and didn't breathe until she was gone and the door closed.

Two hours later, when the house was asleep, I let myself out of Ard-na-Shiel. The dogs accompanied me to the door, silent and watchful. 'Be good.' I patted each warm head, pushed them gently away and closed the door. If they barked, I was done for, but they stayed silent.

The moon was out, glinting on the surface of the loch, turning trees to silver, bathing the house I was leaving behind so that it looked enchanted. I stood for a moment, suddenly fearful, and then I remembered that scene in the hall. How could I bear to see that again or witness it made holy in church?

I settled my bag on my shoulders and made for the outhouse where the bikes were stored, knowing it would be unlocked because no one in the neighbourhood would dream of stealing from Ard-na-Shiel. Two minutes later I was bowling down the drive and turning left for Ballachulish and the bridge.

At first, I felt a sense of elation and relief. I had done it! I was free! The bike seemed to flow along the deserted road. The moon was just visible above the mountain Jamie called Creag Ghorm, but when I reached North Ballachulish a cloud passed across its face, making the night black except for the lights on the bridge. I glanced over my shoulder but there was no sign of pursuit. They had not even noticed I had gone.

I pictured them, safe in their beds. Nella's face well-creamed, her hair tied up in chiffon. Jamie and Sara wrapped in one another's arms, no doubt. Asleep, please God, because I couldn't bear to think of them awake together, making love. Once more the scene in the hall came back to haunt me. He loved her – there was no escape from that. I felt tears upon my cheeks and brushed them away until the bike wobbled dangerously and I had to concentrate on the road.

Once through South Ballachulish I turned for Crianlarich. Ahead, Glencoe loomed, black and forbidding so that I was suddenly afraid. After all, this was a place of death, a doomed place and a lonely one. I could always go back, restore the bike to its rack, creep up the stairs, slip into a still-warm bed. Except that come the morning I would have to face them: the lovers. See them exchange those smug glances, take every opportunity to touch, send eye messages.

'Sara, I goddam hate you!' I said aloud and pedalled on.

Sheer terror overcame me in the glen. The moon had come out again to bathe the slopes in an eerie light. At times the road was edged with rock, at others a dangerous ditch. Once I cried out in fear as something seemed to rush towards me, but it was only a bird: an owl beating slow, ghostly wings as it went in search of prey. I sobbed then and would have turned back, but I was past the point of no return. Easier to keep going.

And then I was through the pass and Rannoch Moor stretched before me: a black vastness edged with mountain peaks. If anyone was going to catch up with me, it would be here, with nowhere to hide. I stopped pedalling and put a foot to the ground as the bike slowed. But when I turned there was no one there, only the road stretching back to nothingness.

When I started up again, there was the gleam of water to either side. I pedalled on, the bike's lamp catching the rocks that lined the road. No rosebay willow-herb here or the yellow flowers that Jamie had called 'Stinking Billy'. There would be flowers at the wedding: roses and stephanotis. They had planned them weeks ago. Roses and stephanotis for the bride, freesias for me. Who would be bridesmaid now? Wear watered silk and Munro tartan? I shook my head to get rid of dangerous thoughts and pedalled on towards Bridge of Orchy and Tyndrum.

An hour later, after a lot of begging and pleading, I was safe in the cab of an articulated lorry and on my way south.

7

It was dawn by the time we reached the border. I shared the driver's thermos – sweet tea at blood heat – and chomped on a proffered doorstep of bread and cheese. We parted company on the outskirts of Newcastle. He was big and red-faced but he had treated me kindly. 'I don't know what you're up to,' he said as he let out the clutch, 'but watch your step.'

I walked on towards the city centre, occasionally glancing back in the hope of a lift. It came at last in the shape of a GPO van. 'Running away?' he asked as I slumped gratefully into the passenger seat. 'Or was it a real good party?'

I mumbled something about being on my way home from youth hostelling and disembarked in a broad thoroughfare that turned out to be Grainger Street. I had decided that hitching all the way to London would be too conspicuous. Drivers would remember someone they had given a lift if there was any kind of appeal on radio or TV. And to London I must go, because it was the only place I knew well that was big enough to hide in. So if it couldn't be hitchhiking, it had to be train or bus – and of the two the train seemed more anonymous. I didn't want the GPO man to know I was looking for the railway station so I murmured something about meeting friends and walked blindly away. As soon as he was out of sight I buttonholed a solitary passer-by and asked for directions. Ten minutes later I was on platform three about to board the eight-thirty train to Kings Cross.

I had considered visiting a Girobank and buying a ticket, but I decided it would take too much of my precious cash. I marched into an almost empty first-class carriage and sank as low in a seat as I possibly could. A few moments later the train moved slowly out of the station, crossed the Tyne Bridge and picked up speed on the other side. I looked down as we crossed the river, seeing the dark, swirling waters far below. It would be breakfast-time at Ard-na-Shiel. Had I been missed by now? If so, they would never think of looking this far afield. I was free, lost in a whirlpool of people. And as long as I avoided anywhere familiar, free I would stay.

What I couldn't understand was the longing I felt to be with Sara. Not my mother, who I really cared for; not Jamie, who I would love for the rest of my life; but Sara. I wanted her there to tell me everything would be alright. But she wasn't and never would be again. I turned my face to the window and cried.

As the train grew level with the Cleveland Hills I saw the ticket inspector enter the compartment. It was time to dry my tears. Without meeting his eye I rose to my feet, collected my bags and made my way to the buffet.

I joined the queue feeling panic overtake me. He was going to move down the train demanding to see tickets or travel documents. What would I say when he came to me? I shuffled slowly towards the counter, desperately thinking of places to hide. If I went into the loo would he pass by or would he be waiting grimly outside when I emerged? Worse still, would he batter on the door and demand to see a ticket? Catching the train had seemed such a good idea. Now I felt trapped.

The man in front of me was paying for his order. My turn next – except that if I had to buy a ticket, even to the next station, I would have nothing to spare for food. He was fumbling in his wallet, extracting money. Something fluttered to the floor but he ignored it. I bent to pick it up and was about to hand it to him when I recognized it as a credit-card slip. A slip made out to British Rail in exchange for a standard fare from Newcastle to

Kings Cross. I slipped it into my pocket, and, as he moved away, asked for a large coffee and a chicken salad sandwich.

A few moments later, I had found a seat in a standard-class carriage and was ready to bluff my way out of trouble. I took out the credit-card slip and studied it. The signature was in simple round script: *EH Horner*. I put it in my bag just as the guard appeared at the other end of the compartment.

When he came to me I smiled my most engaging smile and began to hunt for my ticket, confidently at first and then with increasing anxiety.

'I've got it somewhere…'

His brow darkened and I let my bottom lip tremble. 'I put it straight in my bag after – after my mother bought it for me.' He was smiling the pretend smile of the unbeliever when I pulled my master-stroke. 'She gave me the receipt…'

He took the slip and studied it for a moment then he gave a heavy sigh and handed it back. 'See if you can find it before we reach our destination, there's a good girl. And be more careful in future. Strictly speaking…'

I was never to know what 'strictly speaking' would mean. My guardian angel intervened: a voice boomed out from the inter-com requesting the guard's attendance at the buffet and he went on his way.

I relaxed, feeling almost smug at what I had just pulled off. If survival was this easy, I would be alright. I would not only survive, I would prosper and return to Ard-na-Shiel rich and famous to make them all sorry for their behaviour.

I was granting forgiveness to everyone but Sara when a terrible thought struck me. What if the call to the buffet was from an irate passenger who wanted his credit-card slip back? The chicken sandwich turned to ashes in my mouth and had to be washed down with gulps of coffee. I was contemplating leaping from a moving train when the guard returned, walked past me without a glance and disappeared.

The rest of the journey was uneventful, I pretended to be asleep whenever he appeared, and after Peterborough he lost interest and appeared no more. At last we passed Alexandra Palace and then the outskirts of the city. I had come home. A few minutes later I stood in the melting-pot of Kings Cross, surrounded by scurrying travellers and questing pigeons. It was noon and I didn't know where to go next, but before I made any decisions there was one thing I must do. I went into the telephone booth and dialled the Ard-na-Shiel number.

'Alex?' It was my mother who answered, her voice high-pitched and taut with anxiety.

'Yes, it's me.'

'Where are you? Jamie and Sara are out searching. Tell me where you are and they'll come and get you. You are alright, aren't you?'

I sucked in my breath, trying to decide how much to tell. 'I'm OK. Tell Jamie the bike is at Crianlarich. In the station car park. I chained it up.'

'Where are you? Are you there, too?'

'No. I'm in Newcastle – and don't go spare, Nella, I'm alright but I'm not coming back.'

There was a gasp that was almost a cry from the other end. 'What do you mean? Stop talking so foolishly! I can't stand a tantrum now, Alexandra – not with the wedding hours away. If someone's upset you –'

'*No.*'

I spoke firmly. I could see my money ticking away and I had no intention of using more. 'No one's upset me. I love you all and I hope the wedding is wonderful. I just can't be there. Don't worry. I'll ring again soon. I love you, Mummy.' As I said the word from childhood I felt the tears flow. At the other end of the line my mother was incoherent with fear and incomprehension. I hung up the receiver, picked up my bags and set off for the tube.

I took the Piccadilly line to Hyde Park and walked to the Serpentine. I had a favourite place beneath the bridge, where the ducks would congregate to be fed, and it was nice to be somewhere familiar. It was one o'clock and the day stretched before me, huge and empty. I sat for a while watching a pair of white-faced ducks diving for food. The action was almost comical: a quick flip and they were bottoms up, another second and they were gone with only ripples to betray their passing. They surfaced yards away, bobbed about for a moment and dived again.

Beyond them two crested birds swam towards the barrier under the bridge, turning in a stately circle when they could go no further. I swung my legs back and forth under the seat. How long could I sit here without drawing comment? A runner passed me, elbows in to sides, thighs brick-red and steaming. If I was still here when he came back he might wonder…

I got to my feet and walked the few yards to the outdoor café. In the water a tennis ball bobbed aimlessly, only hurrying when the wake from a rowboat stirred the water. I felt a sudden kinship with the ball. I was bobbing about, too, waiting for a current to carry me somewhere. But where? I bought a coffee and sat down to drink it, brushing pigeons from the table and dashing the crumbs they were after to the ground.

I had eight pounds in cash and nowhere to sleep. Although I looked older than sixteen – at least I hoped I did – it wouldn't do to become conspicuous. I couldn't go home or to a hostel because if Nella alerted the police those would be the first places they would look. I felt safe in the park, but what time did it close? Was it patrolled at night? I tried to remember if there were gates. Surely not; people drove through the park at night. I had done it myself in cars belonging to one or more of Nella's men. I could stay here indefinitely. It was still summer. No one froze to death in Britain in August. And if I took refuge in one of the wooded areas I would be quite safe because no one would know I was there.

I walked back to the bridge and sat down on the seat. The bag was becoming heavy now, although I had brought only essentials with me: a change of clothing, a mac, my Walkman, my jewellery, some toilet articles and cherished souvenirs like Poody, my ratty old childhood toy. So why did the bag weigh a ton and, more importantly, what was I going to do with it?

I waited until there was no one in sight, then I climbed onto the seat and leaped over the spiked railings. It was easy to reach for the bag and lift it over, too, and when I moved only a yard or two back I couldn't see the path, which meant no one on the path could see me. I found a dry area under a dense, spreading bush and tucked in the bag. It would be safe there until nightfall. I climbed back onto the path after checking that the coast was clear and, freed from my burden, set off to explore.

At least I meant to explore. Once on the pavement, fear overcame me. I spent the next three hours in the Odeon cinema, watching *Ghost* and sucking toffees. I told myself I could afford one night off, and Patrick Swayze and Demi Moore kept my mind off Ard-na-Shiel. I wanted to believe that they would all be sitting ashen-faced, mourning my passing, but I feared that their own interests would simply have closed the gap left by my leaving and they would be sitting at the dinner table, drinking Jamie's excellent claret, talking about the wedding and agreeing that I was an odious little monster who had always been a nuisance. I cried over Moore and Swayze, but the tears were really for myself.

When I emerged from the cinema, the sun was low in the sky and Londoners were going home. I thought longingly of Notting

Hill and my bedroom there, and even more longingly of the bathroom. I wanted more than anything else to wallow in a bath – except that more even than that I wanted to be back in Glen Orchy with bee-song in my ear and Jamie climbing the bank towards me. Or in the byre with the calf still bloody from birth and struggling to stand. I wanted Jamie to take me in his arms again, only this time he would be the one to say 'I love you.'

I wanted so many things and I had never been more conscious of the old saying 'I want never gets.'

8

It was getting dark when I returned to the park and there were lights all along the bridge. A notice proclaimed that the park was open from five a.m. to midnight, but I could see a dozen ways of gaining access. Presumably there were park wardens hidden somewhere who might come out at midnight and sweep out lingerers. Somehow I had to remain when that happened because I would feel safer here in the dark than out there on the streets, where anything could happen and lone teenagers might be accosted by passing policemen.

I waited until there was no one passing and then I stepped onto the seat and over the railings. My bag was safe under the tree where I had left it. I took out my thin waterproof and spread it on the ground, pulled a thick sweater over my shirt and T-shirt and settled my back against a tree, then I slipped on my earphones and put in my Sinead O'Connor tape. I was going to be alright here for tonight. Tomorrow I would go into some big hotel and get washed and changed and then I'd work out what I was going to do with the rest of my life.

When the light went, it went suddenly. One minute I could see the outline of the trees against the darkening sky, pick out each branch, each leaf. The next there was only a black line with stars beyond and around me at ground level, impenetrable blackness. I shut my eyes and tried to concentrate on the music. Only a few hours to dawn. The park would come alive then, joggers, workers, mothers with prams. Safety!

I was thinking of Jamie as Sinead sang of lost love. I would always love him. There would be other men in my life, but never another Jamie. I pictured myself twenty years ahead. A white streak in my hair, a line or two on my face but groomed to perfection, I would drive up to Ard-na-Shiel in a car – a Merc or a Rolls-Bentley – and they would stand on the steps to greet me, old and careworn but still recognizable as Jamie and Sara. I would have children with me, a son and daughter. And they would have none. *None!* Because I couldn't bear to think of that. I opened my eyes to the moon above me, looking wise and kind and infinitely cheerful. Please, God, don't let them do it. Not any more!

That was when something ran over my leg. I felt small feet patter across my skin, felt something brush my other leg, heard it scurry into the undergrowth when I tore the headphones from my ears and screamed at the top my voice. I tried to tell myself it was mice or voles. I could stand mice or voles but a voice in my head kept yelling one word: *Rats!*

After that it seemed the shrubbery came alive. Rustlings in the trees above me: wood-pigeons, perhaps, or squirrels – or wouldn't they be sleeping? There were scurryings, too, in the leaf-mould that covered the ground. The last straw was a pair of eyes, red as rubies, that came and stared and vanished. I gathered up my bag, renegotiated the fence and sped along the path to the safety of the café.

The tables looked lonely in the moonlight. No pigeons now to peck for crumbs. The lake was moonlit but that made it look remote and unfriendly. I retreated into the darkness of the colonnades and curled up in a corner. I put my bag behind my head for a pillow, tuned in to Sinead and tried to compose myself for sleep.

I drifted off eventually and when I awoke it was daylight. But it wasn't dawn that had woken me; it was a man crouched beside me, leering at me from puffy eyes.

'Wakey, wakey!'

When he smiled he revealed discoloured teeth and his breath smelled sweet and unpleasant.

'Go away,' I said. He didn't move. 'Please! Go away!' He went on smiling. I tried to move my legs but they were stiff from sleep and he was too near to allow easy movement. I put out a hand and pushed him so that he rocked back on his heels.

'Now, now,' he said. 'Is that a nice way to treat a friend?'

It was then that I noticed his eyes, pupils as big as boiled sweets and dark. He was on something. Not alcohol but something. Somehow just knowing that made me feel brave.

'You're not my friend. Now get out of my way before I really hurt you.'

I scrambled to my feet, not caring if I kicked him or trod upon him. He let me pass, lolling backwards as I picked up my bags and moved out from under the shelter of the colonnade. I turned back.

'Don't follow me or you'll be sorry.'

For just a second something flickered in the boiled-sweet eyes and then subsided.

'Fuck off,' he said languidly and leaned back against the wall. I walked away, feeling the sun on my face, letting it ease the ache in my bones from sleeping awkwardly, hoping against hope he wouldn't change his mind and follow me.

The park was waking up now, ducks moving languidly across the water, birds wheeling and swooping above. I looked at my watch. Four forty-five. Soon the park would be officially open. Joggers would return and mums with prams and people passing through on their way to work.

That was what I needed: a job! I had three pounds left, not enough to get me a night's lodging in London and another night in the park was out of the question. A bench loomed up and I sat down on it. Impossible to walk and think at the same time when I felt tired and dirty and hungry and on the verge of tears. I took out my last toffee and contemplated the options. I could throw myself on the mercy of some good organization like the Salvation Army, but they would probably want to re-unite me with my family. I knew do-gooders.

A job was the answer, but I had an uneasy feeling that any job worth having would require paperwork and once I was entered onto someone's books it would be easy for Sara and Nella to find me.

The third possibility was to pick up the nearest phone and say I wanted to go home. I sat for a long while contemplating this. Undoubtedly there would be recriminations, but in the flurry of the wedding they would be swept aside. I could claim the white dress and follow Sara down the aisle, passing Nella looking divine in palest lilac and waterproof mascara.

I tried to be funny about it, imagine myself beating my sister around the head with wired freesia and stephanotis, but I couldn't be humorous. I had a funny kind of ache inside me, just above the waist, that went up and down and threatened to engulf me. At this moment I couldn't see how I was going to go on living without the sight of Jamie's smile, the sound of his voice, the warm feel of him next to me in the Land Rover or in the Ard-na-Shiel library with dust motes swimming in the sun like tiny glittering moths.

When I stood up, I had made my decision. I would seek out the nearest hostel, give a false name, probably foreign, and pretend to be a sandwich short of a picnic. By the time Sara had rung round all the people I might have run to, I'd have found work and a place to live. If I made sure no one at the hostel knew where I'd gone they'd be unable to give her any help and I'd be free. I wiped my nose, picked up my bags and set off in search of shelter. But not before I had done something to clean myself up.

The cloakroom of the Cumberland hotel provided everything I needed: scented soap, hot water, plentiful towels and even a good dollop of hand lotion. That took care of my face and hands, but I was left with an uncomfortable feeling of the day-before-yesterday's knickers and bra. I stood looking at myself in a mirror that reflected a somewhat thinner face, lankish hair and crumpled clothes. I lifted one arm and sniffed. Was there an odour? The other armpit was no more conclusive, but I didn't feel clean.

I would have bent down and sniffed my nether regions if a woman in a Chanel suit and pearls like hen's eggs hadn't swanned in and looked at me as though I was a reject from an Oxfam shop. I picked up my bag and fled, trying not to think of a bath like the one at Ard-na-Shiel: wide and deep and unbelievably hot!

I had other things to worry about, too. After a lifetime of thinking myself streetwise, I was beginning to realize how little real knowledge I possessed. All very well to talk about a hostel, but how did you find one? I could hardly walk the streets of London in search, still less could I ask a policeman who might already be carrying my description and a wanted notice. Except that they might not want me. They might be carrying on with the wedding, glad to have got rid of the millstone. I felt my eyes prick and turned into the first coffee bar I saw.

I bought a cappuccino, regardless of the fact that I oughtn't to spend more than I had to. It was frothy and comforting but disappeared with horrifying speed. I kept on pretending to drink from the empty cup, glad of the sanctuary and fascinated by the antics of the couple in the opposite booth.

At first they were rowing. 'If you loved me – you don't give a shit about me – you'd say anything to get your way.' The reproaches went back and forward and then suddenly the ice melted and they were all over one another. I watched her nuzzle his neck, he kiss her eyes and mouth, half of me wanting the waitress to stop them, half wanting it to go on forever.

After a while they stopped canoodling and got down to planning.

He had had enough of London and was off to a job in Birmingham. He wanted her to go with him and reluctantly she agreed. The stumbling block was her job. If she walked out now she'd lose wages. If she promised to follow him, he didn't believe she would and he wasn't prepared to trust her.

In the end he won, offering to accompany her to her workplace and demand they pay her up-to-date. When they stood up to leave, I waited till they were at the door and then stood up to follow. The one thing I knew about London was that job vacancies were hard to fill at the lower level, and from the look of her she wasn't an executive. Where she was out, I might just be in! I could promise references and stall for a few days, maybe even weeks. It was a start.

We walked about two blocks and then cut down a back street. It was dingy and empty and I was afraid they'd turn and see me. I needn't have worried. They were so wrapped up in one another I could have hung on their coat-tails without detection. At last they turned into a gateway. I followed cautiously and peeped in at a yard. It looked like the back of a café or hotel because there was the smell of food and steam gushing from a vent in the wall. I saw them vanish through a doorway and then, a moment later, there was the sound of raised voices. I strained to make out what was being said but before I could make sense of it the boy emerged alone.

I was ready to beat a retreat but he didn't attempt to leave the yard. He hung about on the step, and after a few moments the girl joined him, turning on the step to fling 'Go to hell!' into the doorway. The boy raised his eyebrows in query, she showed him a small brown wage packet, swung her bag onto her shoulder and linked her arm in his. I darted behind a telegraph pole, trusting they would go back the way they had come, and watched as they walked off arm in arm, obviously bound for the tube.

I stood against the brick wall for a moment, summoning up my courage. If I'd guessed right and the girl had walked out on her job, that meant there was a vacancy. And she hadn't looked like a fully qualified pastry-chef – more like a kitchen-hand. Well, I could wash up. I picked up my bag and entered the yard.

There was no response to my first tentative knock on the open door so I knocked again. Still no response. I stepped over the threshold into a brew of steam and fumes and cooking smells.

'Hello?'

There was the clashing of pans somewhere and then a muffled shout. 'What you want?'

I moved forward, trying to see the enquirer. He was a short, fat man dressed in white trousers and a double-breasted white top with straining buttons. His brow was furrowed under an untidy white thatch as he jiggled pans on an immense range. He lifted a lid, swore under his breath, replaced the lid and turned.

'Well, what you want?'

He was obviously on a short fuse and wouldn't appreciate any verbal fencing.

'A job,' I said. 'Kitchen work. Anything.'

He looked at me for a moment, obviously dying to say no. Then he looked around him, and then back at me.

'Start now?' I nodded. He gestured towards a pile of dirty dishes. 'Get rid of those,' he said. 'We'll talk when the rush is over.'

Later on I would learn about the breakfast trade. Now all I knew was that a face appeared in a hatch every minute or so and demanded, 'Two rashers, one egg, two pork and beans' or 'Egg well-done on fried and mush.' And sometimes the voice from the other side plonked down more greasy plates to add to the pile.

The huge industrial sink was full of greasy water. I hung up my jacket, rolled up my sleeves and fished for the plug. The water was tepid and full of unidentified floating objects. But I was being paid, and with any luck I might get an egg well done on fried when the rush was over.

There was something soothing about the process of reducing the huge pile. I filled the draining board and then began to dry.

'Good girl,' the little man said when I filled the plate stack.

I smiled and went back to the task. An hour and a half later I had a job.

'You got cards?' asked Mr Papandreou, for that was his name. I shook my head. He clicked his tongue against his teeth. 'You student?' I nodded. He smiled and tapped his nose. 'Little bit extra?' I nodded again. 'OK. If we get inspection you go and sit in café.' He patted my hand. 'We don't get inspected much.'

I was warming to him but also feeling guilty. I had no intention of staying more than a day or two. He was paying two-fifty an hour. I wouldn't survive for long on that and the thought of another night in the park was unthinkable. Still, I filled my plate from the leftover sausage and bacon and crisply fried eggs and wolfed the lot.

I'd no sooner finished than the lunchtime rush began. 'Chicken and chips.' 'Cumberland and mash.' 'Faggots and gravy.' Now I was allowed to stir and drain and plunge great baskets of frozen chips slowly into the fryer.

'Good girl,' Mr Papandreou said.

After a while it became automatic to move from sink to cooking area, from there to hatch and while I washed and stirred I made plans. I had to have a decent night's sleep tonight and I needed more clothes, toiletries and more suitable luggage. There was only one place this could be obtained: my own home in Notting Hill.

There was a key in the back of my purse. As long as I was careful not to let any of the neighbours know I was there, I could use the house for one night at least. I felt a huge weight lift from my shoulders.

At five o'clock my relief arrived, an Asian lady who was obviously vastly skilled and looked at me with deep suspicion.

'Where is Emma?' she said and received a flow of invective in reply.

'This girl good,' Mr Papandreou said and beamed at me.

'What time do I come tomorrow?' The Asian lady was busily cleaning everything in sight, obviously dissatisfied with my levels of hygiene.

'Seven?' Mr Papandreou said and sighed with relief when I nodded.

9

Going home in daylight was out of the question. I bought myself a Bounty bar and ate it slowly while I walked back to Hyde Park.

The hours to nightfall seemed interminable. I sat by the lake, watching the diving birds, following the progress of joggers as they went around the lake, sometimes walking to the café to sip a cappuccino as slowly as I could, to make it last. I longed for something to read – anything to keep me from thinking about Ard-na-Shiel. I didn't regret my decision to leave. I couldn't have stayed to see Jamie pass beyond my reach forever. Nella was different, but if I contacted her again I might give something away.

My mind ran back over all the detective series I'd seen on television. How did they trace people? On telephones if you talked too long. By background noises. By postmarks. I must let Nella know I was OK, but how could it be done? And what if they'd abandoned Ard-na-Shiel and come back to London in the hope of finding me?

By the time it was dark enough to take the tube to Ladbroke Grove, I was half-expecting to see a light in the window, but to my relief, the house was in darkness. I stood on the corner trying to remember which of the neighbours were nosy. There was a street-lamp not far from our door. As I stood on the step to turn the key I would be terribly visible.

In the end I decided I had no other option. I walked up the street, key at the ready, and mounted the steps. Insert, twist, push... the next moment I was in the dark hall, the door safely locked behind me. I had meant to run straight upstairs to the bathroom and wallow. Instead I sat down on the bottom step, put my head against the newel post and howled my misery.

A week ago I had left this house knowing pretty well what the future held. Now I had a few hours at most to sort out my life before I must take to the streets, not knowing when I would have a secure home again. I dried my eyes and went upstairs.

The first thing I wanted was a bath: a long, sudsy, scented, red-hot bath. After that something to eat and then I would pack those things I needed to take with me. There would be no time in the morning if I was not to be late for work. As I lay soaking I gave way to a delicious fantasy, that I could stay here in the house unknown to anyone for as long as Nella stayed on at Ard-na-Shiel. I was nervous about lights, but ours was a cosmopolitan street. There was no one I could think of who would be madly interested in who was in the Morgan house. They were all too taken up with their own affairs.

What if Nella phoned them, though? Surely anyone would be tempted to check up for a neighbour whose daughter had gone missing? I was about to leap out of the bath and douse the lights when reason prevailed. I had work to do, clothes to choose or discard and I must make wise choices. The only thing I could do was make very sure Nella or Sara did not try to look for me in London. I left the bath, towelled myself dry and went to the telephone by Nella's bed.

'Mum?' It was Nella who answered and I felt a pang at the thought of her sitting over the phone hoping for a call.

'Lexy! Is that you? Where are you? We're frantic…'

'I'm OK.' I interrupted. I had vague thoughts about police tracing calls and the need to be brief. 'I'm still in Newcastle. I've got a room with another girl – two girls in fact, and I'm fine and you mustn't worry!'

'*Mustn't worry?* Have you gone mad, Alexandra? Why are you doing this? And on the eve of Sara's wedding –'

I interrupted again. 'It isn't the eve – it's two days yet. And that's why I left. I'm sick of all the fuss about the wedding.'

Impossible to say I was in love with the bridegroom. 'I'll come back when it's over. When you go back to London…' I almost said 'come back' but checked myself in time. Nella was barmy but she could be very quick on the uptake when it suited her.

'Please, Lexy – I'll come to Newcastle. We'll talk. You needn't wear that dress if that's what it is…'

I felt a tear slide down my cheek. If only it were that simple!

'I have to ring off, Mum. Love to Sara – and Jamie. I love you all.' I put down the phone before the break in her voice turned to sobbing, which I couldn't bear.

I had meant to have a meal when I left the bathroom but suddenly I was no longer hungry. I found myself on the landing, half-wanting to slip back into the comfort of the bath water, half-wanting to crawl into bed and go to sleep. Instead, I found myself in Sara's bedroom, breathing in the scent of her, the clean, sensible scent of a well-ordered life, drinking in the sense of order that prevailed, so different from Nella's overflowing, powder-strewn boudoir. I had never had a proper bedroom of my own. At first I had shared with Sara, and then, when she was grown up and needed her own space, I was banished to Nella's dressing room with her going in and out whenever she chose.

I suddenly realized I had wrapped my arms around myself and was rocking slightly on my feet. I wanted my sister, wanted to be held in those capable arms and be small again – small and safe and not tormented by feelings I could hardly understand and couldn't bear. In the end I forgot about packing or choosing or eating. I took Sara's well-worn towelling robe from the back of the door, wrapped it around me and climbed into her bed to cry myself to sleep.

*

When I woke, it was six o'clock and matters had been settled for me because there was no time to pack now, and so I must come back tonight. I opened a tin of grapefruit segments and made myself a cup of tea, then I let myself out of the back door and crept down the yard in the shadow of the wall. A few moments later I was on the tube and rattling towards the café.

Mr Papandreou greeted me with relief and not a little surprise, as though he'd half-expected I wouldn't turn up.

'Watch those eggs,' he said and moved on to the sausage and bacon. I tipped hot fat over the eggs, replacing each cooked egg with a freshly cracked one, taking a pride in seeing the yoke pale under a white film, lifting them before the edges crisped too much, keeping up the flow as the orders flooded in.

At nine o'clock we could relax and sit either side of the table with mugs of hot, sweet tea.

'You're good girl,' Mr Papandreou said. 'Better than that Emma. She walk out on me. You'll stay.' He looked at me beseechingly so that I was tempted to say 'Of course I'll stay,' but there was something so nice about his round face, crinkled like a newborn baby and glistening with sweat, that I couldn't lie to him.

'I can stay for a while. If I can find somewhere to stay, that is. I can stay for a few weeks, but then I'll have to move on.'

Mr Papandreou drained his mug and set it down in front of him. 'You running away?' I didn't reply and after a moment, he nodded. 'Everyone running away. Come to London, big ideas. No milk and honey here! Always moving on. I make you good job if you stay here.'

'I will stay. Like I said, a week or two. Till you find someone else. I can't stay too long…' I took the plunge. 'I don't have any papers – employment cards, those things.'

He shook his head. 'Don't matter. I pay you on the side. But you stay. You think about it. I need a good girl. I teach you.'

I wasn't in the mood to argue. 'I'll stay for the time being,' I said. 'If I can find somewhere to stay. But keep on looking for someone. I can't stay forever.'

'OK.' He put his little hands flat on the table in front of him. 'OK. You stay for now. Where you sleep last night?'

'A friend's. But I can't stay there after tonight.'

He reached out and patted my hand. 'OK. OK. We find you somewhere. Now, you do the potatoes. Chop, chop. Good girl.'

I took a deep breath.

'And I'll need a sub,' I said. 'I'm absolutely skint.'

10

I wandered the streets when I left the café, waiting for dusk, but as I approached home my heart was pounding. What if Nella had telephoned a neighbour? What if there was a police car on the corner, waiting? Tomorrow was the day of the wedding. Was it going ahead or had they postponed it and were even now bearing down on Notting Hill?

I walked past the house twice on the other side of the street before I felt secure enough to walk up to the door and insert the key. Once inside, I put my cheek against the closed door and listened to my heart pounding against my chest wall. This would be the last night in my own home. Tomorrow I would set out on an independent existence.

When my heart ceased to thump, I sat down on the bottom stair. Why had it happened: this love I felt for a man I couldn't have? Did I want him just because he was Sara's? I had always coveted Sara's possessions, envied her effortless achievement of everything she wanted. But it wasn't just envy. Even now, when I thought of Jamie, I felt a strange sensation, a feeling I'd never had before.

So this was love: the thing everyone at school went on about – except that, for them, it came and went. I knew that what had happened to me was not just an overnight sensation, and the thought was terrifying because this feeling wasn't comfortable. I made myself consider that it might be just a schoolgirl crush, but I knew it wasn't. It was too painful for that.

When at last I climbed into my bed, two cases stood at the door, ready for the morning. They contained a sensible selection of clothes, a few souvenirs too precious to leave behind, hair-brush, toiletries, my Giro book, a sewing kit, the leather manicure case Sara had given me when I stopped biting my nails and a photo of the three of us which I had taken out of its frame and put between the pages of my copy of *Watership Down*, from which I could never be parted.

I didn't expect to sleep, but I did – a dreamless sleep until just before dawn, when I woke thinking of Sara and Jamie. Today was their wedding day. I sat in bed, hugging my knees. Had they slept together last night? Were they even now waking, tearing apart, laughing at the prospect of the day? It sounds crazy but half of me wanted it to be like that: a fairy-tale wedding. The other half wanted to be there, at the back of the church, to say those fatal words 'just impediment' that would put them apart.

Except that there was no impediment. I had never mattered to Jamie. He had probably never really looked at me. I had lusted after him in the byre but all he had felt was embarrassment.

While I washed and dressed, I let myself ponder the possibility that the wedding might not take place if I was not there. Crazy thoughts came and went, the two of them arguing over me, Sara criticizing my wayward behaviour, Jamie defending me. I couldn't let Nella into this scenario. The thought of what I was doing to her was too painful to contemplate.

At six-forty-five I left the house, hesitating on the step for a long time because I knew that this time there would be no coming back. Had I packed everything? What had been forgotten? In the end I accepted the impossibility of bringing with me almost seventeen years of life and let the door thud close.

It was better once I got to the café. No time to think, then, about society weddings and tartan and taffeta. We got through break-fasts and sat down for our break.

'You got a place yet?' Mr Papandreou's face was beaded with sweat and anxious.

I shook my head. He pursed his lips and looked towards the bags I'd stashed away in a corner.

'So,' he said. 'So… out on the street then?'

I decided to play it cautiously. 'Not exactly.'

His fat little hands came up in the air in a gesture of exasperation. 'Yes or no?' he said. 'No one lives "not exactly". In or out, up or down? Don't go round houses with me, Alexandra.'

'I did have somewhere but I can't stay there any longer.'

He looked at me expectantly, waiting for more.

'It's not safe,' I said.

There was silence for a moment and then he sighed.

'OK.' he said. 'OK. I heard it before. Pretty girls has troubles.' He rose to his feet. 'Let's cook, then we fix up something.'

By four o'clock he'd found me a room in his cousin Eleni's house. It was small but clean and the window looked over the roofs and backstreets of Edgware. I shared a toilet with the rest of that floor and could use the kitchen downstairs according to rota. Best of all, it only cost twenty-five pounds – a special deal to family – which left me just enough over to live on. For the time being at least, I was OK.

I had terrible pangs of guilt about letting Mr P, for so I had christened him, think I was escaping sexual abuse, but I couldn't even begin to tell him the truth. Anyone hearing my story would decide I was a spoiled brat who had a crush on her big sister's fiancé and send me smartly back home – and it wasn't like that. I wasn't being brattish. I had this pain inside me that I couldn't quite understand and was a little bit afraid of. If this was love, they could keep it. Except that it had been pleasure, too. For a little while.

That night I unpacked my bags and then sat down on the room's only chair. There was a picture of Liverpool Docks on one wall and a chocolate-boxy portrait of flowers on another, but it was warm and clean and mine. For the time being, it was home.

So why did I lie awake long after I had put out the light and see the lights of Ballachulish swim towards me in the darkness?

11

The next few days were comparatively easy. I knew that in all probability Sara and Jamie were man and wife, and somehow that fact was oddly comforting just because it was a fact. No point in wild dreams of Jamie waking up to his mistake and choosing the right sister. No point in thinking Sara would ever leave him. I knew my sister too well for that.

If I daydreamed at all, it was of a life of glorious celibacy, me as a woman of mystery dressed in black and touched by sorrow. Not that there was much time for dreaming, by day or by night. The round of sausage, egg and toast or Pasta Bolognese and chips was remorseless, and Mr Papandreou ever more reliant on me. By the time my replacement arrived each day at five, I was more than ready to leave for Edgware and my eyrie at the top of Cousin Eleni's house.

I had spent the first two nights rearranging the furniture to my liking. I placed the bed so that I could look straight through the tiny window onto the roofs and steeples of Edgware. There was a hint of green on a rooftop opposite and sometimes a flamboyant line of washing fluttering languidly in the soft August breeze. My own washing, rubbed through in the bathroom handbasin, was draped around the room. How had I lived for sixteen years without realizing that the spin dryer was God's gift to the human race?

Each night when I had done my chores, I curled up on the bed and scanned the *Telegraph* I bought on my way home. The notice appeared on the fourth day.

At St Bartolph's Church, Lochmore, Western High-
lands, on August 21st, Sara Emma Louise, daughter
of Mrs Prunella Morgan of Notting Hill, London,
and the late Euan Gilmore, FRCS, MRCOG, of St
Helier, Jersey, Channel Islands, to James Hector
Munro, son of the late Colonel and Mrs Hector Munro
of Ard-na-Shiel, Lochmore, Lochaber, Inverness-shire.

There were no further details, not who had stood up for Jamie
or who, if anyone, had taken my place in attendance on the bride.

Suddenly, tears filled my eyes. I had often imagined Sara's
wedding, the glorious moment when she would move out and
leave the stage to me. I had wished her well on that imaginary
occasion, pictured myself wreathed in smiles that spoke of
sisterly piety and not at all of relief. But then I summoned up the
scene in the hall, the body language of two people beside
themselves with longing. I let it linger for a moment and my tears
dried. I had done the only thing possible. Now I must get on with
the rest of my life.

I couldn't stay with Mr Papandreou forever. Partly because
the job didn't pay enough to live on (not in London, anyway),
and partly because, even in London's teeming streets, there was
always the possibility of bumping into Nella: on a bus, in the
tube, window-shopping in Oxford Street. And even if it never
happened, the possibility that it might would make a normal
existence impossible.

The day after the announcement appeared, I rang the Ard-na-
Shiel number from the café, hoping Nella would still be there.
But when McGregor, the ancient retainer, answered, he informed
me that Mrs Morgan had already departed for London and would
be at her own residence by nightfall.

'Is that the wee lassie?' he asked suddenly.

I panicked and put down the phone.

Outside, when I sought to quell my panic by going out into the yard, the late sun was gilding the rooftops, turning them to orange and apricot, hiding the squalor of the backstreet in a hazy shimmer. In the Highlands, the dying rays would turn the loch to silver and rim the edges of Creag Ghorm and Meall Mor. But Nella was speeding towards London now, no doubt in search of her delinquent daughter. And vague though my mother could be at times, she was possessed of a steely determination when the need arose. If she was determined to find me, she would do it eventually.

Unless I disappeared completely. Unless Alexandra Sacha Louise Mentmore was no more. I turned and went back into the house. Tonight I would ring home from a call box and reassure Nella. Thereafter I would vanish for as long as it took to make my way in the world and come back to lord it over them all. At the back of my mind lurked doubts about exactly how this would be accomplished, but I pushed them aside. One day at a time. In ninety-six hours I had run away, travelled the length of the British Isles, found myself a job and a place to live. What could I do in a year or two?

Half an hour later I said my goodbyes and got ready to quit the café for the day. The Asian lady had softened a bit now that I had failed to supplant her. She accorded me a grudging 'goodnight' and swept only a perfunctory cloth over the waste-taps. I felt oddly pleased by this acceptance and had to resist the impulse to hug her. As usual, Mr Papandreou pressed food on me: mutton in rich, creamy sauce and honeyed figs, all wrapped up in cartons. If I stayed in this job any length of time I would be able to audition for the Roly-Polys, but I knew it gave him pleasure to think he was fattening me up and Eleni was always happy to relieve me of anything I brought home.

There was a phone box on the corner of the next street to the café and I went inside. The telephone had hardly started to ring when it was snatched up and my mother's voice, huskier than usual, belted out the number.

'It's me,' I said. 'Lexy.'

'Darling!' Surely she couldn't be crying. A terrible vision of a honeymoon plane crashing into the Atlantic overtook me. It was a relief when she sniffled loudly and continued. 'Alexandra. Where are you?' Her voice was sharper now, even angry. 'Come home at once. This charade has gone on long enough. You ruined the wedding. If that's what you meant to do, you certainly succeeded.'

'I'm sorry.' Suddenly, I felt mulish. 'I'm sorry if once more I was the black spot on the family portrait, but I have a life, too, you know.'

There was silence for a moment and when she spoke again her voice was softer. 'Darling, I'm sorry. I'm not cross. I'm just out of my head with worry. So is Sara. She rings every few hours to know if there's any news.'

So I was spoiling the honeymoon, was I? There was a certain perverse satisfaction in that. Perhaps I could go home now, be taken back like the prodigal son. But even as I thought it, I dismissed the idea. It would be kisses all round at first and then recriminations. And lots of watching the newlyweds wrapped in one another's arms. Besides, there was no way I could go back to school! Not now, when I had tasted freedom.

'I'll ring soon,' I said, and put down the phone.

That night I sat cross-legged on my bed, making plans. For now I was happy enough at the café and safe at Cousin Eleni's. If I kept clear of the ritzier places there was little chance of my bumping into Nella, and due to my total lack of funds, little or no opportunity to frequent such places. But I couldn't stay in Edgware forever.

I knew how Nella's mind would work. At first she'd play my absence down in the hope that I would come back. She knew I was not in immediate danger from my telephone calls, so no need to inform the police or court publicity just yet.

Eventually, though, she'd get desperate. She was still a minor public figure. Even an almost-Bond girl has a profile. It wouldn't take much effort to get on a TV programme complete with pictures of me, and turn the whole country into a detective service. Before that happened I had to be somewhere else, with another identity and a different appearance. When at last I turned out the light, it was not to sleep but rather to plan how my second escape might be accomplished.

The following morning I waited until our break between breakfasts and lunches and confided in Mr Papandreou. 'I don't think I can ever go home again,' I said.

His nice old face clouded and I felt really mean because I knew what he was thinking. Child abuse! Any minute now he would summon Esther Rantzen to secure justice for me.

'Don't worry,' I added hastily. 'I don't really want to, so I don't mind. It's just that I want to make a fresh start: a new name and another identity. But for that you need documents.'

'Papers,' he said gloomily. 'Everything is papers nowadays.' He shook his head and suddenly I knew who he reminded me of: Gepetto, the kindly old father in the Disney *Pinocchio*. And here was I telling porkies, just like the little puppet. I put up a surreptitious finger to my nose, half-expecting it to have grown an inch or two.

He put out a big hand and covered mine, where it lay on the table. Beneath the sleeve of his white chef's jacket a clean if frayed shirt cuff showed. 'Listen,' he said. 'I ask around. I sort it. Maybe not today but soon.'

I nodded gratefully but I wasn't hopeful. I'd confided in him because I didn't see what harm it could do, but I couldn't see how he could help me. He'd given me temporary sanctuary but the rest would be up to me.

I was wrong to underestimate the old Greek. The following day he greeted me at seven in a state of some excitement. 'We have a visitor today,' he said, but when I asked who, he only rolled his eyes and got on with the sausages. At ten-thirty we subsided into our chairs either side of the table and drew breath.

As if on cue, a man entered from the yard. He wore a donkey jacket in spite of the heat and small rivers of sweat were running down either temple, but he had a kind face and his handshake, when we were introduced, was firm.

He accepted a mug of tea and some baklava and sat down between us. He was staring at me in an odd way and I turned to Mr Papandreou, raising my eyebrows in question. He, too, was staring at the man as if waiting for him to say something. 'Well?' he said at last. And when there was no answer, 'Well?' again.

Suddenly the man nodded and broke into rapid Greek. Mr Papandreou looked pleased and nodded back. Eventually the man put his hand inside his jacket and withdrew a plastic pouch. He laid it on the table and then pushed it towards me. 'Take it,' Mr Papandreou said. He got to his feet, crossed to the till, rang up 'No Sale' and withdrew several notes. The man accepted them, drained his mug, got to his feet, shook my hand again, raised his hand in salute to the old Greek and went out of the door.

Mr Papandreou tapped the plastic pouch and said, 'Papers. They belonged to his daughter. He wanted to make sure you were good girl before he gave you his daughter's name.'

12

Inside the packet there was a passport belonging to a Melina Sophia Vassilides, a birth certificate showing that she was born on June 6, 1970, in Nicosia, Cyprus, and a P45 dated September 14, 1989. I opened the passport and gazed at the photograph. Apart from the long dark hair we could have been sisters. We were not identical but there were similarities. Straight brows above dark eyes, quite a prominent nose... Nella had always said my nose was Roman and I had always made the obvious reply, that it was roamin' all over my face. But the girl in the photograph was good-looking, even beautiful.

'Who is she?' I said.

Mr Papandreou shook his head sadly. 'She died a few months ago. Her father is sad but she left a child – a little girl. For her, he takes money. But first he had to see you were a good girl, worthy of the name Vassilides.'

'You paid him,' I said. It wasn't a question. 'How much?'

For a moment I thought he wasn't going to answer me, but I held his eye until he gave way.

'Fifty pounds,' he said. 'You stay here for a while. It's worth it.'

He turned away then and I was glad because it meant he didn't see the tears in my eyes. 'I'll stay,' I said. 'For as long as I can.'

The next day I dyed my hair in the kitchen sink at Cousin Eleni's. When it was done I looked even more like Melina Vassilides, but the face that looked back at me from the mirror was strange. Older, somehow, and more wary, but puzzled. A month ago I had been an almost sixth-former getting ready to buckle down to A-levels as soon as I had my stint as a bridesmaid out of the way. In the holidays I lived under my mother's roof and was dependent on her for everything. Now I was earning a wage, I had a place of my own and I would never again attend school. It seemed too far-fetched to be true, but it was.

The day after I dyed my hair I phoned Nella again. This time she sounded more resigned but hostile. 'Why are you ringing, Alexandra, if you don't intend to come to your senses?' And then quickly, in case I put down the phone: 'If something's wrong, if someone has upset you, tell me. I'll help you – but *come home*, just come home, Lexy darling.' Her voice broke then and I felt my own chin tremble. Better get this over quickly!

'I can't come home, Mum. Not just yet. I'm safe and I'm fine. I have a job and a nice place to live – and I will come home eventually. I promise you. It's just that, for now, I have to be on my own…'

'But where are you?' she interrupted. 'Tell me where you are. I'll come to you – I must see you, Alexandra. I won't make you come home, not if you don't want to, but just let me see for myself that you're alright.'

'I can't, Mum. You know what would happen if I did. You would make me come home and I can't, not just yet.'

'You're not pregnant, are you? Because if that's it –'

'*Mum!*' My outrage must have sounded convincing because she muttered an apology before she returned to the interrogation.

'Well, where are you? At least tell me where you are? Who are you staying with? It's not someone from school because –'

It was my turn to interrupt now. 'Oh God! You haven't told everyone at school?'

But even as I spoke, I knew that it didn't matter what had been said to my schoolfriends because they belonged in the past.

'I'm in Newcastle,' I said. 'And my money is running out. I'll keep in touch, Mum. I love you. Sara, too. And Jamie. Give them my love and take care. I love you, Mum.' I put the phone down then, although I could hear her still speaking at the other end.

After that I rang her every week. I was always afraid that one day it would be Sara who answered, but to my relief it was always Nella.

Summer was drawing to a close. There were leaves on the paths in the parks of London – only a few at first, but eventually piles that I could scuff through when I walked there on Sundays. The café didn't open then and I loved my day off, although, as the nights began to draw in, my bedroom began to seem a little claustrophobic.

I was managing quite well on my wage from Mr Papandreou, largely because of all the handouts he gave me: food, occasionally a bottle of ouzo, which Cousin Eleni grabbed from me in exchange for a discount on the rent, and sometimes an extra five or ten pounds for what he called 'good work'.

I was lonely, but there was a strange contentment about my life. I was at no one's beck and call, no silly rules to obey, no secret conventions to observe, no appearance to keep up. All I had to do was keep myself clean and get out of bed in the morning. As long as I concentrated on essentials and didn't allow myself to think too much, I was OK.

And so it might have gone on indefinitely if it had not been for the approach of Christmas. Takings in the café dropped but Mr Papandreou was unconcerned.

'People are saving,' he said. 'A little here, a little there – it mounts up and they buy big presents for their family. We make it up in January. Then they think only of themselves.'

That night I sat in my room and thought about Christmas. The café would be closed. So would everything else in London, in all probability. At New Year I could mingle with the crowds in

Trafalgar Square. I'd done that once before with Sara and her then-boyfriend. But Christmas was a family time. Everyone had someone to go to at Christmas.

Everyone but me.

Christmas Day would fall on a Monday, which only made things worse. At first, Sundays had been a welcome relief from the drudgery of the café. I had revelled in a long lie-in, soaked in a bath, enjoyed the autumn sunshine in the parks, a different park each week. Now, though, a lie-in was no longer a novelty. Someone else was always locked in the communal bathroom or, if I got there first, disturbing my peace by trying the handle. And in the park the wind blew chill, sending me scurrying home too soon.

I had a radio, bought in Petticoat Lane, and occasionally Cousin Eleni would invite me to watch her small colour TV. We followed Michael Palin around the world in eighty days and sat open-mouthed as the Iron Curtain was torn down and country after country celebrated freedom, but mostly Eleni's tastes ran to reruns of old black-and-white films, especially if they starred Cary Grant or Gregory Peck – and to be truthful they left me cold. There was only one fantasy for me, and one man to star in it.

At weekends I telephoned Nella, always from a different call box, never for more than a few minutes. She always begged me to come home, but there was a resigned note in her voice now, as though she had accepted my going as a fact.

Somehow her resignation affected me more than her entreaties had ever done. And with the onset of Christmas, everyone was talking of their plans, even Meera, my Asian colleague. There were rapt faces in the shops as women tried to decide between a tie or a shirt for the man in their life and I began increasingly to think about going home.

I had been away for four months, long enough to prove I could survive on my own, long enough to demolish any thought of my going back to school. If I went back there would only be Nella and I could easily vanish during visits from Scotland.

The first weekend in December I set out to make my phone call. All morning the radio had been full of the remake of 'Do They Know It's Christmas?' Bob Geldof and his friends had made the original record in 1984 to raise money for famine relief. Now Kylie Minogue and Jason Donovan and a host of pop stars were doing it again. Which meant that everyone was talking about it and the strains of the original record seemed to issue from every window in every street. Did I know it was Christmas? I could hardly avoid knowing!

As I walked to the phone box I made my decision. Unless Sara and Jamie were coming, I would go back home for Christmas, just the days I had off from the café. I would say I had come up from Newcastle and leave on the Tuesday night, as though to return north. If the two days were bearable, even happy, then we could both consider the future. After all, Nella might be enjoying her freedom, too. But at least neither of us would be alone.

I decided to broach the subject cautiously – as cautiously as you can in less than four minutes. After all, she might have been invited to Ard-na-Shiel. It would be typical of Sara to include Nella in her first Christmas with Jamie. She had come into the world oozing consideration for the midwife so it wasn't likely she would neglect her own mother.

'What are you doing for Christmas?' I said when we'd gone through the inevitable 'please come back' routine.

'I don't know... nothing, really.'

'I thought you might be going up to Scotland.'

'No, not their first year. They asked, but I refused. And Sara doesn't want to travel too far at the moment...' She hesitated then and I felt a sudden horror engulf me. I knew exactly what she was going to say.

'She's pregnant – only three months, but her blood pressure's up a bit. The doctor thinks she should stay put. And I'm going up for Hogmanay.'

I managed to force a laugh. 'You'll have a hundred pipers and a' an' a'.'

'Something like that. They make a lot of New Year up there.'

I murmured something about not getting too drunk and mumbled my goodbyes.

'Where are you spending Christmas?' she said desperately. 'Oh Lexy, darling, please come home.'

But I was putting the phone down by that time, afraid my sniffling nose would betray me.

I pushed open the kiosk door and emerged into the cold December air. I could see Jamie's face in the byre as he had delivered the calf, alight with the wonder of birth. How much more his eyes would shine as his own child came into the world. *A child!* Living proof that they did it, night after night, probably, in the huge bed in the even more huge bedroom with the moonlight shining on the loch.

'I can't bear it,' I said aloud and started to run, not stopping until I was in Oxford Street, people pushing and bustling all around, preoccupied with their own business and not at all interested in a stupid girl wiping eyes and nose on the sleeve of her denim jacket.

The news that Sara was pregnant punctured my last faint illusion of some sort of future in which Jamie and I could be together. Out of sight of them both I had been able to postpone facing up to the truth of their being together, but now that togetherness was a fact – a growing fact. The baby was due in June, so it had been conceived straight after the wedding.

'They couldn't wait!' I said in the privacy of my room off the Edgware Road, lacerating myself with a vision of Sara and Jamie grappling, coupling, sighing with satisfaction, the amalgam of every erotic book I had read in the school dorm, shrieking with laughter at detail, reading some of the goriest bits aloud to a chorus of 'Yuk!' from the other girls. Only in real life it wasn't funny. There were consequences to sex. My sister was pregnant and I cried.

I tried to shut it out, arms deep in greasy water in the café. I tried to think of nothing, of anything except the moonlit loch and lovers awaiting the living proof of mutual desire. But everywhere I looked there were pregnant women; every other shop sold baby clothes. Even Meera proudly announced she was pregnant and patted the swelling mound under her tunic.

I had abandoned any thought of going home for Christmas. I didn't ring Nella the following weekend. Instead, I spent Sunday in the Odeon cinema, watching Harrison Ford play Indiana Jones. The film was halfway through when I realized that he bore a resemblance to Jamie. Thereafter I held my breath through each close-up, searching every feature, squeezing my eyes shut to remember the sound of his voice in the sunlit library, the strength of his hands where they gripped the steering wheel, the warmth of his body against mine in the byre when we gazed down at the newborn calf. I was torturing myself and at the same time revelling in it. I came out into Oxford Street and wandered, tearful, among wide-eyed shoppers clutching present lists like people in search of the Holy Grail.

I was passing M&S when I saw Nella. She was standing on the edge of the pavement obviously waiting for a taxi. She was laden with parcels, but her face was not animated as it usually was at the end of a shopping spree. Instead, she looked sad and somehow older. I came to a halt, half-afraid she would see me, half-afraid she would hail a taxi and be whisked away before I could reach her.

She lifted a hand as a taxi came down from the direction of Hyde Park Corner but it swished past her. I stood uncertain, whether or not to move towards her. And then my courage deserted me. If I made contact she would clutch me, hold on no matter what I did. I would be drawn into a taxi and back into my role as little sister. I couldn't do it. I was turning away when she, too, turned, as though some sixth sense had told her I was there.

'Lexy!'

Her voice rang out across the crowded pavement. A tall black man loomed up, cutting off sight of her and in that moment I turned and ran, not stopping until I had run down the alleyway that led to St Christopher's Court and could be sure she had not followed me. I slowed to a walk then, on and into the maze of streets that led me back to Eleni's and safety. But the safety was only temporary. Now that Nella knew I was in London, the search for me would be relentless.

That night I sat up in bed, hugging my knees, trying to work out what to do next. I must leave London, but where could I go? I had no savings. The money I earned at the café barely lasted me the week; there was never anything left over. Besides, the money

Mr Papandreou had paid out for my new identity was a debt of honour and must be repaid.

If I was going to move to another city I would need train fare and the cost of accommodation until I could find work. I needed a minimum of one hundred pounds, which might as well have been a thousand for all the chance I had of getting it. When at last I lay down to sleep, all I could do was pray for a miracle.

The miracle came at half-past three the following afternoon, in the shape of Meera's excitable husband. With great wringing of hand and a torrent of broken English, he informed Mr Papandreou that his wife had taken to her bed with raised blood pressure, a threat to both mother and unborn child, and would not be back at work in the foreseeable future. Papa maintained his composure until the distraught husband had departed, but then he sank into his chair at the table and clapped both hands to his forehead.

'Why now? Why Christmas?'

I slid into the chair opposite him. 'Will she be hard to replace?'

He looked at me with scorn. 'Hard? Oh not *hard*. Impossible! It's Christmas: you know, Christmas? Big deal? Every shop, every café, every pub has extra trade, extra staff. Where I get replacement? You tell me!'

Ten minutes later I had convinced him that I could do Meera's job as well as my own. 'But only until the New Year,' I said. 'I must go then. There'll be lots of people looking for work once Christmas is over, but for now you need me. I need the money.'

He hummed and hahed over whether or not I could possibly work two shifts six days a week, but he had no other option and we both knew it.

Meera had worked from five to eleven each day, thirty-six hours at two pounds fifty an hour. Ninety pounds a week. If I stayed until New Year's Eve, I would make two hundred and seventy pounds extra, and on that kind of money I could go anywhere. All I had to do in the meantime was keep out of sight.

When I went home that night, weary in the bone at the end of a sixteen-hour day, I knew it was going to be alright. I had grown up a lot in the last four months. Now I knew I could survive.

That knowledge made me bold. I turned into a telephone box and rang home. 'Hello, Mum,' I said, as though I had not run away from her yesterday.

'Lexy? You're in London!'

I feigned surprise. 'London? No, I'm still in Newcastle.'

'But I saw you yesterday.'

'Saw me? Where?'

'In Oxford Street. I saw you. I called out and you ran away.'

'Not me – I'm in Newcastle. You know that. Why would I be in London? And if I'd been there, why wouldn't I have come home? You say I ran away? Why would I do that?'

'It *was* you!' There was a trace of doubt in her voice and I exploited it.

'Sorry, Mum. Not me. I'm still in Newcastle, sharing a flat. I'm fine. Are you OK?'

'But I saw you!' There was real doubt in her voice now and I pressed on.

'I've got a job. A restaurant near the Tyne. And I've been to Northumberland. It was cold, but wonderful countryside.'

'Well…' Her certainty had petered out. 'I was sure it was you. Still, it was crowded. Anyway, when are you coming home? It's ten days to Christmas. I'll send you the fare… Sara rings every day, hoping to hear you're back safe and well.'

'Is she OK?' I listened to the detail of Sara's pregnancy until my money was almost gone. 'Sorry, Mum. Got to go. Cash about to run out.'

'But Lexy –'

'Sorry.' The pips were going and I could hear her protesting on the other end of the line. 'Sorry. Don't worry. I'm fine. Love you.'

I put down the phone and slumped against the side of the kiosk. Still, I had done a good job of putting her off the scent. If she did anything it would be to scour the riverside restaurants of Newcastle. Perhaps she'd ring Jamie and he would speed down and over the border. I pictured him entering, searching with his eyes, going back to the Land Rover and driving to the next bistro. At least it would keep him away from Sara for a while! I jabbed viciously at the door and exited into the cold December street.

I was halfway home when I realized that now I could not summon up a clear vision of Jamie's face. I stopped in my tracks and concentrated. I could see his silhouette, picture the soft, dark thatch of hair, the set of his shoulders... but the face, the features, eluded me. Henceforth I would have to think of Harrison Ford.

In spite of fooling Nella I spent the next week studiously avoiding the centre of London. Not that I had any time to window-shop. By the time I had tackled Meera's shift as well as my own I was exhausted, fit only to crawl home and tumble into bed.

At the end of the first week I received a bulging pay packet.

'Nice,' I said and lifted the flap.

Mr Papandreou was gazing at me fondly. 'You sure it's not too much for you?'

I shook my head. 'It's a doddle. Anyway, it's only until the New Year. I must go then – you know that?'

He nodded. 'I know. You'll be a big miss.'

I had pulled out the comforting wodge of notes and was spreading them between my fingers. 'Those papers you got for me. Fifty, wasn't it?'

He was waving his hand. 'Nothing, it was nothing.'

'How much?' There was that note in my voice that spelled business and he pursed his lips.

'Twenty – twenty pounds.'

'*How* much?'

'Thirty. It was thirty.'

'I know it was more, Mr P. You said it was fifty.'

'Alright, alright. Fifty. But I don't want it back. It was gift for you...'

In the end we settled at thirty-five pounds, honour satisfied on both sides. 'You very determined girl,' he said, fitting the notes into his wallet.

Suddenly I thought of moving on, leaving behind the safety of this steamy, odourful kitchen and his thousand small kindnesses. 'I'll miss you,' I said, and then my arms were round his neck and he was patting my back and all I wanted to do was snuggle in and be comforted more.

'There, there,' he said at last. 'You can always come back. Now,' he looked at the clock, 'time to start again.'

When I crawled home that night, vowing never to go near food again as long as I lived, I separated my usual weekly wage and put the surplus fifty-five pounds in my knicker drawer. I was more than a third of the way to my target of one hundred and fifty pounds, a sum that would take me anywhere, especially if I hitched or kidded my way onto a train. But where would I go? Where would I find work and a roof over my head? Because I would almost certainly have to do it single-handed. Angels like Papa didn't happen twice.

I would go anywhere in the country as long as I could be sure of finding somewhere to live. I still had bad dreams about my night in the park, could still feel the rat running over my leg or smell the beery breath of the man who had pestered me in the doorway of the café.

And it was winter now, and a cold winter, too.

14

The café was chaotic in the run-up to Christmas, but on the Thursday, the rush ended. On Friday, December 22nd, the normal breakfast rush was non-existent. Everyone who could had ceased working to prepare for the great day.

At lunchtime it was the same story. 'Everyone is going home for Christmas,' Mr P said. He looked at me quizzically. 'You going home?'

I shook my head.

'You sure?'

I shook my head again. 'You come home with me, then. We have real Greek Christmas. My niece come with her man and her children, big family, tree, presents. She cooks...' He lifted his bunched fingers to his mouth and kissed them. 'She cooks angel food. *Avgolemono*: egg and lemon soup.' He waved his hands. 'Egg yolks, bay leaf, good stock, lemon juice, little spring onions.' Again he kissed his bunched fingers. 'Chopped mint to garnish! Angel food.'

For a moment I was tempted, but only for a moment. To be part of a family Christmas that wasn't my family Christmas would be more than I could bear.

'Thank you,' I said hastily. 'I'm not going home, but I am going to friends. They live in – Luton. I'm going on Saturday night. They're collecting me.'

'Ah.' He nodded. 'Good. Not good to be alone in London at Christmas. You go to Luton. Sunday, Monday, Tuesday. We open Wednesday, but trade will be thin. Come on afternoon. That be fine.'

'It'll be my last week,' I reminded him. 'I'll finish on New Year's Eve if its alright with you.'

It seemed a good idea to strike out on New Year's Day. The café would close on Saturday night and would not re-open until Tuesday, January 2nd. By then, I would be far away.

'Will you have someone by then?' I asked. 'I could stay but I'd rather get away.'

He promised to ring up the employment bureau the next day but I could see he wasn't worried. With Christmas out of the way there would be hundreds of people looking for work. All the same, I would have liked him to miss me a bit.

As if he read my thoughts he smiled. 'I don't want to lose you, but it's right that you go. You clever girl – good girl. You can't stay in backstreets forever. You go places.'

I could feel a foolish smile spreading across my face even though I wished I shared his confidence in my prospects.

'I'll miss you,' I said. 'And I won't forget you.'

'Pish…' He was shaking his big grey head in embarrassment and I wanted to hug him again but enough was enough.

'What first?' I said. 'Spuds or sausages? The lunch lot'll be here any minute.'

I spent Christmas Day on my own in my room. Cousin Eleni and her family had gone off to spend Christmas with family on the other side of London, so there would be no one to snitch on me to Papa. I had told Eleni I was going to Luton but she had told me to make free with the kitchen and fridge anyway. I cooked myself a TV dinner and ate it in front of Eleni's television, trying hard not to think about Nella alone in Notting Hill, probably eating an identical doll's meal from an identical tray in front of an identical TV picture.

The sight of the Queen was almost too much. Calm and unchanged, hands neatly folded as they had been in every broadcast

I could remember. Was she nervous? Was she real? Did she think about her family troubles as she talked about Commonwealth and country? If all the rumours were true, it was hardly a happy family. Suddenly I felt a shaft of sympathy for her, endlessly keeping her chin up, smiling that serene, forced smile even when her back and her heart were both aching. I leaned towards the screen and addressed her.

'Never mind,' I said. 'Never mind.'

I laughed at first at the ridiculousness of talking to the Queen, of all people, in an empty room in an echoing empty house. And then I cried because another phase of my life was coming to an end, and although it had little to recommend it, it was better than the unknown.

I spent the rest of Christmas in bed, listening to endless yuletide music on my radio and longing for it to be Wednesday so I could go to work. But when the café reopened after Christmas, trade was slack. I gave Papa a glowing account of my time in Luton and filled him in on my plans for the New Year.

'I'll say goodbye on Saturday night, when we close. I'm leaving first thing on Monday and I'll need Sunday to get squared up at Eleni's. Got to leave the place spotless.'

'You're sure it's right to go?' His lovely old face was screwed up with anxiety, making him look more than ever like Gepetto. He pursed his lips. 'When you came I thought – "Pretty girl, silly girl; she won't last a day in kitchen".' He shook his head. 'Me and my bad judgement. You are a good girl – strong. I would like a daughter like you.' He grinned then. 'Daughters work cheap. But I don't want to lose you: not for kitchen, for friendship.' He paused. 'I had a daughter once. Long time ago. Little baby. One hour, then she died. Mama, too.'

'I'm sorry.' It sounded so inadequate but it was all I could think of.

He smiled now. 'Could you stay for little bit?'

'I have to go.' I said it simply because I didn't want to lie to him. He wouldn't understand why I had fled Ard-na-Shiel. No one would understand giving up family for a foolish love, certainly not a Greek to whom family meant everything. 'I have to go,' I said again. 'But I'll come back one day. When I'm rich and famous, I'll come back. You won't know it's me until I order two eggs and toast.' We both laughed then because it was better than crying and then we got on with breakfasts.

He gave me my final pay packet on Saturday night. It bulged suspiciously and I raised my eyebrows. 'You pay me back,' he said. 'When you rich and famous.'

I hugged him and then I went out into the night, all the time wanting to run back into the kitchen and ask for my job back forever. But what I had said to him was true. I *had* to go. The only problem was where.

Sunday was New Year's Eve. During the day I did my meagre packing and cleaned and tidied the room. Eleni was not as warm or as generous as Papa, but she had been kind to me in her way and I owed her that courtesy.

I listened to my radio, hoping for some good news, but everywhere there seemed to be conflict. Earthquake in Australia, crisis in Israel, thousands of Vietnamese refugees rioting in Hong Kong. I turned to a music channel, but strains of 'Auld Lang Syne' sent me scurrying back to the news. I didn't want to be reminded of Scotland.

At ten o'clock I turned off the radio and crossed to the window. There were faint sounds of revelry coming from the house across the road and two men holding one another up as they weaved their way towards the corner.

I looked at my watch. Too late to go to Notting Hill, knock at the door, be drawn over the threshold and into the warm. Nella would be seeing in the New Year at Ard-na-Shiel. I pictured Sara in the panelled hall. Her belly would be carrying Jamie's child and he would be solicitous and I couldn't bear it. I put on my jacket, wound a scarf round my neck and set out for Trafalgar Square.

Long before I reached it I was caught up in a tide of merry-making. Someone shoved a can in my hand, a man drew me into a conga line, a girl peered at me blearily and said, 'Is that you, Gilly?' I felt suddenly elated, part of them, free to drink and dance and hug complete strangers and sing 'Danny Boy' to an Irish fiddle. At twelve we fell silent for the bongs of Big Ben, booming from a dozen hand-held transistors. As the last one split the silence, we cheered and hollered and turned to our neighbours.

'Happy New Year,' I said to the man beside me. He was tall and thin, ginger-haired and freckled but he kissed me nicely and then let me go.

'Same to you,' he said.

I smiled. 'That's not a London accent.'

He put a protective arm around me as the crowd grew even more boisterous. 'Scouse,' he said. 'Liverpool.'

'Ah,' I said. I was about to say I'd never been there when he put up a hand. 'Just don't mention the Beatles,' he said. 'Liverpool FC, Everton, the Mersey Tunnel – anything but the Beatles.'

'I like the Beatles,' I said.

'Me, too. But they do hog the image a bit.'

There was a fine drizzle now, but the revellers splashing in the fountain didn't seem to care. He took his arm away and turned to face me. 'I've got to go. There's a minibus waiting.' I nodded understanding. 'I wish I didn't have to,' he said, 'but it's a long walk if I miss the lads.'

The rain was coming down more heavily now and I shook my head to get rid of the drops on my forehead. He put out his hands and pulled my collar up around my face. 'Go home,' he said 'before I decide to miss the bus.' He kissed me then, on the forehead. 'Tell you what, same place, same time next year?' I nodded and smiled. 'See you,' he said.

'See you,' I answered. 'Second lion on the right.'

He nodded. 'Second lion it is.' He went then and I watched as he melted into the crowd.

I had seen in the New Year with a total stranger, someone I would never see again. But he had done me a favour. Nella was fond of talking of the finger of fate. Tonight it had beckoned. Tomorrow I would go north: to Liverpool, a city I had not only never seen but could not remember ever being mentioned in my home. Liverpool of the picture on the wall in my room at Eleni's. Liverpool, the last place on earth Nella would think of looking for me.

I walked back to Edgware through streets packed with merrymakers. Occasionally a man would reel towards me and lunge but there were always at least two others to pull him away and apologize. I felt safe. I felt almost happy but above all I felt relieved. Christmas and New Year had been a hurdle that had filled me with apprehension, but it was a hurdle I had cleared, and now a New Year lay before me like a brand-new exercise book.

Nineteen ninety-two was mine to make what I chose of it.

15

I took a bus to Liverpool. My nerve for ticketless train travel had deserted me, and besides, I felt rich with my accumulated pay in my pocket. I slept part of the way and woke to sunlight brightening everything it touched. I bought an evening paper as soon as I alighted. The headline was stark: *IRA Kill Loyalist Taxi Driver.* I turned into a café and ordered a cappuccino, but I wasn't expecting to pick up a job from a fellow customer as I had done in London. I didn't need to do that. I had a P45 in the name of Melina Vassilides, and in the morning I would turn up at the Employment Agency and look for work like any other law-abiding citizen. What I needed now was a place to sleep.

The paper had a list of places to rent. I settled for *Clean accommodation, half-board if required, no smoking, DHSS welcome.* The house was in a quiet street near to the dock area, and the rent was twenty-two pounds a week. For this, I had a bedroom and tiny off-shot kitchen and the use of a shared bathroom on the same landing. I declined the offer of half-board, but accepted the offer of high tea –

'Because it's your first night and you'll have nothing in.'

Mrs Concannon was small and wiry and madly in love with Paul McCartney, and tonight he was playing live on stage for the first time in thirteen years. 'I'm made up,' she kept saying, which I took to mean she was pleased. Her favourite song was 'The Fool on the Hill', and as a girl she had once brushed past him in The Cavern.

'I loved the bones of him, then,' she said, 'and I will till I die.'

Mr Concannon took all this in his stride, merely lowering his paper to say 'Give the girl her tea, Mother' whenever she paused for breath.

I told them I was second-generation Greek and orphaned, and marvelled at the ease with which I could lie.

'I'm looking for a job,' I said. 'I'll do anything, really, but my last job was in a restaurant.'

I could safely call the café a restaurant because they'd already told me that they hadn't set foot outside of the northwest in twenty years and didn't intend to, so they'd never see the café off the Edgware Road and realize it was really a greasy spoon.

'You could try the Adelphi,' Mrs Concannon said, spooning more fresh tomatoes onto my plate. 'Or the Brittania.'

Mr Concannon lowered his paper. 'You don't want to go to those places. You want a nice homely place where they treat staff like family. Try the Royal Mersey.'

By eleven the next morning I had a job and, best of all, a room of my own at the top of the building. It was a tiny attic room, and claustrophobic, but it was free. I would work ten-hour shifts five days a week and a split shift every second weekend. My duties would be in the kitchen at first, but if I proved satisfactory I'd graduate to waitressing, which carried with it a uniform and tips. The woman who hired me was small and stout and distracted. All the while her eyes kept shooting here and there, as though she was checking up on a thousand and one things. She examined my P45 and gave me a form to fill in, but I had the feeling she was so desperate for staff she'd'd've taken me on anyway.

On the way back to the Concannons, I tried to suppress my rising euphoria. A job and a place to stay on my first day! Whichever gods had directed me to Liverpool had been benign indeed. I had half-expected Mrs Concannon to be put out at my leaving so soon, but she was delighted at my good luck and insisted on returning half my week's rent. Mr Concannon came in as we were talking and beamed with pleasure when I thanked him for suggesting the Royal Mersey.

'You'll be alright there,' he said. And then, 'Give the girl some supper, Mother.'

As I ate, I looked around the polished shabbiness of their living room and thought of how much better off they'd be if they were more businesslike. Except that they seemed happy, which was probably more important.

I started work the next day, moving in during the morning and starting work at two p.m. I would work until midnight, with half an hour off at five and another half an hour from seven to seven-thirty. The Royal kitchens were vast and steamy and bore no resemblance to Papa's domain. There we had juggled two frying pans on each of two four-burner cookers; here there were huge industrial ranges and most of the meals came deep-frozen and ready-plated. All I had to do was press buttons.

By midnight, however, I was almost asleep on my feet. I hung up my blue overall and climbed the back stairs to my eyrie in the roof. There was a small seat in the window space and I curled up there, trying to decide whether or not to make a nightcap. Across the way and just below me there were lighted windows, some curtained, some open to the night air. In these rooms the people seemed like goldfish swimming in a bowl. I saw a man and woman embracing, oblivious of prying eyes above. In another room a woman stood at an ironing board, her hand moving right to left with patient intensity. And in the room directly opposite a mother was walking the floor, her baby held high in her arms so that its cheek touched her own. I couldn't hear anything but I knew she was crooning to it. And suddenly I remembered Nella crooning to me. *Oh my lula, lula, lula, bye-bye, do you want the moon to play with?* She had always come if I cried in the night. No matter who shared her bed, her child had come first.

I wanted her now, when I was tired and aching and my fingers smelled of Ajax. Wanted to be held and dictated to so that there was no need for me to go on striving. Except that soon there would be another baby to fuss over – *Sara's* baby. Sara's baby by *Jamie!*

I could never, ever go home. I had to make a new life: here, in a city by the sea, in a tiny room with the Mersey just visible between the rooftops and a warm-hearted population around me.

I decided to dispense with washing or teeth-cleaning just for this one night. I dropped my clothes where I stood and the next minute I was in bed and, mercifully, asleep within seconds.

On the way to Liverpool I had worried about how I would fill my leisure time. At the end of the first week I knew I had worried for nothing. By the time I left the kitchen I wanted only one thing: sleep. And when I woke the next day I had hardly breakfasted when it was time to go to work. On my first day off, the Sunday, I bought a McDonald's and carried it into the park to eat while I read the Sunday papers. I had bought two for a treat and they came with a healthy supply of glossy supplements.

On the front page there was news of another killing in Northern Ireland, this time a Catholic taxi-driver murdered in retaliation for the first. I turned quickly to the fashion pages and tried to relax. In an hour or so I must ring Nella, and that thought was depressing enough without thinking of pointless deaths in another country. Except that it wasn't another country. The dead men, both of them, had been as British as I was – had spoken my language and shared my heritage. And now they were dead because of conflicts too far off for anyone to really understand.

At four o'clock I rang Nella.

'Mum? It's me.'

There was a coldness in the voice at the other end, a weariness that bordered almost on indifference. 'Where are you?' Could I go on plugging the Newcastle line? She had probably made enquiries up there and knew I was fibbing or would be if I said it again. 'I'm in Leeds now. I have a job – in a hotel. I live in so I'm quite safe. Are you OK? And Sara?'

'We're fine. Why don't you ask about Jamie?' There was the faint note of suspicion in her voice and suddenly I knew why. I had been left alone up there with him and then I had run away. Obviously she had been thinking things over. Surely she couldn't imagine – even for a second – that Jamie had laid a finger on me? The very thought horrified me.

'I was going to. Is he OK? He was so kind to me when I was up there.' I put enough sincerity into my voice to float the *Queen Mary* and it worked.

'He's fine.' She was mollified, the last lingering doubt swept away. 'He's fine and looking forward to the baby, but, like the rest of us, he can't understand what you're up to, Alexandra.'

I leaned my head against the side of the phone box as she continued. It was pointless to listen because there was no way I could explain. 'I just had to get away,' I said at last. 'And I'm OK. I *will* come back one day. When I've sorted things out.'

'*What* things? I'm going crazy with worry. You're not pregnant are you? I know you said not –'

It was a relief to be able to laugh out loud. 'No, I'm *not* pregnant. I'm not in a relationship, I'm not on drugs and I haven't touched alcohol since I left Ard-na-Shiel. I just want to be free, Mum. Try and understand.'

I cried on the way back to the hotel, with relief that the call was made and over and with a kind of horror that such evil connotations could be creeping into the situation. Jamie was the most honourable of men. If I had made Nella doubt him I had done something very wrong.

However traumatic that call had been, it served a useful purpose. Thereafter, when I rang, Nella did not again ask why.

She continued to beg me to come home. She asked where I was and what I was doing but she seemed to accept that, if there was a reason why I'd run away, I wasn't going to tell it. And increasingly as the weeks went by our conversations were filled with talk of the coming birth.

Looking back on that period I see it as a rewarding time, a time of growing certainty that I was going to be able to fend for myself. At first, I was a kitchen hand dishing up prepacked gourmet meals to the glitterati of Liverpool. The chef ruled the kitchen with an iron hand. He called me 'Butterfly Brain' because I didn't immediately recognize everything on the menu. But as the weeks went by, he became more friendly, treating me with a grudging respect and eventually recommending me for counter service.

I stood behind the huge buffet forking meat onto plates for those who asked for a salad accompaniment, carving great swathes of lamb or beef for those who preferred roast and four veg, or using tongs to transfer rum babas or over-filled brandy snaps to individual plates. Once I had become proficient at counter service, I graduated to waiting on tables in the restaurant. This was a coveted position because it included tips.

My first day in the restaurant found me with damp palms and trembling knees. What if I tipped soup over someone's couture jacket or, worse still, into someone's lap? There were two other waitresses: Agnes, who had been there since the flood, and Reinie, which I later learned was short for Renata.

'Ask if you're stuck,' she told me as we glided between tables. 'And take that look off your face. Sure, no one'll eat you.' She had the smile of a Botticelli cherub and a mass of red hair that threatened to escape the ribbons and pins that bound it. 'Bags me the table in the corner,' she said. 'He's a tenner if I ever saw one.'

That night we agreed to pool our tips, which was generous on her part because she did better than me with her Irish brogue and her blue eyes that twinkled from between lashes so thick she could have used them for dusters. She was one of nine children born to a German father and an Irish mother and had come to Liverpool from Dublin to escape a home she described as 'a madhouse'. She seemed not to want to say too much about her background and this suited me very well because I didn't want to say too much, either.

Her bedroom was two doors away from mine, and gradually we became so familiar that at times we slept together, sprawled on the one bed, or ate together in one another's room, sharing a bucket of Kentucky Fried or cod and chips, hot and crisp and redolent of vinegar. 'Sure it beats the grub you get here,' she said. 'That's all sauce and no substance, it is, and a hideous price.'

It was Reinie who first took me clubbing, tottering on a pair of her high heels on legs still smarting from the Louis Marcel strip-wax she had just used on them. 'You have to make the best of yourself,' she said. 'Even you, with the face and body of a star. There's always room for improvement.' I knew she was only trying to raise my morale but it was certainly working.

So we sat in our rooftop eyrie trying out face-packs and essential oils. She plucked my eyebrows and I did her a French plait that would have done justice to Vidal Sassoon.

'I'm happy,' I said aloud one night, looking up from the toenails I was painting 'Crimson Glow.'

'Good,' Reinie said. 'But don't let anyone know. It's not the done thing to be happy. Angst is the name of the game.'

She sounded unlike her usual flippant self but when I pulled a questioning face she just smiled. We had been friends for seven weeks and two days when I told her my secret.

'God,' she said. 'Isn't that the saddest thing? In love with your own sister's man.' She hugged me then and offered me her thin gold chain bracelet. 'Not forever, mind you. Just till the tide turns.'

16

On the odd occasion we had a night off together we went to a club in the heart of Liverpool. It was not yet really summer but we scorned coats, partly because we didn't want to hide our finery and partly because neither of us had a coat we'd risk being seen dead in. We weren't short of men to buy us drinks. It quite shocked me that Reinie would accept a drink from a man and then turn away from him if something better offered. But as like as not she'd turn back to him when she tired of the newcomer and no one seemed to mind. Sometimes the men we met would try it on but Reinie would be there, slapping a wandering hand or uttering a sharp four-letter word if someone wouldn't move off me.

I drank piña coladas and told myself that this was the way it was in the real world. The old rules of politeness belonged to that other world, the one I had ridden away from more than six months before. That had been a strange old world, too. Lots of surface gloss when underneath things had sometimes been quite grotty. Not that Nella hadn't had her own code of honour. She had, but it hadn't been the same as other people's. Everyone had been 'darling', although some of them had just been ships passing in a night. That was why Sara had meant so much to me. She had been the one area of total certainty in my life, and soon it would be a year since I had seen her.

I will go back, I told myself. *One day it'll all come right.*

In the meantime, there was Reinie and a Liverpool coming alive in the sunshine. The Albert Dock was always awash with people: shopping, drinking coffee, holding hands to gaze down on the strange television weather map floating on the deep, dark water. On my afternoons off I wandered around like any other Liverpudlian, except that on my way home I would step into a phone box and pretend to my mother that I was ringing from Leeds.

I had another worry. The closer I grew to Reinie, the more I realized that the sunny Irish exterior was a cover for something else. At times she looked as though she had been crying. At others she was euphoric, ecstatically happy. A few hours later she would be apathetic to the point of indifference. I wondered if there had been a man in Ireland – married, perhaps or forbidden in some other way. I was screwing up the courage to ask her outright the night we went out to celebrate her birthday.

The drinks flowed more freely than usual, the music seemed louder, Reinie's enjoyment more hectic than usual. At the end of the evening Reinie suggested we went back to someone's flat for coffee. I said yes, although I was really ready to go home. After all, it was her birthday; I couldn't be a party pooper.

'Stick by me,' Reinie said when we were out in the street. 'I'll see you alright.' I was glad of her arm because I felt quite unsteady on my legs.

We sat on the floor of someone's flat, seven of us, no one in pairs, all laughing and wise-cracking. Music thudded in the background: moody guitars and drums. Someone produced a ten-pound note and began to roll it into a fine tube. Someone else spilled out white powder onto the coffee table and then drew it into fine lines using a credit card. The guy with the roll bent his head and a line of white powder disappeared up the tube and into his nose. He sniffed, tossed his head a little and passed the note to Reinie. She hesitated a moment and then snorted the next line, looked up and smiled.

One by one they took their share but when someone proffered the note to me Reinie intervened.

'Not the kid,' she said. 'I need her to see me home.'

They were all looking at me now, waiting. I held out my hand and when Reinie would have stopped me I shook myself free.

'It's OK,' I said.

'*No.*' Reinie's voice was sharp now. 'She doesn't,' she said.

One of the men patted her arm. 'It's only coke,' he said. 'Coke's not like heroin.'

But Reinie was scrambling to her feet, half-laughing, half-crying. I saw that her eyes were glittering, almost as though she felt triumphant about something.

'We're going,' she said. 'Sorry to spoil the party.'

She was pushing and pulling me towards the door. There was silence for a moment and then they turned away, indifferent to whether we stayed or went.

Outside, the cold air sliced at us. I looked at Reinie and saw tears on her cheeks.

'Hurry up,' she said, 'before I change my mind.'

'Are you alright?'

She stopped then and faced me, taking my shoulders in her two hands.

'Am I alright, kid? I am fantastic. I am intelligent, I am beautiful. I am almost fucking airborne. But I'll feel like shit in the morning. I don't want that to happen to you. And don't believe that crap about coke not being as bad as heroin. It's ten times worse.'

We walked on in silence until a cab overtook us and we could get a lift back to the hotel. We parted on the landing, she still euphoric, me half-resentful and half-grateful. I had to learn to survive by myself, as Reinie had done. If I'd tried the coke, at least I'd've known what it was like. I stood by the window for a while, looking out at the sliver of Mersey between the rooftops, and then I climbed between the thin sheets, pulled up the chenille bedcover and was asleep as my head hit the pillow.

17

I rang home at least once a week, more often as the time for the baby's birth drew near. Whenever I thought of the baby, I thought of Jamie, but now I could almost enjoy remembering that stolen week. The Jamie who climbed the river bank in Glen Orchy or ridden, whooping, through Glencoe, the man who had safely delivered the calf and then smiled up at me... that man belonged to *me*. The Laird of Ard-na-Shiel, now awaiting his baby's birth, was my sister's husband, and increasingly the two men were separate – at least in my mind.

One thing I was sure of. I was glad it had happened, that falling in love. I wouldn't have missed it for the world.

The birth was two weeks away when I made my routine call.

'Lexy! Thank God. I didn't want you to see it in the papers.'

My heart leaped into my mouth. It couldn't be – *mustn't be* Sara. All the times I had ill-wished her, begrudged her, wished her out of my way, rose up to haunt me.

'See what? What's the matter?'

'I'm sorry.' Her voice was calmer now. 'I was just so afraid that you wouldn't ring in time. It's your father. He died yesterday. In Hollywood. I didn't know until the papers rang me. Apparently he died alone. Drugs, they think, although they're not sure.'

Drugs! Immediately I thought of Reinie. I had only the most shadowy picture of my father. Coming from the shower, towelling his blond hair, calling out for coffee and the flip-flop of Nella coming into the bedroom bearing a tray. The next day, or so it seemed, he was gone. And now he was dead.

Denise Robertson

'What happens now?' I said it automatically. What did you do when your father died if you hadn't seen him for thirteen years?

'There'll be a funeral. They didn't seem to know who was handling his affairs.'

I had never asked Nella if there had been another woman. At first, I had been too young for the idea to strike me, and when I was old enough it seemed too far in the past to mention. Now I needed to know.

'Did he get married again? Or was there someone else?'

'*Someone?* He had more women than there are days in the year, but no one special, as far as I know. I suppose we ought to be represented, but I couldn't go so far away with Sara's baby due. You could go, I suppose.'

'No.' I suddenly realized I was shaking my head vigorously. 'No. I couldn't go all that way. I wouldn't know anyone. It isn't fair to ask me –'

'Alright, darling. Of course you needn't go if you don't want to. I'll ring Aunty Mamie in LA. She'll go and represent us. She loves occasions.'

'Will it be an occasion?' I had never heard my father's name mentioned – not for years, anyway. I was even surprised the papers had been interested enough to phone Mum.

'I suppose so. Your father made a lot of B-movies. And Americans are very into death. Oh dear!'

There was a sudden intake of breath at the other end of the line.

'I hope he's left enough to cover expenses. He liked living well and I should know – I paid for it long enough. Still, he could have been a great talent, Lexy, if he hadn't thrown it all away.'

She was warming to her theme now, anxious not to denigrate my father in my eyes.

'Such a waste. He had critics eating out of his palm when he made *Height of Passion*. He wasn't the lead, but he stole the

– 118 –

picture, everyone said so.' Her voice changed suddenly. 'Lexy, something like this happening – out of the blue... He was only forty-nine... Come home, Lexy. Let's put an end to this silly nonsense. It's bad enough Sara being so far away, without you – not knowing where you are. You've made your point – whatever it was. You won't even tell me that much. Now come home. Before the baby's born. Then we can go up and see it together. It's your niece or nephew, Lexy. You can't stay away from a baby!'

'I won't. Not forever. But I can't come back just yet. I will, eventually. Mum, my money's running out.'

There was still ten pence showing, but I replaced the receiver. We'd gone over it so many times there was nothing left to say.

Ever since the night I had seen Reinie take coke she had been different. Outwardly she was her usual self, especially at work, but she made excuses not to go out and I could almost feel her slipping away from me. Now, though, I needed to tell her about my father's death.

She was sympathetic.

'What a pity that you didn't get to know him more, Lexy. Still, he'd be proud of you if he'd known you, kid. That's for sure.'

'We're off this afternoon,' I said. 'Let's go somewhere.'

She shook her head. 'Not today, Lexy. Maybe tomorrow.'

But I liked her so much, with her soft voice and her tales of her mammy and her huge brood of sisters and brothers back in Ireland that I wasn't prepared to be shaken off.

'Please,' I said. 'Please, Reinie. Let's go in the park. Or to the dock. I need someone to talk to about my dad.'

That seemed to tip the scale. For a moment she looked at me, a little smile that wasn't a smile on her lips and then she shrugged. 'OK, kid. Let's go to the dock.' So we carried our foil-wrapped parcels into the Albert Dock, past the Beatles

Museum and the shopping mall, and out to the side of the great River Mersey.

We sat on a stone wall and unwrapped our feast, but neither of us was hungry. Instead, we threw tasty morsels to the birds that swooped around us as soon as they scented food. I was searching for words to break Reinie's strange mood when she spoke – but it wasn't my father she wanted to discuss.

'We won't be going out again, kid. And don't think it's anything you've done. It's me.' I started to speak but she shushed me to silence. 'I wasn't much older than you when I started on the stuff. And that was in someone's flat with a bunch I'd met in a club. I watched them snort and I was too intimidated to say no when it was my turn. I thought they were all so clever. If they were doing it, it must be OK. And it *was* OK at first. It made me feel so intelligent, so beautiful... I went home at five in the morning thinking I owned the world.'

I wanted to say something but she wouldn't let me.

'The first hit is always massive. That's why I stopped you that night – I knew how good it would be. It's never as good again, although you don't realize that at the time. The next few days all I could do was think about it. How good it had been, how I could do anything if only I could get more. I had a good job: PA to a magazine editor. I didn't want to do anything that would jeopardize my job. But even weekend using changed me. I began to think people and places where they didn't do coke were boring. I felt incomplete without it.'

Her voice broke then and I put out a hand.

'Don't go on any more, Reinie. I won't ever do it. I promise you.' She didn't seem to hear.

'I'd look at myself in the bathroom mirror and see a dull, ugly face and I'd think, "I'll just have a line of coke and I'll be beautiful again". And I was – to myself. To everyone else I was a useless idiot. That's what my boss called me when she sacked me. "You're an idiot, Renata," she said.'

A seabird was sidling towards her and she threw it a crumb.

'I owed two thousand pounds on credit cards alone. *And* rent. I couldn't afford to keep up my supply without a salary so I started begging for it. I'd let dealers fuck me for a single hit.'

I winced at the way she spat out the F-word but she seemed not to notice.

'I'd have too many lines and when I was coming down, I felt like I had flu. In the end I got so frightened of coming down that I'd take another line – and then another – just to stay up there. I couldn't remember what I'd done so I'd spend hours searching for the rest of a stash I thought should be there. When I rang home, my mother would say, "Are you crying, darling? Come home if you're homesick." But it was just my nose. Snorting scars the lining so that it runs constantly. Winter and summer you feel bunged up.'

She turned to me suddenly, opening her mouth and drawing her lips back from her teeth.

'See my gums? I tried rubbing coke on them until my gums started to recede.'

'They look fine,' I said. 'Honestly.'

But it was as though she didn't want to hear me, only to go on with her confession.

'In the end I was thrown out of my flat, which was actually a blessing because living on the street meant I couldn't party anymore. A woman came up to me one night and shoved a card in my hand. "Use this," she said. "It worked for me." So I rang and they came and fetched me. It was hard, but I came off. I've been clean for two years. Until the other night.'

She stood up then and walked to the water's edge. The great river shimmered and rolled, the seabirds swooped and somewhere far off, a siren hooted. She shook the tin-foil and the rest of her food flew in an arc, to be swooped on before it hit the water.

I stood up and moved to her side. 'You won't do it again,' I said. 'I'll help you.'

She put her arms around me and held me gently for a moment. 'Sure,' she said. 'Sure you would. But I've made up my mind, Lexy. I'm going home. Back to Mammy and all the brothers and sisters and the dull life I couldn't wait to leave. And if you have any sense you'll do the same. We've had our adventure, Lexy. Now it's time to go back.'

I hugged her then and told her I was glad for her. And I was. But I wasn't ready to go home. Maybe I would one day, but not yet.

Before the end of the week Reinie was gone and I was alone once more. But she left me her green enamel shamrock, the one she spit on for luck whenever she backed a horse.

Sara's son was born a week later. I saw it in the *Telegraph*:

> *On May 17th to Sara and James Munro of Ard-na-Shiel, Lochmore, Inverness-shire, the gift of a son, Liam Alexander.*

I tried to be glad, but I was still missing Reinie desperately and gladness wouldn't come.

I rang home but there was no reply. Nella would be in Scotland, wetting the baby's head. I wanted to ring, to say I was pleased and wish them well, but if Jamie answered what would I say? It took three attempts before I actually dialled the number and then I kept my finger poised to cut off the call if it was anyone other than Nella. It was snatched up almost before it rang out.

'Darling, have you heard? It's a boy! He's so sweet: the image of Jamie. You must come and see him. They're calling him Alexander after you. It would have been Alexandra if it had been a girl. He's a Munro, every inch of him, but with Sara's eyes.'

I closed my eyes, imagining what it must be like to hold the baby you had made together. I pictured myself lying proud in the bed with Jamie poised above me, proud and grateful, his mirror image lying on my chest, small and warm and wonderful.

And then the picture changed. I saw Sara, but this time she was not a mother figure; she was naked, holding out her arms. And Jamie, equally naked, was above her and within her and they were doing it – endlessly, endlessly doing it.

'I'm really glad, Mum,' I said. 'Give them my love.'

And I put down the phone.

18

I had never really thought about my father except, when I reached my teens, to think of him as a handsome boy who hadn't wanted to be lumbered with two kids, only one of them his own. I had imagined him living hand to mouth on the fringes of Hollywood, and Nella's fear of being landed with the funeral expenses had only served to reinforce that image. So it was a surprise to find he had left me some money. I put it down to Reinie's lucky shamrock, but Mum knew better.

'He was between wives,' Nella explained. 'There was no will so you'll get it all.'

'That's not fair,' I said. 'You should have some, Mum. And Sara.'

'Don't worry about Sara,' Nella said. 'She doesn't need money and I won't take it. But I won't give it to you, either, unless you come home and stop this nonsense.'

'I can't,' I said, but all of a sudden what I was saying seemed silly. In the face of birth and death what did unrequited love matter? 'I can't come home,' I said. 'At least not now. But we can meet – in London.' I added that hastily in case she suggested going to Leeds, which is where she thought I was.

'Oh, Lexy, darling!' She sounded choked, so surprised and pleased that I felt ashamed at how long it had taken me to make the offer.

'I can't come straight away,' I said, 'because of work. But I'll ring soon and we'll make arrangements.'

A month later I caught a train at Liverpool Lime Street and emerged into the bustle of Euston. My mother had insisted we meet at the Meridien in Piccadilly, which was typical Nella territory. I'd suggested somewhere less ritzy, but she wouldn't hear of it.

'It's not every day you see your long-lost daughter. After a year I want to celebrate.'

I was about to protest that it was less than a year until I thought over what had happened. Since my flight from Ard-na-Shiel I had grown up. I had earned my living, put a roof over my own head, even changed my name. I was, after all, Melina Vassilides. A wicked impulse to tell Nella of the name change was easily resisted. I might need that identity to hide in again. It would be foolish to give it away.

So I dressed in the clothes I had worn that day I left Notting Hill and tried to look as much like Alexandra as I could. I took the tube to Piccadilly and on the way I practised my entry. I would submit to Nella's embraces, smile sweetly but refuse to be drawn back in. There was no way I could pick up Lexy's life again. School days seemed a million light years ago and I knew that Nella would insist I went somewhere to get those qualifications she didn't have herself but so prized in others.

So, I would be a loving daughter again, a concerned sister and a doting aunt when I looked at the inevitable baby pictures, but there would be no going back. If my father had left me a few hundred pounds and Nella could be persuaded to part with it, I would leave Liverpool and go somewhere else – even to Europe.

Just before I left the tube I fingered my lucky shamrock and thought of what I could do with a bit of money behind me. It was a rosy prospect and I was smiling as I walked past the top-hatted commissionaire and into the elegant foyer of the Meridien. We had been apart for just over a year, but nothing had prepared me for the sight of my mother. She looked older and uncertain and for once it was I who moved forward to take command.

'Are you alright?' I asked as we settled into the deep settee and picked our choice of tea. She was looking at me strangely and the courage I had built up for this meeting suddenly evaporated.

As if she sensed this she leaned over and patted my hand. 'It's so good to see you, Lexy. Sometimes…' Her chin trembled and I felt my own eyes fill. 'Sometimes, I wondered if I'd ever see you again. And when I wasn't wondering that, I was wondering what I'd done to make you go off like that. It wasn't because of the car trip, was it? I've asked myself a thousand times why I didn't find the money for another ticket…'

I could bear it no longer. 'Hush,' I said. 'It wasn't anything you did. It was *me*. I – it was what *I* did, Mum. It meant I couldn't stay.'

Suddenly the waiter was there, silver teapot, hot-water jug, strainer at the ready. I watched the clear brown liquid flow first into Nella's cup, then mine, and tried desperately to find something that would satisfy her and not come anywhere near the truth. A second waiter placed the tall cake stand, smiled at us both and departed. Nella allowed the first one to place her napkin, then mine, smiled a dismissal and then fixed me with her gaze.

'What did you do, Lexy? Tell me now.'

And suddenly it was easy to tell the truth, about falling in love in the glen and the dust motes in the library and the moment in the byre when I owned up to loving Jamie. As I finished I bowed my head, waiting for her to admonish me or, worse still, tell me what a silly little child I was.

I was ready for either response. I was not prepared for what actually happened.

'Poor Lexy,' she said. 'And you had to bear all this on your own.'

It was too much. I cried, and with a mouthful of smoked salmon sandwich that was a complicated business. I gulped and wept while Nella proffered a clean white hanky and gave the entire room one of her best almost Bond-girl smiles to show that nothing whatever was wrong.

'So what are we going to do?' she said when I'd composed myself.

'I can't come home.'

The words came out so quickly they were hardly comprehensible.

'No,' she replied calmly. 'You can't come home at the moment.'

'Ever,' I said and even smiled at how dramatic I sounded.

Nella wiped her lips with her napkin and then folded and refolded it. 'One day you'll fall in love again, and then you'll be able to see Jamie and Sara and be perfectly OK. In the meantime…'

'You won't tell them?' I interrupted, suddenly panicked.

'Of course not. I'll tell them we met and you explained that you left Scotland because of boyfriend trouble. Someone you met at school. Sara had already decided that's what it must be. And I'll tell them everything's OK, and you'll be in touch. You must ring them, darling, or write at least.'

'What will I say?'

Now there was an almost schoolmarm note in Nella's voice.

'You'll stick to the script, Alexandra. A love affair gone wrong which is over now. But you've tasted the pleasures of independence so you're not coming home for a while. They'll buy that. They're so taken up with the baby.'

She must have seen a shadow cross my face at the mention of the baby because that was the last thing she said on the subject. Instead, she reached in her bag and took out a letter.

'Read that. And by the way, now that I'm over the shock, I like the hair colour.'

The letter was written on headed paper, some firm with about four names in it. I hardly looked at the words because my eyes were fixed on the figures. *Twelve thousand pounds.* My father, the father I could hardly remember, who had never seemed to amount to a row of beans, had left me *twelve thousand pounds.*

'Surprised?'

I nodded and Nella smiled. She raised her hand then to summon a waiter and it was my turn to smile because she did it with the air of a mega-star – and, as always, it worked. A waiter materialized at her side and she asked him in the sweetest tones for fresh tea.

'We talked too much,' she said. 'It's a little cold.'

When the fresh tea was poured, she took a scone and anointed it with jam and cream. 'The money's in my care until you're twenty-one,' she said. I nodded. 'But I'm prepared to let you have some of it now – on certain conditions.'

'I can't come back.'

'I know that. We've been over that. But I need to know where you are, Lexy. I need to be able to contact you. What if something went wrong with Sara or the baby? Surely you'd want to know?'

'Of course I would. And I will keep in touch.'

To prove it I told her about Liverpool but I didn't mention Reinie. The very mention of drugs would be enough to spook Nella.

'But you don't want to stay there?'

'No,' I said. 'It's a lovely city but I'm ready to move on. Not back to London, but somewhere in the north, I think. York, perhaps, or Leeds.'

'What are you going to do? To earn money, I mean? If you have a little money behind you, you could train for something. I can't imagine you in a restaurant. You never showed the least interest in food. Sara is the good cook.'

She said the last sentence absently and I tried not to scowl. Sara was good at everything. That was a fact and all the wishing in the world wouldn't change it.

In the end we agreed that I should go back to Liverpool and give in my notice. While I was working it, we'd both think about where and how I'd continue my independent life. I hadn't told her about Melina Vassilides, not even when she commented on my hair colour, and I decided not to. There were bits of my story I needed to keep to myself.

We parted on the pavement in Piccadilly where I saw her into a cab.

'Be careful,' she said as we kissed. 'And let me know what you want to do about the money. Some of it, anyway.'

'I will,' I said. And then: 'Mum, you won't ever tell them why I left, will you?'

She reached out and touched my cheek. 'No, my little stormy petrel. I'll never tell them. They wouldn't understand. But *I* do, Lexy. I understand.'

And I knew she did.

I waved until the cab was swallowed up in traffic and then I turned towards the tube. Twelve thousand pounds! Even the thought was exciting. I hugged it to myself all the way to Euston and carried it onto the Liverpool train. As it gathered speed I closed my eyes and gave thanks that I'd made my peace with Nella. She was wrong about my getting over Jamie one day, but she had been unbelievably reasonable today and I loved her for it.

19

The meeting with my mother seemed to sap my energy. I wanted to move on, but where to? I had money – or at least the prospect of it – but somehow that seemed to cause more problems.

For the first time in my life, almost, I had choice – and it confused me.

I went out on my morning off, down to the Albert Dock where there were several small boutiques clustered round a studio where they made a programme for morning television. I was standing at the dock-rail watching a weather forecaster caper about on a floating map of Britain when a man pushed through the crowd to stand beside me.

'Hello,' he said and I was just about to freeze him when he smiled and said, 'Trafalgar Square? Name's Rick, by the way.'

'Lexy.'

I grinned foolishly, wondering how I was going to explain what I was doing in Liverpool. I could hardly say I came there because he kissed me on New Year's Eve. He would think I was following him. Which I had done but not in the way he would interpret.

To my relief he didn't ask the obvious question. Instead, he said, 'Fancy a coffee?'

A few moments later we were seated in a café, two cappuccinos in front of us and the noise of the crowd shut out by glass.

I cleared my throat. 'I didn't expect to see you again.'

It was his turn to grin. 'Snap. I'm only here for forty-eight-hours. Then it's Germany, Holland, Belgium, France and Denmark.'

'I'm impressed. It sounds like a fabulous holiday.'

'Touring,' he said. 'I'm in a group. We've just done a British tour, which was a drag. You don't get the audiences in this country – not for live music. Europe's a different story.'

'What do you play?'

I expected him to say a guitar because my impression of groups was men holding guitars stepping backwards and forwards in time to music. But he wasn't a guitarist; he played keyboards and composed and arranged most of the music they played.

He talked for a while about his job and I liked the way he did it. Not boastful but proud, and, as far as I could judge, very knowledgeable. He'd toured Europe for the last three years and obviously loved it.

'What kind of music is it?' I asked, and he pursed his lips.

'Rock, I suppose. More melodic, but rock-based. Anyway, what about you? I had you marked down for a Londoner.'

'You're right. But I'm working in a hotel here.'

I gave him a mock-up of my life, leaving out anything lethal like running away or having a film-star mother – not that he was likely to remember Cleopatra's handmaidens or the girl who got bumped off in 'Murder on the Night Train to Munich.'

'So I'm moving on,' I finished. 'Further north, I think, and not waitressing. It kills the feet.'

I almost asked if he needed a groupie for the tour, but he didn't look the type to appreciate it and, anyway, I wasn't too sure what a groupie's duties included. But I liked him, or rather the look of him. He wasn't handsome, but he had a nice face. Humorous and kind and, like Jamie, I felt safe with him. But he wasn't Jamie; he didn't stir me. I closed my eyes momentarily, remembering bees and heather and a heron poised on a rock. When I opened them he was looking at me quizzically.

'Am I so boring?' And then, when I started to stammer explanations: 'What time do you have to be back? It's our last gig tonight. If you wanted to come…?'

But the gig ended at eleven and I was on duty till midnight.

'So that's it then.'

He sounded disappointed but not devastated, and it piqued me.

'I'm afraid so. Still, thanks for the coffee.'

I held out my hand. His hand was warm and the pressure just right.

'I'm off tomorrow,' I said, but they were leaving at six a.m. to catch the Dover ferry. We parted on the dockside, a wind from the Mersey twisting our hair so that we both put up a hand to clear it from our brows.

'Trafalgar Square 1992?' he said. 'We promised, remember? Second lion –'

' – on the right' I finished for him.

'It's a date.' I watched as he was swallowed up in the crowds. He had played a big part in my life and he'd never know it. New Year's Eve seemed light years away. Would I see him again? I turned and made my way back to the hotel just in time to start work.

My second customer of the night ordered smoked salmon followed by minted lamb, and when I brought him his starter the table in front of him was littered with small carvings.

'Netsuke,' I said as he pushed them into a velvet pouch.

He looked up, startled. 'How did you know that?'

I was about to tell him we had once had a cabinet full of them back home in Notting Hill when I thought better of it.

'My mother had one,' I said. 'I used to play with it when I was a kid. I liked the carving so I found out about them.'

While he cleared space for his smoked salmon I gave him chapter and verse on netsukes, the ivory carvings that had been Nella's passion until she had to sell them for school fees.

'They're toggles, aren't they? Fasteners for their purses. The signed ones are more valuable – well, usually – and there are a lot of fakes about.'

He smiled at me. 'Go on,' he said, so I obliged.

'If it's plastic and not ivory, it'll melt if you hold a hot needle against it, and in a genuine one the hole for the cord is almost invisible. If they're wood, that's OK as long as the carving is good.'

When I'd finished, he reached in his pocket and gave me his card. 'You're a bright girl. If you're ever in my part of the world, look me up.'

He had a nice, twinkly face so I took the card and smiled my thanks. 'I just might do that,' I said.

Back in the kitchen I examined the small oblong of pasteboard. *Bedan Antiques. Durham. Proprietor K McEwan.*

Durham! I knew it had a cathedral and a university. It was as good a place as any to go to.

Two weeks later I caught a train at Lime Street station and settled back for the journey to Durham. I had money in my purse, part of the five hundred pounds Nella had advanced me, and a ticket. A year ago I had stolen a ride in the opposite direction. Now I was travelling legally. Things were looking up.

As the train crossed the Pennines I let myself think of Sara, pictured her holding her baby, felt the same old mixture of hatred and yearning she always evoked in me. But I daren't let myself picture Jamie – above all, daren't think of those thin, brown hands tending the baby, loving its mother...

Instead, I squeezed my eyelids together and thought about Rick. He was too thin and his hair was red, but he had nice eyes, a kind of greeny-grey. He had long, musician's fingers and he was tall enough to be called lanky, but he was the very best kind of imaginary lover because I would never see him again.

BOOK TWO

Durham
1995

1

There were still daffodils here and there as I walked along North Bailey. This was my favourite route: North Bailey, South Bailey, past Watergate to Prebend's Walk, the river on my left, the cathedral looming on my right. There was only one thing missing – a dog! I wanted one desperately, but my hours at the shop would hardly be fair on a lively animal. Besides, there was the added complication of Ian, who was constantly asking why I didn't move in with him and who hated anything with four legs.

I liked Ian – even half-loved him, I suppose, as I slept with him – but something inside me resisted the idea of getting closer. I had had my great love; anything else was bound to be second-best. So Ian and I ate together, slept together, spent holidays in the sun and snowy winters by the fireside, but resolutely kept two establishments. Expensive and probably silly, but still the way I wanted it for now. I was only twenty years old. Plenty of time to hear my biological clock ticking.

I crossed Palace Green, making for Owengate and home. There were people everywhere, enjoying the public holiday they'd been given to celebrate the fiftieth anniversary of the victory in Europe. In London, they would be thronging Hyde Park, gathering outside Buckingham Palace, even dunking in the Trafalgar Square fountains. In Durham, they were more sedate. Liverpool would be livelier.

I smiled to myself, thinking of Rick, the boy I had met on that bleak New Year's Eve of 1991. So much had happened since then. I was settled in Durham with a job I adored and a flat in the shadow of the cathedral – and, according to the show-biz columns,

Rick was a rising star. I hadn't seen him since that meeting at the Albert Dock, but I could still remember his kiss: soft and dry and tentative. So different from Ian, who was hungry and forceful in passion and only half-aware of me out of it. He was an academic, and I suppose that took up most of his mental energy.

As the flat came in sight I felt in my pocket for my key. Once inside I would put my feet up and watch TV. Much as I loved my job, it was nice to have a day off – a whole day to please myself. Ian was in Munich at a seminar and wouldn't be back until tomorrow; I had soup and salad in the fridge and half a Patricia Highsmith to curl up with later. Bliss!

As I turned the key in the lock the phone rang. Ian? But it was Nella, ringing from London.

'What's it like in Durham? The crowds here are tremendous.'

She sounded girlish and excited and I felt my mouth curve in a smile. Good old Nella! Never one to let a celebration pass her by. She rattled through a description of the scene so far and then described the party she was due to attend that evening.

'With Giles – you remember Giles? He drove you to Ard-na-Shiel for the wedding.'

And suddenly it was there again. Rannoch Moor and Glencoe and the lights of Ballachulish springing up in the darkness. Moonlight on the loch, the lazy sounds of bees in heather, the clutching at my breath that had told me I was in love. I felt tears prick my eyes as I tried to concentrate on what Nella was saying but it was no use.

In the three and a bit years I had been in Durham, I had seen Jamie and Sara twice. Once in London for Nella's fiftieth birthday, and once when they had called on me in Durham as they drove down to London. Each time I told myself that the pain would be less, especially the last time, when Ian and I had been lovers for a year. But if anything, the pain had intensified. I loved Jamie now with a tenderness I would not have understood as the child I had been in 1991. Loved each new line on his face, the slight greying at his temples, the way he seemed to grow in stature as his family increased.

What had changed was my attitude to Sara. I no longer resented her. She was no more to blame for being born first than I was responsible for being born second. What had happened to us was an accident of Fate – a misfortune. She had fallen for the only man I would ever love and he loved her. When I hugged her at Nella's party I felt a flood of relief that now we were close again. She had long since forgiven me for my flight on the eve of her wedding, putting it down to teenage rebellion. Sometimes I had seen a questioning look in Jamie's eyes, but if he suspected, he never said. And Nella was magnificent, making excuses, spinning tales, so glad to have her daughters reunited that she would have done or said anything to make it work. Sara was expecting her third child and if I couldn't exactly be glad, at least I didn't resent it.

When at last I put down the phone, I switched on TV. Dame Vera Lynn was singing her heart out outside the Palace, flanked by Harry Secombe and Cliff Richard. I switched off and went through to the kitchen. Everything I had intended to do today seemed suddenly meaningless now that I had been reminded of Ard-na-Shiel.

In the end, I gave up trying to get on with chores and walked round to Ken's. I had been in Durham for three months, working as a hotel receptionist, before I called in at his shop. He had looked up as the bell clanged that day and said, 'It's the netsuke girl. What are you doing here?' Three months later he gave me a job. It paid less than my job at the hotel, but there was commission on sales and, above all, the opportunity to learn. Now I was becoming something of an expert on ceramics, an area that didn't interest Ken much but accounted for forty percent of our sales. And he was not only my employer – he was my friend.

He was red-eyed when he answered the door, but immaculately dressed in honour of the occasion.

'Come in, Lexy. I'm so awash with emotion – have you seen it? The old boys seeing one another in Hyde Park after fifty years? I must be getting soft.' He wiped his eyes with a Liberty silk square and reached for a glass. 'Sit down. Take my mind off it, for Christ's sake, before I dissolve.'

An open bottle of wine stood on the sofa table in front of him. He filled my glass and then refilled and raised his own.

'The Queen and all those bloody old heroes.'

We drank solemnly and then he switched off the television set. 'That's enough of that. It's making me maudlin. What are you doing with yourself with the don away?'

He always called Ian 'the don' and I was never sure whether it was said with respect or sarcasm.

'Not much.' I smiled and stretched my legs in front of me. 'I've been for a walk along the river. Otherwise, I've slobbed around.'

A companionable silence fell then. We were such good friends that there was no need to speak unless we had something to say. I had worked for him for six months before I realized he was gay, partly due to my own naivety and partly because of his discretion. Since then I had seen him hurt by more than one broken relationship and once seen him cry. Now I spoke aloud.

'I'm very fond of you, Ken –'

He put a hand to his mouth in mock alarm.

'You're not going to propose, are you? Because I tell you now, I'm not up to it!'

'No, I'm not, you old sod. But I am fond of you – and grateful – and I just wanted you to know.'

He wiped imaginary sweat from his brow. 'What a relief! I'm quite fond of you, too, funny little thing that you are. Especially when I hear the till ring.'

We bantered for a while, teasing one another about whose sales figures were best, both knowing that Ken only had to sell one piece of furniture to equal twenty sales of mine. Still, I knew what I was doing now and I knew he appreciated it, which was nice. By the time I left him, I had lost most of my misery and was looking forward to the evening again. In a week's time I was going to London to spend a few days helping Nella move house. It would be hard work and I knew my mother too well to doubt there would be a round of social engagements, so the more peace I got now the better.

Ian rang me just after seven. 'Missed me?'

He sounded slightly drunk and very contented and I resisted the temptation to say 'You obviously haven't missed me!' Instead, I said what I knew he wanted to hear: that Durham without him was a wasteland and I could just about manage to keep breathing until he got back. But afterwards, as I dressed my salad and poured a glass of wine, I wondered if I had really missed him in the way you should miss the man in your life.

By the time I rolled into bed, squeaky clean from the shower, my mouth tingling with toothpaste and my clothes neatly laid out for the morning, I had still not made up my mind.

2

I travelled to London the following Saturday. We had three days to pack up Notting Hill. On the fourth day we would transfer Nella's possessions to the house she had bought in Windmill Walk, on the south side of the Thames. She was talking bravely about the South Bank being the only place to live nowadays and how the move would give her a nice lump of cash, but I wondered if she was moving from choice or from necessity.

I had mixed feelings about the move. Nella had kept my old room after I left, school textbooks in the bookcase, childhood souvenirs on the walls and in the drawers. Would dismantling my childhood bring back painful memories? When the train reached York, I gave up pondering the uncomfortable and opened my paper.

It was full of the impending wedding of a minor pop star to an equally minor footballer. At twenty-one, she was just a year older than me and yet she looked incredibly serene and mature. I studied her picture carefully. Was she genuinely in love or a spoiled little madam opting for six pages in *Hello*? Only time would tell. I turned the page, trying not to think about weddings. They always made me feel uncomfortable, with their reminders of white watered silk and tartan sashes. I folded the paper and closed my eyes and managed to think about nothing at all until we reached Stevenage and it was time to gather my bags.

We started work on Sunday morning, each of us dressed for action in jeans and T-shirt. Looking at Nella, it was hard to believe she was my mother, harder still to see her as grandmother of two. She had just finished a bit part in a film for Channel Four and her hair was cropped and highlighted so that it circled around her head like a halo. She was still reed-slim and the shadows that had clouded her eyes at our first reunion were gone – banished, no doubt, by the thought of soon being out of debt.

I felt a pang of guilt. Perhaps I should move back to London and share expenses – except that something in me had the need to be free. I tried to tell myself it was because I wanted my own space and a bed I could share with a man of my choice, but I knew it was more than that. I was still on the run and with no prospect of turning to face that which I feared. I might be able to meet Jamie now, make conversation, act the dutiful sister-in-law, but my longing to possess him had not diminished at all.

Perhaps it never would.

We spent the first day picking things up, regarding them and then subsiding into chairs to reminisce.

'It won't do,' Nella decreed eventually. 'A whole day gone by and we haven't achieved anything.' In typical Nella fashion she had the remedy. 'We'll stop now and go out for a nice meal. Early bed and when we start tomorrow we won't speak to one another. Not a word!'

I pointed out that we could keep on working now and put the evening to good use, but she wouldn't hear of it.

'No, you go back on Wednesday and we must have one night off! You bathe, I'll shower. And dress up, darling. No point in doing things by halves.'

By the time I'd bathed and changed into the one good dress I'd brought with me, she'd turned into a fashion model: pale grey Jean Muir, old but still stunning, pearls in her ears and a veritable mist of Femme.

'Will I do?' I asked.

She held me at arms' length, cogitated and then nodded. 'You're so good-looking now, Lexy. Not pretty, but definitely *Je ne sais quoi*!'

'Thanks,' I said faintly but was unable to ask for a definition of *quoi* because the cab she'd summoned was at the door.

'Rules,' she said as she subsided into her seat. I opened my mouth to protest at her extravagance but she held up an elegant hand. 'Don't say a word, Lexy. I'm working again, I've made a bomb on the house sale and I feel like celebrating. Besides, I want to show you off.'

We ate in the dark, atmospheric restaurant that was reputedly London's oldest. Between bites Nella gave me a rundown on any diners she recognized.

'There's Germaine Greer; don't know who she's with but I'm sure that's Caroline Charles she's wearing.' Or 'That's Malcolm McDowell. Isn't he ageing well? I wonder who *she* is? Not in the business... probably his agent.'

After the first four or five tables I ceased to listen and concentrated on my osso bucco until she leaned forward to jog my arm.

'See him? Corner table, half-turned to us? I know I've seen him in the paper but I can't remember the name.'

I looked across, quite sure that if the woman who devoured *Hello* magazine couldn't place somebody, then my chances of doing so were nil.

I was wrong. The profile in the corner was familiar to me. 'It's Rick Paul,' I said, trying to sound phlegmatic. 'He's a musician.'

Nella's face lit up. 'I knew I knew him. He wrote that 'Starlight' thing they play incessantly. He's very talented.'

I kept eating, hoping her eye would flit on. She pushed her food around her plate for a moment, then laid down her knife and fork.

'How do you know who he is?'

I shrugged in what I hoped was a nonchalant way.

'I just do.'

I might have known she'd guess I was being devious.

'You *know* him, don't you? I know you: always got your nose in an antiques handbook; you never read the showbiz pages. Come on, tell me: have you met him?'

I gave her a watered-down version of my acquaintance with Rick and then tried to get her interested in dessert, but all the while I could see her eyes flicking towards Rick's table.

'Mother!' I fixed her with a glare. 'If you embarrass me I'm going back to Durham tonight. Be warned!'

Her lashes flew skyward and a hand fluttered to her breast.

'*Moi?*'

I firmed my lips. 'Forget the Miss Piggy impersonation, Mother. Just remember what I said.'

She smiled sweetly. 'I love it when you call me "Mother". Such a nice change.'

We ate mouth-watering crêpes and shared the last of the wine and then I saw Rick stand up. Should I warn her again or hope she hadn't noticed? Before I could decide, he had threaded his way towards us.

'Hello Lexy,' he said.

I smiled up at him, noticing changes. His eyes looked tired now and the freckles over the bridge of his nose had faded. I sought for words but he forestalled me.

'You didn't keep our date.'

It was too much for Nella. She reached for his hand.'She was very silly if she stood you up. I'm her mother. I'll see to it that she mends her ways.' And then she was pulling out a chair and gesturing for him to sit down. I looked at his friends, waiting for him to move on, and felt my heart sink.

'I'm sure you're on your way somewhere. I was very pleased for you when "Starlight" was such a success. Please forgive my mother for hanging on to your hand; she's like that. Anyway, good to see you.'

He was grinning now but not attempting to disengage his hand.

'Are you in London permanently? I'd love to stay, but we're on our way to something. Maybe we could meet up…?'

'She's staying with me.' Nella let go of his hand and fished in her bag. 'There's a card, but don't waste time. She goes back to Durham on Wednesday. She's only here to help me move in – but that's the new address on the card.'

'I'll ring,' he said, pocketing the card and then he inclined his head to Nella and went on his way, his entourage close on his heels.

'Now,' Nella said, wiping her mouth and throwing down her napkin. 'What date did you break and when and why have you kept it quiet?'

'I hardly know him.'

Even as I said it, it sounded weak.

'That's why he calls you "Lexy": a family name? I didn't come up the Thames in a banana boat, darling. And why did you stand him up? Did you notice his hands? Heaven! And that jacket was Paul Smith.'

I shook my head. 'You're letting your imagination run away with you again. I met him one New Year's Eve and then again in Liverpool. We had a coffee. That's it.'

'But he asked you out.' She had elbows on table now, her chin supported on her hands, eyes wide.

'No,' I said. 'Well, he said we'd meet in Trafalgar Square the next New Year's Eve. He was off on a tour, I was leaving Liverpool. I never thought he meant it.'

'But he did. He must have turned up to know you didn't.'

I threw up my hands to show how silly the conversation was, but she had suddenly sobered.

'Are you over it – the thing with Jamie? I haven't liked to ask. I just hope, when you mention Ian, that you've come to terms with it.'

I reached to pat her hand.

'I'm over it. I'll always like him – love him – but I've got my head around it, so don't worry.'

'Good. Shall we have coffee? And an Armagnac, I think. And then we'll plan what you'll wear for Rick Paul.'

'He won't ring, Mother. You'll see.'

She was smiling at the waiter who was advancing on us, but her words were for me.

'Trust one who knows, darling. It's been a painful learning curve but I think I know men by now. He'll ring.'

3

I should have trusted Nella's superior knowledge of men. Rick rang the following day, but not before a bouquet had arrived for Nella (roses and stephanotis), together with a card wishing her well in the new house. She took the phone from me as soon as she realized who was ringing and thanked him profusely then curled up on the sofa to listen in as I spoke to him.

He asked if I was free that night and I felt a strange mix of pleasure and alarm.

'I suppose I could be.'

Nella's eyes rolled heavenwards and I covered the mouthpiece of the receiver to glare at her. 'How do you know what he's saying?' I mouthed.

She knelt in her enthusiasm and mouthed back, 'Say yes!'

At the other end of the line I heard Rick chuckle and knew he knew exactly what was going on.

'What time and where?' I said, anxious to bring the call to an end. He named a restaurant I'd never heard of and offered to pick me up, but I said a firm no. 'I'm coming in from somewhere else,' I said and saw Nella's eyes roll again.

'Where's he taking you?' she asked before the receiver had reached the phone rest.

'La Bamba,' I said and saw her shoulders heave with pleasure.

'It's *heaven*,' she said. 'I've never been, but everyone raves about it.'

I tried to concentrate on putting the house to rights while she went through her wardrobe like a terrier, regarding and discarding one outfit after another.

'I won't wear any of them,' I warned her, but I could have saved my breath. In the end I accepted the loan of her dusky pink Jean Muir: straight dress and loose jacket. With pearls in my ears and my hair tucked back it looked discreetly chic, and honour was satisfied on both sides.

I knew I looked good when I entered the restaurant and saw his face as he rose to greet me. I couldn't tell a label from the cut of a jacket like Nella, but I guessed his was Armani and the shirt beneath it had the sheen of quality.

We ordered and sat nervously, fingering the stems of our glasses, until he broke the silence. 'Where do we begin? We've got some catching up to do. Shall I start or will you?'

You first,' I said. 'You went to Europe. How did that go?'

But even as he told me about the tour of Europe, sleeping in the van, eating well in one place, starving in another, the break-through with the one melody that no one could stop humming, I was rehearsing my own story. How would it sound if I told him about running away because I coveted my sister's bridegroom, taking a dead girl's identity to get a job, living like a mouse in a hole, afraid of friendships until I fell for a man who came into the antique shop where I worked to buy a *pliqué a jour* pendant and took my virginity that same night?

Suddenly I was filled with a feeling of anger towards Ian, seeing his face, smug and sensual, bearing down on me as though it had been his right.

'Penny for them?'

I came to and found Rick's eyes on me, amused and a little hurt.

'Was it that boring?'

I spent the next hour devouring his every word and shifting three delicious courses and a fair quantity of excellent red wine. He was easy to get on with, laid-back, witty and seemingly oblivious of the fact that other diners cast curious eyes in his direction from time to time. And yet, at the same time, he seemed shy.

'What's it like, being famous?' I asked after two people had threaded their way between tables to get a closer look at him.

He shrugged.

'Irritating sometimes, nice at others. You get letters – they say the music meant something to them, that's... pretty satisfying.' He grinned then. 'Quite a few kids came into the world on the back of "Starlight", or so they say. Now *that's* a responsibility.'

It was ten o'clock now and I began to hope I would get away with a few short phrases about the transition from a Liverpool restaurant to a Durham antique shop. I was wrong.

'Right,' he said, as they served coffees and Armagnac. 'Nineteen ninety-two: Liverpool. Begin there.'

So I gave him the sanitized version. How I kept Ken's business card and when I found myself in Durham, renewed the acquaintance. How he let me hang around the shop until I'd acquired some expertise and then took me on full-time.

'I really enjoy it now,' I finished, hoping it would end there.

'No relationships?' he said. 'I've told you about my groupies. Do they have an antique equivalent?'

I felt my cheeks flush. 'Not really. But there is someone – he's a lecturer at the university. We don't live together...'

That last came out too quickly and I realized that I didn't want to discourage Rick by making him feel I was already involved. Which was odd, because I hadn't really wanted to come tonight. Was I trying to tell him Ian didn't mean a lot, or was I trying to quell the feeling of disloyalty to Jamie that always overcame me if I was even faintly stirred by another man?

'Let's stick to you,' I said. 'You've never mentioned your love life.'

'There've been one or two relationships in the last few years,'

Rick said at last, 'but not as many as legend would have it. I come from a pretty strong family. Mum's Liverpool, Dad's Welsh. Odd combination, but they've stuck together for nearly forty years.'

He must have seen me doing calculations in my head.

'I'm the baby of the family: two sisters, one brother and then me. Anyway, that's what I'd like eventually. Something that lasts.' He put down his glass. 'What about you? I've met your mum. What about the rest of the family?'

It was easy to explain my father, to laugh over some of Nella's exploits. Sara and Jamie were harder. I stammered through an account of Ard-na-Shiel and their kids and then looked at my watch. 'Goodness! I'd love to go on talking, but we've a strenuous day ahead.'

It was a relief when we were out on the pavement. I turned to look for a cab, but a dark limousine was pulling out from the opposite kerb and gliding towards us. The driver leapt out and opened the back door and I let myself be handed in to a deep seat.

'The trappings of success,' Rick said wryly. 'Now, where do we go?'

As we rolled towards the South Bank he wrote down my address in Durham. 'We seem destined to meet on the eve of my taking off for foreign parts.' He had told me earlier of his departure for New York the following day. 'I'll be back next week. Where will you be? And is it OK if I ring?'

'Of course!' I sounded so surprised that he started to explain.

'I don't want to butt in if there's someone else... I mean, just say –' He was suddenly disconcerted and I found it appealing.

'Ring me!' I said, and then, as the car came to a halt: 'I'd ask you in but we're still in the throes of moving.'

We climbed out and stood together on the pavement. 'Goodbye again, then.'

'Yes. Again.'

'Let's hope it's not another five years.'

'Yes. Let's hope…'

'Good night, then …'

Out of the corner of my eye I saw that the driver was staring rigidly ahead. Was he used to farewells like this? Or just well-trained? But the lips that came down on mine were too uncertain to be over-used.

'I enjoyed tonight,' I said as we moved apart.

'Me, too.'

He stood while I fumbled for my key and opened the door. I kept thinking about Ian that night, following me into my flat, taking over. Again I felt anger, and Rick seemed suddenly so dear that I almost turned and went back to him. And then I remembered that none of it was real emotion – real love. I had known that once, still knew it, and this wasn't to compare.

'Good night,' I said again and went into the house.

'Good night?' Nella was in her dressing gown, curled up on the sofa. She was smiling, but there was something lacklustre about her question. When I'd left, she'd been avid for detail. Now she was simply going through the motions.

'What's wrong?' I asked and put down my bag.

She didn't argue but shook her head as though she couldn't believe what was happening. 'It's Jamie. Sara told me he was going for a check-up, just routine: something to do with insurance. She rang tonight. They've found something. It may be benign. There's a fifty-fifty chance of it being benign.'

I couldn't trust myself to speak. Instead, I walked through to the kitchen, lifted the kettle to check it had water in it and clicked the switch. *Get down two cups, one spoon of coffee granules in each, two sweeteners from a dispenser, hot water, add milk…* I made the coffee automatically, a singing in my ears that precluded thought. It was not until I sat down with Nella, nursing my mug in both hands that I could seriously contemplate what she had told me.

'Drink your coffee,' I said automatically.

She raised the mug to her lips and I noticed that her hands were shaking

'Don't worry,' I said, trying to sound convincing. 'They're clever nowadays. He can afford the best treatment. Sara's a doctor, for God's sake!' And then, when I could no longer spout platitudes: 'Where is it? What do they say it is?'

'It's his lungs – a shadow, they say. It could be TB, but Sara doesn't believe that. I could hear it in her voice.'

'She's bound to think the worst.' Even to my own ears I sounded desperately unconvincing.

'We'll have to help her,' Nella said.

I nodded. 'Of course. Anything...' I felt a rising panic and knew I mustn't let it show. The man I loved was in mortal danger and I couldn't let my terror show; it wouldn't be fair. Once again, it was Sara who had the right to sympathy, support, even tears. *Damn you, Sara.* I shouted it so in my head that for a moment I was terrified I'd said it aloud.

Nella's composure was returning.

'Tell me about tonight. Is he as nice as he seems? When are you seeing him again? Was the restaurant good? They say it's hideously expensive...'

'It was good,' I said. 'Very good. And he's a nice guy. When will I see him again? The year 2000 probably, if we keep to the pattern.'

I couldn't have cared less about Rick at that moment. I wanted to get upstairs, into my room. Climb over the boxes and bales and burrow into my bed like a wounded animal.

'I think I'll go up now,' I said and managed to contain my tears until I got to the hall.

4

I went back to Durham two days later, outwardly confident that all would be well. That was how Nella wanted to play it and it suited me.

'Ring Sara,' she said as I got into the cab. 'And keep in touch.'

I nodded.

'I promise. Don't over-do the settling in. I'll try and come down again soon.'

In the train, I tried to work out what to do for the best. I wanted above all else to see Jamie, to put out my hands and touch his flesh, feel it warm and alive and untouched by disease. But I had no excuse, no right to rush to Ard-na-Shiel. And suddenly I could feel the wheels of the Bentley bumping over the bridge at Ballachulish and see the white stones lining the driveway to that great, gaunt house. I turned my face to the window, wishing it would rain and drown the sun that struck against the glass and made the landscape outside bright with the promise of the summer. I didn't want time to pass, seasons to change – not if it meant that Jamie wouldn't be there in his Highland kingdom, in my heart, young and unchanging forever.

I didn't ring Ian when I got home. If I did, he would come round and I was in no mood for sex. I spent a night wide-eyed in the dark and it was a relief when dawn came and I could get ready. I paced the floor until half-past seven, a time when I could decently call on Ken.

He was still in his dressing-gown when he answered the door.

'Come in. Coffee's on.'

I moved past him into the hall.

'It's not a social visit, Ken. I've had some bad news.'

'Not your mother?'

There was genuine concern in his voice. He had met Nella several times and rejoiced in finding someone as eccentric as himself.

'No, it's not Nella. It's Jamie, my brother-in-law.' I had told him of my flight from Ard-na-Shiel but allowed him to think of it as teenage trauma. Now I was truthful. 'I love him, Ken. I'll always love him. That's why I ran away: because I couldn't bear to see him and not have him. And now he may have cancer.'

'So you're afraid you might lose him altogether?'

I nodded.

'Well ...' He moved towards the armoire that housed his drinks collection. 'Brandy, I think. With the merest hint of soda.' He handed me a heavy tumbler and sat down opposite me, serene, as though there were nothing odd about brandy before breakfast. Underneath the brocade dressing gown his pyjamas were navy-blue silk, his slippers gorgeous creations of beadwork and silver wire. Any other time I would have smiled at the vanity. Today it didn't matter. Usually he was immaculate; today he had a faint stubble and his silver hair looked somehow fluffy and vulnerable.

He's getting old, I thought.

'Right,' he said when we had both sipped. 'Tell me everything.'

He listened attentively while I repeated the conversation with Nella.

'So it's not a confirmed diagnosis?'

I shook my head. 'And even if it is malignant, they're clever nowadays. I'm always reading about new research.'

He leaned to pat my hand, his stubbled face crinkling with concern. 'Wait and see, Alexandra. If it comes to the worst he can afford the best treatment. He's young and fit. Don't give up on him yet.'

By the time I left Ken's house I felt, if not comforted, at least back in command of myself. I rang Sara as soon as I got home. She sounded her usual, serene self.

'They're doing a biopsy today. We should have the results by Saturday. They'll start treatment then, if –' Her voice trembled for just a second and then she carried on, but I was remembering the scene in the hall, the two of them melting into one another.

'Sara, I'm so very, very sorry. If you need me, I'll come: take care of the children'– for little Alex had a sister now – 'anything. You only have to say the word.'

When I put down the phone I went into the bathroom and ran a bath. Lying in it I tried to sort my jumbled feelings. Talking to Sara a moment ago, I had cared about her, worried about the coming baby – for she was pregnant for the third time – wished I was face-to-face to put out my arms and comfort her. And yet she had ruined my life, always stood between me and what I wanted.

I had sat on the stairs in Notting Hill one night, long after I had been put to bed, hearing her laughing with my mother behind the closed sitting-room door. I had wound my fingers around the balustrade then and wished, with all my heart, that she would die so that I could be the one within that special mother-daughter relationship. And yet I had loved her and she me. I could remember her hands: pulling up my wayward socks, plaiting my hair for infants school, showing me how to do fractions, buying me my first two-piece bathing suit out of her earnings from a holiday job.

I closed my eyes and leaned back against the edge of the bath, wishing I had the courage to sink below the level of the scented water and put an end to all ambivalence. Did I still love Jamie? My love for him had revolutionized my life, so it must have been exceptional. But could love that was not returned last for years? Did I still love him, or did I cling to the idea because it freed me from commitment to anyone else? Had my love for Jamie become merely a creed I was ashamed to renounce? Even as I wondered, I knew that it burned as brightly as it had ever done and if he died part of me would die, too.

Ian arrived just after I left the cooling bath, appearing in the hall as I came out of the bathroom. As usual the sight of him pleased me: dark brows under blond hair, eyes almost permanently crinkled in a smile. He was a charmer and he knew it, but he could be the best company in the world.

'I missed you, Lexy. Tell me about the move. But first...'

He had propelled me as far as the bedroom door before he accepted I wasn't in the mood.

We wound up against the jamb of the door, he not smiling for once, me trying to explain that my lack of desire had nothing to do with him.

'I've had some bad news, Ian. My brother-in-law – Sara's husband.'

Suddenly he was all concern.

'I'm sorry, darling. I'm an idiot.'

He led me to the kitchen, sat me down at the table and turned to switch on the kettle. Even in my present mood I couldn't help admiring the elegant figure inside the well-cut sports coat. He had been a tennis blue and could still beat anyone who came up against him in straight sets.

'Now,' he said, spooning instant coffee into cups, 'tell me what's happened.'

I repeated my conversation with Nella as he mixed the coffee and gave us each a mug.

'So it's not definite yet?'

He managed to make it sound as though we were talking about a bout of flu and it irked me.

'Sara's a *doctor*. She wouldn't get agitated if she didn't see a real danger.'

'Of course not.' He was using the soothing tone that had such a devastating effect on his female students, but I didn't want to be soothed – I wanted to be understood. Sympathized with, helped to cope. Ken had been better than this.

'Of course there's danger – well, risk – but nothing's definite. This time next week it could all be over: a false alarm.'

He stood up and moved towards me, putting out a hand to take my face in his palm and urge me gently to my feet. Once pressed against his chest, feeling his hands move over my back I felt better. His lips came down on my hair, my forehead, my mouth. We moved to the bedroom, he guiding me and somehow managing to divest himself of jacket and tie at the same time.

'There, there,' he said. 'I'm here now. It'll be OK, you'll see.'

And I gave in because I didn't care enough to resist. As usual he was a more than adequate lover. My body responded but my mind was strangely resistant. He wanted sex. My family turmoil was merely a hiccup to be soothed out of the way so he could get what he needed. As he gave a last convulsive shudder and rolled away, I was thinking of the hall at Ard-na-Shiel and two bodies almost liquid with desire for one another but still respectful and tender.

That was what I wanted: what Sara had with Jamie and what had been denied to me.

There was none of the usual post-coital *badinage*. He seemed preoccupied; I felt resentful. And yet I needed him – wanted him to hold me and tell me everything was going to be alright.

I leaned against the headboard and thought about all those times when there had been sounds of discord from below as Nella battled with one man or another and I had thought it the end of the world. Sara would come into my bed then, or let me burrow into hers. 'It'll be alright in the morning,' she would say, and I had nestled into her warmth and hung on to her words and believed in her – even when it wasn't alright in the morning and the man in question had packed up and left. Was Jamie hanging on her words now, clutching at her for warmth and reassurance?

I felt tears prick my eyes and brushed them away. Mustn't cry in front of Ian. And suddenly I wanted him out of my bed, my bedroom, my life. What good was a man if you couldn't cry in front of him, couldn't snivel and whinge and wipe away snot and still be loved?

When he'd gone, trying to hide his relief that I didn't want company, I lay on the bed and thought about things. When Jamie got better – and it had to be *when,* not *if* – I would get on with things. That first devastating experience of a love that couldn't be mustn't influence the rest of my life.

I wanted a real relationship. It might not have the heady scent of clover but it would have a magic of its own. And if I never found it I would be content with all the other things I had to be glad about.

I prayed for Sara then, squeezing my eyes shut, apologizing for daring to pray after years of indifference to anything remotely spiritual, and then for all the years I had begrudged Sara's happiness. *She only has to crook a little finger, things fall into her lap, it isn't fair* – that had been the mantra of my adolescence, and if I had not voiced it lately, I had still felt it. Now I asked the gods to let her keep her family intact, and if they had a little good will left over, to give me the grace to be glad about it.

The day after I returned from London, flowers arrived from Rick. After that it was postcards: the Manhattan skyline, Vermont in the fall, San Francisco's Chinatown. I would have been pleased that he was remembering me, but as the days and weeks went by, fears for Jamie obscured every other emotion. The biopsy found a malignant tumour. They removed it, but the outlook was still uncertain. Nella went north to look after the children, and I could tell from her voice when she telephoned that things were not looking good.

Each night when I put down the receiver, I sat, arms around myself, a kind of singing in my ears at the horror of what might be happening. I tortured myself with tiny glimpses into the locked cupboard of my days in Ard-na-Shiel. The sunlight in the library, the storm sweeping over the loch as we ran for cover, that one moment of enlightenment beside the Falls of Orchy when I felt the first physical manifestation of love. I felt it now, that welling up of feeling in chest and abdomen and groin. I wanted Jamie – wanted to hold him in my arms, kiss his brow, his eyes, his lips, infuse him with my love and strength and make him well.

What I did *not* want was sex with Ian.

At first I tried to explain.

'I'm worried for Sara, Ian. Besides, I *like* Jamie – I couldn't bear it if anything happened to him.'

His answer was to cluck sympathy and then draw me into an embrace at first comforting and then, as soon as he thought he decently could, erotic.

'Don't – please –'

'For God's sake, Lex. What difference will it make? I'm sorry for the guy. I hope he's OK. But we can't just turn off. He's your *brother-in-law*. Christ, I can hardly remember my brother-in-law's face.'

For a moment I was tempted to explain, but only for a moment. How could you explain to your lover that he had never, ever been the love of your life? Never had and never would be? Instead, I submitted to sex when it couldn't be avoided, my detestation of Ian growing with each thrust, each groan of selfish satisfaction.

Afterwards, I wept.

'It shouldn't be like this,' I told myself and even, sometimes, took a guilty satisfaction in blaming Sara for my present pain. Without Sara there would have been no Jamie, no love, no loss. I would have stayed at school, got two good A-levels and be a rising City executive by now. And yet, without Jamie, there would have been no edge to life, no dazzle, no moment on a heathered bank when I came close to heaven.

At the beginning of September they told Sara there was nothing more to be done. The cancer had spread throughout his body.

'They say six weeks,' Nella said. Her voice was bleak and she sounded old and defeated.

I tried not to cry because it wouldn't help.

'Don't give up,' I said. 'Don't give up.'

I sat on the bathroom floor, my arms round my knees, and cried for all of us. Even Sara – no room for enmity now. It grew dark while I sat there, the light from the window paling until lamps flared up in the street outside, sending shafts across the white tiles, creating lagoons of darkness here and there. I thought of Rannoch Moor, the moon glinting off water left and right, the darkness of Glencoe and the Ballachulish bridge that led to the house above the loch. I thought of Ard-na-Shiel and knew I had to go there one more time.

'Of course you must go,' Ken said, when I told him. 'I can manage here. Stay as long as you need – as long as you want to…' He held me in his arms then and for a few moments I felt safe.

'I don't know what I'd do without you,' I told him when we moved apart and saw a gleam of pleasure spring up in his eyes before he diffused the tension with a joking remark. Once, when we were talking about life as a gay man, he had said he believed it honed your sense of humour. 'You have to see the joke in everything,' he'd said, 'or else you'd cry.'

Ian was not so supportive. 'Of course,' he said. 'If it's the end...'

He made it sound as though a wearying burden was shortly to be lifted from him and I itched to strike him. Instead, I moved to him, smiling as though with gratitude, put my hands on his upper arms and looked into his eyes. I felt a glimmer of movement in him, surprise turning into elation at the prospect of sex at my invitation. I waited for as many seconds as I dared before I spoke.

'Fuck off, Ian,' I said. 'And don't come back.'

5

Two days later I caught the eight-fifteen to Glasgow, Ken shepherding me aboard and fussing over my seat.

'I'll be fine,' I said, and waved until the train pulled away and castle and cathedral were lost to view.

I tried to concentrate on the changing countryside as we moved towards the Scottish border. The trees were a darker green, conifer-like, the landscape magnificent but bleaker than the south. I watched it flit past and felt an imaginary nip in the air because we were going north. But try as I might I couldn't blot out the purpose of my journey. I was going back to Ard-na-Shiel because Jamie was dying.

Twice I went to the lavatory to splash my eyes with cold water and wipe away the traces of my tears. I must not arrive at Sara's home looking sorry for myself. She was the one who was entitled to cry. Although it seared my soul, I couldn't stop imagining the end of Jamie's life, the moment when he would slip away. I played the scene in my mind, holding him, putting my lips to his cheek, telling him all was well and we would never be parted.

Except that it wouldn't be me who held him. It would be Sara who heard his last soft breath, kissed his tired eyes shut, held his still-warm hand. Sara who walked with dignity behind his coffin as it journeyed to the church at Onich, all eyes upon her because she was his wife. In death, as in life, she would be there before me, occupying my place, stealing even that last precious moment. Even when he was gone she would have him inside her in the body of her unborn child. And I hated her for it. I damned her in my mind, cursed her, whipped her with a silent tongue and then gave way to tears because nothing really mattered except that soon I would have to surrender my dream of one day being with him.

It had always been there, the hope that, somehow, without anyone being hurt, he and I could be together. Now there would be no more room for dreaming. The agony that rose up in me at that thought could only be subdued by conjuring up another emotion: rage. I cursed Sara, coldly and efficiently because, by being alive, she had robbed me of the years I might have shared with Jamie. *I hate you,* I told her image in my head, and invented a thousand coldnesses with which to punish her.

She was waiting at the barrier when I stepped from the train, reed-thin except for the swollen stomach on which her hand rested in the age-old gesture of pregnancy.

'Hello,' I said aloud, but in my head I tried to think *Bitch, bitch, bitch.*

She was sheltering within her the flesh of Jamie's flesh: a child who would bear his name. She who already had so much would have more and I would be left with nothing! Suddenly she moved towards me and leaned her head on my shoulder. I did nothing for a second; it was usually she who comforted me. And then I sensed the need in her and it was easy to put my arms around her and hug her till she almost gasped for breath.

'Don't worry about anything. I'm here and I'm staying.'

As the car drew away from the station, I thought of Jamie, stepping out from the portico that first night, bending to restrain the dog, drawing me from the darkness into the warmth of the house. My teenage awkwardness had melted in the warmth of his welcome and within a week I had grown up. I suddenly realized I was smiling and glanced hastily sideways in case Sara had seen. But her eyes were on the road ahead, her mouth compressed into a thin line of concentration.

Nella was waiting at the door when we reached the end of the drive, the children beside her. Alex was the image of his father: a sturdy little toddler who smiled up at me but betrayed his unease in a dozen small ways. Fiona wasn't yet two, clinging to her mother now as though her life depended on it.

'I've spent too much time away from her,' Sara said. Her voice was devoid of emotion, her words a simple statement of fact that conjured up an image of a hospital room and hope receding.

'Let's get inside,' Nella said. 'I expect you'd like some tea.'

I wanted to kneel down and take the children in my arms, but I was almost a stranger to them. I moved forward to follow Nella into the darkness of the porch and then I felt a small hand insinuate itself into mine. I looked down at the boy, but he was staring ahead. Behind me Sara was scooping her daughter into her arms, McGregor bringing up the rear with the bags. I closed my fingers round the hand of Jamie's son and let him lead me into the hall.

6

Jamie came home the following day. Nella took the children into the walled garden, fearful of overwhelming him at the door. I waited in the hall, surrounded by long-dead Munros seemingly unmoved by the fact that the Laird of Ard-na-Shiel was coming home to die. I waited while the sun came and went outside the door and came again so that my first glimpse of Jamie was against a brilliant backdrop which threw his face into shadow. But even before I saw his features I knew death was upon him. He had shrunk inside his clothes so that the tall frame was stooped and hung with flesh rather than covered by it.

'Lexy?'

He was smiling at me and I felt my chin tremble. I moved towards him because I could not bear to look at him, meaning to bury my face in his shoulder in a pretence of greeting. But there was no shoulder for me to hide against – only a figure so fragile that I felt I was clutching a bird.

'Welcome home,' I said and then stood back to let Sara lead him through to the room where a day-bed had been prepared.

We settled him there, all the while making conversation as we plumped cushions and helped him discard his outer garments.

'Are they here?' He was looking hopefully at Sara and I knew he wanted to see his children.

'I'll get them,' I said, and left them there, holding hands as though to give one another strength.

As I went towards the walled garden I tried to summon up anger, anything to dull the pain. *She is there,* I told myself. *She is there, like always, where you should be.* But it wouldn't work. I couldn't feel anything but pity for her now, facing the loss of what mattered most to her. She loved her children, but not in the way she loved Jamie.

I led them through to the breakfast room, relinquishing their hands at the doorway, letting them run, whooping with glee at the sight of their father, praying their onslaught would not be too much for him, and then I turned away, not daring to watch.

He was well enough to stay up until the children were bathed and kissed goodnight and carted off to bed, but all the while I could see the energy draining out of him. Fiona sat on his knee to be kissed, looking up at him occasionally in a puzzled way, knowing something was wrong but not quite sure what it was. The neck, once corded with muscle, now sat inside a collar at least three sizes too big. The hands, still beautiful, were strangely bleached as though a long time out of sunlight. I looked at the prominent wristbones and the teeth suddenly larger than the mouth that contained them.

I had never seen death, but I recognized its coming.

When the children were gone, I tried to make conversation: about Durham, about antiques, about Ken and was sometimes rewarded with a smile, but when Sara came down from putting the children to bed he looked at her with relief.

'I think I'll go up now, if you don't mind. It's the first day home... tomorrow will be better.'

'Of course it will.' Nella and I spoke in unison and stood as Sara led him away, both of us longing to help but knowing his dignity demanded we do nothing of the sort.

'We have to do our best,' Nella said when they were gone. 'It's terrible for me, it must be worse for you – but we can't let them down.'

'We won't,' I said, grateful for the acknowledgement of my particular grief.

And then I went to her and clung, neither of us crying because it was too bad for tears.

Nella broke away first and looked at me dry-eyed. 'We can't do much for him, but his children need cherishing and he – *they* both deserve that we do it well.'

When Sara came down, we picked at the salad meal McGregor had laid out in the dining room and then carried coffee to the library, making a desperate fuss over cream and sugar to delay the need for conversation.

I saw Nella open her mouth to fill the silence, her eyes desperately seeking something – anything – to say, but before she could speak Sara put down her cup and spoke.

'This baby's going to be a boy and I'm going to call him Jamie.'

For a second Nella's eyes shut, as though in pain, and then she recovered herself.

'Darling. That's wonderful. I didn't realize you knew its sex.'

'I don't.' Her voice was matter-of-fact. 'But it will be a boy.'

I could see Nella seeking words that would not come.

'The children have grown,' I said. 'It's an age since I saw them, but I was still surprised.'

This was safe territory. Nella's eyes flashed gratitude and Sara's face lost something of its quiet despair.

'Yes,' she said. 'They have grown.'

After that no one spoke again until Sara put down her cup and rose to her feet.

'I think I'll go up now. It's been quite a day.'

7

The next two days were a blur of secret tears and public smiles, of trying to amuse two children horribly aware that their world was crumbling and trying to maintain a semblance of normal life when we met for meals in that strange lull when children and patient had been put to bed.

The third day Jamie did not come downstairs.

'Not much longer,' Nella said at the breakfast table, and I felt at once relief and black despair as she continued, 'She can't stay up there all day.'

I nodded.

'Will you go up or shall I?'

But before we could resolve this question, Sara appeared.

'I want to take the children out for a while. Will you take something up and read to him, Lexy? He's sleeping, I think, but he likes to hear a voice.' Her own voice was steady and I felt my throat contract. 'It will be tonight, I think. I want to get out for an hour and then I'll stay with him.'

It was so matter-of-fact and yet it was not cold. There was a wealth of meaning in the words and in the way she said them.

'Good girl,' Nella said, but when she would have reached out, Sara stepped aside.

'I'm OK,' she said. 'Really, I'm OK.'

I moved across the great hall and entered the library. It was still there: the small volume of Dowson.

They are not long the days of wine and roses,
love and desire and hate.

I think they have no portion in us
after we pass the gate...

Dust motes were swimming in the shafts of sunlight just as they had four years before, but the words had lost their romance now that I knew their meaning. If Jamie died...

I put it aside and, before I mounted the stairs to his room, chose the volume of Scott he had read to me that same day. He looked small in the wide bed and the waxy hand on the coverlet looked too big for the wrist that supported it. His eyes were closed as I sat in the wicker nursing chair by his bed and opened the book at random. In front of me on the page was the 'Lay of the Last Minstrel.' I began to read aloud.

'The way was long, the wind was cold ...'

I looked up and saw he had opened his eyes. His hand lifted as though to point and then he spoke.

'The sixth canto,' he said. 'Turn to the sixth canto.'

I leafed my way through the long poem until I found what he meant.

'Breathes there a man, with soul so dead, who never to himself hath said, this is my own, my native land.'

As I read on, he smiled, his eyes closed again and as the poem ended I saw that he slept. I sat on watching him, wanting to reach out and touch his hand but afraid I might wake him. Eventually I closed my own eyes until I heard him clear his throat. I looked up to find his eyes open and fixed on my face.

'Lexy?'

I smiled at him. 'It's me. Is there anything I can get you?'

He seemed not to hear. Instead, his eyes turned to the window. 'It's a grand day for a picnic. Is Sara...?'

'She's with the children. They've gone for a walk. She won't be long.'

He fell silent then and I waited, uncertain whether or not to make conversation. His eyes closed and I thought he slept until he spoke again.

'Do you remember the heron?'

'Yes.' I felt my heart rise up until it threatened my throat. 'And the falls and the heather and the common ragwort.'

He smiled. 'Stinking Billy. You've remembered that!'

I wanted to tell him I remembered everything – that I would always remember. That I loved him and would love him till I died. Instead, I said. 'I remember the calf – McKechnie's calf. Did it live?'

For a moment I thought he wouldn't remember and then his face cleared. 'It lived. It's in the meadow now – somewhere…' He half-smiled again and then he closed his eyes.

There was a pulse beating in his neck. I watched it, seeing in it his fight for life. His eyes were closed but his breathing had suddenly become louder, almost a rattle, as though he needed to cough. There was water on the bedside table and I was reaching for it when the rattling ceased. He seemed not to breathe but the pulse in his neck beat on.

'Jamie?'

His eyes flew open then, imploring.

'What is it?' I said, but I knew what his eyes were saying. He tried to speak but no words came.

He's dying, I thought and suddenly I felt a surge of triumph. I would be with him. *Me!* For once it was my turn. I reached for his hand, suddenly feeling strong.

'It's alright,' I said. 'I'm here.'

But his eyes were still beseeching.

I sat there, knowing I could ignore his plea, telling myself it didn't really matter. This was my chance to hold him in death as I had never held him in life. My chance to win something from

Sara for the first and only time. For one full minute I fought my own inclination and then I rose to my feet.

'I'll get her, Jamie. Hold on, I'll get her for you now.'

I sped down the stairs, all the time asking God not to punish me, to keep him alive until Sara was there so that I would not need to be forever tormented by that one moment of hesitation. I found her coming up from the loch, the children trailing behind.

'Hurry,' I said. 'Please hurry. I think it's almost over.'

It was as though the pregnancy fell away from her in that minute. She moved across the grass, her feet scarcely seeming to touch, not looking at me or at the children she was leaving behind. They looked surprised and fearful and I held out my hands.

'Come here,' I said. 'It's going to be alright.'

We walked on slowly to accommodate childish footsteps, them leading me because I could not see for tears. And in my mind was the picture of Sara and Jamie melting together in the hall the night I ran from Ard-na-Shiel.

Nella was there when we entered the house, her head turned to the staircase.

'Is it …?'

I never answered her question, for at that moment Sara appeared on the landing. She was smiling as though she had suddenly found a solution to a great burden.

'He's safe now,' she said, and moved to take her daughter in her arms.

8

The funeral cortège wound its way to the Episcopal church at Ballachulish just as the wedding procession must have done four years before. Nella and I rode with Sara in the first car, along with two of Jamie's kinsmen and McGregor, suddenly old and exhausted by grief. Neighbours and friends and local dignitaries brought up the rear. The children were with the wife of a tenant farmer for the day. Nella had arranged it and taken them, eventually, from Sara's arms, both of us fearful she would refuse to let go of them.

Now she sat erect, dry-eyed, staring out of the window as though the passing scenery demanded scrutiny. Only Nella dabbed her eyes occasionally, for I dared not permit myself the luxury of grief. If I let go, even for a second, I would howl like an animal. I had not only lost a loved one, I had lost the dream on which my life had been focused: the faint possibility of union with Jamie. I had known it was fantasy but I had clung to it nevertheless.

Now it was gone.

At the church we stood in sunlight streaming through stained glass, knelt to pray and listened attentively as the minister spoke of Jamie with affection and respect.

'He loved the land that bore him, he loved his proud heritage, but he loved his family most of all.'

I heard Sara's swift intake of breath at that, but that was her only sign of emotion as she sat and stood and lowered her awkward bulk to the floor to pray.

In the churchyard, we stood amid handsome granite tombstones to see the Laird of Ard-na-Shiel laid to rest among his forbears. Here and there were still-bright floral tributes, evidence that the dead were not forgotten. I felt the breeze from the loch on my brow and closed my eyes to remember the day we had run, laughing, from the storm that swept over that great water.

The churchyard was in a hollow, the banks heather-covered above and deep in green ferns below; behind them the quilted mountains, fold on fold, and everywhere wild aubrietia splashing colour. *It's peaceful here*, I thought, and was comforted.

Until I heard the minister bend to Sara.

'It's hard for you,' he said. 'But God will comfort you.'

What about me? I shouted. *How will I live now?* But I shouted only in my head.

Sara had refused to arrange for funeral meats, ancient tradition though it might be. Nella had protested in vain.

'They're coming from all over the Highlands, Sara. You can't turn them away with nothing.'

But Sara's eyes were unflinching, her mouth set.

'I can do anything I like now.'

So we rode back to a silent house and parted in the hall, Sara to seek the children, Nella to repair her by-now ravaged face and me to change into jeans and sweatshirt and run as far away from Ard-na-Shiel as I could, the Labrador padding dolefully behind me as though following a cortège.

When I had run until my lungs ached and my legs felt like stones, I sat down by the edge of the loch and gave myself over to grief. The dog appeared to understand, wriggling closer and closer until his muzzle rested on my knee. I saw that it was flecked with white. He had been little more than a pup the night that the Bentley crept between the white stones to the house on the hill. Now he was full-grown and soon he would be old, and I envied him that, knowing I must live for decades without Jamie in my life.

I sat there, grateful for his companionship, until it was time to dry my eyes and go back to the house. Whatever I might feel, I must keep it to myself. It was Sara alone who was entitled to sympathy now.

That night it seemed we all found new strength to play with the children and laugh and talk as though the world was still turning. It was only when they had been carried off to bed that gloom settled over us like a pall. We picked at the food McGregor had laid out in the dining room and then carried our coffee through to the morning room, but even there we seemed lost without that frail figure in the chair. He had been an invalid for only a few weeks, back home for only a day or two, and yet that was the ghost that lingered rather than the fine figure of a man who had once been Laird of Ard-na-Shiel.

'What will you do now?' Nella asked when the silence had stretched to breaking point. The answer came swiftly, delivered in the flattest of voices, a voice that brooked no argument.

'I'm going away.'

'What about the baby?' We spoke in unison, my mother and I, but all she did was repeat her words.

'I'm going away. As soon as I can – after the birth.'

'What about the children?' Nella sounded unusually stern, a grandmother anxious for her grandchildren.

Sara was equally determined.

'They'll come with me, of course. I've thought it all out. We need to get away.'

'For long?' My own voice sounded weak and I tried to firm it up. 'I mean, are we talking holidays, or something more permanent?'

Sara rose. 'I haven't decided. The important thing is to get away. I'm going to bed now. Ask McGregor if you need anything.'

We would have moved to kiss her – or at least wish her a good night's rest, but she gave us no chance. As she walked away, my eyes met Nella's, the message in them the same: that the woman who was daughter to one and sister to the other was now a stranger.

9

I went back to Durham two days after the funeral. I had been away for ten days and it wasn't fair to Ken to stay away longer. Not that he urged me to come back. When I spoke to him on the telephone he was adamant that I should stay as long as was necessary, but there was an odd gaiety about him that made me anxious to know exactly what was going on. Apart from which, there was nothing for me now at Ard-na-Shiel.

It was difficult to leave, with Sara still withdrawn and silent and Nella's eyes filled with anxiety.

'I'll come back as soon as I can,' I said. 'Ring me every day; if you need me I can be with you in hours.'

I meant what I said, but Sara seemed not to care and Nella still looked wretched.

My flat had the stale atmosphere of abandonment when I pushed open the door. There was a pile of mail on the mat and a mountain of newspapers and I cursed myself for forgetting to cancel. I put down my bags and carried post and papers to the kitchen. Once I had a mug of coffee in my hand I felt more like tackling them, putting the bills and circulars to one side and going for the hand-written, personal envelopes first.

There were three notes from Ian, increasingly petulant until the last. *As you don't seem to return my calls or notes, I write to express surprise. I thought we had something, Lex. Sorry if I was wrong. I'm willing to overlook your little outburst so get in touch when you're ready.* There was a letter from Rick, too, full of news about his travels and messages for Nella and for me. I smiled as I read it and then it, too, was put aside. I would have to explain about Jamie eventually but it could wait.

I finished my coffee, binned Ian's messages and the circulars and went in search of Ken. I stood on the step when I'd rung the bell, turning back to look at a garden already browning now with the approach of autumn. Ken was fond of his garden, but there were unexpected signs of neglect here and there: the lawn untrimmed and weed-ridden, a peony trailing across the ground, lupins ravaged by greenfly. I knew he wasn't ill from our phone conversations, so why was he neglecting his beloved garden?

The reason answered the door: tall, blonde and unnaturally brown against his white T-shirt. He looked like a catalogue model as he looked me up and down, one arm against the jamb, the other ruffling his fashionably untidy hair.

'Yes?' he said.

I resisted the impulse to push past him and was about to ask if I could speak to Ken when he appeared in the hallway behind.

'Lexy!'

He sounded overjoyed to see me and the youth stood aside to let me pass.

'Lexy, this is Jack,' he said, glancing up at the boy as he spoke in a way horribly reminiscent of a doting parent.

'Hello,' I said and held out my hand. Jack's grip was what I had expected: damp, cold and unenthusiastic.

'Hi,' he said and turned back to the kitchen.

'Darling!' Ken's arms were as welcoming as ever and I let him hug me, reminding myself that Ken's friends were Ken's business and not there for me to detest on sight. While we sipped wine in the sitting room and I told him everything that had happened at Ard-na-Shiel, I could hear a stereo blaring away in the kitchen. At one stage it seemed to grow louder, as though it had been turned up, and Ken made a little moue of apology.

'He's mad about his music,' he said.

I couldn't resist my next question.

'Who is he, Ken? And what's he doing here? He looks as though he lives here.'

The sudden flicker in Ken's eyes was answer enough, but I let him blunder through a welter of explanations. The boy was a dealer in a minor way, very good on kitsch and an absolute lamb underneath the bravado. He'd had to leave his last place in a hurry through no fault of his own, his money would come through soon and then...

The 'then' was never specified and I groaned inwardly. I'd seen one or two 'Jacks' already and they never made Ken happy, not in the long run, anyway.

'Be careful,' I said, seeing him looking bright-eyed and vulnerable in a black Moschino T-shirt that had obviously been bought with an eye to looking young and trendy but actually had the opposite effect.

As I walked back to my own flat I felt my eyes prick. I had looked forward to coming home, to being consoled and welcomed and able to pour out feelings I'd had to conceal in front of my mother and sister. *It isn't fair,* I thought and then realized that I was as guilty of wanting to use Ken as Jack undoubtedly would be before long – if he wasn't already.

The shop bore the same signs of neglect as the garden when I got there the following morning. There was a quantity of kitsch in the back, bought from Jack no doubt and not at all our usual items. An earthenware Alsatian stood guard over two jugs that might have been Clarice Cliff on a bad day and a 1950s plastic dufflebag ornamented with signs of the zodiac. I picked up a pair of tumblers ornamented with a transfer-print of the Beatles peeping from behind a door. The tumblers were ugly and heavy, the transfer already disappearing so that the boyish faces were blurred and ghost-like. What place did trash like this have among our Doulton, Lalique and Sheraton? I sifted through a box of Bakelite – ashtrays, tableware, jewellery cases, a set of napkin rings in the shape of roosters. Fascinating examples of the pre-plastic age, but not – emphatically *not* – what Ken would have countenanced when he was in his right mind.

The only worthwhile piece in the lot was a Goldscheider earthenware wall mask of a young woman with cat-like eyes and spiralling orange hair. It was worth perhaps a hundred and twenty pounds and Jack had dumped it in a boxful of kitchenalia where it stood every chance of being chipped! I took it out and put it in a place of safety before I got on with opening up the shop.

The rest of the day veered between farce and tragedy. Ken looked and sounded so happy that it was hard to be firm with him, but it had to be done.

'I hope you're selling that junk on,' I said, our eyes meeting across the tableful of kitsch.

'Well…' he began, fingering the alsatian.

'Ken!'

My tone was ominous and he winced.

'He means well but he's got a lot to learn about the trade,' he said, and again winced an apology.

I doubted Jack would be willing to learn anything (at least as far as antiques were concerned) but I let it go. Ken's love affairs were usually over in a few weeks. Jack could hardly bankrupt us in that time. Besides, I had other things on my mind. Sooner or later, I would have to face Ian. I knew him too well to think he would give up. My resistance would only make him keener to conquer, so before long I would have to find a way of convincing him that we were permanently through.

Added to this was worry over Sara and the coming baby. Did a child in the womb know grief? Did it suffer because the body that carried it was in pain? I asked myself these and a dozen other questions over and over again without coming up with a single answer. And Ken, who I might have relied on, was walking around like a seventeen-year-old in the flush of his first sexual encounter.

Each night I telephoned Ard-na-Shiel. Always it was Nella who answered, and although she made an effort to ask after me and make conversation, we soon got around to discussing the one thing that preoccupied us both.

'She won't talk, Lexy. At least, not about anything important. She's busy all the time – fiendishly busy: clearing cupboards, answering letters… Yesterday she packed all Jamie's clothes and took them to the charity shop in Oban.'

'It's better than hanging on to them, I suppose.'

The words were hardly out of my mouth when Nella erupted. 'It's *not!* It's *not*, darling! She needs time to mourn, she needs to cry over his things. It'd be healthier if she was up there crying into his closet, hugging his sweaters. It's so cold-blooded, what she's doing. It's unnatural.'

'She'll be better when the baby comes,' I said, not because I really believed it, but just for something to say.

Privately, I understood what Sara was doing. She was putting Jamie and everything belonging to him away from her, much as I had done the night I ran away from Ard-na-Shiel. And that action had not been cold-blooded; it had been necessary to save my reason.

'Oh, well,' I said, 'things'll probably be better when the baby's here. Hang in there, Mum. It's not much longer now.'

In the end, the baby came early. I had accepted Ian's third invitation to dinner and we had endured a polite tit for tat across a restaurant table when the proprietor came to say there was a call for me.

I followed him to the reception desk, mystified. Only Ken had known I was here! For a moment, Jack's face swam before me and terrible thoughts of elderly gays murdered by young lovers ran through my mind until I realized that murder victims didn't phone restaurants.

'It's a girl,' said the voice at the other end. 'Mother and baby doing well. Your mother will phone you in the morning.' It was the old Ken, sensible and reassuring and delighted at a new life in the world.

'Thank you for ringing me, darling,' I said. 'That's a huge relief.'

If anything served to kill the last spark I might have felt for Ian it was his polite disinterest as I told him the news.

'Wonderful,' he said, but his eyes were already flicking over the dessert menu. I felt a wave of shame that this was the man who I had so willingly given myself to.

'I need the loo,' I said, and got to my feet.

In the cloakroom I steeped my wrists in cold water and tried to meet my own eyes in the mirror. It wasn't easy. On my way back to the table I asked the *maître'd* to order me a cab and was assured one would be there within ten minutes.

I refused dessert and sipped a coffee as he drooled over tiramisu, then I saw the *maître'd* nodding at me and got to my feet.

'It's over, Ian,' I said as I got to my feet. 'Dinner was nice and I wish you well, but don't call again.'

I smiled at him sweetly from the back seat of the cab, seeing his rictus grin turn into a mouthed 'bitch' as I did so and sped off home feeling that at least one of my worries was out of the way.

We'd drunk a fair amount of wine with dinner, but when I reached the flat I sat nursing a tumbler of whisky and water and cried for Jamie, the man I had lost and the new baby who would bear the surname of a father she would never know. When the phone rang, I wiped my nose and composed myself. Mustn't let Nella know I was upset.

Except that it wasn't Nella – it was Rick.

'I'm in Berlin. Next stop Copenhagen. Only eight more gigs and I'll be home.'

It was some consolation. Although we hardly knew one another, I liked the feeling that he was out there, on the periphery of my life. I downed the whisky and climbed into bed, make-up and all.

But sleep wouldn't come. I turned from side to side, trying first to think about nothing, then trying to concentrate on the shop or my wardrobe or changes I might make to the house. It was Rick who helped me to sleep eventually. I thought back to that day in Liverpool, his face earnest beneath the red hair, his eyes alight when he talked of his music. One day I would have to think seriously about Rick, but not yet.

Instead, I imagined him taking me to an awards ceremony, the band playing his music and flash bulbs popping. Halfway down the red carpet, I slept.

10

Over the next few days Nella kept me abreast of developments. The baby was a dark-haired, eight-pound wonder with pianist's fingers, Sara was on her feet within hours, the whole of the estate was making ready to celebrate the christening.

'You'll come, won't you?'

I heard the doubt in her voice and dispelled it.

'Of course I will.'

Nella's sigh of satisfaction could have travelled without benefit of telephone. 'She hasn't mentioned anything yet, but she'll want you to be godmother, I expect.'

Neither of us remarked on the fact that estrangement had prevented me being godmother to Alex or Fiona, but we both thought it.

'She was set on it being a boy,' I said. 'Is she disappointed?'

'She doesn't seem to mind,' Nella said, then added: 'She doesn't seem to care about anything.'

I quite liked the idea of being godmother to the fatherless baby, who was to be called Imogen. Fierce protectiveness rose up in me as I imagined myself being there for all the salient moments of her life. I even picked out a christening gift: a silver porringer dated Birmingham 1812 and ornamented with a florid letter 'I' in a circlet of laurel leaves.

I needn't have bothered. Sara came home two days after the birth and two days after that she began to pack. For the first time ever, I heard my mother cry. She had kept her chin up in every crisis of my life, never being more than suspiciously bright-eyed. Now, two hundred and fifty miles away at the other end of a phone, she sobbed her fears for her daughter, for her grandchildren and for herself.

'She expects me to go with her, Lexy, but I don't want to go. I think the whole idea is crazy. Running away – that's what she's doing. And it won't work. It never does.'

For a moment I considered offering to go in her place, but only for a moment. I was increasingly worried about Jack's influence over Ken. Now was not the time to embark on someone else's crazy escape from reality.

'Where does she intend to go?'

There was a sigh at the other end. 'That's just it! She won't say. Thank God she's breastfeeding. I can't think how we'd manage if we had to buy baby food. And what about nappies and school for Alex? And oh, Lexy – I'm frightened.'

I told her you could buy Pampers in the jungle and Alex would love the travel and probably wind up multilingual, but in reality I was terrified for all of them, Nella especially.

'Look, I said, before the call ended, 'We'll speak every day – or almost – and I'll come if you need me. Just ring and I'll be there.'

They left two days later, first stop Paris, and I made up my mind that, at the first hint of trouble, I would hop on a plane and fly to them. Nothing in my life now could compare with what Sara must be going through. I couldn't and wouldn't let her or Nella down.

Once they were actually on their way, Nella regained her composure and I was glad, because things were going from bad to worse where Jack was concerned. He was making changes in the shop, cramming windows we had kept tastefully bare, insinuating his dreadful kitsch into prominent displays and helping himself from the till with muttered promises to pay 'some time'. And all the while Ken looked uncomfortable but besotted and said precisely nothing. There was a pretence at subservience on Jack's part, to be sure, but who was on top was never in doubt. He would make mock gestures of apology when he did something outrageous and then lean over to ruffle Ken's wispy hair or pat his cheek. It was arch and horrible to watch.

I kept on doggedly doing my job and hoping every day that Jack would get tired and go. Except who would tire of life in a beautifully appointed house in the shadow of a world-famous cathedral with an open till to pillage whenever you needed cash?

Sara stayed in Paris for a week and then decreed a move to Rome.

'It's costing the earth,' Nella told me when she rang. 'She doesn't seem to care about money, or how things are back home.'

'What's she like with the baby?'

I felt anxiety well up in me as I asked the question. I had never seen the baby, but I felt as though she was all that was left of Jamie. If she wasn't receiving the love she needed, I couldn't bear it.

'She doesn't coo over her the way you normally do, but she holds her – clutches her even. I don't know; it's all too much for me.'

'Cheer up,' I said. 'She'll get homesick soon and everything will get back to normal.'

There was silence at the other end of the line and then Nella spoke. 'What will "normal" be, Lexy? I can't see her living alone in that house. And who'll manage the estate? Jamie did so much – he understood it. And the children... she'll need help.' She paused then, but I had got the message.

'You wouldn't want to live there permanently?'

She sighed and for a moment I thought she was going to cry.

'I'm getting older, Lexy. Oh, fifty-three isn't old – not *really* old. But it's when you start to think about time, about it running out. I've never really done anything properly – except give birth to you two. I'm really proud of that. But other things… acting: I only fooled around. I was a fool with men. I haven't achieved a thing. And soon it'll be too late.'

I hesitated, unsure of what to say.

'I was offered a part in a soap,' she went on. 'Just before Jamie had the first op. I turned it down when I realized Sara needed me.'

'Oh, Mum,' I said. 'Oh, Mum: I'm sorry.'

'It's nothing,' she said. 'I expect there'll be something else.' She made an effort to brighten up. 'If we can get Sara sorted, everything will fall into place then.'

Long after I'd put down the phone I sat thinking about the future. Perhaps I should offer to live with Sara for a while. Living in a house filled with memories of Jamie would be hard, but there would be compensations. The baby, for one thing, and getting away from Jack for another.

I thought about it as I lay in the bath and almost talked myself into resigning forthwith and heading north, but as usual it ended in tears. I lay there, letting the tears run unchecked until they mingled with the bath water, remembering love and Ard-na-Shiel and feelings I would never, ever know again.

Eventually I wrapped myself in a towelling robe and poured myself a glass of Chablis. I was about to refill it for the second time when the phone rang.

'Remember me?'

It was Rick, ringing from Bruges. He would be home in two weeks and was I free on Friday the twenty-first?

'Shall we meet in Trafalgar Square or the Albert Dock or shall I come to Durham?'

We were still debating the venue when I realized I had ceased sniffling.

11

The following day I had my first open row with Jack. I had been at a house sale in Yorkshire, where we'd hoped to pick up some nice Edwardian oak. I'd done reasonably well and I knew Ken would be pleased, so I drove straight to the shop, although it was after five and I could have gone straight home.

It was raining quite heavily when I reached Durham, and for once there was a parking place outside the shop. I pulled into it and gathered up my bag and catalogue. The lights were on in the shop and I saw Jack's blond head bending over a showcase. There was a girl beside him, dressed in the drab, loose garb of a student. As I watched I saw Jack straighten up and hold aloft something that gleamed as it hung from his fingers. It was a pendant of some sort and the girl reached out and took it from him.

I sat back in my seat, unwilling to enter the shop and perhaps break the bubble of a potential sale. Ken must be there somewhere. Since Jack's arrival in his life the two were seldom apart. In a moment he would come forward to clinch things and give her a better price, something he was wont to do with students. But no Ken materialized. The girl considered for a few minutes, holding the pendant away from her then against her neck and then again at a distance.

Eventually she put it down and opened her shoulder bag. I saw money pass and then Jack was wrapping the purchase and smiling the girl to the door. I sat still as she hurried up the rain-swept street, watching Jack inside the shop, waiting for him to go across to the till and deposit the money. Instead, he went into the back of the shop and a moment later I saw the lights begin to go out, one by one.

I got out of the car against my will, wanting desperately to stay there, switch on the ignition and go home, knowing that I must tackle this now and hoping against hope that Ken was in there somewhere and would tell me my suspicions were totally unfounded.

As the last light went out I opened the door and the bell pinged. The light flared again and I saw Jack's mouth open to tell a potential customer he was closing.

'Oh,' he said. 'It's you.'

I brushed a raindrop from my forehead and moved forward.

'That customer – the girl who just left. Did she buy anything?'

'No.' He sounded genuinely regretful and for a moment I almost doubted what I had seen. 'She was a student. You know the sort... lots of arty-farty ideas but no money. She liked that jade pendant, there...' He was pointing at a jade piece that had been craftily moved so that no telltale space was left beside it.

There were two choices. I could go on questioning him until he tripped himself up or I could come straight out with it. I chose to do the latter.

'I saw you,' I said. 'I saw you take money, I saw you wrap something up. What I didn't see was you ringing up the purchase or putting money in the till. You sold that girl something and I want the money for it.'

Suddenly he was cocky.

'Well, I hate to disappoint you, petal, but I don't know what you're talking about. And now, if you'll get out of my fucking way, I'd like to go home. Ken's waiting.' He smiled suddenly, a leer of pure insolence. 'He's making some of his foreign muck: bweebays... whatever that is. "Marvellous," I'll say. That's what the daft old git likes to hear, so that's what I'll give him. Come round if you like. It'll stretch to three. But don't bother peddling lies about me because we both know he won't believe you.'

I wanted to smack his grinning face. Instead I let him walk past me and out into the rain because I knew he was speaking the truth. Ken wouldn't believe me because he was too besotted to acknowledge that he was in love with a thief.

When I'd locked up the shop I went back to the car feeling unbelievably depressed. Where would this business with Jack end? In tears, undoubtedly, and if it went on too long, probably in bankruptcy. Nor could I draw any consolation from my own life. Nella would ring tonight with another tale of woe or news of a move somewhere even more outlandish.

I'd been looking forward to a night with my feet up and something good on the telly. Now, above all, I wanted to go out, somewhere bright and noisy and full of people without a care in the world. I even, for a moment – but only for a moment – contemplated ringing Ian and suggesting a meal. Except that I wasn't that desperate. I had a date with Rick to look forward to, after all. Only eight days more and he'd be in Durham.

Nella rang while I was still working out what to wear. I tucked my legs underneath me on the sofa and prepared to lend a sympathetic ear. Everyone was well, a sympathetic Italian had taken Sara to a museum and she was sleeping better.

'Wonderful,' I said. 'I could do with some good news.'

Nella was alert at once. 'What's wrong?'

I laughed out loud.

'Nothing's wrong. I'm fine so don't start dreaming up troubles. Tell me about you.'

12

I woke before daylight and thought about the day ahead. It was Friday, the twenty first of August, and Rick would arrive before lunch.

It was difficult to work out what that meant to me. I liked him, was even excited by the idea of seeing him, but I couldn't imagine ever loving him, let alone sleeping with him. And yet I had slept with Ian, who I had liked a damn sight less. Was that because I could have sex with someone who didn't matter because that wasn't betraying Jamie's memory? And with Rick it might be different – it might matter?

I had known Rick for four years, but we had spent less than a day together. We kissed now when we met or parted, but they were the kisses of brother and sister – at least on my part. With Rick, it was different. I knew that from his eyes, which lit up when he saw me. From the tone of his voice, his hand on my elbow if we crossed the street, the affection in the writing on his postcards. He fancied me and I was glad. Which was wrong of me, because I had little or nothing to offer in return.

The phone rang while I was still wrestling with my feelings. I looked at the clock. *Five forty-five!* Who would be ringing me so early in the morning?

In the few minutes it took me to sit up and fumble for the receiver I had arranged funerals for Nella, Sara and all three children.

'Lexy?' The voice at the other end was almost hysterical.

'Yes, it's me. What's wrong?'

There was only muffled sobbing.

'Mum, pull yourself together. What is it?'

There was a loud sniff at the other end and then some vigorous nose-blowing. 'I'm sorry,' Nella said at last. 'It's just that I've been up all night waiting. I didn't want to ring you till I had to – because of the time difference.'

'Waiting?' I was almost shouting now. 'Waiting for what?'

'For Sara. She hasn't come home and I don't know where she is.'

'Have you tried the police?' In my head I could see the tabloids: *Widow Murdered in Italian Capital.*

'No, we don't want to involve the police. I don't know where she is, but I know she's with *him*.'

I struggled to make sense of what she was saying. She couldn't mean Alex; he was barely three years old. 'Who's "him"? Who are you talking about?'

'I told you! The last time I called, I told you then about this man, this Italian.'

It was chilly in the bedroom and I shivered as I tried to remember the last time Nella and I had spoken on the phone.

'Do you mean the man who joined you for dinner? The one who took Sara to the museum?'

'Yes. He's Italian. Cesare something or other – she calls him "Carlo". I don't like him, Lexy, but even if I did, we've known him less than a week and she's spending the night with him. It's not like Sara.'

It wasn't at all like Sara – except that Sara grieving was unlike the Sara we had known before. I tucked the receiver under my chin and pulled the duvet up around my bare breasts. I was trying to think of something comforting to say, but Nella wasn't waiting.

'You must come out here, Lexy. Now – today. You can't leave it all to me. Besides I'm tied with the children. If anything's happened to her...'

She broke down then, not thespian weeping but real sobs that caught at her breath and made me realize just how much the last few months had taken out of her.

'OK,' I said. 'I'll ring about flights as soon as they open. Just hang in there, Mum. I'm on my way.'

I left from Newcastle Airport five hours later, thanking heaven that Ian had forced me into getting a passport for a trip to Paris the year before. It was in my own name, for I had laid Melina Sophia Vassilides to rest the year after I came to Durham.

There was rain on the tarmac as the plane took off for Brussels on the first leg of the flight. As I settled in my seat, I wondered what Rick would make of my message. He had already left when I phoned so I had asked Ken to intercept and explain and left a limp explanation on his answerphone. I didn't think he'd believe me and in a way that didn't displease me. If he decided to take offence, I would never have to put my feelings to the test.

I closed my eyes, trying to think of Ken, left behind at the mercy of Jack. And then there was Sara. What had happened to my lovely, sensible sister? I knew the pain of my own grief; hers must be so much more unbearable. I would have to try and help her. Above all, I must make sure she was safe. If the Italian was a pleasant diversion, that was fine. If he was a threat, he would have me to deal with.

'She's back,' Nella said when I phoned her from Brussels Airport. 'She walked in at ten o'clock as though she'd never been away. "Are the children alright?" she asked, ran a bath and went to bed. She's sleeping now, but thank God, you're coming, Lexy. What is she going to do next?'

'Was he with her?' I pictured some fat, greasy Italian fortune-hunter with pudgy fingers and liquid brown eyes. I'd soon get rid of him.

'He brought her to the door,' Nella said. 'I heard him say something in Italian, some loving thing, then he went. *Ti amo*, I think, something like that. Please hurry, Lexy. Try and get here before this evening. I can't stand the thought of what might happen then.'

I was about to say I was coming as fast as I could when she spoke again.

'*Te adoro, Sara* – that's what he said. *Te adoro*. It means "I adore you", I suppose.'

'But she's only known him for two days!'

'Five,' Nella corrected, 'but you see why I need you.'

On the flight from Brussels to Rome, I tried to compose my thoughts, but I wasn't helped by the sight of the dishy Italian stewards, all wearing wedding rings but making eyes at any female passenger foolish enough to meet their gaze.

One leaned over me.

'Signorina?' he said. And then in English, 'Anything I can do for you?' His eyes were twinkling and impenetrable.

'I'm sure there is,' I said dryly, 'but I'm alright just now, thank you.'

The next moment the crew were buckled in their seats and we were airborne.

Above the cloud layer there was brilliant sunshine. It sparkled off the glass like moonlight reflecting from the windows of Ard-na-Shiel and I thought of Jamie striding out from the great door, the dogs at his heel. But Jamie was dead and his widow probably canoodling with an Italian. Was I still painting myself a romantic picture? Was that what it had become: a fantasy I cherished in order to avoid real life? I was twenty years old and I had never had a real relationship. I had faked things with Ian, moaned and sighed in what I hoped were the right places. But I had never experienced anything remotely as stirring as that moment by the Falls of Orchy. Sara had lost her true love, too, but at least she was trying to get on with her life even if it was driving my mother half-mad with anxiety. I resolved to pour oil on troubled waters when I got to Rome, closed my eyes and fell asleep.

When I woke, we were experiencing turbulence. The captain was pouring out a soothing message and no one around me seemed too perturbed. The next moment we were in soft white cloud, and when it broke there were tantalizing glints of water below and then the Alps, looking for all the world like the top of a Christmas cake. In my whole life, this was the furthest I had travelled and I felt a little shiver of excitement.

See Rome and die. Someone had said that – or was it Naples? I had told Ken I would only be away for a few days, but I meant to make the most of it and see as much as I could of the Holy City once I had sorted out the over-amorous Italian.

And that would take no time at all.

The airport was a disappointment: smaller than I had imagined and filled with touts who plucked at my clothes and tried to commandeer my luggage. I clung determinedly to my bags and queued for the official taxis, feeling the excitement draining away from me minute by minute.

The hotel restored a little of it. It was vast, all marble and gilt and rococo mirrors.

'It must be costing the earth,' I said to Nella after she'd hugged me like a drowning man embraces a lifebelt.

'It is,' she said, 'but Sara seems not to care. I think Jamie left a lot of money.'

'I hope he did,' I said, looking round the huge sitting room of the suite. 'Where is she? And where are the children?'

'The baby's asleep next door. She's taken Alex and Fiona to the Borghese Gardens – to meet *him!* It's some sort of public park. He jogs there, apparently. I want you to go after them, Lexy! I know you must be tired, but what if she doesn't come back? Please, go there now; you'll easily find her with the children. Make her come home!'

I got into a cab, clutching the Italian phrase book Nella had thrust at me. 'The Borghese Gardens,' I said, and sat back as the cab hurtled down narrow streets, and then along wide boulevards past wonderful statuary. The cab driver pulled up at a flower-filled roundabout that seemed to have roads spinning off in every direction.

'Jogging?' I said hopefully. He shook his head. I scrabbled through the index at the back of the phrase-book. *Ruby ... rucksack ... rudder ... ruin ... rum ...* After that we were on to *sacristan, sacristy, saddle* and *safety-pin*.

'Run?' I tried again and tried to mime someone jogging along.

He shook his head and looked pointedly at the meter, which was still ticking.

'I can't get out here,' I said desperately.

He nodded. 'Get... out,' he said.

I opened the phrase book at random. I could say *C'e'vento*, 'It's windy', or *Sono protestante*, which meant 'I am a protestant', but if there was anything about running it was well-hidden.

I climbed out and held out a bunch of lire. He took what looked like an alarming amount and then drove off, leaving me in the middle of the crossroads. There were signposts everywhere but none of them mentioned jogging.

I did a quick eeny-meeny-miney-mo and went down the left-hand road. Five minutes served to convince me that the gardens were vast. One road led always to another; between the trees stretched green vistas which might easily have been English except for the intrusion here and there of an exotic palm or a classical statue. I passed under arches, paused at columned temples, came upon a lake that shimmered in the sunshine and reflected temples and trees.

Occasionally I came upon an incomprehensible signpost. Sometimes runners passed me, but they were going both towards and away from me and I couldn't work out where their base might be. At last, in despair, I decided to stop the next one who overtook me. He was panting and shaking his head as though to restore consciousness but his legs kept pounding just the same and he ignored my polite request for help.

I followed as fast as I could on the basis that where there was one runner there might be two. At last a building came in sight. There were tables in front of it, umbrella-topped. At the furthermost table sat Sara, Fiona on her knee, Alex at her side. I felt my knees tremble with relief and fatigue as I walked towards her.

'Sara?'

She looked up at me and for a split second I thought she didn't recognize me. Alex's eyes were fixed on me as I bent to kiss him, but I couldn't work out the expression in them; the nearest I could get was wary. I kissed Fiona and then my sister's cheek. It was moist with sweat and her hair clung wetly round her hairline.

'What are you doing here?' she said and then supplied the answer. 'I suppose Mum sent for you. I don't know why. I'm perfectly alright.'

'Mum didn't send for me,' I lied. 'I had a few days off and I got a cheap flight. Aren't you pleased to see me?'

She smiled, and suddenly she was the old Sara again – kind and sensible. 'Have you just got here? You must be weary. Let me get you a coffee.'

The waiter was large and slow and heavy-footed, but the coffee was perfect. I sipped it gratefully and wondered how I could broach the subject of what she was doing in the park. I was about to ask her straight out when her face lit up suddenly. She put Fiona down and stood up as a man came towards us. He was walking but sweat gleamed on his limbs and stained his white designer T-shirt. He was tall and dark and when he smiled at me as we were introduced I knew exactly why my sister was behaving like a woman bewitched. The eyes were more liquid, the chin more cleft but the overall impression was of a tall, dark man who would have looked at home amid heather.

Why had Nella never mentioned the resemblance to Jamie?

I breathed in to calm myself and held out my hand.

'It's good to meet you,' I said, and was proud that no evidence of my confusion showed in my voice.

'Why didn't you *tell* me?' I asked Nella as soon as we were alone.

She looked at me blankly. 'Tell you what?'

'That he looks like Jamie?'

There was genuine amazement in her face. 'He doesn't. Well, he's tall and dark, I suppose. But...' Her voice took on a note of outrage. 'He's nothing like Jamie. Not in the least.'

I decided to let it drop, but however hard I tried to think about other things, his face was there: sometimes Jamie Munro, sometimes Cesare Giulini.

'What are we going to do?' I said. 'Should we do anything? At least she's happy. Maybe we should leave things alone.'

Before Nella could answer, Sara came into the room. She was carrying the baby but she was not looking at her; Imogen lay on her mother's arm rather like a sheaf of flowers. The other children trailed at her skirts, but she seemed not to notice them, either. She sat on the window-seat looking out over the rooftops of Rome, but her mind was obviously elsewhere.

At last she spoke. 'We're going to the Palazzo Falconieri tonight. You will keep the children, won't you.'

It was a statement, not a request, and Nella nodded her head to show she'd heard.

Sara left while I was bathing Fiona, putting her head round the door to say goodbye. She looked beautiful but strange, and I found myself staring at her. She was recognizably Sara, my sister, but there was something different about her. Something about her eyes.

When the children were all in bed I went out for a breath of air.

'I won't be long,' I told Nella, 'and I won't go far.'

I was crossing the foyer when a concierge approached me.

'Signorina Alessandra?' I nodded and he held out an envelope. 'What's this?'

He smiled, a melting smile designed to convey incomprehension.

'Who gave you this? Why didn't you bring it up to the room?'

He shrugged and held out his hands, palm upwards. I held his gaze and at last he spoke.

'For you only, signorina. Only for you.'

He turned and went and I carried the note to a velvet sofa and sat down to read it. It was signed *Cesare Giulini* and its contents were simple.

> *For your sister's sake, please meet me tomorrow. Tell no one, especially Sara or your mother. I will explain when I see you. I will be waiting in the Piazza Venetia at ten o'clock. Please, for Sara's sake, grant this request.*

I sat for a moment, wondering whether I should take the note straight to Nella and then I remembered what had been strange about Sara tonight.

It had been her eyes that were different.

They had reminded me of Reinie's eyes.

Sara came home that night, much to Nella's relief, but I lay awake long after we were all in bed, conscious of the note hidden in my vanity case, wondering whether or not I should do as Cesare Giulini had asked. Why had he asked me not to tell Sara or our mother? And if I went, how was I going to explain my absence?

In the end, curiosity overcame my fears. I announced that I wanted to go sightseeing for an hour or two.

'Where?' Nella asked, and I improvised rapidly.

'Oh, the Trevi Fountain, the Colosseum, St Peter's Square… you know, the usual places.'

Nella looked at Sara and I knew what she was thinking: if Sara took the children, she could come with me. But all Sara said was:

'We could take you. But not today. Carlo has a business meeting and then we're meeting friends of his.'

She didn't suggest Nella should come with me, and before it could enter her mind I made my escape, promising to be only an hour or two and to ring at once if I got into trouble.

'She is twenty, you know,' I heard Sara say reprovingly as I left the room.

The Piazza Venetia was vast and thronged with people. I moved towards the huge building that occupied the centre and stood uncertainly. Was he coming, or had it been a ruse to draw me away from the hotel?

Suddenly he was there, smiling uncertainly and looking even more like Jamie than I remembered

'Thank you for coming.' His voice was as tentative as his smile. 'I didn't know if you would.'

His eyes were moist and filled with an expression I could not fathom. But they were brown, not blue, and he was really not like Jamie at all. I steeled myself to interrogate him.

'I can't imagine why you needed secrecy,' I said, 'and I can't be missing for too long.'

His answer was to cup my elbow with his hand and guide me away from the piazza. The red car we had ridden home in from the Borghese Gardens was parked halfway down a narrow street. He held the door as I climbed into the passenger seat, and then we were off through a maze of streets and onto a wide road.

I had no idea where we were going, but I knew we were speeding away from the city centre.

'Look,' I said, as firmly as I could. 'I want to know where we're going and, more importantly, why.'

He kept his eyes on the road ahead as he answered.

'Bear with me, Alexandra. Please, I can explain better when we get there.'

I looked at my watch. It was twenty minutes past ten.

'I'll give you ten minutes more,' I said,' and then we're turning for home.'

There were thirty seconds of my ultimatum left when we came to a halt on the brow of a hill. Around us the fields were lush and green, but Cesare was pointing towards a house half-hidden by trees. It was large and beautiful, the warmth of its stone walls a contrast to the dark foliage surrounding it.

'That was my home,' he said, 'and all this land was ours. But we are not a businesslike family. Now, all this belongs to *il commerciante* – a shopkeeper.'

It was said with venom and I stayed silent, although I longed to ask why he was telling me this.

Instead, I gazed out at the landscape and for a moment he, too, was silent. A large bird rose from a field, and then another and another, until there was a skein of geese flying above us, on and away.

'Come,' he said at last. 'We have to go now.'

This time I couldn't resist.

'Why have you brought me here? I'm sorry if you lost your home. but what's it to do with me? I hardly know you.'

'I tell you for Sara – for your sister's sake. You are the strong one. I saw that yesterday. *La sorella giovane*, but still the guardian. Now, *prego*, one more place and then I take you home.'

We went back to the car in silence: he, locked in his thoughts; me, so bemused I couldn't think of anything to say. He turned the car and we sped back the way we had come.

When I recognized the church we had passed soon after we left the Piazza Venezia I began to relax. Almost home, except that he was turning into a side street full of tall, shuttered houses. He pulled up at a kerb and came round to open the door.

'Where are we now?' I asked.

He didn't answer. Instead, he took my arm again and guided me through wrought-iron gates into a courtyard. I could hear water playing somewhere and the air was cool after the heat of the street. He pushed open another gate and I saw a fountain set in the centre of a courtyard. A stone nymph stood at one corner, water cascading from the basket she carried, and there were lilies floating on the surface of the water.

I was about to move forward when a dog came bounding from the shadows to throw itself upon my companion. It was a West Highland White terrier, but all I could see was the hand that bent to stroke its head – so like Jamie's hand the night he had tried to restrain the Labrador. Ahead of me was a huge door and I was filled with a sense of *déjà vu*.

'Come,' he said, when the dog ceased to leap. We moved through a high arched doorway and into a lofty hall. As our footsteps rang out on the marble floor, a woman appeared as if from nowhere. She was small and swarthy and dressed in black, but her face lit up at the sight of Cesare. She gabbled away in Italian for a moment, but all he said was, '*Bene, bene,*' until she turned on her heel and led the way to a large salon.

There was magnificent furniture there, but the upholstery was threadbare, the wood desperately in need of polish. She went to a huge chiffonier that would have had Ken drooling and picked up a tray of glasses. She put them on a sofa table and then withdrew, appearing a moment later with a bottle of wine. It was half-empty and Cesare looked at it ruefully before pouring it into two glasses.

I took one and sipped appreciatively. 'It's good.'

'Very good, and also the last,' was his reply.

Embarrassed, I looked around and selected a gilt chair.

'I'm going to sit down for a moment and then I must go.' It was almost twelve o'clock. I couldn't stay away much longer.

Cesare raised his glass.

'To Sara,' he said. 'And to *la madre* who loves her and *la sorella* who comes running to the rescue. Except that there is no need, Lexy. I have nothing to offer your sister. This house, but that, too, will go with time. So she is safe from me. I am not inclined to be a *gigolo*.'

'You've only known her a week.'

It was the only thing I could think to say.

'A week... ten days. But your sister is in pain. She wants to stop the pain. She thinks – she *knows* – I could do that. And I would like to, I would like that very much. But I cannot and I will not. Your mother sent for you...' He saw my shake of denial and shook his own head. 'I *know* she sent for you, Lexy: to save your poor sister from a fortune-hunter. That is why I had to show you – *convince* you – that what you fear will never happen.'

His eyes gleamed with conviction and I felt a sudden wave of compassion. He *was* good, after all.

He put down his glass then and moved towards me. I stood up and put down my own glass.

'Dear Lexy,' he said and stooped to kiss my brow. As his lips brushed my skin I remembered that other kiss, that night at Ard-na-Shiel. Or had there been a kiss? Difficult now to tell reality from dreams.

I had a sudden, mad impulse to move into his arms, but all I said was, 'Thank you for telling me. And now I need to go home.'

14

When I came back to the hotel, my mind was in turmoil. 'Why did you ask me to meet you?' I had asked as we parted, and he had looked straight at me and replied, 'I love your sister.' He had turned away then, leaving me to wonder what his words meant. He had virtually declared that he would not, could not marry Sara, so why bother to recruit her sister as an ally? And yet he had nothing to gain by displaying his comparative poverty. If he were the fortune-hunter Nella believed him to be, then surely he would have pretended affluence.

I kept my thoughts to myself until Nella and I were alone. Cesare and Sara had gone off to meet the friends Sara had mentioned earlier and we were sitting on the terrace of the hotel, watching the children playing with other children in the small walled garden. Their laughter rang out over the distant buzz of traffic in the street outside. It was pleasant in the shade of a canopy, cool drinks in tall glasses in front of us, the baby asleep in her carry-cot on a chair beside us.

'I met Cesare today,' I said. Nella put down her glass.

'While you were window-shopping?'

'No.'

It was my turn to place my glass carefully on the table, playing for time.

'No. I met him. He asked me to meet him, so I did.'

'Without telling anyone? And why you? What did he want?'

I struggled to find words, aware that I didn't know how to answer her question because I didn't know the answer myself.

'He took me to his family estates – well, the estate that his family once owned. And to his house here in Rome. It's very grand but very shabby. He's pretty hard-up...'

Nella let out what could only be described as a snort. 'I never imagined anything else. Why else is he so interested in Sara?'

She was being so unfair that I felt tears of anger sting my eyes.

'It's not like that. He's not interested in her money; in fact, he sees it as a barrier between them. That's why he was so honest with me: because he wants us to know he has no intention of marrying Sara.'

'So he's fooled you, too.'

She said it quietly, and somehow that was chilling.

'You're being unfair,' I said. 'I think he's simply an honourable man who won't take advantage of a situation. And anyway, if he was a fortune-hunter, he'd surely be after bigger game than Sara. She's not poor, but she's not in the millionaire class.'

'She is.'

Again, Nella spoke quietly, glancing at the baby as she spoke.

'Jamie never made a great show of his worth, but in land and other assets his estate was over five million.'

We sat silently for a moment, each trying to grasp what five million amounted to. So *that* was why Cesare was over-awed. Sara must have told him and I could understand how he felt.

I sipped my piña colada, wondering what to say to Nella, all the while feeling a glow inside me. For once I possessed an advantage over my sister – I had no wealth to come between me and a lover. I thought of Cesare's face as we had stood looking over the land to his old home. I could remember every feature, the way he had smiled, the little motion of his brow that expressed regret. There had been no sound of bees in heather, but I had been moved in the same way as in that moment by the Falls of Orchy.

'That's a lot of money,' I said at last, and tried to keep the satisfaction out of my voice.

That afternoon we took the children to a public park, the Villa Doria-Pamphili. It had been recommended by the concierge as a paradise for children, and so it proved. Alex and Fiona came alive at the sight of moorhens nesting in the thick vegetation around the ponds and lakes, and screamed with delight at the sight of magpies, six and seven deep on the undulating lawns. We walked past cascades, grottoes and fountains too many to count, until Fiona tired and I had to carry her, piggyback-style back towards the gates where we might pick up a cruising taxi.

Nella walked beside me, pushing the pram, silent as she had been for most of the day. It was sunny and I could feel sweat trickling slowly down the small of my back. Fiona's arms were wound about my neck, her chubby legs threaded through my arms. It was strange to carry Jamie's child, feel her skin against mine, her breath warm on my ear. I closed my eyes momentarily, remembering, but now it was not Jamie's face I saw; it was Cesare, his expression gentle but rueful as he surveyed the remnants of his fortune.

Suddenly, I realized Nella was speaking.

'Where did they say they were going?'

Her voice was full of suspicion, and I tried not to sound resentful as I reminded her where they had gone, but try as I might, I couldn't fool my mother.

'It's no good blaming *me*, Alexandra. I'm not responsible for this debacle.' I would have argued but she didn't give me time. 'My previously sensible daughter has gone mad. She's running around a foreign country with a man she's known for five minutes and you expect me not to worry? She's neglecting the children, one of them hardly born; she's left her home and responsibilities to God and good neighbours and...'

She hesitated suddenly and her voice faltered. I hoisted Fiona further up and turned to look at Nella.

'And what?'

For a moment I thought she wasn't going to answer but she halted in her tracks and began to rock the pram.

'She's taking something,' she said flatly. 'I don't know what and I don't know where she's getting it, but I know – I just know she is.'

'She's a doctor,' I said. 'She knows what she's doing.'

But I was thinking of Reinie, of those suspiciously bright and yet curiously vacant eyes that I had seen in Sara back in the hotel.

'That's just it: I don't think she does. I know we've always relied on her – me, too, I admit it. I made her old before her time because I wasn't grown up enough to mother her – or you, either. But she's changed, Lexy. And I don't know if I'm up to shouldering the responsibility of it all. I'm like your Ken: I'm getting older and I'm lonely. That's why he's clutching at that ruffian you detest so much. I want to clutch at something. Instead…'

She shook her head despairingly and I wished with all my heart my arms were free so that I could comfort her. I shifted Fiona further onto my shoulders and made my voice as confident and reassuring as I could.

'It won't last, Mum. You'll see. Cesare doesn't intend to take things further. I know he means that and I'm glad. She'll get tired of wandering and go home. She needs a good estate manager. We'll help her get the best there is. And then she'll want to take care of the kids and you'll be free, I promise.'

I sat in the back of the taxi, Fiona now asleep across my knee, Alex heavy-eyed beside me. Nella sat with her eyes closed, the sleeping baby clasped in her arms. She looked weary – even, for the first time I could remember, looked her age. I shivered a little, thinking of the responsibility that would be mine if anything happened to Nella and Sara failed to come to her senses.

It didn't bear thinking about.

Outside the car, the myriad churches and statues of Rome sped past. We crossed a bridge and turned onto a tree-lined street. Fiona stirred, opened her eyes, recognized me, smiled briefly and lapsed back into sleep. *She trusts me*, I thought and was suddenly overwhelmed with love. I could care for these children if I had to – except that Sara would soon be the old Sara again and I could get to know Cesare and find out if what I thought I felt for him was real or illusion.

15

The next morning I woke early and lay thinking of Cesare, alone now in the shabby house in the tree-lined street a mile away. Soon he would break off the relationship with Sara; I had seen it in his eyes yesterday. There would have to be a decent interval, but then I could come back to Rome, back to the Eternal City where even the worn pavements seemed welcoming.

Embarrassed at my own mushiness, I turned my face into the pillow – but thoughts persisted. Except that they were jumbled thoughts. I imagined an embrace, a kiss, a hand on my breast. But whose hand? There was the warmth of an Italian sun but also the sound of bees in heather. I felt my muscles contract and give suddenly, as though for a lover, but the body that entered and fused with mine was not one man but two. I pulled myself upright and covered my face with my hands to hide my shame. This was madness – an adolescent fantasy.

The sound of children in the next room got me out of bed and out of my misery. They were obviously in with Nella now, which meant Sara was up and about. I pulled on a robe and went out onto the balcony that led to Nella's room. As I neared her window, I heard her voice, raised in argument, and when I entered the room, she and Sara were facing one another, each holding a child in their arms but glaring at one another like Kilkenny cats.

'I'm going,' Sara said. 'Like it or not, I'm going!'

'You'll take the children, then. I won't be responsible for them.'

This was Nella, spitting out her words in a way I had never heard before.

'Please!' Sara's face was agonized, her eyes two dark coals in a

too-white face. She threw up a hand in supplication and I moved to take Fiona from her arms. The child whimpered and clung, but Sara helped me detach her little arms from around her mother's neck. She did it without looking at the child or attempting to soothe her and I felt a surge of anger. How *dare* she treat Jamie's child like this?

'What's going on?' I asked.

'She wants to go off for two days!' Nella's voice was dramatic, her eyes full of rage and contempt. 'She wants to leave her children and go traipsing off with her boyfriend and God knows when we'll see her again. *If* we see her again!'

'You're being ridiculous.' Sara turned to me as she spoke. 'Carlo wants to take me to Amalfi. He says it will do me good. I'll be back on Friday. I'm only a few miles away if I'm needed. Please, Lexy, make her see sense.'

I swallowed, trying to think. I didn't know much about Italy but I'd heard about Amalfi: a beautiful village creeping down to a turquoise sea! A perfect place for romance! And then I remembered Cesare's voice: *I cannot and will not.* Now I knew the purpose of the trip to Amalfi, it was to put an end to the affair.

'I think you should go,' I said. 'I'll help with the children.'

An hour later Sara was gone, Nella standing tight-lipped, refusing a loving goodbye. 'I hope you know what you're doing,' she said to me as the door closed.

'Trust me,' I said, hoping with all my heart that I was right.

The two days passed quite quickly in a haze of child care and visits to any and every attraction that might provide the older two with amusement.

We were returning from the Villa-Doria at four-thirty on the second day, me carrying a sleepy Fiona as usual, Nella with the baby, when Alex said, 'Mummy'll be home soon.'

I ruffled his hair. 'Of course she will,' I said, glad that soon it would all be over.

I was smiling as we lifted the children into the hotel, the various porters and doormen fussing adoringly round as only Italian males can fuss over children. The concierge came from behind his desk, an envelope in his hand.

'For you, signora,' he said, handing it to Nella.

We stood in the gilded lobby, its vaulted ceiling so fine it might have graced the Vatican, while she opened it and scanned the single sheet inside. She read it twice and then her shoulders slumped suddenly and she sighed.

'Read it,' she said, handing it to me.

Carlo and I were married this morning. Be happy for me.

That was all, except for a scrawled signature and two crosses to indicate kisses. I crumpled the paper in my hand. So he had lied to me: Cesare of the liquid eyes and the sad history. Conducted a charade to defuse any hostility until he had achieved his object. *You fool*, I thought, and felt ashamed.

'Well?' Nella said flatly.

Before I could answer, the concierge approached again. 'Telephone,' he said. 'For the signorina.'

I half-expected to hear Sara's voice at the other end but it was Ken – a curiously disconcerted Ken.

'Can you come home, Lexy?' he said. 'As quickly as you can?'

I felt tears fill my eyes and squeezed my lids to dispel them.

'I'm coming,' I said. 'Now. Tomorrow. As soon as I can.'

I didn't say more. That he was in trouble was obvious and right now I didn't want details. My business in Rome was finished anyway. Once more Sara had won. Except that perhaps Cesare wasn't such a prize after all.

I went back to Nella and held out my arms for the baby.

'What shall we do, Lexy?' Her eyes were wide and scared and I patted her arm.

'Nothing, Mother. Nothing – except hope for the best.'

16

The moment I read Sara's note I had wanted to go up to my room and pack, run through the streets to the airport and get on a plane – any plane. After all, I had the best of excuses; an old friend, who happened also to be my employer, was in trouble and needed me. I had every reason to go home. But within minutes of Sara's bombshell I realized Nella needed me more.

'How *could* she?' was all she could say as we went up in the lift. 'How could she do this?'

And silently, inside my head, I echoed her words. Except that I said 'he' instead of 'she'. How could he, the man who had bared his poverty, if not his soul, to me only hours before, go back on everything he had said?

The only explanation was that he had lied to me, lied skilfully and comprehensively so that I would do exactly what I had done: allow Sara to escape from the hotel. And yet he seemed so sincere, in that shabby room of faded glory, holding the half-empty wine bottle up as though to advertise his unfittedness to marry a rich wife.

You're a fool, I told myself even as I tried to invent excuses for his perfidy. *And not only fool but traitor to see even a glimmer of resemblance between him and Jamie, who was all things honourable and true.*

In the melée of child care and mother-soothing that followed, my own troubles had to take a back seat. I telephoned Ken and told him I would be home as soon as possible. He sounded less distraught, but there was an odd air of resignation about him that frightened me even more.

'Are you alright?' I asked, and was assured that he was.

There was a pause then, neither of us sure what to say next, and then he spoke, quite flatly and without emotion.

'He's gone.'

I was about to say 'Thank God' when I heard him speak again.

'He's left a hell of a mess, Lexy. All I can say is, I'm sorry.'

I couldn't work out what he meant. A physical mess? A wrecked shop? Or an emotional mess? For a second terrible thoughts of HIV coursed through my mind, but Ken was too sensible not to have got the safe-sex message.

'Never mind,' I said at last. 'Whatever it is, we'll work it out. As soon as I get home.'

The next two days passed in a blur of crying children and an uncharacteristically stony-faced mother. I would have liked it better if Nella had ranted and raved. Perhaps then I could have given vent to my own anger and resentment. Except that I could never publicly admit to feeling twice robbed, to making a habit of falling for my sister's man. What would a psychiatrist make of a woman of twenty who was unable to feel for any man except one she couldn't have? Who, moreover, had felt instant rapport with a stranger in a foreign park, even when her sister's proprietorial hand was upon his arm?

The newlyweds came home on the third day, sweeping into the suite as though nothing out of the ordinary had occurred. While Sara fussed over the baby, Cesare came over to where I stood in the open window, distant sounds of Roman traffic drifting up from the street below.

'I owe you an explanation,' he began, but I cut him short.

'Tell me one thing,' I said. 'When you handed me that spiel about being unable to marry because of Sara's money, did you know – had you already arranged this marriage?'

He shook his head.

'Lexy, *per favore*, I did not know. Sara arranged *la cerimonia civile* – a civil ceremony. We will be married in church as soon as possible.'

I said nothing and he reached for my hand. I felt nothing at the touch of his fingers.

'I couldn't help myself, Lexy. I love her. But I will take nothing from her, that I promise you. All is for his children, as it should be. I will work; we will make it happy: for us, for the children.' He smiled then. 'And for the family, too? I hope so.'

I looked over to where Nella stood, the older children at her skirts, her arms protectively around them and a look of implacable hostility towards Cesare on her face.

'We'll see,' I said quietly. 'For all our sakes, I hope it does work out.'

The following day I left Rome, seeing it melt into a blur of domes and spires and faded pink palazzos. I had hugged my mother before I left and promised her all would be well.

'They love each other, Mum. OK, so it was quick and Sara hardly knew what she was doing, but he loves her. He loves her and she needs him. If she protects the children's welfare, as he says she will, it'll be OK. We just have to trust him.'

'I *don't* trust him,' was her bitter retort. 'I don't trust him one bloody centimetre!'

'Then trust Sara. She's always been sensible. *I'm* the crazy one. I took off, remember? And it all came right in the end.'

She hugged me then, properly, as she hadn't done since the whole affair began.

'That's true, my darling. You're a good girl and a great comfort.'

'There, then,' I said when we disentangled. 'She'll sort herself out, I'll get back to work and you can have a life.'

'I hope so.' Her eyes narrowed. 'But I'll be watching him, Lexy. Every inch of the way.'

As the plane gained altitude and the pattern of fields gave way to a bed of clouds, I made myself a promise. Once I had sorted out Ken I would get my own life in order. It was my turn now.

I put my head back against the head-rest and began to plan a future which, if not rosy, would at least be realistic.

BOOK THREE

1999

1

Outside the window the Thames flowed, broad grey water flecked here and there with the dying wakes of boats moving up and down the river. I turned back into the room as Rick entered, towelling hair wet from the shower.

'That's better,' he said and held out his arms.

I went into them willingly enough, resting my cheek against his chest, feeling him nuzzle the top of my head.

'It's growing dark,' Rick said at last, his voice a little husky with desire.

I raised my face for his kiss, knowing it would lead to bed and finding that thought not unwelcome. We had been lovers ever since I returned from Rome, licking my wounds after Cesare's deception. I went to ground in Durham and Rick sought me out. He was taking a sabbatical from touring and had time and patience, but I was the one who initiated sex. I wanted to be held, loved; I wanted a man to take me so forcibly that I stopped thinking for a while.

At first he was cautious. I knew he was trying to work out what was going on in my head. I made it obvious that what I wanted was passion and he gave it to me. I exulted in being wanted, and almost pushed Cesare Giulini's duplicity from my mind.

It was not just that he had deceived me; it was my own gullibility, my wanting to believe him, which had hurt. That and the knowledge that, once more, I was coveting my sister's man. Was there something evil in me that made me want whatever my sister had?

Unhappy and unsure, I came home and fell into Rick's arms. He supported me through the messy business of sorting out the shop and dried my tears when I cried for Jamie and for the foolish dream that Cesare had been. Now we shared a bed whenever he was in Britain and I loved him – but I was not *in* love with him, and there is a difference. Twice he had proposed, treating it as a joke but meaning it all the same. And twice I had deflected his proposal with a jibe.

Perhaps I took him for granted. If so, it was very wrong of me. Certainly guilt fanned my ardour. Now I twined my arms more tightly round him; mine was the tongue that probed and teased. I opened my eyes as he drew a little way from me.

'Hey,' he said. 'What have I done to deserve this?' And then, as I opened my mouth to answer: 'No. Don't answer. Just keep going.'

We made love in his wide bed, greedily at first and then companionably as long-time lovers do. Outside it grew dark and lights sprang up along the river.

'Happy?' I asked and felt his lips brush my forehead.

'Yes. You?'

I nodded but I didn't speak. I wanted so much to satisfy him, but I could not honestly claim satisfaction myself. I had come satisfactorily enough, and come again, but that last elusive piece was missing – as it was always missing.

I lay watching light dapple the ceiling, wondering, as I often did, how to extricate myself from the bed. Usually Rick would raise himself on an elbow, lean over to tease me or plant comfortable kisses on my closed eyes. Tonight he, too, lay still, but he did not contemplate the ceiling for his eyes were closed.

We stayed like that for a long time, until I felt a wry chuckle forming inside my head. This was a Mexican stand-off. Sooner or later one of us would crack and make a move. I was just about to take the plunge when Rick spoke.

'So, Lexy, what happens next?'

I raised my arms above my head and gripped the iron rails of the bedhead.

'You make some tea?'

I said it jokingly but he wasn't amused.

'Be serious, Lex. You know what I mean. I mean what happens next to *us*?'

I was tempted to ask another question: 'We get up?' or perhaps 'We have a gin and tonic?' But even in the semi-darkness I could see he was not in a joking mood. And I wasn't in the mood for discussing the future. I sat up and reached for my shirt.

'I don't know, Rick. We go on as we are, I suppose. Unless you want something different.'

I tried to sound nonchalant, but to my own ears my voice came across as strained.

'You know what I want.' He was raising himself on the pillows. 'I want your undivided attention, Lexy. I want – just for once – not to be part of three-in-a-bed.'

'I don't know what you mean.'

But even as I spoke, I knew I was lying. Knew that whenever I was in a man's arms, I wanted, even imagined them to be Jamie's. His was the mouth that covered mine, his the limbs entwined with mine, his the paradise thrust. And he was the reason I had turned my face into the pillow and wept when Rick and I first made love.

For a moment Rick said and did nothing, and then, suddenly, he catapulted from the bed and made for the shower.

'Tea or coffee?' I called out, but he didn't answer – or if he did, his voice was drowned by the sound of cascading water. After a moment I, too, sat up and began to shrug into my clothes. I wanted to go home – or at least back to my mother's house. I wanted to turn back the clock and be a girl again in Notting Hill, stealing my big sister's make-up and dreaming dreams.

But there was no going back. Not to Notting Hill or Ard-na-Shiel. Not even to the little café off Edgware Road. I had gone there once, as soon as I had some money and could completely repay my benefactor, but the café was gone, replaced by a slick coffee bar run by young men in tight-fitting shirts...

Nothing lasted. Nothing at all.

When I was dressed, I called out goodbye – and then I fled Rick's apartment.

2

As the train left Kings Cross I sat back in my seat and reached for my newspaper. Outside the train window London fell away and we ran between September fields scattered with neat, round bales of straw or green with late-sown crops.

'You're a fool,' Nella had told me over breakfast. 'Rick's everything you could want and you keep him dangling. You'll be sorry one day.'

I had turned away without speaking because it was impossible to explain how I felt. Impossible because how could you explain what you didn't understand yourself? Even trying to understand brought pain nibbling at the edges of my mind, and I opened my paper, desperate for diversion.

There was a picture of that new London wheel, one of the millennium stunts, wobbling skywards. Tony Blair was calling for 'a new national moral purpose' alongside some alarming statistics on pregnant twelve-year-olds. How wonderful to be twelve again, having learned from your mistakes. My mistake had been to hanker after a dream, and in doing that I was letting a real man slip through my fingers. I could feel Rick withdrawing from me.

'Call me,' he had said the last time we parted. 'Call me when you're ready to get real.' But that was my problem. After Jamie, nothing had been real at all – Cesare for a second or two, but no more. Rick was dear and familiar and safe. To thousands of women he would have been the answer to prayers, but to me, he was just a friend. We met when we could, we made love, we parted and none of it seemed real at all.

And now he was expressing dissatisfaction.

I sifted through the newspaper looking for something cheerful and found it on the TV page. It was a picture of Nella in her guise of Emily Guinn. She was the gay divorcee in the BBC soap, *Langley Meade*. It was a good picture and not even the blonde wig she wore as Emily could disguise her charm. I realized I was smiling foolishly and looked around guiltily, but the other passengers were either asleep or deep in their own papers. I folded mine, closed my eyes and thought about my mother.

She had never lost her mistrust of Sara's husband, but she had channelled her distress at the wedding into a new zest for her career. There had been a couple of one-off roles in *The Bill* and *Casualty* and then *Langley Mead* had been launched. Nella went to audition for a minor role and came away with the part of Emily: a rich, slightly daffy divorcee living in a Dorset village alive with scandal. She had been given a three-month contract, but now Emily Guinn was almost a household name, and Nella, if not rich, was at least off the breadline and had a rolling contract.

As for Sara, she had her beloved Carlo and her children. We saw them occasionally. Nella went up for two weeks whenever she had time off and I'd been twice: once for Alex's fifth birthday and the second time to keep Sara company when Cesare went home to Italy for a week. Sara had been as welcoming as ever. So had Cesare – except for a wariness in his eye, as though he feared I might be questioning his motives. If he thought that, he was right: I still found myself wrestling with the problem of whether or not he had lied to me on that Italian hillside. He had told me he could not, would not, marry Sara and three days later he had done so. Did he know then that they would be married two days later?

Nella had made sure that Sara's will benefitted the children, so Cesare was getting nothing from the marriage except a very easy lifestyle. Against that, he was miles away from his own country and I was not sure that the life of a Scottish laird suited him. At first, we had feared he would persuade Sara to sell up and move to Italy, but that hadn't happened. There was now an efficient steward – a 'factor' as the Scots called him – named Cameron in charge of the estate, and Alex's inheritance was safe. Most importantly, Sara was happy – or at least, she *seemed* to be happy.

Sometimes, watching her, I wondered...

Thinking of that kingdom by the loch was a mistake. I heard again the sound of Orchy waters, smelled the scent of heather and that moment of closeness in the barn, before I had spoiled it all with my foolish declaration of love. Why couldn't I forget it all – or, if not forget, at least put it to the back of my mind? Why was it still more real than what had happened between Rick and me last night? I had detected a change in him then, a resignation. As though he was finally accepting that we were friends and nothing more. 'Call me when you're ready to get real,' he had said. What did 'get real' really mean?

I opened my eyes and saw the Cleveland Hills on my right, dear and familiar, the gateway to the kingdom of Northumbria where I was now so at home. I wiped an almost-tear from my eye and thought about home and the shop. Thinking about Rick was too complicated.

In the case on the rack above my head were the proceeds of my trip to London: three Jumeaux dolls, each with a wonderful, waxen face and dressed in their original clothes. I had paid three thousand pounds for them and would probably resell for four thousand five hundred – a nice profit.

I had come back from Rome to find Ken near bankruptcy and Jack vanished. In the end, I used the money my father had left me to pay off Ken's debts. In return he made me a full partner and retired to his house to lick his wounds.

At first I had been afraid, but quickly I came to relish the responsibility. My first big buy was a doll: a German bisque-headed doll which turned out to be a Kestner. The seller wanted five hundred pounds, and we settled on four hundred and fifty after I'd had an anxious conversation with Ken. When I sold it on, it made nine hundred pounds and I was hooked. Now Ken was back to superintend when I was away, we had a nice part-timer called Pauline, and I specialized in dolls: Kestners, Jumeaux, Heubacks, Brus and the twinkling-eyed Kewpies. I felt almost maternal towards each one; Rick had even accused me of turning potential buyers away because I didn't like the look of them and he was probably right.

Rick! We were almost at Darlington now, one more stop to go, and I couldn't afford to go down that path. I wasn't being fair to him and I didn't need Nella to tell me so.

I busied myself with my bags and dismissed uncomfortable thoughts. Instead, I thought about Max, the object now of almost all my affection. He would be waiting: black and beautiful, bounding with delight at my return. Part Labrador, part retriever, he had been mine for a year now and I couldn't imagine life without him.

I went straight to Ken's flat when I reached Durham – partly to collect Max and, if I was honest, to swank a bit about the dolls. I found him in his garden, glass in hand, Max glued to his knee until he saw me and remembered where his allegiance lay. We settled on a wooden seat in the shelter of the house, sipping Sancerre and contemplating the glories of the September garden. It was a rich mix of blue, red and gold, and if leaves were already browning at the edges it hardly showed.

'We sold the Davenport,' Ken said. 'I let it go for nine-fifty. She obviously wanted it.'

I nodded. Even at nine-fifty we had made a profit and I had

grown used to Ken's habit of looking for good homes for stock rather than exacting the last penny.

I told him about the dolls and he whistled appreciation.

'Three! Well done.'

I narrowed my eyes until the garden was a blur of colour. I felt suddenly at peace. It was safe here with Ken, talking about beautiful objects, being careful of one another's feelings. He knew about Rick and approved of him, but he would not cross-question me about him, just as I never referred to his fleeting relationships; since Jack, he had been wary of entering into any kind of permanence.

We sat on as the sun sank and the air temperature dropped. Once I almost turned to him and said, 'I love you, you know,' but mercifully the words didn't come. We neither of us cared much for displays of emotion. In the end, I whistled up the dog and made my way home, still glorying in the safeness of my life in Durham.

I was almost at my door when I saw a familiar figure ahead of me. It was Ian, the rangy coat and the flowing hair was unmistakable. What was not familiar was the child he carried in his arms: a boy of about two. A girl (she was hardly old enough to be called a woman) walked beside him pushing a pram. She looked like and probably had been, a student. So Ian had been hooked! I found I was smiling maliciously and slowed my pace so there would be no chance of catching them up. I was simply filled with a sense of thankfulness that he would never again come knocking at my door, and if he did I would have a legitimate excuse for turning him away.

When I entered the house, the scent of roses assailed me, a fresh loaf lay on the kitchen bench and there was milk in the fridge. My eyes filled at the thought of Ken's kindness as I set my tray with my Coalport cup and Arthur Wood teapot. I was carrying it into the sitting room when it struck me.

'You'll end up an old maid,' I said aloud, and waited for the phrase to hurt. Except that it didn't. Old maids lived fulfilled and untroubled lives. I had had my moment of magic once beside tumbling waters and another, illusory one on an Italian hillside. They would never come again.

I poured my tea, switched on the TV and watched as they made one more attempt to raise the Millennium Wheel. I felt suddenly cosy and contented and safe. This New Year would be a special one – the start of a new millennium. It was really quite exciting. The news had ended and a documentary begun when the phone rang. It was Sara, sounding subdued – hushed, even.

'I can't quite hear you,' I said, cupping my other ear with my hand.

'I can't shout,' was the answer.

I thought of the echoing space of Ard-na-Shiel. If you couldn't speak up there...

'What's wrong?' I said, but the only response was a click as the receiver was replaced.

3

I slept fitfully, worrying about Sara's phone call. I had dialled Ard-na-Shiel again and again, only to hear the engaged tone. The operator declared a fault on the line and the TV weather report spoke of Highland gales. I went to bed trying to convince myself that a falling tree had cut off contact, but the sound of Sara's voice and the click as it was cut off reverberated in my head. It was a relief when the bedside clock showed six a.m. and I could drag myself out of bed.

At seven-thirty I rang Ard-na-Shiel, half-expecting still to hear the *burr-burr* of engagement but it was Cesare who answered.

'Lexy?' He sounded alarmed. 'There's nothing wrong, is there?'

I stood barefooted, feeling foolish. What was I ringing about that was urgent enough to ring at such an early hour?

'No.' I hurried to make amends. 'No, nothing's wrong. It's just that Sara rang me last night and we were cut off. They said there was a fault on the line.'

It sounded foolish, even to me, but he appeared not to notice.

'A fault? Probably one of the kids knocked an extension phone – they rush about; it happens. I'll get Sara for you now.'

A moment later she was on the line, sounding perfectly normal if a little sleepy. Had I imagined the change in her voice last night? It certainly seemed so, as she talked about children and weather and the latest episode of Nella's soap.

I felt myself relaxing as we talked until we reached that stage of having to think what to say next that heralds the end of conversation.

'Oh, that'll be lovely, Lexy,' she said suddenly, as though

replying to something I had said. 'I was hoping you'd be coming up soon.'

'Coming up?' I stupidly repeated her words.

'Good,' she said. 'Yes: as soon as you like.'

I hesitated but only for a second. 'You mean you want me to come up?'

Her answer was unbelievably light-hearted. 'Yes, of course. See you tomorrow, then.' After that there was only the burring of a dead line.

I sat down in a chair and tried to remember what had been said. Chit-chat about the children, Nella, rainfall and seasons... and then: 'Oh, that'll be lovely, Lexy.' Just that. Six words in a perfectly normal tone of voice and yet making no sense because I had never suggested coming to Ard-na-Shiel. And then: 'See you tomorrow,' she had said – when tomorrow had never been mentioned.

Tomorrow! That meant 'Come quickly, come now'. I reached out for the telephone to dial Nella's number, but then drew back. Mustn't worry Nella until I knew there was something to worry about.

Instead, I whistled up the dog and walked him down by the river, trying to make sense of my jumbled thoughts. It was quiet on the riverbank. Only the faint sound of the water and the snapping of twigs underfoot. Max snuffled ahead of me, nosing holes that might have held rabbits and starting suddenly at every unexpected noise. You could tell from every line of his body that this was doggie heaven, and I envied him his contentment.

What had Sara said? 'Come tomorrow!' And suddenly I knew that what she had meant was different, more urgent. *For God's sake, come tomorrow* was the true message. I whistled for Max and turned for home.

I settled him when we got back, refusing the pleading eyes that begged to come with me to the shop. Today I needed freedom to think and plan my journey to Ard-na-Shiel. It was five to nine when I set out for Ken's. He was taking a day off to recuperate from being in charge during my London trip. How would he take having to step in again? I knocked on his door, praying that he would already be up, rehearsing my apologies for a change of plans. The door opened, I opened my mouth to speak and then shut it again as I gazed into the face of a stranger.

'Hello?' He was smiling at my discomfort and I felt myself smile back. 'You expected to see Ken? Come in.' He moved aside to let me enter. 'I'm Leo and I imagine you're Alexandra.'

His hand was warm and firm and drew me into the kitchen where Ken stood, slightly flustered but happier than I'd seen him for quite a while.

'You've met,' he said, somewhat foolishly, and then reached to the dresser for another mug.

We sat round the table, drinking coffee and making conversation. Leo was forty-fiveish, greying at the temples and tanned. Handsome in a comfortable way a million miles from Jack. He had nice hands, too: slightly work-roughened but with well-kept nails. *I like him,* I thought, but I still wished he would go so that I could talk to Ken.

As if he read my thoughts, Leo rose to his feet. 'If you'll excuse me, I must get my things together. Will you be here when I come down?'

I held out my hand. 'I have to open the shop, but it's been good to meet you.'

He shook my hand, smiled and was gone.

'What d'you think?' Ken said with the fervour of a teenager. 'He arrived unexpectedly last night. I wasn't keeping it from you.'

'He's lovely,' I said. 'But be careful, Ken. You hardly know him.' I might as well have addressed the air so I let it go. When

Ken took a new lover, reason deserted him. 'Ken, I hate to do this to you but I've got to go to Scotland. Sara needs me.' I tried to describe the telephone conversation, but half his mind was upstairs with Leo.

'Of course it's alright,' he said. 'Take as long as you need.'

I kissed him on both cheeks, told him not to come into work until his lover had departed and set off for the shop.

For a blessed hour I immersed myself in stock, entering the dolls, listing what I'd paid for them and adding our mark-up, checking what had been sold in my absence, drooling over a Minton tile Ken had bought, circa 1875: a background of blue and beige with a central illustration of waterbirds. He had also acquired a Victorian silver travel clock, the surround richly embossed, the dial marked *A. Jones of Regent Street*, and a nice pine wardrobe, probably Dutch, with a mirrored door and two drawers in the base. All in all, a good week.

At eleven, my mobile shrilled.

'Lexy?'

I reached behind me for a chair and subsided onto it.

'Rick! I'm so glad to hear you.'

There was a rather grim chuckle at the other end of the line. 'I'm not used to such fervour.'

At the back of my mind I registered surprise at my own pleasure on hearing his voice, but there was no time for introspection. I gabbled through my account of Sara's phone call and my own call the next day.

'So what do you think?'

At the other end of the line he whistled softly. 'Well,' he said at last, 'my guess is they've had a row, she wants a shoulder to cry on, but doesn't want him to know she's involved you.'

'So he was listening?' I moved the phone to my other ear but didn't miss a word.

'Oh yes,' Rick said. 'Oh yes, I think he was listening.'

We talked then about my going up to Scotland. He got me train times from the Internet and forced me to confess to Nella.

'You have to tell her,' he said. 'But you don't need to alarm her. Say Sara invited you and you're going. That's enough. With a bit of luck you can sort it out and she need never know you had doubts. If she has to get involved – if it's serious – well, at least you didn't lie.'

When I put down the phone I felt comforted. I would get to Ard-na-Shiel and find everything was fine, and when I came back I would do some serious thinking about my relationship with Rick.

Ken came in at one o'clock, still starry-eyed over Leo. Leo was a rep for a huge cosmetic firm and came to Durham several times a year. 'I've known him for ages,' Ken said, 'but just lately….'

I hadn't the heart to remind him of Jack, and, anyway, Leo seemed a different proposition. Instead we sorted out a few loose ends of business and I went home to pack, promising to get back as soon as I possibly could.

I filled my case and then dialled Ard-na-Shiel to arrange for someone to meet me at the other end. The line was engaged, just as it had been last night. I rang again before I left the house, but it was still busy. I hadn't time to check with the operator; I would just have to use my mobile on the train. I took a last look round, gathered up Max's lead and favourite toy and let myself out of the flat.

Max was overjoyed to see Ken again and the joy was mutual. I left rejoicing in my choice of partner and resolved to slaughter Leo if he harmed a hair of Ken's shiny head. The train was on time and I settled into my seat, accepted my complimentary coffee and dialled Sara's number. Still engaged. I leaned back in my seat and watched Durham become Northumberland. Once or twice I dialled again and heard the operator. 'There is a fault,' trilled the ghostly voice. 'Try again later.' I closed my eyes and thought of Sara. *I'm coming*, I vowed silently. *I'm coming as fast as I can.*

4

I tried to reach Ard-na-Shiel again as the train crossed the Scottish border, but the line was still engaged. We were nearly into Glasgow when I heard the regular ringing tone and then a man's voice giving the number.

'McGregor?'

There was a moment's hesitation and then: 'Is that you, Miss Alexandra?'

Around me people were getting to their feet and reaching for luggage. 'McGregor, I'm on my way. I'm changing in Glasgow Can you ask Sara to meet me at Bridge of Orchy?'

Again there was hesitation and I was about to speak when he answered. 'I'm not sure the mistress is here. I've just got in myself. But someone will meet you. When will you be there?'

I gabbled my arrival time just as we entered the station and the line broke up. I put my phone away, praying the information had gone through, and then collected my bag from the rack. I had to wait an hour before the other train was due. I thought about ringing again but decided against it. McGregor was as reliable as the seasons. If Sara wasn't waiting for me, someone else would be.

In spite of a pale moon, it was black outside as the train thundered towards Ard-na-Shiel. Sometimes I could see the lights of a far-off house, once or twice a lit-up pub and strings of lights along motorways but otherwise almost uniform darkness. I thought of Rannoch Moor. There would be light there, reflecting from the myriad lochs and waterways. I ran over the journey in my mind: first the moor, then the black vale that was Glencoe. If it was Sara who collected me, we could talk in the car. The children would long since be in bed so she would come alone. Or perhaps Cesare would bring the Land Rover. We would cross the bridge at Ballachulish, a string of lights over the loch and then the road up to Ard-na-Shiel.

But this time there would be no Jamie stepping out from the canopied door.

I dozed then, waking as we neared Glen Orchy and collecting my things for journey's end. There was no one on the platform as I alighted and I stood, feeling foolish. I should have rung again. I was reaching for my phone when I saw McGregor. He looked older than I remembered and there was no smile of welcome on his face.

'You're here,' I said. 'I was beginning to worry.'

He had reached me by now, but he made no move to take my bags. Instead he swept his tweed hat from his head and began to twist it between his hands.

'Couldn't Sara come?' I said and suddenly ceased to speak as I saw his chin was trembling. 'There's something wrong ... what is it? Tell me, for God's sake...' I would have shaken him if he hadn't opened his mouth.

'There's been an accident, Miss Alexandra. A terrible accident.'

All I could think of was the children. 'It's not Alex?' He shook his head. 'It's no the children. It's your sister – it's Mrs Giulini... I'm so sorry. There was nothing we could do.'

I heard his words and wanted to reply, but there was a singing in my ears that became a roaring. Then my head was cold and I felt myself falling through space, except that I was still standing there, still holding my case and my coat, and the platform was empty except for me and the old man who stood before me, tears running now from his rheumy eyes into the seams of his cheeks.

I saw a seat a few feet away and managed to make my way to it.

'What happened?' I said. 'Was it the car?'

He shook his head. 'She fell, Lexy.' He who was usually so

formal had lapsed into the use of Sara's name for me. 'I went to look for her after your call. She wasn't in her room. The children were asleep so I knew she'd be there, somewhere in the house. She'd never have left them alone.'

'Where was Cesare?'

His eyes dropped. 'He wasn't there. The Land Rover was gone. I saw that as I came into the house. I looked for the mistress and when I couldn't find her in the house I went outside. She was in the courtyard, she was under her window... I knew she was dead. Her eyes...'

His voice broke and I suddenly saw the scene: the glinting windows casting light on a figure lying on the flagged courtyard.

'Did you get a doctor? Where is she now? Where are the children? Is Mr Giulini back?' And then, because I couldn't help it, 'Are you sure?'

'I telephoned for the factor. He came, and the doctor from Fort William. He was there when I left. The fall killed her, Miss Alexandra. He said she died at once and that's a blessing.'

'Who's with the children?'

I was on my feet now and moving towards the exit.

'The factor was there. We didn't wake them. We thought that should be for...' he hesitated. 'Well, we left them sleeping.'

'Where is Mr Giulini? Has anyone tried to contact him?' I was fumbling in my bag as I got into the car, intending to telephone Nella. And then I looked at my watch. It was ten o'clock. Should I tell her now? She couldn't catch a train before morning. I let go of the phone and instead fastened my seat belt. 'Did you hear what I said?. Has anyone got hold of Cesare?'

'No one knows where he is.'

Something in his voice chilled me. Sara dead and Cesare gone! How had she fallen from her window? I had been thinking 'accident', but the window ledges at Ard-na-Shiel were broad and high. Even if she had reached for a window to close it, she couldn't have over-reached and fallen. It didn't make sense. As we sped over the moor and through Glencoe, thoughts scurried round and round in my head.

'Tell me again,' I said. 'Where were you? Who was there when you left the house? Has anyone called the police?'

He seemed to welcome the barrage of questions. His voice steadied and he gripped the wheel more firmly.

'They were all there this afternoon. Fine as could be with the little ones. They had tea at half-past four, when Master Alex and Miss Fiona came home from school. I carried it in and they were watching the television. I said I would like to go down to the village and Miss Sara said that was fine and I could take her car. They wouldn't be going out themselves.

'I went to visit Jock Craigie. We had a game of chess and a dram – just the one before I set off home. I saw the Land Rover was gone when I came into the courtyard. That was a surprise: that they had – that one of them had gone out after all. I let myself into the house. I was taking my coat off when you telephoned. I went to find Miss Sara, then, and I found – what I found. I rang the factor and then I checked the children. They were sleeping like lambs. I went back down and I put a blanket over her, but I knew. I *knew*. So I stayed with her until they came, the factor and the doctor and the district nurse from South Ballachulish. Then the factor said to fetch you. I'm so sorry – to bring you news like that.'

I reached to pat his hand. 'Thank you. I was coming because I felt…' I almost told him of the strange conversation I'd had with Sara but something held me back. 'I felt something was not quite right. I'll have to tell my mother – but I need to talk to Cesare first. Where can he be?'

He shook his head. 'He didn't go anywhere much, not without

Miss Sara. And not at night. Unless they were going to the theatre in Glasgow or out for a meal somewhere. They were home-bodies, both of them.'

Why was he talking of Cesare, too, in the past tense?

'The police will find him,' I said. 'They'll put out a call for the Land Rover. And he may be home by now.'

But there was no Land Rover in the courtyard when we swept in, raking all four corners with our lights. Other cars were there: two police cars and a pick-up truck. A police constable stood in the hall, looking solemn and absurdly young. And then Cameron, the factor, was coming towards me, his face grey with worry.

'Thank God you're here, Miss Alexandra. The police are asking for next of kin, but no one knows where – can you come?'

I followed him into the library. There were three men there, none in uniform. One of them introduced himself as the doctor. There were little bottles of pills on the table in front of him and he stirred them with a finger.

'Did you know your sister was taking so many of these?'

I shook my head. 'She never said. I thought you looked after her health. I didn't know anything was wrong with her. Except...'

The older of the other two men leaned towards me. 'Except? Except for what?'

'I spoke to her on the telephone yesterday. There was something odd – nothing definite.' I felt tears prick my eyes. 'I came to reassure myself that everything was OK.'

'You and your sister were close?'

I felt tears well up in my eyes. Not close enough – *that* was the truth if I dared to utter it. I had begrudged her almost everything. Most of all her marriage – her *marriages*.

'We were close,' I said aloud. 'We didn't meet often. She was a long way away. But we kept in touch. I didn't know anything was wrong. Neither did my mother. I was with her in London two days ago. She thought everything was fine.' Inside me a reluctance to answer questions was growing. 'Can I see my sister?' I was amazed at how firm my voice was, almost defying them to say no.

They led me into the morning room, where a collapsible trolley stood with a black body bag on it, the end unzipped. Her face was framed in the opening, wisps of hair escaping onto the edge of the plastic, one strand across her forehead. She looked to be sleeping except for the pallor of her face. But the pale face was swollen, almost distorted. She must have put on at least three stone since I saw her last.

I closed my eyes, feeling the room swirl around me. But I couldn't, mustn't faint. I opened my eyes and stood for a moment, wanting to kiss her, wanting to say sorry, suddenly remembering a thousand tendernesses I had received from her when I was young. Before Jamie. Before Ard-na-Shiel. In the end, I kissed my fingertips and then placed them on her cheek. It was strangely puffy but also ice-cold, and I knew then that she was dead. Inside that bag her body must be broken or why else had she died?

I felt a hand on my elbow and obediently turned away. We came into the hall and I glanced towards the stairs, half-fearing I would see three frightened children there, asking why there were strangers in the house. But there were no children; only a commotion at the outer door as Cesare burst through, brushing aside the policeman as though he was merely a curtain. He saw me and stopped.

'What's going on, Lexy? What are you doing here? They say there's been an accident.'

The older policeman was stepping forward.

'There has been an *incident*, sir. A fatality. I'm very sorry, sir. You are Mr Giulini?'

Cesare nodded, his eyes seeming to grow darker as his face paled.

The policeman cleared his throat. 'I'm sorry, sir. I'm afraid your wife – is dead.'

Cesare let out a moan and for a moment I thought he was going to fall to his knees but the policeman was continuing. 'Can I ask where you've been, sir? We made every effort to find you.'

Cesare shook his head, as though to clear it. 'I was just driving. Driving around.'

I saw the two policemen's eyes meet and then flick away. Cesare seemed not to notice.

'Where is Sara? Where's my wife? Where are the children? Do they know?' He looked at me. 'Can you see to them, Lexy?'

I nodded as the older policeman moved to Cesare. 'I'll take you to see your wife, sir, and then we'll be removing the body to the police mortuary in Glasgow.'

'*No!*'

But even as the word burst from Cesare's lips, he seemed to realize the inevitability of it all. He let the inspector lead him towards the morning room, leaving me to mount the stairs towards the children's bedrooms, my feet more leaden with every step I took.

5

I sat for a long time in the moonlit bedrooms, regarding first the sleeping Alex, Sara's son, and then the girls, Fiona and Imogen. No point in waking them to tell them their mother was dead. Morning would be time enough for that. And how could I tell them something I didn't really believe myself? Was that my sister, swollen-faced, lying in the morning room inside a body bag? Were these children orphaned now and I part-guardian? Or would Sara suddenly appear, calm and smiling and let me off the hook of responsibility as she had always done?

When at last I accepted that it was no dream, I went downstairs to telephone my mother. She would need to make arrangements. I couldn't leave it until morning. McGregor stood in the hall like a sentinel, dejection in every line of his body.

'Where are they?' I asked.

He pointed towards the morning room. I looked at my watch. They had been in there for almost an hour.

'Do you think I could have a drink, McGregor? Anything: whisky, brandy…'

I needed something to fortify me before I spoke to Nella. While I waited for McGregor to bring the alcohol I rehearsed my opening words. *Mother, I hope you're sitting down…* Stupid! *There's no easy way to say this…* Equally banal! In the end I took a long drink of the brandy and soda at my elbow and launched straight into it.

'I'm so sorry, darling, but I have bad news. It's very bad. Sara is dead.'

Whatever I had expected to hear at the other end, it did not come. Instead, there was a pause and then Nella's voice, quite measured. 'Where is he?'

'Who?' Even as I said it I felt foolish. There was only one 'who' – one 'he': one man against whom Nella's face had always been set. 'He's with the police. He was out when it happened...' I suddenly realized I had given no explanation and she had not asked for one. 'She fell from her bedroom window. It was instantaneous. You know the height... she didn't suffer.'

'He killed her.' The voice was calm and matter-of-fact. 'I knew he would, sooner or later.' And then, as I sought desperately for the right words, 'I'll be with you in the morning, Alexandra. For God's sake, watch over the children.'

The police left at three a.m., leaving Cesare standing in the hall, his features frozen into an expression of horror.

'They think I did it, Lexy. They think I killed her.' He staggered then, like a drunken man, and I moved towards him and took his arm.

'Let's sit down, we need to think. Go into the library. I'll get you something to drink. Have you eaten?'

'*Eaten?*' The word shot from him like a bullet. 'I couldn't eat. I'll never eat again. She's *dead*, Lexy. My darling Sara, *cara mia*, is dead. I can't – I can't...'

He stumbled again and I led him, weeping to the room that had been Jamie's favourite, the place where she had nursed his children and fondled his dogs and made his telephone calls. I had settled him into a deep armchair when McGregor arrived with strong black coffee and the brandy decanter.

'Now,' I said, when I'd poured two cups and added sugar, 'tell me what happened tonight.' To my own ears, my voice sounded cold, even hostile, but he responded with a look of gratitude.

'We argued, Lexy. No point in denying that. I was worried about her – she wasn't herself and she was taking something.'

'What? What was she taking?' I leaned forward to interrupt. 'Do you mean drugs?'

He shook his head. 'Pills of some sort. She always dosed herself, you know that. But lately it's been worse. She was... she was not Sara. Tonight – last night – I begged her to stop. She flew into a rage...' He saw my look of disbelief and half-smiled. 'Yes, it's hard to imagine Sara losing control, isn't it? But I told you: it wasn't the old Sara.'

I would have argued, but I was remembering Reinie and the way her personality had fluctuated. 'Go on,' I said. 'She flew into a rage and you argued. What happened then?'

'I took the Land Rover and drove off. I wanted to cool down but most of all I wanted her to collect herself. We needed to talk: I couldn't go on just letting it go as I had done.' He shook his head again, like a man trying to shake off a blindfold. 'I've been hanging on, Lexy. I'm unhappy. I have been for a long time. Scotland is beautiful but it's not for me. I wanted Sara to come back to Italy. I wanted to get her away from Ard-na-Shiel and all its memories. But she was adamant. This was her children's heritage. She had to stay here. And now...' He threw up his hands. 'What will happen now? God alone knows.'

He sounded utterly sincere and utterly broken and I had to steel myself not to go to him and put my arms around him. I summoned up the picture of him on that Roman hillside, the utter sincerity in his voice as he told me he would never marry Sara because her wealth stood between them. And all the time he must have known they would be married within the week. Whether or not he was the murderer Nella believed him to be, he was not a man to trust.

'Why should I believe you, Cesare? You've lied to me before.'

He flinched, as though my words had actually struck home. 'Yes,' he said at last. 'Yes. I lied and I schemed. But I *loved* her, Lexy. I *loved* Sara. But I could never make her forget him: her *real husband.*' He spat out the last two words as though they were burning his tongue. 'He lay between us in the bed, all these years.' He looked at me, expecting a response, but there was nothing I could say because I knew exactly what he meant.

'We'd better get to bed,' I said, rising to my feet. 'There's nothing we can do here now. We'll sort things out in the morning.' I was halfway to the door, the loaded tray in my hands, when he spoke.

'I didn't do anything to hurt her, Lexy. I don't know how I'm going to prove it, but I hope you, at least, will try to believe me.'

I turned to face him. 'Where did you go when you drove off from here?'

Again the shake of the head like a dog emerging from water. If he was acting, it was Oscar-winning stuff. 'I just drove: on and on – across the bridge, through the glen. I went on towards Glasgow. I went into the outskirts, I was almost in the city centre when I realized how much time had passed. I phoned her then, but there was no answer, so I turned the car and headed home.' He paused for a moment. 'I saw the police car, the light turning, flashing. I think I knew then that something terrible had happened.' He stood up and came towards me, holding out his hands to take the tray. 'Let me have that. You look like a ghost. Poor little Lexy.' He was smiling down at me and his eyes were kind. 'Go to bed, dear sister. I'll see to this.'

For a moment I thought he was going to bend to kiss my forehead and I panicked.

'Goodnight,' I said and bolted for the door. McGregor stood in the hall, his face a thundercloud. He took the tray from Cesare without a word and turned towards the green baize door to the kitchen.

'Goodnight, Miss Alexandra.'

I saw Cesare's face contort at the snub. For a moment his mouth trembled and then he collected himself.

'I'll look in on the children,' I said to him. 'You get to bed.'

I stood at the bathroom basin for a long time, staring at my face in the mirror. I did indeed look like a ghost. I felt like one, too. How could this be happening? And if Sara really was lying in some far-off police mortuary, how was I bearing it? I wanted to cry then but no tears would come. Instead, I drew my dressing gown closer around me and went to check the children. They were all asleep, and I smoothed the dark hair Alex had inherited from his father, tucked in the girls and then put out the light.

There was no sign of Cesare as I crossed the landing to my own room. I switched off the lamp as soon as I'd turned down the bed and then crossed to the window-seat. The loch lay serene in the moonlight, the only sign of trouble a police car parked far below on the road and a dark figure moving up and down in the garden.

I curled up on the seat and tried to let the peace of the night sky enter into me. Was there a heaven? I had discussed it with Sara in childhood when one of our pets had died and she had declared herself ambivalent about the idea of an afterlife.

'There must be something,' she'd said. 'I just don't believe it's clouds and harps and everyone wearing nighties.'

I found myself half-smiling in the darkness at the memory of that far-off conversation. Her words had comforted me then; I had curled up in her bed and gone to sleep next to her. How sweet that had been, when she had been my comforter, before I had come to hate and envy her...

Forgive me.

I almost spoke the words aloud and might have done if I had not heard the creaking of floorboards outside my door. The next moment I saw the brass handle move in the moonlight that lay across the floor and touched the further wall. The door eased open and a figure stood in silhouette against the light from the landing.

'Goodnight, Lexy,' Cesare said. 'And thank you for not locking your door. It means a lot to me.'

6

Amazingly, I fell asleep almost immediately but awoke in a still-dark world, trying to convince myself that the night before had been no more than a nightmare. But even as I told myself I'd imagined it, I knew I hadn't. There was a strange stillness about Ard-na-Shiel, as though the house were holding its breath.

Eventually I got out of bed, wondering why every joint in my body was aching, and went to the bathroom. There was no sound from any of the other bedrooms, but I could hear faint noises below, and as I went back to my room McGregor appeared on the stair.

'You're up, Miss Alex.' He sounded relieved. 'I've got a pot of tea down below.' As he spoke, the bell clanged in the hall. It was Nella, white as a sheet and as unkempt as I had ever seen her but still the most welcome sight I had ever laid eyes on.

We sat either side of the kitchen table while McGregor hovered with toast and offers of porridge. Nella smiled as she accepted a cup of tea and then changed tone.

'For goodness sake, man, sit down. We haven't time to eat.'

I looked at my watch. 'How did you get here so soon?'

She grimaced. 'Fast car through the night. But never mind that, now. Where is he?'

I knew who she meant, but I looked at McGregor for an answer.

'He's still abed. I'll hear if he stirs.' He eased into a chair then and we both looked to Nella for guidance.

'How was she, McGregor? On that last day? Was she sad enough to kill herself?'

His eyes were fixed on the table and he took a long moment before he answered. 'She was confused. Ill. Ill in the mind and taking too many pills. But she'd never have left the children. Never.'

'So what happened?' I heard my own voice without forming the question in my mind. He shook his head.

'I don't know, Miss Alex. Mebbe she fell. If she leaned out for air – mebbe. But… but…'

'But what?' We spoke together, my mother and I.

'You can't leave it there,' Nella added. 'Did he kill her? You know I feared it. All along I knew he meant her harm.'

This was getting out of hand. Questions were one thing – allegations another. 'They were married for four years, Mother. If he meant her harm, it would have happened before now.'

She shook her head stubbornly but she didn't speak. It was McGregor who broke the silence.

'She wasna' well – not at all. Something changed her.'

'What do you mean?' Nella leaned forward for an answer, but he pushed back his chair and lumbered over to the dresser. He fumbled in a drawer for a moment and then produced a photographic wallet.

'You sent young Alex a camera for his birthday.'

I nodded.

'He took photos all day, then I took the film into Crianlarich.'

He took two photographs from the wallet and laid them on the table.

'I kept these out for fear they upset her.'

We each picked one up and studied it. They had been taken in the walled garden. Cesare was there laughing into the lens, Imogen in his arms. Fiona was running in the background but my eyes were drawn to Sara: a Sara bloated almost beyond recognition, her slender body a barrel, her face round and moon-like so that her eyes were almost slits. I had seen it when I looked down on her in death. The old slender Sara was gone.

'My God,' Nella said. And then again: 'My God.'

I closed my eyes, remembering the day I had climbed into the

Bentley outside the house in Notting Hill. She had waved me off, slim as a reed, smiling, exhorting me to take care of the size ten wedding dress; I had folded my size sixteen into the Bentley's soft leather and hated her for being slender. And now I was almost a twelve and she...

'But she must have known,' I said. 'She was a doctor. Why would she overeat to that extent?'

'She didn't overeat.' His voice was sombre. 'She hardly ate enough for a bird.'

'*He* did it,' Nella said. 'He destroyed her.'

McGregor and I looked at one another, not knowing what to say. We might have gone on standing there except for the voice from the doorway.

'Why would I destroy her? I *loved* her. She was my *wife*.'

Cesare looked haggard and unshaven, his dark hair curled around a tortured face.

'Answer me, my dear Prunella. Tell me why I would ruin my own life!'

Nella raised her chin defiantly. 'For money! To get your freedom! I don't know why, I just know it's so.'

He moved forward, creakily, like an old man, and subsided into a chair. For a moment, seeing his mouth tremble, I thought he was going to cry and I felt an unbidden wave of tenderness. But before I could say anything, he spoke.

'For money? If I killed her for money I was foolish. It all ends now – all this. I made her tie up her fortune for her children. For me there is nothing – not a penny. Ask her solicitor. He will tell you.'

Even Nella was taken aback, but she soon rallied. 'You could challenge the will. A husband has rights.'

He nodded. 'I could, but I won't. As for saying I did it for freedom, I could have gone at any time if I'd wished to. I had no need to stay. She was self-sufficient as the rich are always self-sufficient. So if not for money or freedom, tell my why?'

No one spoke and then he raised a fist and brought it down with such force that cups jumped and rattled in their saucers. '*Why?* Don't just sit there in judgement. Bring out your evidence – your motive. Then you can hang me, dear mother-in-law. As if I could care if you did.'

Again I felt the urge to reach out, to comfort him. He had answered the accusations; why didn't Nella climb down?

I stood up and walked to the stove. 'I think we should all cool down,' I said, 'before the children come.'

A few moments later they were there, Imogen holding Alex's hand, Fiona bringing up the rear.

'Where's Mum?'

The boy's face was creased with anxiety, as though he already knew something was wrong. Cesare moved towards him and hoisted Imogen into his arms.

'We need to talk,' he said and led them out into the sunlit garden, leaving Nella and me behind.

A moment later there was an anguished cry from Alex and then sustained sobbing from Fiona. Only Imogen remained almost unmoved, looking from face to face as though trying to decide who was telling the truth. When Nella and I reached them, Alex had regained his composure. Only his eyes, liquid with tears, betrayed emotion. Otherwise his face was stony. Fiona was sobbing, almost angrily, occasionally beating her fist against Cesare's chest. When I held out my arms to her she turned her head away and buried it in her stepfather's jacket. Only Imogen consented to be held and comforted by her grandmother, leaving me feeling superfluous in the face of such distress.

We had given the children a breakfast they didn't want and taken them into the garden to play when the inspector arrived. He walked across the lawn towards us, looking every inch a police-man, his sergeant a pace behind.

'Good morning.' He smiled at the children. 'How are they?'

I looked at Cesare, expecting him to answer but his eyes were fixed on the inspector's face and he stayed silent.

'They're as well as they can be in the circumstances,' I said. 'My mother's here now. That's helped.'

The children had fallen silent and moved closer to one another, and I smiled at them as reassuringly as I could.

'Your mother – that would be the lady from the television?' The sergeant leaned to whisper Nella's name. So, they'd been doing their homework!

'Yes,' I said. 'She came this morning – from London. Do you want to speak to her? She's in the house somewhere. I can call her.'

'Thank you. I will need to speak to her later. For the moment, though, I need to speak to you, sir.'

Cesare let out his breath in a sigh but he didn't speak.

'It might be easier if you came to the station. With the chil-dren here…'

It was delicately said, but it was an order nevertheless. I moved towards the children and put my hand on Alex's shoulder as Cesare turned and followed the policeman towards their waiting car.

We had coffee in the morning room, trying to make a show of drinking it for the children's sake, both of us acutely aware of the hours ticking away. From time to time our eyes met: Nella's increasingly satisfied as time passed, as though it meant they had something to go on. I was increasingly uneasy.

If it was true – if Sara's death had been no accident – what would it do to the children? They were at ease with Cesare; they had grown up with him, especially Imogen. They had lost their mother. If they were to lose their stepfather too, how traumatic would it be? The older two were not asking questions; that meant they were afraid of the answers. Imogen had asked where Cesare was when we sat down at the table and I had fobbed her off. The older two had said nothing and that was unnatural.

It was a relief when the ritual coffee was over and we could leave the table. The sky had darkened outside and there were storm clouds over the loch, which ruled out a walk.

'What do you want to do?' I asked, imagining Scrabble or Monopoly in the library.

'We could watch a video,' Nella said. 'I brought two new ones with me.'

Fiona's face lightened, but Alex shook his head. 'I'm going up to my room.' He left without a backward glance at his sister, who was looking decidedly disconsolate.

'Come on, peach,' Nella said, giving her a hug. 'We'll watch a video, shall we? Just the four of us. You, me, Imogen and Aunt Lexy.'

We were shepherding the children across the hall when we heard wheels on the gravel outside. And then he was there in the doorway – triumphant this time in the half-light of the great hall and achingly like Jamie.

'I'm back,' he said, a huge smile of relief on his face. 'I've told them everything. They know what happened. It was a tragic accident. The inquest is tomorrow. There has to be an inquest. After that, we can make arrangements.' His voice broke then and he dashed a hand across his eyes before he swooped on Imogen and raised her aloft. 'Now, what shall we do with the rest of the afternoon? I've missed you.'

They followed him towards the morning room, leaving Nella and me behind.

'He's going to get away with it,' Nella said slowly.

I shook my head. 'Don't say that. You heard him: there'll be an inquest. They'll find out all the facts. You're letting prejudice overcome you. Be fair.'

Nella moved to the stairs and mounted the first one before she replied. 'It's not prejudice, Alexandra, it's instinct. There's a difference. You'll understand when you have children. That man killed my daughter and I won't rest until I've proved it.'

For a few moments she stood there, her face implacable, until suddenly it crumpled.

'I want her back, Lexy. I want my daughter – my child. I want to hold her, smell her, feel her, hear her say, "Oh, Mum" again, the way she did when I was outrageous. I want her back and she's *gone*, Lexy. I'll never see her again.'

She slid down onto the stair then and I moved to sit beside her.

'There, there,' I said. 'There, there.'

I could think of nothing else to say.

7

Cesare had arranged two cars to take us into Oban for the inquest, which was just as well as Nella could not bear to be in his company. Mealtimes were scratch affairs, and only affection for McGregor brought us to the table together. He was to give evidence at the inquest. Neither Nella nor I had been called, although she was adamant that she had much to contribute.

'This is only a preliminary hearing,' I told her over and over again, but it was no use. She wanted Cesare indicted and hauled off to jail – or, better still, the gallows. I was thankful that I had not told her about the phone call from Sara that had brought me to Ard-na-Shiel.

In the end, I rode into Oban with Cesare and Nella came with McGregor in the Land Rover. We set off early, as soon as we had seen to the children and left them safely in the care of the factor's wife. Imogen was clingy and inclined to be weepy, calling out sometimes for her mother in a way that tore at the heart. Each time I looked towards Cesare and saw his eyes gleam with unshed tears. If he was not genuinely grief-stricken, Italy had lost a fine actor.

Now, as we passed over the Ballachulish bridge, I saw that the muscles along his jaw were clenched, as though to stem emotion. He did not speak until I prompted him.

'I know you don't like talking about it, Cesare, but have you thought what you're going to say today?'

His answer came swiftly. 'I'm going to tell the truth, Lexy: that we argued and I left the house. That I drove for long enough to convince myself I'd been a fool and then I turned back. But too late!' As he said this he lifted his hands and smote the steering wheel. 'It was *my* fault, Lexy. Whether or not she fell or...' He hesitated. 'Whether she fell or she threw herself down, I should have been there. I'm to blame. I'll tell them that.'

'You can't say that!' I was surprised at the vehemence of my own rebuttal. 'We'll never know what happened, but it could easily have happened while you were there. You couldn't watch over her every minute. Besides...' Now it was my turn to hesitate until I felt his eyes on me, willing me to continue. 'Was there any reason to suspect she'd do something foolish? She was strange when she spoke to me on the telephone. Not like herself at all. And –' I was going to tell him about McGregor's photograph but something stopped me. 'And – well, I just wondered if she'd been herself lately?'

'No. She was not herself. She had not been the old Sara for a long time. She was open about it. She was still grieving for Jamie. I understood that. But I thought when we – I thought I could make a difference. I thought there would be children and for a while I think she wanted that, too. She stopped taking pills – at least she told me she had stopped depending on them. Perhaps she was playing with words.'

He was silent then.

'I was here twelve months ago. She was quiet, but I thought she was happy. She was never one for getting excited about things.'

I was staring ahead, watching for shards of bright water amid the rocky terrain, until I heard him sob. I turned to look at him, tears coursing down his cheeks, and then I put out my hand and covered his where it lay on the wheel. It seemed the right thing to do and I left it lying there until we were pulling into the car park of the courthouse in Oban and it was time to resume my place as nothing more than a sister-in-law.

*

McGregor gave evidence first, his eyes never once glancing in Cesare's direction. He had served an early dinner to Mr and Mrs Giulini and then brought them coffee in the morning room. After a time he had heard raised voices. The argument had lasted awhile – probably ten minutes or so. When things quietened down he had left to visit a friend in the village. When he got back the phone was ringing. It was his mistress's sister, asking to be collected from the station. He had gone in search of someone to deliver the message... He broke down then and had to have water before he could describe finding the body.

The court was quiet as Cesare replaced him at the witness stand. There were two men scribbling away in a corner and I took them to be reporters. Beside me, Nella sat erect, her chin tilted almost to a defiant angle, her ungloved hands clasped on her handbag. I had never seen her look so bleak, and her expression did not change as Cesare told his tale.

'My wife was normally of a very serene disposition, but lately... there have been – difficulties. We argued over something trivial. I can't even remember how it started. She was getting more and more upset. I asked if she wanted to be left alone. She didn't answer. She simply took the keys of the Land Rover from the mantelpiece and threw them at me.'

Beside me, I felt Nella stiffen and I knew why: Sara had been constitutionally incapable of throwing anything at anyone, and yet Sara had been constitutionally incapable of carrying an ounce of spare flesh until now...

Cesare was telling of his drive across the moor.

'I just drove on and on. I wanted to give her time to cool down. I'd done it before and when I went back usually things were easier.' He looked down at his hands as though examining them before he continued. 'This time I went too far – I was away too long. I found myself on the outskirts of Glasgow; there was a public house and railings – a park, I think, or perhaps a cemetery. I reversed the car and started back. If I'd turned back sooner – I feel I am to blame. I was away too long.'

I waited for the coroner to offer some words of comfort, but none came. Instead, he asked a question. 'Can anyone confirm that you drove as far as Glasgow? Did you call in anywhere for petrol or ask directions?'

'No.' Cesare's voice was firm. 'There is no one to confirm my story. It's the truth, but I have no way of proving it.'

Everyone in the courtroom knew what the coroner was getting at. If Cesare really had driven as far as Glasgow, he could not have been there when Sara fell. If he had not... The question hung in the air as the inspector took the stand. He gave evidence of taking the factor's call and proceeding to Ard-na-Shiel. He had cordoned off the incident scene and delivered the body to the police mortuary as soon as the police surgeon had pronounced death and photographs had been taken. Enquiries were continuing.

It was the turn of the pathologist now, a small, grey-haired woman with rimless glasses and a mole on her upper lip. She confirmed that death had occurred between nine and ten p.m. and had resulted from multiple injuries consistent with a fall from a great height, but there were other factors she wished to pursue. Tests were ongoing and she would know more in a day or two. When the coroner queried the nature of the tests she tried to avoid answering but, under pressure, said she believed the deceased had been taking or had been administered a number of prescribed drugs, among them anabolic steroids.

I saw the coroner's eyebrows twitch at this and Nella let out her breath in a little sigh as the coroner adjourned the inquest for a further week in order to allow enquiries to continue. He added that he would have liked the deceased's general practitioner to be in attendance and hoped the inspector would see to it for the next session. The inspector bowed his head in agreement and we all rose to our feet.

On the steps of the court Nella clutched my arm.

'She'd never have taken steroids. She was a *doctor*, Lexy. She knew how those things destroy you.'

But I was remembering the bloated face in McGregor's picture.

'Don't think about it now,' I said. 'We'll find out more. We'll find out what really happened, I promise you.'

I felt Cesare's hand on my waist then, his voice in my ear.

'Go back with your mother, Alexandra. She needs you now.'

I half-turned to smile but he was gone, striding towards the Land Rover, one hand dashing the hair from his brow – or was it tears from his eyes?

8

The following day Cesare was arrested. The two older children had left for school at eight-thirty a.m. and Nella was still with Imogen in the nursery when the inspector arrived. I heard the bell clang and then McGregor's footsteps on the hall tiles. I had finished breakfast in the morning room and was wondering how I was going to fill another tense day, so the prospect of a visitor was not unwelcome. I was halfway to the door when I heard Cesare's voice raised in protest.

'I'm sorry, sir.' The inspector was polite but implacable. 'It'll be much easier all round if you come along with us now.' I had reached the door to the hall by this time and I could see Cesare standing at the foot of the stairs, hand clutching the newel post, face ashen.

'You can't think I had anything to do with my wife's death.' Again that wounded shake of the head as though to brush away cobwebs. If he was lying, he was good.

'I don't think anything at the moment sir, except that we need to talk further. You can contact your legal adviser, from the station, if you wish to do so.'

Cesare turned towards me. 'Alexandra…' He was giving me my proper name and I tried to keep my voice steady as I responded.

'Go with them, Cesare. The sooner this is cleared up, the better. Who is your solicitor? I'll get him to meet you at the station.'

Nella had appeared at the head of the stairs, Imogen peering from her skirts. There was a terrible, almost drooling satisfaction on her face and it stiffened my resolve. I crossed the hall floor and laid my hand on Cesare's arm.

'Off you go. You'll be back soon.'

I realized my mistake as soon as the gesture was made but it was too late to withdraw. The inspector had seen me reach out for my brother-in-law and would read into it what he chose. I turned on my heel and went into the library to telephone the name Cesare had given me.

I had finished the call and replaced the receiver when Nella came in, closing the door behind her.

'Why are you doing this, Lexy? Why are you helping him?'

There was genuine distress in her voice and I tried to explain.

'I don't know if he had anything to do with Sara's death, but he deserves the chance to explain – to prove his innocence. You surely wouldn't deny him that!'

'Oh, Lexy!' She put a hand to her brow and then subsided into a chair. 'I wish I could explain how I feel – how certain I am – but I can't. It's just a gut instinct. Something that told me from the beginning that he meant trouble.'

'But they were *happy* – he made her happy. They've been together for four years. If he meant to harm her, why wait so long?'

She shrugged. 'I don't know. Perhaps he fell out of love with her – if he ever was *in* love. Perhaps he's playing a long game. I don't know. You saw that photograph. Why didn't he step in, why didn't he ring me? Or you? Why didn't he get treatment for her? Obviously something was terribly wrong and all he does is drive off into the night. It doesn't make sense.'

That was the one thing on which we were agreed. It didn't make sense, and someone must find a way to sort it out. I got the keys of the Bentley from McGregor and drove to Oban to see Cesare.

At first I thought they were going to refuse to let me see him, but I persisted and at last the inspector gave grudging agreement. We sat either side of a table in a small, bare room with a woman police constable perched on a chair by the door. Cesare was pale but composed. They had taken his belt and the neck of his shirt was open, making him look strangely vulnerable.

'Are you alright?'

He nodded. 'Yes. Are the children – is Imogen OK? What will you tell Alex and Fiona when they get home?'

I shook my head. 'Leave that to me. What did your solicitor say?'

Cesare shrugged. 'Very little. He listened while they interviewed me. Once or twice he intervened – told me not to reply – but I want to tell them whatever they want to know.'

'What did they ask you?'

He threw back his head. 'Did I love your sister? Did I have another woman? Why did I leave the house, where did I go? I told them: through the Glen to Crianlarich and on to Glasgow. They just raised their eyebrows at that. But where else would I go? Where else on that blasted moor?'

'*Think*,' I said firmly. 'Did you pass anything on the road? A distinctive vehicle? We could check…'

He shook his head and I wondered if he was even listening to me, much less concentrating.

'When you got to Glasgow, you said there was a park with railings – a public house – can you remember its name?'

Again, a shake of the head. There was silence for a moment and then his eyes met mine.

'Yes?' I said, urging him on.

'There was something. Near the pub – down a side street when I was turning back. There was a fire engine. I saw the light reflecting on their helmets. There was an engine and one or two firefighters but no fire. No smoke, no flames.'

I felt my body tense. 'What time was it then? Think hard – it's important.'

Behind me a door opened and the inspector entered the room. 'I'm afraid time's up.'

There was dour disapproval in his voice, the kind reserved for women foolish enough to consort with their sister's murderers.

I stood up and faced him. 'I was just going, inspector. I got what I came for.'

I drove on from Oban until I reached the centre of Glasgow, but not before I had phoned Nella on my mobile and tried to explain.

'If there was a fire between nine and ten, if he really was in Glasgow that night, it means Sara's death was an accident. If he's lying, I'll find out. Please understand, darling: I'm not doing it for him; I'm doing it for us – so we can all have peace.'

She gave me her blessing, but she gave it grudgingly. 'Try the local paper,' she said as the call ended. 'They know if a leaf stirs.'

The newspaper was available in the local library, its address at the bottom of the back page, so I went there. The girl behind the counter was helpful.

'The 23rd you say…' She checked her computer. 'Jimmy was on news then.' She vanished, to return in a moment with a ginger-haired boy of about nineteen.

'I'm trying to find out about a fire,' I said. 'At least, it might have been a fire or a cat up a tree or anything that would call for a fire engine. It was about ninety-thirty at night. Somewhere on the outskirts…' My voice trailed off as I realized what I was asking. In a huge and sprawling city like Glasgow, there were probably twenty incidents a day requiring a fire engine.

The boy remained unfazed, however. 'Nine-thirty?'

I nodded. 'About then.'

He turned on his heel and exited. When he returned he had a computer printout in his hand and he flicked through a couple of pages. 'The twenty-third. Nine-thirty.' He shook his head. 'There was a chimney fire at 8.15 in Broad Street. And a chip-pan fire in Soley Terrace at nine-oh-five – number four. Engine and full crew out in both cases. After that, nothing till after midnight. And before that peace from four forty-two. A cat up a tree. They didn't send a tender, just offered assistance. Any good?'

I scribbled down the two addresses, offering to kiss his feet in gratitude as I did so, and went in search of a Glasgow A-Z. Broad Street was nearer and I drove straight there. It was a narrow terrace among a dozen other narrow terraces and no sign of a pub or a park with railings. I drove on towards Soley Terrace with a sinking heart – until I saw the green expanse of a cemetery with ornamental railings and then a splendid pub on the corner. This was where Cesare had turned back.

Number fifteen was a shabby house, divided into flats. I played eeney-meeny-miny-mo with the doorbells and rang.

'This is going to sound crazy,' I said to the man who answered. 'But did you have a fire here four days ago?'

He had not had a fire but the tenant above him had. 'Not there two minutes,' he grumbled 'and all of us out in the street for fear of it taking hold. What kind of a wifie fries chips for hersel' at nine o'clock of the night? That's what I want to know.' He offered to ring her bell to summon her, but I shook my head. I already had what I wanted.

I drove to the office of Cesare's solicitor and laid the facts before him, then I turned the car for Ard-na-Shiel, satisfied now that Cesare had been where he said he was when Sara had fallen to her death. Had she fallen or jumped? We might never know, but at least we could be sure no one else was involved. If I could convince my mother of that, we might be able to come to some decisions about the future.

9

If I felt any satisfaction at proving Cesare had not been at Ard-na-Shiel when Sara died it evaporated as I tried to explain to Nella what I had done and why. There was a coldness in her expression that I had never before seen and it was obvious that she felt I had betrayed the family.

'I don't care what you think you found, I know that man is *wrong* – wrong through and through, Alexandra.'

There we went again, the use of my proper name. I was certainly in the doghouse.

'But if he didn't do it…' I persisted. Her answer shot back before I had finished my question.

'Didn't do *what*? I never said he threw her from the window. What brought her there, Lexy? Ask yourself that! Calm, serene Sara. Have you forgotten how steady she was? A rock, to me and to you. What drove her to the desperation we saw in that photograph? Why did she take steroids? If, indeed, she *did* take them?'

There was no mistaking the meaning of that last remark. If Cesare had not propelled my sister from a high window, he had fed her enough toxins to induce her to do the job for him. And hard as I tried to tell myself the idea was far-fetched, I had to acknowledge that it was easier to believe than that sensible, medically trained Sara had administered them to herself.

'But she must have known!' The words burst out of me as though I was resentful of Sara's self-neglect. 'She was a doctor. She must have known! She was obese. She must have realized.'

'Perhaps she was drinking and it affected her judgement – I don't know. Perhaps she was just so besotted she didn't even notice. Can't you see, Lexy? Or won't you trust my instinct that he is bad?' It was on the tip of my tongue to remind her that her instinct about the men in her life had hitherto been a hundred percent wrong, but I bit the words back. The present was enough to contend with without dragging up the past.

Cesare was released the following morning. A police car delivered him to the door just as we finished breakfast. He swung Imogen up into his arms, bent to kiss Fiona and ruffled Alex's hair before he turned to me.

'My solicitor told me what you did. I can't find words to thank you, Lexy.'

Behind me I heard a swift intake of breath from Nella. He heard it, too, and gave a wry smile.

'I'm sorry, dear Prunella. I know you need a villain of the piece but, really, in the end there is no crime here. Just enormous sadness.'

It was said quietly and with affection and I looked at Nella, hoping for at least a softening of expression. To my amazement I got more. She smiled, a sad, resigned smile and reached to pat his arm.

'You're right, Cesare. It's sad, but we must make the best of it. The children are what matter now.'

My relief lasted for the few minutes it took him to excuse himself and go in search of a shower.

'If that's his game,' Nella said, when he was safely out of earshot, 'I can do sad resignation, too. And don't you think it's time you told Rick what has happened? I don't think you've given him a thought since you got here.'

There was disapproval in her voice and I accepted the rebuke. Rick was hundreds of miles away, but that was no reason to exclude him from my life. I went to my room and rang him. He was both horrified and sympathetic when he heard my story.

'I'll come,' he said. 'I can catch a flight this evening.'

'No.' The word escaped me too quickly. 'No, there's no need. Really. There's nothing you can do.' I was shutting him out and we both knew it.

Two days later, we drove into Oban for the resumed inquest, this time travelling together in the Bentley with Cesare at the wheel. Sara's GP was the first to give evidence. He had not seen Mrs Giulini for some considerable time. As a trained physician herself, Mrs Giulini had not needed the services of a doctor except during her pregnancies. He had not prescribed any medicines for the deceased, had no knowledge of any steroids and could not imagine any reason why a physician would take them, knowing their potential for harm, unless they had been properly prescribed. To the best of his knowledge his patient had been in good health, although he had noticed on social occasions in the aftermath of her first husband's death that she appeared somewhat depressed. He coughed then and made a mumbled reference to alcohol consumption.

The pathologist took the stand. Her enquiries confirmed the presence of anabolic steroids administered over a prolonged period. There had been potentially disastrous effects and the steroids were probably the cause of a dramatic increase in weight. There was also some evidence of raised alcohol consumption over a period of several years, and traces of the antidepressant Ziagen in the blood samples. However, the actual cause of death was an internal haemorrhage: direct result of a fall. The coroner asked one or two questions, and then the inspector gave evidence. He outlined the various steps taken to check the movements of everyone connected with the deceased. It would appear the deceased had been alone when she met her death. As to how she had fallen from the window, in spite of extensive forensic examination there was nothing to show whether the fall had been accidental or as a result of deliberate action on her part.

The coroner pursed his lips and then addressed his audience. In the absence of conclusive evidence that Mrs Giulini had been severely depressed, and pending further investigation, he felt he had no option but to adjourn the proceedings. He gave his condolences to the family of the deceased, especially her husband and children, and freed the body for interment.

Beside me, Cesare seemed to slump in his seat. Nella collected bag and gloves and rose to her feet.

'Shall we go?' she said sweetly. 'We've a lot to discuss before the children get home from school.'

We sat in the morning room, a tray of coffee in front of us. Cesare's eyes were liquid with unshed tears, Nella was calm to the point of serenity. I found it hard to analyze my own feelings. We were about to discuss the disposal of my sister's body, and yet I felt almost nothing.

At any moment I expected her to come through the door, look around with the amused tolerance she had always shown when Nella or I were in a pickle, and then say, 'Leave it to me.' The thought of how much I had resented her help – her 'interference', as I had called it – rose up to rebuke me. I had not only resented her, I had *hated* her. And yet I had loved her, too, admired her more than anyone else in the world, longed to be like her, above all longed to have what she possessed: Jamie and Jamie's children. Cesare, too – except that that had been so ephemeral, so totally Hollywood, that it had scarcely seemed real.

I looked at him now, staring blindly ahead as he raised a cup to his lips. What kind of man was he? Would I ever know?'

'Well?' Nella said, purposefully. 'We have arrangements to make.' Amazingly, it was settled without argument. There would be a service in the church at Ballachulish, where Jamie was buried. I expected Nella to suggest that Sara be buried there, too, but she agreed to Cesare's suggestion of cremation. I felt a little shiver of satisfaction at the thought that she would not lie with Jamie in that quiet plot – until revulsion at my own self-obsession made me gag on my coffee.

'But I don't want her ashes scattered,' Nella said in a voice that brooked no argument. 'For the time being, I want them kept here. You'll grant me that, Cesare, I know.'

His face had grown lined suddenly under the faint stubble. He nodded like a man who would agree to anything because he had lost the will to argue. I looked at my mother, wondering what she could be up to. What could you prove from dust? Because she meant to prove something, that was sure.

I left the house then, ostensibly to get some fresh air, in reality to howl aloud my grief and shame. I had not valued my sister in life, and in death I was begrudging her her rightful place at her husband's side. Except that Cesare was her husband.

In the end I gave up thinking at all. I lay down in the heather and hoped there would not be the sound of bees to remind me of when everything had seemed possible.

10

All the way to the church at Ballachulish I was remembering that other mournful ride and I knew that Nella must be remembering, too. But this time Sara was not sitting between us; she was riding ahead in a satin-lined coffin piled high with flowers and it was Cesare – who might or might not have brought about her death – who sat next to me.

My mind raced backwards and forwards. *It's alright, Lexy.* That had been my sister's mantra through all those childhood years when I had clung to her and trusted and felt her warmth protecting me. How had I come to hate her – to envy and begrudge her as I had done? Was it only Jamie who had come between us? If we had stayed in childhood innocence, big sister and little sister, would everything have been alright? But my resentment of her had started long before my fat-filled, angst-ridden teens. It had sprung up as soon as she entered into the half-world of adolescence and enjoyed its freedom while I was left behind: the baby in the nursery. That had not been her fault, but it had taken me all those years to realize it.

I glanced sideways at Nella, wondering what she was remembering. At Jamie's funeral, she had dabbed continually at her tears; now she sat dry-eyed. *Implacable,* I thought. *That's what she is now.* Nella, who had swayed with every wind of fortune, had become rock-like and devoid of tears – and that meant God help Cesare.

He was unnaturally composed. Only the occasional tremor of a dry sob betrayed his grief. I wanted to reach out and give him a consoling pat but I daren't for fear of discomposing him – and, even more, for shame that Nella might see.

There was a crowd at the church when we arrived, local gentry and tenants from the estate, all downcast and respectful, and one or two sightseers anxious to see the grieving husband who had spent time with the police and just might be a villain.

One or two of the older men raised their heads to look directly at Cesare and their gaze was far from pleasant. These would be men who remembered the laird and saw Cesare as an interloper. One of them turned his gaze from Cesare to me and inclined his head in acknowledgement. So did the woman by his side, and it was she I recognized although, it was eight years since I had last seen her being led through the rain to the ambulance.

I halted as I passed them. 'It's Mr and Mrs McKechnie, isn't it?' I said, suddenly engulfed in nostalgia for that long-ago moment in their barn, close to Jamie, feeling my body come alive with a love I had not known before or since.

'Indeed it is, Miss Alexandra, and a sorry day this is.'

It was my turn to bow my head. 'Yes,' I said. 'It's very sad. We must speak afterwards. I want to hear about the baby.'

This brought a smile to the woman's face. 'No' a babby, now' she said, her voice full of pride.

As I took my place in the pew beside Nella, I was still remembering but it was hard to remember detail. Only the sensation was unforgettable. The baby born that day would be a sturdy boy now and my memories were older, too.

We sang 'O Love That Will Not Let Me Go', and then the minister moved to the lectern. In front of him the coffin lay like a long table, its brass trimmings gleaming in the sunlight, just as the brass on Jamie's coffin had gleamed that day in 1995. Four short years, yet long enough to turn the world upside down. Beside me I felt Cesare stiffen and turned my attention back to the minister.

'But if we can not be sure of the circumstances of her death, we can be very sure of her place in the hearts of her family...'

He was looking directly at Nella and at me and not – quite pointedly not – at Cesare. So Ard-na-Shiel had made up its mind. Defiantly I turned my face to his and smiled at him. His eyes looked back, grief-stricken and afraid, but grateful just the same.

Only a handful of mourners followed us on the long drive to the crematorium. Canned music and then the dreadful sound of marching as the coffin was lost to view. I heard Nella's breath as her mouth made an 'O' of anguish. Cesare's face was impassive, but his knuckles where they clutched the pew in front were white.

'Nearly over now,' I said. 'Hold on.'

Back at Ard-na-Shiel we made polite conversation with people we hardly knew, friends of Sara's from church and the livery she had used, some of the tenants and one or two civic dignitaries who had come to pay their respects to the widow of the laird rather than Mrs Cesare Giulini. For all the sympathy or attention paid him, Cesare might never have intruded into Sara's life.

I made a point of talking to the McKechnies, reminding them of the day their son had been born. He was one of three now, so their family had closely mirrored Sara's own.

'How will the bairns manage?' Mrs McKechnie enquired.

I shook my head. 'I'm not too sure what will happen. We've lived from day to day for the last week, as you can imagine. We'll make very sure that they're alright. It will be as Sara wanted.'

As I stood in the hall to bid the guests goodbye, I was thinking furiously. What *would* happen to the children? Whose responsibility were they now that Sara was dead? More importantly, who had the right to make decisions? Would Cesare want to go back to Italy and, whether or not he did, would he wish to be encumbered with another man's children? There was the question of Ard-na-Shiel, too. It was Alex's property now, but he was still a child. Even with the best of factors, who would oversee the running of the estate?

My sense of *deja vu* deepened as Cesare played with the children, restored to the house by the same tenant's wife who had cared for them while we buried Jamie. Alex was silent, Fiona tearful at times. Only Imogen had heart for games and her little face wore an air of puzzlement as though she knew something was wrong but couldn't decide what.

By the time we had got them to bed and McGregor had brought sandwiches and coffee into the drawing room, I was ready for a repetition of the speech Sara had made that first funeral evening. 'What will you do now?' Nella had said when the silence had threatened to engulf us. And Sara had answered: 'I'm going away.'

I couldn't bear to wait through another long silence, so I said it straight away. 'What's going to happen now, Cesare? We need to make arrangements.'

He was standing staring into the fire, one hand on the mantel the other in the pocket of his jacket. He turned as I spoke, his eyes widening in surprise.

'What do you mean, Lexy? What arrangements do we need to make? Life here will go on as before. I shall hire a housekeeper. McGregor is getting older and deserves a peaceful retirement. But otherwise... I was already overseeing the running of the estate. I intend to keep the children's lives as unchanged as possible.'

Nella had sat silent through this exchange. Now she spoke. 'Shouldn't we wait for the reading of Sara's will? She might have expressed wishes for what would happen in the event of her death.'

She spoke quietly and I was full of admiration for the evenness of her tone. She was not going to provoke a row – not yet at any rate.

Cesare moved to the table and took up his coffee cup. 'If she expressed a wish, I will try to carry it out, Prunella, but the legal position is quite clear. I adopted the children over a year ago, so I am, in every sense, their guardian.'

'I see,' Nella said, again apparently serene. 'That's settled, then.'

She rose to her feet. 'I have to go back to London, of course. I have key scenes to film. I'll leave tomorrow, I think.' She smiled at us both. 'So I'll say goodnight. Look in as you come up, Lexy. Unless it's too late.' A moment later she was gone.

We sat in silence for a moment.

'She doesn't like me,' Cesare said at last. He said it flatly, without a hint of anger.

'I'm sorry.' There was nothing else I could say except those two words. Except – there was one question I must ask. 'Cesare, Sara gained so much weight. She had lost sight of herself or she'd never have let it happen. Why didn't you do something?'

He looked at me with what amounted almost to amazement. 'Why didn't I do something? Because I didn't care what she looked like. I hardly noticed that she put on weight. I *loved* her, Lexy. Loved her, her spirit. To me she was still beautiful – always will be beautiful.'

I sat on, wondering what to say next, wishing I could be whisked up to my room without the need to take my leave.

It was he who made it easy for me, holding out a hand to haul me from my chair. 'Thank you for today,' he said.

I shook my head. 'I didn't do anything…'

He reached for my other hand. 'You were there,' he said. 'I couldn't have managed it without you.'

We were close together now and I could feel his breath warm on my forehead. 'Oh, Lexy.' He was drawing me closer, neither of us moving our feet but allowing our bodies to sway inwards until they were almost touching. I felt a terrible shame come upon me, realizing that I wanted him, wanted to be held in his arms, swept up the wide staircase, folded into his bed and his body… I tugged my hands free, or I would have done if he would have let them go. And then he did release me, but not before he had leaned to kiss the side of my mouth. 'Goodnight,' he said then and turned back to the fire.

11

I spent a sleepless night thinking about the relationships I had had with men. If I was honest, none of them had really mattered. I had given my virginity to a man I had not even liked, and now I could scarcely remember his face. For even as I had sighed and groaned and clung and promised, there had been a single image in my mind: a dark and smiling Celt climbing towards me up a riverbank and somewhere a bee humming in heather.

And yet… I struggled to remember Jamie's face, but even that was vague now. What had not faded with time was the sensation of that moment. An orgasm of joy – pure and unadulterated. That was what I remembered and had never been able to replace. Not even with Rick, who was good and kind and loved me.

Until Cesare! I knew him to be at best weak, at worst villainous but still he obsessed me. I had no difficulty at all in recalling his every feature, each nuance of his voice. I felt a strange compulsion to protect him and excuse his every wrong move. At least Jamie had been worth obsession. I could not say the same for Cesare.

As soon as it was daylight I started packing. The sooner I was back in Durham and getting on with my life, the better. I told Cesare at the breakfast table.

'So soon?' He was genuinely taken aback. 'I thought you would stay…' His voice trailed off and I felt a surge of guilt.

'Are you worried about the children? I could take them back with me for a while, if that would help.'

'No!' His reply was emphatic. 'I want everything to be as normal as possible for them. They need their school-friends, they need familiar surroundings. They need *me*.'

Outside in the hall I could hear Alex and Fiona gathering their possessions for school. What he said made sense. Should I stay and help them come to terms with the loss of their mother? His eyes were on me, not beseeching but waiting nevertheless. If I stayed... I thought about last night, the moment when we had stood close to one another. If that happened again, I knew what would happen – and if it did I would never forgive myself.

'Very well,' I said. 'I must go back and see to the shop. I can't impose on Ken much longer. But I'll keep in touch. If you need me – if the children need me – I'll come at once.'

He drove Nella and me to the station to catch the train to Glasgow. We didn't speak much on the journey, each of us busy with our private thoughts. Nella gave a curt nod as she left the car and then moved ahead. I held out my hand as the train chugged up to the platform but Cesare ignored it. His lips on my temple were stiff.

'Try to think well of me, *cara*. I loved Sara. I hope you know that. If I could change things I would, but...' His shrug was a despondent one, his eyes, as they met mine through the train window, misted with tears.

I felt a sense of relief as the train moved away and he was left behind. It was all too confusing, too full of unanswered questions. Whatever happened on the night Sara met her death was only the climax of something else, the mystery of why a sensible trained physician would turn into a shapeless hulk without the wish to live.

I turned to the window to watch the Highlands slipping away and tried to dismiss the meaning of the photograph from my mind. That must not be the image of Sara that stayed with me. And yet I had always hated her for her elegant slenderness, blamed her for my own ungainliness. In the end, we had changed places, my sister and I, but now I could gain no satisfaction from it. As the miles increased between us and Ard-na-Shiel, I felt a sense of relief. I kissed Nella before I alighted at Durham, and the sight of the shop, as the taxi drew up at the door, brought tears of pleasure to my eyes.

Over the next few days I settled back into my old routine. It was comforting to switch on the television and see Nella back in her soap opera, but the smiling persona on screen was very different from the woman who telephoned me every night. She was still obsessed with the mystery of Sara's death, unable to accept the inquest verdict.

I tried reasoning with her, but at best my arguments were half-hearted. I knew that Cesare had been miles away when Sara died. How else could he have known about a small fire in a nondescript street in a Glasgow suburb unless he had seen it for himself? But I could still not accept the weeks leading up to Sara's accident. Why had there been steroids in her bloodstream? Why had she made that call to me, the call that had drawn me to Ard-na-Shiel? And if she had undergone some terrible personality change, as Cesare had suggested, why had he not contacted Nella or me?

I was still puzzling over these things when he rang me. It was eleven at night and I had just come home from walking Max. The phone was ringing as I let myself into the flat.

'Lexy. At last. I've been ringing all evening.'

I loosened the neck of my coat and moved the receiver to my other ear. 'What's the matter? Are the children all right?'

His tone was definite. 'They're fine.' But the emphasis on the first word suggested that although they might be fine, he was not.

'How are you?' I said, wondering if I was being manipulated into asking the question. 'Damn you Cesare,' I added under my breath. I knew him to be a liar and a cheat but the sound of his voice could still rob me of my self-possession. I closed my eyes and leaned against the hall-stand as he told me of his loneliness. When at last I put down the phone I felt a weariness of spirit that could not be shaken off until, in the early hours of the morning, I fell asleep.

12

For the next few days I tried to be a responsible antique shop proprietor. By night I prowled the area around the cathedral, buttoned into my oldest, most shapeless coat, hands thrust in pockets, chin sunk into my collar, Max padding along behind. Passing students barely gave me a second glance. They were always going somewhere, full of anticipation, sharing a joke with their companions, no time to spare for a solitary figure who looked as though she might be walking an invisible dog.

The weather was kind that week. A full moon rode the night sky, its face kind as it looked down on mankind in all its folly. Against that brilliant sky the towers of Durham stood out like story-book castles, but I could only see the moonlit splendour of the water, the Ballachulish bridge and the brooding peaks above the loch. I had much to occupy me in Durham but I wanted to be in Ard-na-Shiel.

One saving grace was that Ken was once more his old self. Safe and happy in his new relationship with Leo, he moved round the shop, tweaking a vase here, moving a chiffonier there. I marvelled at the difference love could make and envied him his new-found certainty.

Especially when Rick eventually rang.

'What's happening?' he asked. 'Will you come to me or shall I come to you?'

I felt a sudden panic. I couldn't cope with Rick. Not now.

'Leave it for a few days,' I said. 'Just to see how things settle down.'

For a moment there was silence at the other end.

'OK,' he said at last. 'If that's the way you want it, Alexandra.'

He did not often use my proper name and it was awhile before I grasped the finality in his tone.

Nella continued to ring me each night, but where before she had been obsessed with the subject, surprisingly she now seemed reluctant to talk about what had happened or anything to do with Ard-na-Shiel. She was ringing to check on the children, she told me, and all seemed well, but Cesare's name scarcely passed her lips.

What are you up to? I asked, but only in my head. Nella had been an actress far too long to have difficulty with dissembling. When she was ready, she would tell me. Until then, it was pointless to waste time with questions. Not for the first time I marvelled at how exactly Nella fulfilled her Gemini birth sign. She was certainly two people: one of them totally frivolous, even 'scatty', but the other was frighteningly focused.

In that first week I spoke twice with Cesare and each time he telephoned me. He would tell me about the children and the way in which the new girl from Ballachulish was settling in as nanny-cum-nurserymaid. He would ask about Ken and the shop and mention that Nella had called, and then he would fall silent until he forced me to make some inane remark about the weather or an item I had heard on the news.

I longed for him to ring off but felt powerless to terminate the call myself. It was as though the open line connected me with Ard-na-Shiel, so that even as I fretted over what to say, I found a curious peace there.

I didn't sleep much, preferring to sit at the window and watch that awesome moon, sometimes until I heard birds cheep in the darkness and knew dawn was not far away. It was pleasant to creep into bed then and watch the light filter noiselessly into the room. And while I waited until I could decently get up and begin the day, my mind filtered back and forth, to a childhood where

Sara had been my rock and mainstay, to adolescence when she had been a focus for resentment, to the moment when I had let myself out of Ard-na-Shiel and begun the moonlit ride to Crianlarich and freedom, or what had passed for freedom at the time.

Would things have been different if I had stayed? Would she have been alive and well and mistress of her estate – and if that had somehow been possible, was it what I wanted?

I would sit up then, bathed in perspiration, knowing that I couldn't be sure, aware that I was truly the bad sister of the fairy tales who wished her sister ill. And we had fitted the fairy-tale image, Sara and I: she the good princess, blonde and saintly; I the wayward one, dark-haired and even darker of soul.

At the end of the second week I gave way and ran back to Ard-na-Shiel.

'Are you sure?' I asked Ken a dozen times, half-hoping he would say, 'No. It's not convenient.' But he was happy enough to care for things, serene as he was in his relationship with Leo. I left a message on Nella's answerphone, ringing when I knew full well she'd be rehearsing, told a delighted Cesare what time I'd be arriving and caught the Glasgow train from Durham station.

He was waiting on the platform at Bridge of Orchy, Imogen in his arms, the others at his side. They swarmed around me, chattering, tugging at my jacket to get my attention, full of tales of their doings.

They're happy, I thought. *He's making them happy.*

The first night it rained, but it seemed not to matter. We had sent the nanny off to her family croft and sat now in the morning room using Alex's Playstation or playing Fiona's Four Square. When the children began to flag, we took the younger two upstairs, leaving Alex the dignity of half an hour's grace. I led Fiona by the hand, Imogen sat astride Cesare's shoulders and urged him on.

We splashed like mad things in the bathroom and then folded two clean but weary children into their beds, standing together for a moment to watch them snuggle down.

I wanted, longed, for his arm to come around me in mute acknowledgement that he shared my contentment. It did not come, but he did touch my hand to signal that it was time to tiptoe away. We went down the broad staircase side by side, and I felt as happy as I had felt in a long time – until I made the mistake of looking down into the hall.

There was only one image that belonged there: Sara and Jamie as I had seen them on the night I left Ard-na-Shiel. And my happiness turned to ashes in my mouth, because being happy with Cesare was like dancing on my sister's grave.

I stayed with Cesare for three more days, days in which we indulged the children, shared suppers by the fire and avoided any subject that might puncture the illusion that all was well. McGregor came and went until the last day, when he announced that he was going into Oban for two days to visit with family.

It was a curious exchange. He did not ask Cesare's permission. He simply announced it in perfectly polite tones, which nevertheless conveyed insult. If he was trying to provoke his employer, he was wasting his time. Cesare sent him on his way with his blessing.

'How will you manage?' I asked when McGregor was gone, racking my brains to think of an excuse to Ken to allow me to stay two more days. But Cesare was convinced he could manage without McGregor's help.

'Believe me,' he said, the ghost of a twinkle in his eyes, 'in some ways it will be easier.'

So I caught the train from Bridge of Orchy, leaving them standing together, father and children, looking for all the world like a united family. Only one thing missing: a mother. I closed my eyes as the train chugged on towards Glasgow and wondered if I could ever occupy that missing place. *Only for the children.* I told myself that over and over again. I would care for Sara's children as if they were my own, and if that meant also being Cesare's wife, well, I could tolerate that if I had to. But all the time I tried to deceive myself I knew that what I wanted was to be with Cesare. That old urge not only to take what was Sara's but to *be* her had not left me.

When shame had come and gone and returned and been driven off once more, I forced myself to concentrate on work. It was time we had a stock-taking followed by a clear-out and restocking. I would travel to sales up and down the country and acquire magical artifacts at knock-down prices. As for my dolls, I could fly to the States. Dolls were big over there. I could even set up a branch in New York...

It was crazy stuff, but it did the trick. By the time I stepped out at Durham I was my reasonable self and I stayed that way until eight o'clock the following morning, when the phone shrilled in the bedroom just as I'd stepped into the bath.

'Yes?' I said ungraciously, clutching a towel round me and trying not to drip on the duvet.

'I'm coming, Lexy. Today.' It was Nella at her most imperious. 'There's no time to waste. Can you meet me?'

I moved the receiver to my other hand and let the towel go. 'I'll be very glad to see you, Ma, but why the rush?'

She wouldn't tell me details but she was obviously simmering with excitement of one sort or another. I closed the shop at four-thirty and went to collect her from the five o'clock train.

'Not now,' she said after she'd kissed my cheek. 'Let's get home.' Only when we were seated either side of the kitchen table would she begin, and even then not until she had turned down my offer of coffee and produced a bottle of Merlot from her handbag.

'I had to do something, Lexy,' she said as the wine glugged into glasses. 'I didn't tell you because I knew you'd go berserk, but it had to be done.'

My heart sank as I realized she was talking about Sara's death. I sipped my wine and tried to subdue guilty memories of picnics and laughter and the touching of hands in the quiet bedroom.

'I went to a detective: a very sensible man, someone on the show used him over a divorce. They said he was trustworthy. You'll like him. He has this divine place in Camden Passage –'

'Get on, Ma, for God's sake. You went to a detective and...?'

'I couldn't accept the way that man provided an alibi for himself. Let us all think he couldn't prove he was elsewhere and then, when it's almost too late, he remembers something useful.'

'But he couldn't have faked it. I've seen the street, remember? It's a side street miles off the beaten track. It never appeared in the paper and if he followed the fire engine in search of a cover story, he still wasn't at Ard-na-Shiel between nine and ten.'

'Of course!' She brushed my objections aside. 'Of course he couldn't have known if it happened by chance. But what if it *wasn't* chance? What if that fire was timed to occur at just the right moment?'

'When he was passing?' I was trying to work out where she was going but it wasn't easy.

'No, silly – not when he was passing. When he *wasn't there at all* because he was back at Ard-na-Shiel murdering my daughter.'

'But how did he know about the fire?' I felt an urge to shake some sense into her, but it was she who struck out at me.

'Lexy, use your brain! He set it up – the fire. He fixed for there to be a fire at nine o'clock so that he could claim to be there and have seen it but he was never there at all. He knew it was happening because *he'd made sure that it would!*'

She came up with the details then. A flat in Soley Terrace had been rented on a short lease.

'Cash payment,' Nella said. 'Mark that.'

A woman had moved in, a strange woman who had put out no feelers for friendship and rarely crossed the doors until the night of the twenty-second, when she had run screaming into the street shouting that her kitchen was alight. The Fire Brigade had been summoned, the fire extinguished and the woman had retreated back inside her home. Three weeks later she was gone.

'And you think she was something to do with Cesare?'

'Yes,' Nella said without a note of triumph in her voice. 'I think he recruited someone and paid them well to stay in Glasgow for four weeks. They had only one task to perform. At an appointed hour they'd create a fire, call for help and sit back.'

'How can you be sure?'

Nella shook her head. 'We can't. She's gone – vanished. She could be anywhere now: out of the country probably. That's why we have to go on, Lexy: find out more. He's clever, but I'm cleverer and I'm not surrendering my grandchildren to his mercies.'

14

Two days later I was in Glasgow. Nella had left me no choice, threatening to give up her part in the soap if I wouldn't go. I couldn't summon up any enthusiasm for what amounted to looking for a needle in a haystack, but she was adamant.

'Mr Gray...' She spoke of the detective almost in tones of reverence. 'Mr Gray says she is a Glaswegian – well, Scottish anyway. Perhaps she comes from Edinburgh. Cesare hasn't been away from Ard-na-Shiel for more than a day in the last six months, so he must have found her locally.'

'Wouldn't that be too risky?'

She shook her head emphatically. 'Not if she came from a big urban area like Glasgow. And he'd hardly recruit from the villages around Ard-na-Shiel. She was Scottish, we know that from the neighbours, so she came from a Scottish city or town and chances are she's still there.'

Her certainty was having an effect on me. At first I'd thought the idea crazy; now it seemed possible – even feasible. And yet... was Cesare capable of such premeditation? She saw the doubt on my face and leapt on it.

'You don't want to believe he could plan something like this – well, prove me wrong. Find her and have her tell you she's never heard of him and if you believe her, I will.'

I nodded agreement on that promise, but I knew that if the woman denied involvement fifty times over and I believed her implicitly Nella would go right on believing in conspiracy.

Mr Gray met me at my hotel. He was small and stout, wearing a belted raincoat and a Rupert Bear muffler. He looked like a chubby train-spotter but his looks belied his ability to ferret out the truth.

'I think I've found her. She kept herself to herself while she was in Soley Terrace, but she bought cigarettes and papers at the newsagents. The girl there remembered her because she got them to order a specialist magazine – something to do with sugar-craft.' He smiled at the incomprehension written large on my face. 'That's cake-icing to the rest of us. I checked with the wholesaler. A surprising number of Glaswegians take it, but not too many to check. She was eleventh on the list – if she's the one, that is. She fits the description of the woman in the flat and she was away from home at the relevant time.'

I shook my head. 'It's too far-fetched. If she lives in the city doesn't she run the risk of someone recognizing her?'

'And saying what? She hasn't committed a crime – not on the face of it. I doubt he told her what he intended to do with the alibi. And remember they'd never count on anyone checking – just the original enquiry. Did she have a fire? Yes, she did. End of story.'

'They reckoned without Nella.'

He nodded. 'That they did.'

I went up to my room then and rinsed my face in the bathroom. I felt agitated, as though something dreadful was about to happen. When I took the towel from my face I regarded myself in the mirror. I looked troubled and I knew why. I didn't want Nella's theory to be correct because I didn't want Cesare to be an out-and-out villain. I had long accepted that he was a liar and probably a parasite, but a murderer? That was something else. I felt a sudden, desperate longing for life to be peaceful, and then a surge of anger – most of it, however illogical, directed at Nella.

If she had been different, an ordinary mother who cleaved to one husband, none of this mess would have happened. Sara and I would have been full sisters with only a year or two between us. We wouldn't have had to move from house to house and pay lip-service to so many 'daddies' and I would not have needed to hate my sister. And if I had loved her, if we had been more of an age, she might never have married Jamie. I might have been mistress of Ard-na-Shiel and lain in Jamie's arms night after night.

I felt the familiar fingers tighten around my heart and turned away from the mirror. There was only one true reason for the way I felt. I was, and always had been, the bad sister. It was as simple as that. I put on my coat and went downstairs to meet Mr Gray.

We drove to the woman's house in a neat little hire car and parked across the road.

'She lives on the second floor,' he said. 'On her own most of the time, although she has had men living there from time to time. She has some sort of disability pension. One of the neighbours thinks she was a nurse years ago – hurt her back lifting patients. She doesn't work, doesn't socialize much, but drinks at the local club...' He was looking at his notebook. 'Buys gin at the off-licence and does cake-decoration for a local bakery. Quite good at it, they say. Specializes in woven baskets, if that means anything to you. And she's a practising Catholic and superstitious with it.' He flipped the notebook shut. 'If she keeps to routine she'll be off to mass soon.'

Ten minutes later she came out on the step. I had occupied myself during the wait by wondering if she was Cesare's mistress. Why else would a woman leave her home for four weeks and agree to perform such a bizarre act? But as soon as I saw her I dismissed the idea. She was thin and stooped, peering from behind Dame Edna specs and clutching a shapeless camel coat together at her neck. She had long brown hair which straggled over her collar, and her feet were clad in leopard-skin ankle boots that made her thin legs look even weedier.

We left the car and followed her on foot, down past the shops, around the corner and then into the cool half-darkness of a

Roman Catholic church. Statues gleamed in the light of a hundred flickering candles and the air had the warm, musty smell of incense. She walked to the front and slipped into a pew. After a moment's hesitation, I followed and sat on the opposite side of the centre aisle. She bowed her head in prayer, supporting it on one hand. I could see that her nails were long and horny, her index and middle fingers yellowed with nicotine.

Somehow the sight of her hand made me gag as I pictured white icing being spun into the thin struts of a trellised basket. She lifted her face then and I saw that she was lined and wizened behind the horn-rimmed glasses.

She settled back in her pew, staring ahead at the altar. I stared ahead, too, trying to work out what to do next. I could hardly buttonhole her and accuse her of being an accessory to murder. On the other hand, I must do something. I sat on, hoping for inspiration, as she walked to the confessional box and went inside. As soon as the door closed on her, Mr Gray slipped into the seat beside me.

'What are we going to do?' I asked.

He, too, was staring ahead but he turned as I uttered my question. 'What do you want to do?' he replied.

I was watching the door of the confessional, terrified that it would open. 'Get this over as quickly as possible?'

He nodded. 'Might as well. There's nothing to be gained by waiting.' He stood up and I followed him back up the aisle and out of the church.

We waited by the car until she emerged, blinking at the onset of daylight, still clutching her coat to her throat. We moved towards her and as she saw us her eyes flicked back towards the church, as though in search of sanctuary.

'Miss Logan?' For a moment I thought she was going to deny her name, but Mr Gray persisted.

'You are Miss Mary Logan, aren't you?'

'Yes.' The eyes behind the glasses were wary and I stepped in.

'I believe you lived in Soley Terrace a few weeks ago?'

She began to shake her head in denial then thought better of it. 'I did, but only for a week or two.'

I made my tone sympathetic. 'There was a fire, I believe. That must've been upsetting.'

'No,' she was glancing left and right now, planning escape. 'It was nothing – no harm was done. Anyway, what's it to you? There wasn't an insurance claim. It's all done with.'

'Perhaps we could go back to your place and talk about it,' Gray said, reaching to take her arm. She pulled away from him, twin spots of colour appearing in her sallow cheeks.

'I told you. It's over and done with. I never claimed. It was only smoke, anyway. Now, I've got to go…'

She was turning on the high-heeled boots and I felt desperation.

'Why did you go there? Were you paid to live there? Please tell me.'

She was trembling now, whether with indignation or fear I couldn't tell.

'Paid? I never heard of such a thing. I don't know who you are but leave me alone.' She was moving fast now and we followed, still throwing questions at her. She turned. 'I'll call the police!' She turned back and then suddenly lunged sideways onto the road. I saw the bus before I heard the screech of brakes and then she was down under the wheels and I felt the rush of air past my face as it screeched to a halt in front of me.

People were screaming, a man was jabbing his finger at a mobile phone, and all I could do was stand there, thinking that Nella would never, ever believe, that it had just been an accident.

'Come on,' Gray said quietly, tugging at my arm. We'd better get out of here.'

15

I decided to tell Nella face to face. That way, I might just be able to convince her that Mary Logan had not been Cesare's second victim. We waited until Bob Gray made sure she had been dead on arrival at hospital and then boarded a train for the long trip south. I tried to concentrate on the landscape as we sped through fields of clustered sheep or grazing cattle, but all I could think of was the impossibility of convincing my mother that the Logan woman had not died at Cesare's hand. I had seen it happen and I still found it hard to believe. It was too convenient, too pat for Cesare Giulini not to look guilty. And yet I knew he was innocent. Perhaps he was just as free of the guilt of that other crime.

I closed my eyes as the train crossed the border and admitted to myself that that was what I longed for: to see him free and clear of any suspicion. If I had not seen what happened to Mary Logan I would have almost certainly blamed Cesare and I would have been wrong. Perhaps the rest of our suspicions were equally ill-founded. We were almost at Peterborough when I remembered to check my phone. There were three messages from Rick, but I didn't feel up to dealing with them there and then. I would do it when I'd spoken to Nella.

From Kings Cross we took a taxi to the South Bank. Half of me was hoping Nella would be off rehearsing; the other half wanted to get it over with. She answered the door almost as soon as Bob rang the bell and let her breath out in a big sigh when she saw my face.

'You're here! I've been ringing everywhere. Did you find her? Has she admitted it?'

She was still firing questions as we trooped through her tiny hall and into her sitting room. I looked at Gray but he was looking at me.

'Well?' Nella said.

I sat down and loosened the neck of my jacket. 'You're not going to like it, Mum. We found her – or rather, Mr Gray found her. And yes, she was away from her home at the relevant time and she did fit the description of the Soley Street woman – but she wasn't going to admit to anything –

'We must make her – the police will make her.' Nella got to her feet as she spoke, as though she was going to ring the police straightaway.

I shook my head. 'It's not that simple. We were following her, – interrogating her, I suppose – and…' I felt my throat constrict. 'There was an accident. And before you say it wasn't an accident, it was a double-decker bus. A Glasgow bus. She walked into it. No one's fault – unless it was our fault for pursuing her. We'll never know now.'

Nella had turned to look at the detective. 'Is it true? Is there any possibility that it was somehow engineered?'

He shook his head. 'It was an accident. Pure and simple. But if it's any consolation, she admitted she was the woman in the flat. And she knew we were onto it being staged and not just an accident.'

There was silence for a moment and then Nella got to her feet and moved to the mantelpiece. She fiddled with the ornaments there and then turned back to face us. 'What now, then?'

I had arrived feeling guilty. Now I felt a twinge of irritation.

'There's nothing we *can* do – you must see that. And I'm still not sure you were right.' I was opening my mouth to advance my next argument when she moved towards me like a cat.

I felt her breath hot on my face as her fingers dug into my

forearms. 'Don't you see, Lexy? Don't you see? Now that she's gone it will be the *children*.'

I half-shook my head. 'He wouldn't. He's fond of them. They're just babies…' I turned to Gray for support but it was not forthcoming.

'I think your mother may have a point. Legally he's their next of kin. Under the terms of your sister's will, Giulini was modestly provided for, but the estate went to Alex. Adoption is a legal procedure. If the children should die, their adoptive father would be the legal heir.'

I felt my tongue swell suddenly in my mouth until it threatened to choke me.

'But they would know – he wouldn't dare –'

It was Mr Gray's turn to shake his head now. 'You wouldn't dare. Nor would I. But I think Mr Giulini may be a different proposition. He'd be broken-hearted, he'd be hurt that anyone could suspect him, but he'd take the money just the same. After all, with that kind of money you can put distance between you and your accusers. If they couldn't prove enough to have him charged he could simply walk away.'

I felt my shoulders slump as his words went home. Of course Cesare was different. Hadn't he proved that again and again? If I had made that renunciation speech on a Roman hillside I couldn't then have gone through a wedding ceremony. But he had, and then he'd faced me and brazened it out.

'What should we do?' I said, turning to the detective and listening as he outlined the next move.

Forty-eight hours later we flew out of Heathrow on a flight to Rome. I had agreed because I knew Nella's threat to throw up her soap role still stood. If I didn't go, she would ruin a career that had only just come back to life. So I boarded the plane and settled in a seat next to Mr Gray, who was new to foreign travel.

He ate his own meal and then turned mine down twice before accepting gratefully and gobbling it up. After that he slept all the way to Rome.

'It's small, isn't it?' he said as we moved through the airport. He sounded disappointed and I realized he had been expecting something grand. I steered him past the taxi touts and into the official queue and tried to listen to his commentary, mostly critical, as we drove through streets lined with houses in various stages of disrepair.

'Cheer up,' I said at last. 'The city centre is breathtaking. Just wait and see.' And then we were entering our modest hotel and I was relieved of the need to make small talk.

Alone in my room, I slid back the shutters and looked down on the surrounding buildings. Everywhere there was decay. Rome was old and sad – almost as old and sad as I felt at that moment.

I lay down on the bed and closed my eyes. I felt wretched and still horribly, unbearably ambivalent. I wanted to find evidence, concrete evidence, that Cesare was a villain. Then I could go back to Durham and buy and sell dolls and collect porcelain and never again be tormented by feelings. But the other half of me, the foolish part, wanted to find evidence of innocence, so that I could go back to the house by the loch and hold out my arms and feel his body next to mine, warm and comforting and safe.

In the end I turned on my side and slept, but only to dream of bees and heather and a bloated body lying limp as a rag doll in a Scottish courtyard. I woke as daylight filtered through the shutters and realized I had forgotten to return Rick's message. I read the three messages, the last one a curt *Anyone there?* and texted an answer.

I wasn't in the mood for conversation.

16

Bob Gray was waiting at the breakfast table when I got downstairs the following morning.

'It's serve yourself,' he said cheerfully, pointing to the buffet where a dark-eyed Italian matron presided. 'There's some funny stuff,' he said, sucking his teeth. 'Still, it's all tasty.'

I looked at his plate, piled high with sliced cold meats and cheese and smiled. 'I'm glad you're enjoying it.' I collected orange juice and rolls for myself and went back to the table.

'I'm just going to potter a bit today,' the private investigator said between mouthfuls. 'Find my bearings and so on. It's bound to be different here, but I dare say it'll boil down to the same system in the end. And I've got some useful contacts.'

I nodded. 'So you won't want me today?'

'Not unless something crops up. You get out and see a bit of Rome and check back here from time to time. I'll leave a message if something happens. Otherwise I'll see you tonight. I've checked the time for dinner. It's seven o'clock.'

So Mr Gray liked his food. I kept my smile to myself and thought about how I was going to fill my day.

In the end I went to the Sistine Chapel. The taxi dropped me in a street lined on one side by shops and pavement cafés, on the other by the Vatican wall. I waited patiently, shuffling forward behind a queue chattering in every language under the sun. And then I was through the door and into a place that looked remarkably like an airport. A narrow escalator took me skywards, packed liked a sardine among people silent now, their rapt faces turned upwards as though they expected to see the Pope himself waiting on the top step. I glanced sideways. A young nun stood next to me, soberly dressed and coiffed but with a Gucci bag slung over her shoulder. Truly, this was a place of paradox.

And then we were on an upper floor, buying a ticket, shuffling forward into room after room packed with *objets d'art*, in each of them a king's ransom, collectively enough to halt world poverty for at least a few hours. As I moved forward I fantasized. If they sold one item each day, each week, they could feed, heal, educate untold numbers of people. By the time I reached the Sistine Chapel I felt submerged by affluence and acquisition. The Michaelangelo ceiling was as beautiful as I had expected, the colours glowing, but outside lay the the money-changers' tables, selling copies of everything until nothing seemed sacred.

It was a relief to get back to the cool half-darkness of my room in the hotel. I lay on my bed with the shutters closed, listening to street sounds, my mind racing over the sights of the day. So much opulence, such wealth, such an enclosed kingdom, such a money-making machine! And in Africa and Asia people were dying for the want of bread...

In the end I slept, waking to darkness. What time was it? I switched on the bedside light and checked my watch. Quarter to eight! I had promised to meet Gray at 7.30! I sprang to my feet, sluiced my face with cold water and sped downstairs.

He was waiting in the foyer and the satisfied look on his face told me he had news.

'Not now,' he said when I questioned him. 'I'm starving. We'll order first.'

I controlled my impatience while we scoured the menu. I chose antipasto and seafood pasta. For Bob, it was prawns in garlic and oil and a Lasagna verdi. He ordered wine and then reached for his notebook, taking what seemed like forever to open it at the right page.

'I think I've found the house,' he said. 'It's on the Via Furnese. We'll go over there when we've eaten, but I'm sure it's the place. There's a gate and a fountain as you describe. No dog, but it's deserted so they may be away.'

'How did you find it?' I was lost in admiration of anyone who could pinpoint a single house in the seething mass of dwellings that was Rome.

'It wasn't difficult. I looked up his birth details before we left Britain. He was born in Ruspoli – that's a village nine miles out of Rome. There were people there who remembered the family. His father was killed in a road accident when Cesare was seven.'

I widened my eyes in appreciation. 'Go on,' I said.

'His mother left the village after her husband's death. Cesare was an only child. He went with her. She got work with a family named Ponti, a wealthy family who owned land on the outskirts of Rome, and a town house in the city. I went there to see if there was anyone who remembered his mother, and there it was: just as you described it.'

'So he took me – and Sara, too – to the house where his mother worked –'

'– and passed it off as his own. Tomorrow we'll visit the Ponti estates, but I'm pretty sure we'll find the place you went to with him.'

'So he just adopted the Ponti lifestyle…'

I would have gone on, but our food arrived then, and apart from coming up for air occasionally, Bob was preoccupied for the next half hour. I sat and sipped a filter coffee while he downed half a pint of tutti-frutti and then we were ready to go.

As the hire car threaded its way through Rome, I struggled with my emotions. Was Cesare Giulini a cynical liar, a conman? Or a little boy who had lost his father and found sanctuary in a rich man's house so that he felt a part of it?

'That woman,' I said. 'Do you think that was his mother?'

I was remembering the whispered altercation, the way her eyes had flashed at him, half-angry, half-loving.

'Probably.' Bob guided the car to a standstill and there it was: the street of tall, shuttered houses. I got out and walked up to the wrought-iron gate. The house was dark and silent in the moonlight. Even the fountain was still, but the stone nymph was there, holding her basket.

'What happens now?' I said and turned back to the car.

We sat long into the night at the hotel, sipping a thin Italian liqueur that smelled and tasted of lemons and discussing Cesare.

'He must have made money somehow,' Gray said. 'He had the trappings of a man of means when he met your sister, so there's been money somewhere. I need to check all that. What's he been up to since he left Ruspoli? That's what we need to know.'

'What can I do?'

He didn't answer straight away and I knew he was pondering.

'I need to check out that estate tomorrow. After that…' There was a pause. 'I think it would do no harm for you to go back and pay your nephew and nieces a visit. I know I said I needed someone here, but now – well, I think someone should be with those kids.'

There was something in his tone that chilled me.

'Alright,' I said at last. 'If that's what you think I should do.'

I made my good nights and went upstairs to phone Nella.

She was quiet as I relayed Bob Gray's new information.

'What happens now?' she asked when I was finished.

I licked lips suddenly gone dry. 'I'm going to Ard-na-Shiel. He – Mr Gray – Bob – thinks someone should be there. I must go back to Durham first, to see Ken. After that, I'll be on my way.'

I half expected her to demand the right to go herself, to protect her beloved grandchildren. Instead, all she said was, 'Be careful, Lexy. For God's sake, be on your guard.'

17

I was halfway back to Durham, sitting in an almost-empty train, when it occurred to me that I had not thought of Rick for days. There was another message on my phone and a letter from him in the pile on the mat. He was puzzled, at times almost angry that he did not know where I was. My hasty message before I had left for Rome and the text while I was there hadn't been enough to satisfy him.

'I need to see you, Lexy, as soon as you get back. I'm flying up to Edinburgh tomorrow. I'll break my journey at Newcastle and come over to you. I just hope you're there.'

As the automatic voice intoned the time the message had been received I checked my watch. It was September 3rd today. His message was dated September 2nd. He was only an hour or so away.

I felt my heart leap into my throat but it was not in glad anticipation. It was panic that gripped me. It wasn't that I didn't want to see Rick. I liked him; I might even have loved him if there had been no Jamie and now the pale and perhaps menacing shadow of Cesare. But he would make demands on me. Not the cruel sexual demands of an Ian; what Rick would ask of me would be honesty – but how could I be honest when I didn't even know where truth lay? Did I love Rick? Was I besotted with Cesare? If not, why did I yearn to find evidence of his innocence and cringe from the very thought that Nella might be right and he was guilty? Just thinking about it made me feel weak.

I sank into a chair and contemplated the mess I was in. In a day's time, two at the most, I must go back to Ard-na-Shiel and face him. Smile, exchange polite conversation, face him across a meal table – all the while not knowing whether or not he had murdered my sister. The thought was so unbearable that I put it away. Right now I must face another man and try to mend fences.

I had showered and changed and was unpacking my case when Rick arrived, stepping from a cab and looking up at the house as he got out of the taxi. He didn't pay the fare, just spoke to the driver and left it standing there. He looked tanned and fit, a well-cut jacket over a silk polo-neck. *He's matured*, I thought, remembering the boy in Trafalgar Square seven years ago. *Seven years!* It felt more like a lifetime. He was my lover, too: a kind and gentle one I truly didn't deserve.

I opened the door before he knocked.

'Rick! Good to see you.'

He didn't move to kiss me, which was a surprise.

'You're back,' he said, and moved past me into the hall.

'Look, Rick –'

I was about to launch into an explanation when I thought better of it. What could I say? I had been called away on urgent business, I was in the middle of a family mess. But none of that explained why I hadn't phoned him, written, made at least an effort.

I made tea and carried it through to the sitting room. He had perched on the window-seat, one twill-clad knee over another, his palms either side of him, flat on the polished sill.

'Tea?' I had already suggested a drink and he had turned it down, but right now I needed one. I poured him a cup of tea and collected a whisky and dry-ginger for myself. 'I know it's early but I just got back from Rome and my time clock's a bit awry.'

'So,' he said at last. 'Tell me why all the drama.'

I raised my brows in query.

'You left suddenly, Lexy. One short message and then nothing for days except a text. I think you owe me an explanation.'

I wanted to tell him everything, but the words simply wouldn't come. 'It was Nella. You know what she's like: she has some bee in her bonnet. I had to go to Rome...' It sounded weak and the words tailed off. Why didn't I tell him the truth: that the bee in Nella's bonnet was murder and Cesare was in the frame?

As if he read my mind he smiled. 'Rome? The Italian connection. Is *he* there?'

'Who? Oh, you mean Cesare. No – no, he's still at Ard-na-Shiel.' My voice sounded high and foolish, like an ingénue in a West End farce.

Rick was half-smiling now. 'And you're going up there soon?'

'Well, yes, actually. You see, Nella thinks...'

He stood up. 'Don't bother, Lexy. I came to say – well, I'm off to the States in a week or two. You're going up to Scotland again. We'll exchange postcards, I expect.' He was moving towards me, putting his cup on the table, fastening the button of his jacket with one brown hand. I tried to work out what was going through my mind. Relief? Regret?

'Rick, I'm sorry.'

'So am I, Lexy. So am I.'

He was abreast of me now and reaching out for me. His kiss was hard, searching at first and then final. 'See you,' he said, when it ended. A moment later he was gone and I knew I would never see him again.

I cried then, but it was not for Rick or the loss of him. I had never really wanted him, so it would be hypocritical to mourn the losing of him. I cried because I knew that if I couldn't love Rick, who was eminently lovable, the probability was that I could never love anyone. And then, as I realized that was untrue, the tears came faster. I *was* capable of love. I loved Cesare Giulini, had loved him from that moment in the park where, for a split second, I had seen Jamie standing there.

And the man I loved was definitely a liar, most probably a cheat and maybe even a murderer.

18

I hired a car in Glasgow and drove the last stage of the journey. Not until the car was mine and I was ready to set out did I ring Ard-na-Shiel. I had wrestled with the problem on my way from Rome to Heathrow and all through my brief meeting with Nella. Should I give notice of my coming, or take Cesare by surprise and if the latter, how did I explain the discourtesy? In the end I settled for half measures. I would ring him from Glasgow, a buying expedition in Scotland as my pretext. Now that I was so near, I couldn't go home without seeing the children. *I had a car, could I drive over?*

I had psyched myself up to make the call, but I was still unprepared for the sound of his voice. Warm and kind and, above all, delighted to hear me.

'*Cara*, of course you must come! They'll be so excited.'

I could hear him in my head all the way across Rannoch and on through the glen.

Today the moor looked bleak, the stretches of water that scored it lacked sparkle and looked sinister. As I entered Glencoe it seemed even more intimidating than I had remembered, and it was a relief when at last Ballachulish came in sight and I could rattle over the bridge and on through Onich.

I swung the car right when I came abreast of Ard-na-Shiel and there it was before me, as it had been all those years before. For a second I squeezed my lids together, as though by concentrating I could wipe out the intervening years and bring Jamie forth from the pillared entrance, the dogs leaping around him. But it was Cesare who stood in the doorway, every inch the laird until you got up close and could see that the shoes were Gucci, the jeans designer and the shirt undoubtedly Italian.

I smiled at him, remembering Nella's final words as I left her at Heathrow. *Don't forget, darling – like the fox.* So I smiled a fox-like smile and let him enfold me in a bear hug. I gave first one cheek, then the other, to be kissed and moved, within the shelter of his arm, into the great hall.

'Where are they?' I said, looking around for the children.

'Alex and Fiona are at school. Imogen is with the nanny. She's from the village, but you'll like her.'

'Do they like her?' Something in me rebelled at the idea of Sara's children in the care of yet another woman, but what other alternative was there?

His tongue clicked against his teeth in mild reproval. 'Of course they like her, Lexy. Would she be here if they didn't?' He shook his head and took his arm from my shoulders. 'I take very good care of them, you know. For Sara's sake.'

I felt my mouth dry. If I didn't know how this man could lie I would believe him. Implicitly.

'Good,' I said and moved away to a chair by the fireplace. A moment later a woman appeared, bearing a tray of tea. I had never seen her before, and she didn't look like a Ballachulish villager.

'Here?' she said, nodding towards the sofa table.

'That's fine. Thank you.' He turned to me. 'This is Belsy. She's taken over from McGregor. Belsy, this is the children's aunt, Aunt Alexandra. If you are very good to her she may let you call her Aunt Lexy.' The woman smiled briefly and set down the tray. *He's enjoying this,* I thought and gave the woman as friendly a smile as I could muster. We were playing some kind of cat-and-mouse game here and as yet I didn't know the rules.

When she had left the room, I accepted the cup he held out to me and then, speaking as lightly as I could, I said, 'She seems nice. Does she come from the village?'

He shook his head. 'No. From Glasgow, I believe. I got her through an agency. She's efficient. Keeps herself to herself.'

I concentrated on my teacup, trying not to think what Nella would make of the woman. *A woman!* I could hear her voice rising. The woman had had the air of a former prison warder sacked for overzealous discipline, but Nella was bound to see her as a femme fatale. I was still seeking words to disabuse her when I heard the children's voices in the hal,l and a moment later they entered the room. Their eyes flicked over me and then turned to their stepfather. They moved towards him, and the next moment Imogen was on his knee and Fiona in the protective curve of his arm. Only Alex moved to me and gave his cheek for a kiss.

They're clinging to him, I thought, *because they're afraid he, too, will vanish.*

The girl with them was freckle-faced and bonny, her bosom straining the buttons of her flowered blouse. When Cesare introduced her as Kirsty she smiled with her eyes – not her mouth as the other woman had done, and I knew I was going to like her. He was making a great show of reminding the children who I was. It was only a few weeks since I'd seen them, but the girls seemed almost disinterested in me. Cesare was obviously the centre of their universe, and I struggled not to let my emotions show as I reached out to touch Fiona's smocked dress and tell her how pretty it was.

'Now,' he said, when the overtures were over. 'What shall we do with the rest of the day?' He turned to me. 'Are you tired?'

I shook my head. 'Not at all.'

In fact I was longing to go upstairs and lie down on my bed, but he obviously had something in mind. He looked at his watch.

'Shall we take Aunt Lexy to see the boat tomorrow?'

There was a chorus of approval from the children.

'It's settled then,' he said and gave the nanny leave to go.

'We're off to Moidart tomorrow, Kirsty,' he said. 'Take the morning off. We'll be back about six, in time for the children's bedtime. We'll see you then.'

She beamed all round and made her goodbyes to the children.

'Good,' Cesare said. 'Now we're alone we can plan our picnic.' He held out his hands, one to the children, one to me. Almost against my will I moved towards him. He caught my hand and pulled me close. 'It's good to have you here, dear Lexy. We've missed you.' He turned to the children. 'Haven't we?'

Alex nodded. 'Yes,' he said. 'It's good to see you again, Aunt Alex.'

He sounded suddenly so grown up and I felt my throat constrict.

We moved together, like a family, to the morning room. I had dreaded coming back to Ard-na-Shiel, but now all fear vanished. We spent the evening laughing over KerPlunk! and, when the little ones were in bed, over Scrabble with Alex. Once or twice our eyes met and his were warm and welcoming. I put my doubts to one side and let the peace of Ard-na-Shiel permeate my bones.

19

We discussed the boating expedition over the breakfast table. Cesare had decreed a day off school for Alex and Fiona in honour of my visit, and they were obviously looking forward to some fun. 'The boat is at Roshven,' he said, 'on the coast of Moidart, near Lochailort. We could go by way of Fort William but I think we'll take the Corran ferry today.' He beamed at the children and they beamed back. Obviously the ferry was a special treat.

We were packed and away by nine-thirty, piled into the Land Rover with a picnic hamper. We turned left when we reached the road and then right half a mile later. There was a steep ramp lined with waiting cars, and then the ferry came into view and began to disgorge its load. The children counted the cars and lorries as they toiled up the ramp and passed us.

'Twelve,' Fiona said, but Alex shook his head.

'Thirteen.'

They entered into a spirited argument over whether or not motorbikes counted as one or a half and Cesare caught my eye. *See?* his eyes seemed to say. *They're happy, aren't they?* And I couldn't deny that truth.

Then we were on the ferry, packed in rows of cars and vans with the boat rolling under us as we crossed the loch. It was narrow at this point, between Corran on the east side and Ardgour on the west. In only a few minutes, we were driving off and turning right onto the A-861.

The road ran alongside the loch. It was narrow – single-track mostly – with passing places and lined with hedgerows.

'Rhododendron,' Cesare said. 'In June you drive between aisles of blossom, pink, white and mauve, and yellow iris in the ditches.'

It sounded beautiful and he said it in the tones of a lover. Perhaps he had taken to Scotland after all. I looked out at the place names as we went. Trislaig, Camusnagaul.

'We're abreast of Fort William now,' Cesare said. 'When we turn, we'll be edging Loch Eil.'

The car was headed west once we turned and the road was more open with mountains either side. We passed through Glenfinnan, Loch Shiel on our left, and on to Ranochave. Loch Eil had petered out now and suddenly there was Lochailart and the Sound of Arisaig, the Cuillins in the background.

There were islands in the sea. 'Rhum and Eigg,' Cesare explained as the children chanted, giggling as they did so. This was obviously a regular joke. I simply gazed at a vision of paradise. 'Yes, it is beautiful,' Cesare said, as if he read my thoughts. And then we were at the boathouse and examining the smart little motorboat moored inside. I closed my eyes momentarily as I saw the name painted on its prow. *Sara's Dream.*

'How old is she?' I asked. The boat was eight or nine years old. That meant it had been Jamie's boat – Jamie's and Sara's. I felt my throat constrict at the thought of them sailing together, turning their faces to the wind, laughing into the spray...

'Come on, Lexy.' His hand was on my arm. 'Let's have lunch first and then we'll take her out.'

We picnicked on the rocks, sandwiches for the children, cold meat and salad for Cesare and me, washed down with red wine, and orange juice for the children. There was no time to muse as I cut off crusts for Imogen or wiped an orange moustache from Fiona's upper lip.

'Not only the good sister,' Cesare said indulgently, 'but the good aunt.'

I smiled, but the fact that I was enjoying myself was also a knife in my heart. For years I had blamed Sara for taking what was mine. Now I was taking what should have been hers.

After lunch we packed away the picnic and returned to the boat. 'No room for you, Lexy,' Cesare said apologetically. 'Usually I take all three children but today I'll leave Imogen to keep you company.' He bent to lift first Alex and then Fiona into the boat, helping them into life-jackets and firing up the outboard motor.

'Bye bye, Aunt Lexy.' Alex was waving as they moved out and away into the sound, beyond it the Atlantic Ocean.

As I watched the boat far out on the water, I couldn't help but feel peaceful. The lapping of the water soothed my fears so that for a little while I felt divorced from my worries. Cesare was in charge, calm and confident. The children carrying out their small duties were utterly content and Alex had the making of a fine little sailor. Surely this was what Sara would have wanted for her children? They went out for a mile or two, until the boat was a dot on the water. Even with binoculars I doubted I could have seen movement aboard. And then they were turning and heading for home.

I stood holding Imogen as Cesare and Alex made the boat secure at its moorings and then we walked off the jetty.

'Let me take her,' he said. 'She gets heavier as she gets sleepier.'

He was smiling the smile of an indulgent father and I felt my heart leap. If only it could be alright – if there were no mystery, no plot, no possibility of Sara's death being anything but a tragic accident. I surrendered Imogen to him, her head already lolling, and as he took her I felt his lips brush my cheek. It was no more than a feather-touch, but I felt my skin prickle.

'I'm glad you're here, Lexy,' he said and turned towards the place where we had left the car.

I would have been almost happy if it had not been for a little frisson of fear.

No room for you, Lexy, he had said. Only room for one man and three children. And once they were at sea no one else to see what happened – no one else at all.

'We'll come back tomorrow,' he promised, as the children clamoured for more.

And a chill descended upon me at the thought.

20

I awoke to the sound of rain drumming against the window and when I crossed to look out at the loch, I saw that its surface was lashed into foam. No sailing today, then, and I felt a sense of relief that rain would hold us all in the house for a day and give me time to think.

They were all at breakfast when I went down. The morning room was dark without sun streaming in at the window, and conversation round the table was muted. The nanny sat between the two younger children. Alex sat next to Cesare and the woman from Glasgow moved back and forth between table and sideboard, replenishing milk and toast, taking away the empty plates and filling cups from a silver-plated coffee pot. Sara had always had tea at breakfast time, but Sara was gone. I accepted my coffee meekly and buttered myself some toast.

Alex was looking anxiously at the clock, and eventually Cesare pushed back his chair. 'Time to go.' He turned to me. 'I'm taking Alex and Fiona to school. They might as well go as the weather is bad. I won't be long.'

When they'd gone, the atmosphere around the table seemed to ease. The nanny began to joke with Imogen, the other woman disappeared – to the kitchen presumably – and after a while we were sitting, elbows on table, enjoying childish chat.

When at last it was time to leave, I said, 'What happens now?'

Kirsty shook her head. 'We go for a walk usually, but not today.'

Outside the rain had eased, but it still ran in gentle zigzags across the window-panes.

'Let's go up to the nursery,' I suggested. 'We could do jigsaws.'

Imogen nodded excitedly.

The nursery was much as it had been in Sara's day: a fairyland mural on one wall, matching curtains at the window. We settled on the rug in front of the fireplace and Kirsty got out the jigsaws but when she put them down there was a shabby box on top of the pile.

'That's no' a jigsaw,' she said apologetically. 'I was clearing out the wee cupboard over there and it was tucked away. Young Alex said it was likely yours, so I put it by for you.'

I lifted the battered lid to reveal an album. The cover was faded but the title page was written in Sara's hand. Not the clear, incisive script of her adult years, but the still-unformed hand of a teenager. *Alexandra's Book,* it said, and there I was, smiling in my pram, demolishing the sandcastle she had made for me the year we went to Eastbourne, gap-toothed in my seventh year.

'Yes, it's mine,' I said and replaced the lid. Some impulse came over me then, to put it away before Cesare's return. They were only photographs, but they were private. I hurried to my room and put it in my case before I returned to settle down to jigsaws.

I was fitting the last piece into a Pokémon character when Cesare came back. He slumped down onto the floor and began to sort through the remaining pieces. It was obvious that he spent time here. He was perfectly at home, Imogen accepted his presence, Kirsty merely smiled at him briefly and got on with the puzzle. I thought of Nella's warning. *Don't let him get under your skin. He's a liar, Lexy. A liar and a murderer.* But it was impossible to believe this amiable bear of a man, crowing with triumph as he fitted a corner piece, could be either of those things.

We ate lunch, all of us together, and then Kirsty took Imogen upstairs for a nap.

'It's still raining,' Cesare said. He stood up and reached for my hand. 'Come!'

He pulled me to my feet and led the way across the great hall to the library. I looked round for the worn, leather chair that had enveloped me all those years ago but it was gone. At first I felt a pang of regret and then relief; I wouldn't have wanted to see anyone else sitting in Jamie's chair. I was glad, too, that the old dogs were dead and gone. They had been part of Jamie and not to be passed on. The books and the glowing panelling were still there, however, and dust shimmering in the pale sunshine. I closed my eyes for a moment and remembered. When I opened them, Cesare was stacking CDs into a music centre and a moment later Verdi filtered out into the room.

We sat for an hour, not talking except about the music. I felt myself relaxing with each mellow note. If only the past could be wiped out and I could be here with this man in this room, a sanctuary from the storm outside. I was indulging in a private daydream when the music clicked to a stop, and he looked at his watch

'Time to collect the children. How do you fancy seeing a film? The new Disney is on in Oban.'

I was carried away by his enthusiasm as he bounded upstairs to get Imogen dressed and then he was back, my coat over his arm.

'Come, *cara*,' he said. 'I don't like to keep them waiting.'

We ate pie and peas in an Oban café and then sat in the dark watching images flicker across the screen. Imogen sat half the time in her seat and half on Cesare's knee. Fiona sat beside him. Alex sat between us, small and intense, his hands on his knees, his eyes glued to the film. I felt a sudden surge of affection for this, my sister's child. I looked across him and saw that Cesare was watching me. Was that a smile on his lips? In the darkness I couldn't be sure.

Fiona was sleeping as we drove back to Ard-na-Shiel and I put a protective arm around her. Her head lolled against me, surprisingly heavy for such a little girl. Alex was wide awake.

'Did you enjoy it?' Cesare asked indulgently, and the boy and I answered together. 'Yes.'

Imogen was ready for bed when we got back.

'I'll just walk Kirsty and the dogs down to the village,' Cesare said when Imogen was tucked in. 'I asked Belsy to lay out some supper. Pour yourself some wine. I'll be back in fifteen minutes.'

I kissed Alex and Fiona goodnight and then they mounted the stairs, rubbing sleep from their eyes as they went.

There was cold salmon in the dining room, chunky potato salad and ciabatta bread in thick soft wedges. I poured myself wine from the bottle open in the ice bucket and switched on the television set by the fireplace. Belsy appeared in the doorway.

'Everything alright?' she said and without waiting for a reply. 'I'm away to my room then.'

She was at once polite and insolent. I couldn't work out what her attitude was except to know that I didn't like it much.

Cesare was as good as his word. Inside fifteen minutes he was pulling out my chair at the table, striking a match to light the candles in the middle and helping himself to wine. He sat opposite me and sipped appreciatively.

'I love children,' he said, 'but this moment, the moment they are safe in bed, is the best of the day.' He was smiling as he said it and I grinned.

'You sound like a harassed mother.'

'Not mother,' he said. 'Not harassed, either. I'm enjoying the children. They seem happy, don't they?'

He was wooing me with his eyes and I felt myself melt. We would eat and drink and talk and afterwards, unless I was careful, make love. I could see it there in his eyes, in the way his fingers caressed the stem of his wineglass. I struggled to remain sensible.

'I might as well be honest,' I said suddenly. 'Nella has employed a private detective. We know the house in Via Furnese isn't yours and never was.'

If I had expected to shock him, I was disappointed.

He nodded solemnly. 'And?' was all he said.

I raised my glass to my lips to buy time. 'And what?'

He shook his head indulgently. 'Oh, Lexy, Lexy: let's not play cat and mouse.'

I dabbed my lips with my napkin before I answered. 'We know your mother worked there. Was she the woman who was there the day you took me to the house? And the estate – the one you had been forced to let go?'

My voice sounded more sarcastic than I had intended.

'Is that all?' His voice was quite flat and I wanted to rise from my chair and batter some emotion out of him.

'For the moment,' I said. 'He's still working on it.'

'Why does your mother hate me, Lexy?'

He sounded genuinely distressed.

'Because you lie, Cesare. You lie about everything. 'You've always lied: to me, to my mother. For all I know to Sara.'

'No!' This time his voice rang out. 'I never lied to Sara. I lied to you for Sara's sake – because I was penniless, a nobody. She wanted you to like me, to accept me. But she knew the truth and she accepted it.'

He pushed back his chair and stood up. Almost automatically I followed suit.

'You have to believe me, Lexy. Sara and I loved one another. And I miss her. I wake with her name on my lips – urgent, because I can't find her. But she's gone, Lexy. Sara is gone but we are here, you and I.'

Our chairs were three yards apart and yet the distance between us seemed to disappear. Suddenly, his arms came round me, pulling, kneading as he tried to draw comfort. And I was lifting my own arms to his neck and cradling his head in my hands.

'There,' I said. 'There, there.'

When he kissed me, I felt his tongue gentle against my lips, flickering, probing. I opened my mouth and let him enter me. My lips felt weak and only his arms supported me.

What would have happened then I don't know, but far off I heard a child cry out. For a moment his mouth slackened on mine and I pulled away. His eyes were clouded and dark.

'That's Imogen,' he said.

'I'll go.'

I left him standing there, slightly breathless, his head hanging forward like someone winded. As I sped up the stairs towards the crying, I felt a sense of relief and then, straight afterward, a bitter sense of disappointment that I could not, must not, descend the stairs again.

Instead, when I had settled Imogen I went to my room and took out the album. My whole life was in there: photographs, school reports, a cutting from the *Standard* when I had won a competition. All saved by the sister who had loved me and who I had never loved enough. Her love was there in the notes under each item. *Lexy scores again* as I posed with a croquet mallet. *Lexy tames the wild beast* as I wrestled with the ancient poodle which was all our grandparents left us. And it was there in a letter begun in 1990 and never sent. My last year at school – the year that Sara had met Jamie and the sky had fallen.

Dear Lexy, it began. *The house is quiet since you went back. Roll on half-term. I miss you when you are away. No one to pinch my best shoes or leave the lid off my face cream. No Lexy to share my weak jokes or make cinder-toffee at half-past ten at night. Seriously, kid, I do miss you and I'm very proud of the way you are growing up. I can hear you snorting when you read this and covering your ears but a bit of mush between sisters is…*

Here the letter petered out. Something must have disturbed her and it was never sent. I laid it carefully upon a snap of her and me together and closed the book.

21

I rang Nella before I went down to breakfast. She sounded miffed.

'I thought you'd ring last night. I waited up.'

How could I tell her why I hadn't felt able to pick up the phone? I couldn't even analyze my emotions myself. When Nella or Bob Gray pointed out the facts, I agreed – I *knew* – that Cesare was at least a liar and a cheat. When I was with him, alone or with the children… it was different.

'It was late when I came to bed. I didn't want to wake you.' Before she could break in I hurried on. 'He was talking quite freely and I didn't want to interrupt the flow.'

'Well…' She was a little mollified but not much. 'Mr Gray is coming back today. He told me to warn you to be on your guard. He means it, Lexy. He says be careful.'

'But why is Carlo keeping me here?' I sounded anguished and I was. They didn't see what I was seeing, didn't recognize the temptations – and he wanted me here. That much was clear.

'*Carlo*?' Nella's tone was dry. 'So he's *Carlo* now, is he? How sweet. Perhaps he's keeping you there because he wants a witness, Alexandra. Have you thought of that? I've been talking to a doctor, Lexy – a pharmacologist, whatever that is. Anyway, she specializes in drug abuse. She says paranoia can be induced in three ways: chemically, surgically or psychologically. Perhaps he didn't lay a finger on her, but it was because he didn't need to. He'd already done his worst. Anyway, I'm coming to Glasgow. Today. Ring me on my mobile later and I'll tell you where I'm staying. I want to be close by.'

I stayed at the window after I put down the phone. The loch was calm now and the sun was shining. The view exuded peace.

How could I contemplate scheming – even murder – on a day like this? But suddenly a picture flashed into my mind: a swollen body beneath a window. I turned away and went downstairs.

I could almost smell the excitement as I approached the breakfast table.

'We're going out on the boat!' Alex said. 'A whole day! Belsy is packing a picnic.' For a second his face clouded. 'Will you be alright by yourself? On the shore, I mean. You should come with us.'

'Of course she will come with us.' Carlo's voice was warm as syrup. 'And she won't be on the shore all the time; we'll take turns. Now, upstairs and get your things. We're wasting good sailing time.'

I had buttered myself some toast but it was proving difficult to chew. 'Is it safe on the water?' I said. 'They're very small.'

He put out a hand and covered mine. '*Cara*: would I take them anywhere dangerous? They have life-jackets. I'm with them. We are never far from shore. And you are there. You, the bold Aunt Lexy. You would swim out and save them.' He was laughing at me and I felt foolish. Everything he said was true. 'You *can* swim, can't you?' His eyes were quizzical.

'A bit. Just breast-stroke – school stuff. I suppose you swim well?'

He shook his head. 'Just like you. I can do enough. Still, don't worry: no one is going swimming. We're in a boat, remember? Now, stop playing with your toast and let's get away before the heavens decide to cry again. Mustn't waste a good Saturday.'

I went upstairs to collect a windcheater and change my shoes. I could hear the children laughing in their rooms and outside the sun was shining. It seemed impossible to think of anything criminal on such a day. My heart leaped a little – we were going to have a nice day. Everything would be alright. Yes, he was a rogue and a chancer, but life had made him that way. Now that he had no need to lie and cheat, he wouldn't do it.

I slipped out of my shoes and padded over to the window where my trainers were lying. The loch was still calm and smiling and down below, in the yard, the Land Rover was waiting. I was turning away when I saw him coming towards the vehicle. He carried a picnic hamper which he loaded into the boot then he straightened up and looked around him.

There was something animal-like in the movement, a craning of his neck from side to side. The next moment he reached inside his jacket and brought out a bundle. I couldn't see anything except that it was quite long and wrapped in some sort of cloth, perhaps towelling. The next moment he had leaned into the boot to place it, straightened up, closed the boot and turned back to the house.

I turned away, too, trying to convince myself that what I had seen was someone packing a car boot for a picnic. But in my heart I knew it was more. I went out onto the landing to find Cesare mounting the stairs.

'Ready?' He was smiling, his face alight with anticipation of a happy day ahead.

'Yes,' I said. 'I've got everything here. I'm just going to check on the kids. Do you know where they are?'

He was past me now and moving along the landing. 'They're downstairs somewhere. I won't be long.' As soon as he was out of sight I sped down the stairs, across the hall and out into the courtyard, praying all the while that he hadn't locked the boot.

To my relief, it gave to my fingers and I leaned over the picnic basket. A folded rug, a jerrycan, some tools – and then the bundle. I moved the ragged towelling surrounding it and saw what was there. It was a snorkelling tube and a face mask. I stood for a moment, half anti-climaxed, half puzzled. The coast was not the place for snorkelling. The water was cold and the bottom too deep for cursory exploration. I closed the boot and moved back into the shelter of the house.

Denise Robertson

I was still standing there when the children came tumbling out of the door carrying their assortment of toys. I put out my hand to Imogen and felt her small hand slip into mine. They were all small, all vulnerable – even Alex who tried so hard to be a man.

And suddenly I saw it all. The boat just far enough out to prevent intervention from the shore. A little injudicious stalling of the engine and over it would go. Three children in the water and one man with the equipment needed to swim underwater. Easy enough to don it in the lee of the capsized boat. One by one the children going down, no sign of Cesare. Just me on the shore to say how very accidental it had been. He could swim away when it was done, underwater without a ripple breaking the surface. And then, while boats searched and helicopters hovered, he'd struggle ashore somewhere, dazed and distraught, begging to know that the children were safe. That was why he had made me so welcome. He needed an unimpeachable witness.

Could it be true? It was too fantastic to be true. Except... except that I couldn't afford to put it to the test. I had to stop the trip to Moidart. I looked at Alex.

'Hey, I think we need more grub. Could you go and ask Belsy for some biscuits?'

He went willingly enough and as soon as he was too far away to say he didn't want them, I sent the other two scampering after him.

The next minute I was crouching by the side of the Land Rover. The valves were stiff to my fingers but I persevered. One, two, three, four – by the time the children came back, Carlo bringing up the rear, the Land Rover was down on its rims, and best of all, it was blocking the entrance to the garages. No vehicle would be leaving Ard-na-Shiel for quite some time.

I would have felt a sense of relief if it had not been for the sight of Kirsty, over by the corner of the house. How long she had been there I did not know but I knew what her eyes were saying.

'Why have you sabotaged the children's day out?'

Cesare came into the courtyard then.

'What the hell ...?'

I stood there, knowing guilt was written all over my face, waiting for Kirsty to speak up and denounce me. He was bending down, first at one tyre, then another.

'So that's it ...' He stood up, dusting his hands, looking over to the garage entrance. 'I'll have to get someone out from Oban.'

He bent down again. 'How did it happen?' He was feeling the tyres, probing the treads for punctures. Surely now she would speak up. I snatched a glance at her. She looked troubled but she stayed silent.

Cesare stood up again and turned towards the house. 'Tell the children the trip to the boat is off. We'll do it tomorrow.'

A second later he was gone. Kirsty was turning away, too, as though to follow him.

'Kirsty,' I called her name. 'Please. I know you saw me. I had to do it. I had a reason. Will you let me explain?' For a moment she hesitated, uncertain whether to follow Cesare or to listen to me.

'Please. If you let me explain, you'll understand. Look, let's get the children, we can take them for a walk. I'll explain then. If you don't believe me you can tell Mr Giulini when we get back.'

Another hesitation and then she nodded. 'I'll get the children.'

We walked down the drive and crossed the road towards the loch. I waited until the children were well ahead of us and then I spoke. 'You never knew my sister –'

She interrupted me then. 'I did. Since I was a wee girl. My mother worked for Mr Jamie, and then for Miss Sara.'

'Then you know how – how –' I was seeking the right word and she supplied it.

'She was very kind. My mother liked working for her until...'

Now it was her turn to hesitate and I carried on.

'I think someone poisoned my sister – that's what you were going to say: that she changed. I think someone fed her drugs. Not enough to kill her, but enough to make her sick and very unhappy.'

'But she was a doctor? We couldn't understand why she got – like she did. Some people said it was a tumour. And…' She licked her lips. 'They said it was a tumour and they couldn't operate and so she killed herself.'

'There was nothing the matter with her, Kirsty. They proved that at the inquest. She had drugs in her system and they'd caused some changes, but there was nothing else. Besides, I'm not sure that she killed herself. I don't know for certain but I think there might have been someone else there when she died.' I was careful not to mention names but I could see that what I was saying was fully understood.

'I'm frightened for the children. I'm afraid they might come to harm. That's why I had to stop the trip today. I don't think they're safe out on the water – they're too little. I can't risk it.'

'He'd never hurt the children. He worships them!' She was shocked now and disinclined to believe me.

'Look,' I seized her arm. 'Can we go and talk to your mother? Let's see what she thinks.'

I saw her slight frown disappear to be replaced by a half-smile. 'Yes,' she said. 'Mammy will know what's best.'

We called the children then and turned towards Ballachulish, making conversation as the children came abreast and walked alongside us. We walked Indian style across the bridge and then cut down into the village, getting some curious glances as we went. The Munro children on foot in the village was not a common sight and I was a stranger. It was a relief when we turned in at a white-painted gate and up a path bordered with marigolds.

'Mammy' was small and bright-eyed and at first a little flustered, snatching washing from a clothes-horse by the fire and whisking newspapers and slippers out of sight. I sat in an armchair and agreed to have a cup of tea. Kirsty was shepherding the children out of the single living room and into the back garden.

'They'll be away to see the rabbits,' her mother said complacently. I wondered how long that mood would last once I told her why we had come.

In a few moments tea and cake and creamy drop scones were laid on a small table and she sat down to pour. Kirsty came back into the room then.

'They've got the wee 'uns out in the run. They'll be alright for a while.' She sat down between us and reached for a cup. Our eyes met and she nodded. So I was going to have to broach the subject.

'This is going to sound crazy,' I said carefully, 'but I need – I desperately need you to believe me.'

They both listened while I outlined our suspicions, mine and Nella's.

'So you see why I had to stop the trip today?' I sounded as desperate as I felt. Even to my own ears it seemed insubstantial. How could I expect her to believe me, a stranger?

'I always wondered,' the older woman said at last. 'He was awful fine, but I always wondered. What are you going to do now? He'll have the wheels mended by the morrow morn.'

I nodded. 'My mother's coming. She'll be here by tonight. She'll know what to do. In the meantime, I need Kirsty to keep quiet about the tyres.'

'He'll know.' She shook her head ruefully. 'Four tyres canna be accidental. He's bound to know it was you. He'll be aye watching.'

'I know. But as long as he doesn't know for sure he won't bring it into the open. So please, please: will you just keep quiet about it? At least until my mother gets here?'

The woman took one more sip from her cup then she put it back on the tray. 'Our Kirsty will say nothing. But that's all she can do, mind. She canna get mixed up in anything.' She turned to her daughter. 'You're no' to say anything. Just keep your eye on the bairns.' I would have thanked her but she waved my thanks away. 'Just see to Miss Sara's bairns, that's all. She was a fine lady and that 'yun did her no good – no good at all.'

I had to carry Imogen on the way back to Ard-na-Shiel, and by the time we got to the foot of the drive, the other children were lagging behind. Cesare came out onto the drive to greet us.

'Where have you been? It's past lunchtime.' He was smiling as he said it, and I saw that he had regained his composure. 'It's a pity about the trip. I can't imagine what happened to the tyres but they're fixing it now so we can go tomorrow.'

Did I imagine it or were his eyes twinkling, as though we were sharing some private joke?

It was a struggle to eat the food put before me. Belsy kept up a constant muttering about food being spoiled, but I had no appetite. It was a relief when I could escape to my bedroom and close the door. I sat on the bed to punch Nella's mobile number into my phone and a moment later I heard her voice.

'Lexy? Is that you?'

'Oh Mum,' I said. 'Where are you?'

'We're passing Carlisle now, darling. Hang in there, that's a good girl. We'll be in Glasgow in a couple of hours and then we're coming to get you. Don't talk now. I'll ring you at seven p.m. Be sure you're alone then. And don't worry. We'll be with you soon.'

I had put down the phone before it occurred to me to wonder who she had meant when she said, '*We'll* be with you soon.'

22

Somehow we got through the afternoon. The children were still tired after their long walk and inclined to whinge about the lost trip to Moidart, but Cesare was endlessly patient, cajoling and entertaining by turns. We ate high tea in the morning room, all of their favourite foods on his orders. I felt rather than saw Kirsty's eyes on me, questioning whether or not this man could be a threat to the children he was even now dandling on his knee. I had to force myself to remember one unpleasant picture after another: his face utterly sincere on that Roman hillside when he had told me he would not marry Sara; her face bloated and strange inside the body-bag; most of all the snorkel nestling in the boot of the Land Rover.

But even as I thought these things I was making excuses. He had meant what he had said in Rome, Sara had changed his mind. He had tried to wean her off the tablets that had brought about her downfall. And the snorkel could be there for perfectly ordinary reasons. If only we could have proved some real connection to Mary Logan, or find positive proof that the fire in Soley Street had been deliberately set – but we couldn't and I was left in limbo.

The meal was over and we were playing a last round of Snap when Belsy came into the room and suddenly something clicked. Mary Logan, the woman who had gone under the bus outside the Glasgow Church, had reminded me of someone. Now I knew who.

I felt a cold sweat break out on my brow and my hands holding the Snap cards were trembling.

'Lexy?' Cesare was looking at me, half smiling, half curious. 'It's your turn!'

I mumbled an apology and managed to stumble through the rest of the game.

Alex elected to stay downstairs with Cesare while Kirsty and I took the girls upstairs to bathe. I had my eye on the clock. Half-past six. In half an hour I could confide my suspicions to Nella. Cesare came with us to the foot of the stairs and kissed the girls tenderly.

'Goodnight, *cara mia*. Go straight to sleep. We're going sailing tomorrow so you need your rest.' He smiled at me then and his eyes were warm and soft with sentiment. I felt my heart leap – and then I remembered Sara's face and turned away.

Once we were all safe in the bathroom and the water gushing from the taps I steadied my voice and spoke to Kirsty.

'How long has Belsy been here?'

She looked up at me, wrinkling her brow. 'She came a long time ago. Last summer. She was here for a while, for a few months. But she didn't see eye to eye with Mr McGregor. She went away then.'

'And she came back?'

'Some time after Mrs Munro died. Aye, I remember because she was here when we finally cleared out all the mistress's clothes.'

'Tell me,' I tried to keep my voice steady. 'Does she go to church?'

Kirsty shook her head. 'No, I've never seen her in church.' Her face lit up. 'Anyway, she's Catholic. She mentioned it once. Said she didn't agree with the Pope all the time but she was still a Catholic.'

A Catholic! Like the woman in Soley Street. Were they sisters? Cousins? Bob Gray would be able to find out.

'What's her surname?'

Kirsty's thought hard for a moment. 'It's Belsy – Belsy – Leckie!' She finished triumphantly. 'Isabel Leckie.'

I left her to finish the bathing and went to my bedroom to wait for Nella's call. It came at seven on the dot.

'I'm here,' she said.

'Where?'

She sounded a long way away.

'Here,' she answered. 'We're not far away from you.'

'Who's *we*?' There was a pause and then she said, 'Never mind. Just someone who's helping me.'

'One of your men,' I said stupidly.

'Yes.' There was a chuckle in her voice. 'You could say that.'

I was so anxious to tell her my suspicions that I let it go. I would find out which besotted admirer she had called on in due course.

'Listen, Mum. Cesare's got a woman working here called Belsy – McGregor's replacement,' I said, cupping my hand round the mouthpiece although there was no one within earshot.

Nella was alert now. 'Yes.'

I lowered my voice even further. 'Tell Mr Gray to check her out. She looks – well, she reminds me of Mary Logan. There might be a connection. Her surname is Leckie – Isabel Leckie. But tell him to hurry!'

'OK. Calm down. What's happening now?'

I tried to concentrate. 'Cesare's downstairs with Alex. Fiona and Imogen are in the bath – Kirsty's with them. But we're going sailing tomorrow unless the weather breaks.'

I didn't mention the snorkel in the boot and even as I passed over it I wondered why.

'You can't go, Lexy. You must stop it. It's only for a little while. One day, two at the most and then we'll have you out of there. But you mustn't risk anything in the meantime.'

'Why can't we go now?' I was twisting the flex in my fingers, almost cutting off the circulation. 'Come now – please.'

'It's not that easy, Lexy. We can't just walk in the door and abduct those children.'

'Why not?' My tone was petulant as the strain told.

'No.' Nella's voice was firm. 'He'd be within his legal rights to prevent us taking the children – I've checked. We've got to get them out of there, Lexy, and keep them hidden until Bob comes up with something conclusive. But it can't be done tonight. Tomorrow, perhaps. We're making plans.'

'I don't know how I can keep them away from the water...'

Again I thought of the snorkel and again I didn't mention it.

'Well, you must. Do whatever you have to do. Now, how will you get out of there?'

'I don't know. We can't go out at the front and all the other doors lead to the courtyard and then back to the drive. He'd see us. And I couldn't hurry them. I'd carry Imogen, but Fiona's so small – and they might not want to come.'

'Can you come down the bank? Out of the windows at the back of the house and down through the trees?'

'I'm not sure. It's a steep bank. And in the dark?'

'Lexy! Don't be defeatist. Can you or can't you? Tomorrow he's taking them out to sea and even if you stop him there's another day. Dare you risk it?'

'No.' She was right; I daren't risk it.

'Where will you be?'

And all of a sudden I heard Jamie's voice, that day by the loch: *That bank is steep but it can be climbed,* and I knew we would be alright.

'We'll be directly below the walled garden. I'll make sure of that.'

Nella was into her stride now, issuing orders. 'Wherever you get out, make straight for the wall and then come straight down. It's not as steep there as it is towards the other end of the house.'

By the time I put down the phone we knew what we were doing. I only needed a time. There was one snag: I could carry Imogen, and Fiona would come if I asked her. Alex was a different matter.

If he refused or – worse still – threatened to tell his stepfather, what would I do? I put my worries resolutely aside and went back to the bathroom.

Alex was coming up the stairs when I went out onto the landing.

'Off to bed?' I said pleasantly, conscious that Cesare was probably listening at the foot of the stairs. The boy held up his face to be kissed and I took it between my hands. 'Do you know how precious you are, Alex?' He grinned sheepishly but he didn't pull away. I kissed his forehead and let him go. There were things I had to do before I took him into my confidence.

I found Cesare in the library, stacking the music centre.

'I thought we'd have some wine and listen to some music.' He turned to me as the first strains of music filtered out.

'Songs from the Auvergne,' I said. 'Maria Callas?'

He shook his head. 'Victoria de los Angeles. The best.'

He was close enough for me to smell him: a faint, pleasant odour of soap and wine. I could smell it on his breath as his mouth came down on mine. And even as I closed my eyes so as not to see his face I felt my own mouth surrendering to his.

'I must see to the children,' I said when he released me. 'I promised to tuck them in, but I'll be down as soon as I can.'

I put all the promise I could muster into my words and he smiled as he put out a finger to touch my cheek.

'Hurry, *cara*. Hurry, please.'

I mounted the stairs slowly, my mouth still moist from his kiss. I felt as though I was in a hall of mirrors now, first thin then thick then thin again, depending which way I turned. Upstairs I sluiced my face with cold water and ran a comb through my hair. If I stuck to one thing at a time I would manage. I kissed the children goodnight and then made my way back downstairs. Somehow, by hook or by crook, I had to stop tomorrow's expedition and this time I had a feeling the tyres would be well-protected.

The music was still playing when I returned to the library. He held out a glass of wine and motioned to a seat. 'Dinner won't be long. Come and sit by me.'

I moved obediently to him, rehearsing my excuses for taking the children somewhere else tomorrow. And then he spoke.

'I've been thinking,' he said. 'Let's not go to Moidart tomorrow. I fancy a day closer to home. I don't want to go out in the boat and leave Aunt Lexy alone on the shore.'

I felt weak with relief until I realized that he was playing with me, teasing me. He must have seen me looking in the boot. Or perhaps he knew I had let down the tyres? Or perhaps it was all a sad misjudgement of him after all. If he did know, he gave no sign of it. We went in to dinner when Belsy summoned us and he played the perfect host, finally seeing me to my room on the stroke of midnight.

'Goodnight, little sister,' he said, and this time when he kissed me, I did not pull away.

23

His back was smooth under my hands, rippling with muscle like a snake. I parted my thighs and felt him enter me, sighing with satisfaction as we fused and began to move together. Rhythmically. Slowly at first then faster, faster. *Yes!* I woke as he exploded inside me and stretched my empty arms to the wide bed.

I was alone.

Humiliated, I turned on my side and curled my knees into my belly. Had it been Jamie in the dream? Or Rick? Or some imagined hero? But in my heart I knew it had been Cesare, and the words in my ear had been his words, sibilant and soft.

He was there at the breakfast table when I had washed away the odours of imagined sex and came down the wide stair. I could hear the children chattering as I joined them.

'We're going on a boat!' Imogen said happily.

I looked towards Cesare. He was buttering toast for Fiona and he looked up and smiled. 'We're not going to Moidart today. We're taking a boat on the loch, Lexy. A nice little boat on the nice quiet loch. With room for us all.'

I slid into my chair and reached for my napkin. 'That's nice,' I said, and smiled at the three expectant faces. Cesare did not look at me. He poured coffee for me but he did not meet my eye.

'It's an old boat,' he said, and then to Imogen: 'Chug-chug.' She squealed with delight. Obviously 'chug-chug' meant something.

I understood when we had trooped down to the shore and waded out to the *Alla-Beg*. She was a broad-beamed boat fitted with an outboard motor, and when we were safe aboard, the engine gave out a satisfying *chug-chug*, much to Imogen's delight.

Away to the right I could see the Corran ferry. Cesare took us out to the middle of the loch, but we could clearly see both shores. I relaxed a little. If we could see them, then they could see us. No spot for an accident. Besides, he had fastened each child's life-jacket, tugging the straps home, and I could swim moderately well.

'Now,' he said, 'shall we head for Fort William or down to Ballachulish?'

Before we could answer he had turned the boat for the head of the loch and we were away.

The sun was strong but there was a breeze over the surface of the water. I felt myself relax as we moved between the shores. Tiny white houses here and there, hotels probably, and beyond them, the peaks covered in scree and heather.

I was holding tight to Imogen as the boat gathered speed. Alex was close by Cesare, his face turned into the wind, a look of determination on his face. He looked so like his father, or as his father must have looked on this loch thirty years ago. I felt a wave of nostalgia, and then Cesare was reaching out his hand to me.

'Come forward, *cara*. Come here beside me.'

I shook my head and grasped Imogen even more firmly lest she be tempted. But it was Fiona who stood up from her wooden seat and began to move towards him.

'Careful,' I said, but Cesare was laughing and holding out his hand. She came abreast of her brother, hesitated for a second and then stepped onto the wooden shelf that ran around the boat. Her feet in their tiny trainers wobbled, righted themselves and then he had her hand, was hauling her to safety. And then suddenly she was in the water, a blur of bright red shirt and life-jacket, her head – her blonde Sara head – sinking suddenly into its navy folds.

I screamed then and Cesare opened his mouth, shouting in

anguish at me to take the tiller. I moved, still clutching Imogen, lurching as the boat rocked, grasping a tiller which bucked in my hand and he was diving, like the heron at the Falls of Orchy, to emerge thirty yards away with Fiona in his grasp.

How I turned the boat around I do not know. Alex helped me, slowing the engine so that it idled until we came abreast of the pair in the water. I thrust Imogen at her brother and leaned to haul the child from the water. Cesare pulled himself over the side as we leaned back to counteract his weight. And then he was shaking himself like a seal and we were heading for home.

'You saved her life,' I said, as Imogen whimpered against me.

'No.' He shook his head impatiently. 'No. I almost lost her life. My fault, Lexy. My stupid fault.'

He was subdued as he carried the girls ashore, brightening only when everyone was warm and dry and Belsy had laid out a meal in the morning room. I watched him almost croon over Fiona, calling her his brave girl, and knew he could never ever harm these children. We put them to bed together, reading stories to the little ones, praising Alex for his seamanship and leaving him to devour his *Harry Potter*.

Then we walked along the landing, side by side. Not speaking because there was nothing to be said.

That night I did not sleep alone.

24

He was not there when I woke in the morning. I lay for a moment, trying to remember last night. We had checked on the children, seen Fiona sleeping none the worse for her ordeal, and then we had moved as one to my room. The curtains weren't drawn and we didn't put on the light. Instead we undressed slowly, standing in the moonlight that lay across the loch and the garden and streamed through the window until it touched the bed.

We climbed aboard the moon trail and made love. He was a tender lover but as he touched me, roused me, entered me and lifted me to a loud climax, I knew there had been many women. The whisper of his lips across my ear, the way he lifted and turned me and took me again... for him it was a well-travelled road.

Now, in the morning light, I thought about his lovemaking. Shivering first with guilt that I had done it at all, then that I had enjoyed it and then, drawing up my knees and turning on my side, shivering with pleasure at the memory.

It was laughter that got me out of bed. Children's laughter. They were down in the walled garden and Cesare was throwing a ball for them, feinting so that they ran hither and thither in anticipation and then, when it left his hand, racing to see who could catch it first. I realized I was smiling foolishly and hurried to get dressed. Before I went downstairs I phoned Nella.

'Lexy?' She sounded alarmed. 'There's nothing wrong is there? We're almost ready – you can come now. Tonight.'

'No.'

My voice was sharp.

'No, Mum, you're wrong about Cesare. I know that now. We

need to talk – now, this morning. There's a hotel in Glencoe; you can't miss it. When can you get there?'

'What do you mean, "we're wrong"?'

I told her then, about Fiona's fall from the boat and the way he had rescued her.

'So you see, he does care about them.'

For a moment there was silence and then Nella sighed.

'Oh, Lexy, Lexy. How did she fall? Was she, by any chance, somewhere near him? And she just toppled in – and there he was, Sir Galahad saving the day. Think how that will sound in court. "He couldn't have drowned them, m'lud, because he'd already saved their lives". And you'll make the perfect character witness, my poor, deluded little daughter. We're coming for you, Lexy, you and the children. Now, tonight – before he brainwashes you even further.'

'You're wrong,' I said. 'Completely wrong.'

I put down the phone but I felt suddenly dispirited. No matter what course my life and his would take, Nella would remain remorseless. I stood for a moment, wondering if I should ring her again and try once more to make her see sense. In the end, I walked out into the sunshine to join the children.

Almost as soon as I reached the garden it began to rain, huge drops that splashed and soaked. I felt it run into my hair and collect and trickle down my forehead. It felt cleansing and I stood still, waiting for the children who were screaming with delight at the downpour and running for the shelter of the house.

We spent the afternoon playing games in the library while rain lashed the windows and dripped sonorously from the eaves. Tea was egg and chips – a rare treat for a wet day – and after it we watched a Disney video, *The Hunchback of Notre-Dame*, which enchanted Fiona and held Alex's attention but left poor Imogen bemused. At last Kirsty decreed bedtime and shooed them upstairs.'

'We'll come up and tuck you in,' Cesare said indulgently. 'Hurry up now. Tomorrow it will be sunny and we'll go to Moidart and sail the boat.'

When they had gone he moved to my side. 'Happy?' he said, reaching for my hand. I nodded. He stood up then, pulling me to my feet.

'I want to make love to you, Lexy. Is that wrong of me?'

I shook my head. 'I want it, too.' I moved into the circle of his arms and they closed around me. I felt safe with my face against his chest, feeling his heartbeat. We would have kissed then but the phone shrilled out. He released me and moved to lift the receiver.

'Ah yes. She's here.' He held out the phone. 'It's your mother.'

I took the phone from him and he moved away. 'Lexy? Please listen. We're down on the road below you. A dark-blue Mercedes. You *must* come. Come down the bank if you can't bring the children out by the door. We'll help you. But come, for God's sake. Mr Gray has found out about that woman. Her name is Isabel Leckie but she was born Isabel Logan. *Logan*, Lexy. Mary Logan is her sister.'

I stood, uncertain of what I should do or say.

'Did you hear me, Lexy? Her name is Logan. She was dismissed from the Prison Service for some offence – we don't know what yet. After that she worked in a bar. He probably met her there. You've got to get out, Lexy. Come now, quickly, before its too late.'

I put down the phone then and turned. Cesare stood with his back to me, pouring gin into two glasses.

'Everything OK?' he said.

I licked lips that had gone dry. 'Yes, fine. She's in London, working hard.'

He moved towards me and held out a glass. 'I like your mother. In spite of everything, I like her. Will she ever like me?'

'Of course.'

I was battling madly for time to think. Could it be more coincidence that the woman from Soley Street had a sister working at Ard-na-Shiel? Coincidence or not, I couldn't take the risk.

I made some excuse about a bath and went upstairs. My fingers felt numb as I fumbled with my phone.

'Are you still there?'

She was and I almost cried with relief.

'I'm coming,' I said. 'We'll be there in twenty minutes.'

I went out onto the landing to see Cesare at the head of the stairs. 'We forgot to say goodnight,' he said and walked ahead of me to Alex's room. He was sitting at his desk playing a computer game. We said goodnight and made him promise not to be too long before he went to bed and then we moved to the girls' room. There was much kissing and arms wound tight around our necks, and then we went back to the landing.

'I'm going to take a jog now the rain has stopped,' Cesare said. My heart leaped. 'It'll be wet underfoot but I need the exercise. Why not pour us both a drink? I'll get back as quickly as I can.'

'Don't hurry.' I poured what I hoped sounded like lust into my voice. 'I want to get a long, long bath before I join you.'

He hesitated for a moment and then he nodded. 'You're right, *serenissima*. But don't be too long.' His lips brushed my hair. 'I need you, Lexy. Don't keep me waiting.'

I looked into his face and smiled. 'I'll hurry. Pour a glass of wine when you get back. I'll be there before you need another.'

It was suddenly easy to lie to him.

When I got back to the girls' bedroom they were dressed in pyjamas and dressing gowns. Kirsty was folding their clothes and I put out a hand to stop her. 'We've got to get them dressed, Kirsty. Please help me. I've got to get them out of here now!'

For a moment I thought she was going to refuse and then she picked up Imogen's dungarees.

'Come on, wee'un. You're going for a nice walk.'

I left her dressing the children and made my way to Alex's room. He was still sitting in front of his computer but he turned as I came in.

'I need to talk to you, Alex. It's very important.' I sat down on the edge of the bed. 'I'm going to tell you things you may not want to believe. But you have to believe me, darling, because I need you to help me.'

I had his attention now but the tone of my voice had alarmed him and he looked more than ever like a baby. I tried to speak calmly, giving him a watered-down version of the truth, not enough to shock him, just enough to make him believe we had to go. When I came to the end of my tale he didn't speak. He didn't look at me in the eye, either, and I knew that meant he didn't fully believe me.

Kirsty came into the room then and his eyes flickered with relief. She moved towards him and held out her hand. 'Get ready, Alex. Fiona and Imogen need you. You have to go.'

There was a long moment's hesitation and I felt despair engulfing me.

'Please,' I said. 'Granny is waiting for you on the road. In a Mercedes.'

He looked at Kirsty again. 'Should I go?' he said and his voice was trembling.

'Yes.' She was calm and measured, more like a woman of forty than a teenager. 'It's best you go with your aunt and grandma. They'll sort everything out and then you'll be back. Be a good lad, now, and wrap up warm.'

When the children were dressed we shepherded them onto the landing. 'Stay here,' I said and moved to the head of the stairs. To get to a window which gave onto the bank above the road we would have to navigate the stairs, cross the hall and get into the morning room. And at any minute Cesare might come through the front door.

I stood for a second, deliberating, then I swallowed deeply to summon up my courage.

'Now,' I said. 'As quick as you can.'

I don't think I drew breath as we descended the stairs. At any moment Cesare might arrive or Alex might rebel or Imogen cry out. Her eyes were wide in a frightened face. She didn't know what was going on but whatever it was she didn't like it.

It seemed to take an age to descend the creaking stairs. I could hear Kirsty's agitated breathing as she hurried the children along and then we were through the morning room door and Kirsty was closing it behind us. For the moment at least, we were safe.

I looked at my watch as I tucked the pocket torch into my jeans. Seven-forty. 'We have to hurry,' I said. Any moment Cesare would come in search of me. I looked at Kirsty. 'Once we're safely out of here, get out. When he finds we've gone, he might blame you.'

'Don't worry about me. I'll be away home before long, likely. Now, out you go.'

I waited until the moon went behind a cloud and then I went first, lowering myself from the sill until my feet touched solid ground. I had pulled on a sweater but the dampness still chilled me. Alex came next, scrambling over the sill and dropping easily to the ground. Imogen began to whimper as Kirsty handed her down but Alex shushed her. Fiona came next, wriggling and protesting at the dark and the cold.

'Good luck.' Kirsty shut the window and a moment later the light in the morning room was extinguished.

'Right,' I said, shifting Imogen in my arms. 'Alex, can you hold Fiona's hand?' I reached for her other hand and tucked it into my belt. 'Hang onto that and don't be frightened. Gran is down there. We'll be with her soon.'

I hadn't realized how wet the ground was. We began our descent, moving from tree to tree, slipping and sliding. Once I slipped and fell forward until the stub of a tree caught me sharply across the shins. I yelped with pain but cut it short. Mustn't frighten the children. Once more I remembered what Jamie had said that day, that the bank could be climbed. Now I was proving it.

When we were about halfway down I took out my torch and shone it downwards. Any moment I expected light to flare out behind me and hear Cesare's voice. The torch cut through the darkness but all I could see were shrubs and trees. I switched off the light and moved on, the child in my arms a dead weight. Imogen began to cry in earnest now and this time Alex did not shush her. I felt tears on my own cheeks. Were we in the right place? Had Nella given up and gone? I knew that was ridiculous but I was wet and tired and scared. A thorn caught the back of my hand and tore the skin.

'Hold on,' I said desperately and then suddenly someone was looming up in front of me, Imogen was being lifted from my arms and a firm hand was on my elbow.

'Have you got the others? Hang onto them, we're only feet away from the car.'

'Rick?'

I knew his voice and yet I couldn't believe it. 'What…?'

He interrupted me. 'No time for explanations. Let's get you somewhere warm and dry, then we'll talk.'

It was heaven to sink into someone being masterful. I followed him meekly down the rest of the bank and then Nella was hugging and kissing everyone and we were safe in the car and speeding towards safety.

25

I had expected to feel safe once we were in the car, and Rick's presence should have reinforced that feeling, but terror persisted as the car negotiated the narrow road and turned on to the bridge at Ballachulish. There were several miles of road ahead, mostly rock-lined with no way to escape. And then the glen: a vast, boulder-strewn canyon with no place to hide. After that the moor, the road twisting and winding but visible for miles. If Cesare realized what had happened and followed us, we would only have speed on our side.

As soon as we had crossed the moor and reached civilization once more, I started to relax. We were among habitations now. There were side-roads. No one, not even Cesare, could be quite sure which way we had taken.

At Crianlarich we branched right. I had expected we would take the left-hand route, straight on to Callander and then the border.

'Where are we going?' I asked.

Nella patted my knee. 'Don't worry, it's all arranged.'

Ahead of me, Rick was concentrating on his driving. Bob Gray was staring at the road ahead.

'What's arranged?' I persisted.

Mr Gray half-turned. 'We're going to Cameron House. It's a hotel on the banks of Loch Lomond – a big place. We've got a lodge there, in the grounds.'

'It's too near!'

I began to feel agitated again, but Nella hushed me.

'It's alright, Lexy. Rick has been very clever. He took the lodge three days ago, as soon as he got here. He's been there with children

– children of friends of his. If Cesare goes to the press, no one will link him with us because it will look as though the children were there before our children left Ard-na-Shiel.

'No!' It burst out of me. 'It's too near. He'll find us.'

Even as I said it I knew I was being paranoid, but they didn't know Cesare as I did. I was still afraid of his power to find us and exercise his legal right to repossess the children. Or, even worse, persuade me to give them back. And that last fear I could not confess to my mother.

Now Rick glanced over his shoulder. 'Relax, Lexy,' he said, turning back to the road. 'It's near for a purpose. He'll think we've made for the border. He won't think we're here, under his nose. As for other people, we'll be a family: mum, dad, kids and grandma.'

In the dark I sensed he was grinning. Nella, too.

'I hope you're right,' I said, and settled back in my seat. On my left I could see the loch now, glinting in the moonlight. And then we were turning into a wide gateway, skirting a large house, with the loch now a huge expanse of water illuminated by a full moon. A moment later we had passed through another gate and were in a cluster of timbered lodges.

'Here it is,' Rick said, threading the roads, and bringing the car to a standstill. It was a relief to get out and begin to lift the sleeping children from the car.

Rick hefted Alex out easily. The boy stirred and his eyelids twitched but then he went back to sleep. I handed Imogen to Nella and reached back into the car for Fiona.

'I'll come back for the bags,' Rick said and kicked the door shut with his heel.

The lodge was one of the last in the complex, set high above the others. The lower part of the building was stone, the roof slate and between them vast expanses of glass. The door opened into a hall with doors leading off to left and right.

'Two bedrooms down here,' Nella said, 'both en-suite. The sitting room's upstairs, so is the kitchen. And there's a pull-down bed up there if we need it.'

We mounted the stairs, the children awake now, and came into a huge room, handsomely furnished. Lamps burned here and there, and through the window the loch glinted.

'Sit down,' Rick said and moved to draw the curtains.

Nella was busy in the state-of-the-art kitchen.

'This can't be cheap,' I said, looking around.

'We'll worry about that tomorrow,' Rick said. He was unbuttoning Fiona's coat and smoothing her hair from her face. 'I think bed's in order for someone,' he said. But then Nella bustled in with coffee for Rick and me and chocolate for the children. They drank eagerly enough but they still looked tearful.

'Let's get to bed now,' I said to Alex. 'Tomorrow we'll talk. I'll explain everything then.' He looked at me impassively for a moment then he started to unzip his anorak.

'OK,' he said, but it was a grudging answer.

The downstairs bedrooms adjoined one another, one containing a double bed, the other two singles. 'You share with Alex,' Nella decided. 'I'll take the other two in with me.'

Her face was serene enough but her voice was edgy. Was she shirking the questioning that was bound to come when Alex awoke? He had been vociferous enough in the car before he slept. There were sure to be more questions when he woke. I was wondering where Rick would sleep when he came back with the bags. As if she read my mind Nella spoke.

'Rick has his own room in the hotel,' she said, 'so we've plenty of space.'

I sat down on the edge of the bed, wishing we had only one room so that we could all huddle together. I was feeling afraid again, but this time it was not a physical fear – it was a terrible realization of what we had done: kidnapped three children from their legal guardian. If Bob Gray didn't come up with some real evidence quickly, we were in trouble.

As soon as we had got the children to bed and returned to the sitting room, Rick reappeared, a bottle in one hand, three glasses slotted onto the fingers of the other. 'Brandy,' he said. He opened the bottle, then poured three large shots. He reached into the pockets of his coat and brought out some small cans of soda, but we all elected to drink the spirit neat.

'That's better,' he said when the glasses were drained and refilled.

I found myself avoiding his eye, yet wanting somehow to express my gratitude.

'We'd never have managed without you,' I said at last and felt my cheeks flush at the memory of our parting in Durham, when he had simply walked out on me – and, if I was honest, I had felt relieved.

It was Nella who spared my blushes, launching into a string of questions about what we should do next.

'Bob's gone off with the car,' Rick said. 'He'll leave it in Glasgow, then he's off to Italy again. I'm afraid it means we're marooned here for a while, but Bob and I thought the car might have been seen below Ard-na-Shiel and it's quite distinguishable. I'll hire another tomorrow.'

'What do you think Cesare will do?' Nella looked apprehensive as she asked the question.

I shook my head. 'I don't know. Are you scared he may find us?'

'I'm not afraid of facing him,' she said vehemently, 'but he's such a liar, Lexy.'

I nodded, but again I felt that impulse in me to defend him.

'What happens next?' Rick asked.

Nella lifted her hands, palms upward. 'I don't know. Hopefully, Bob will come up with something…'

'What?' I said desperately. 'Unless Cesare's a mass-murderer, what can Bob find that loses him his legal right as the children's guardian? And he's not a mass-murderer – even you must admit that.'

This time Nella's shake of the head was rueful. 'No. I don't think he's Bluebeard. When Sara met him I thought he was a sponger – a gigolo. I didn't like him and I wanted her to see through him, but not in my wildest nightmares did I think it would end the way it did. Has. Will. Because it's not over, Lexy.'

'You didn't see him with the children. I can't believe he'd harm the children.'

'Then why did you spirit them away?' She said it triumphantly and I was floored. 'You see?' She reached to pat my hand. 'It's not in you to hate, Lexy, so you make allowances. I trust my instinct and I know we had to do it.'

'She's right,' Rick said. He rose to his feet. 'I'm just going to stretch my legs. I won't be long. I think I'll stay here tonight, just in case. I'll use the bed upstairs.' He crossed to the door and let himself out into the night.

Nella reached for the brandy and poured two generous tots. 'It was good of Rick to help, wasn't it?'

But I wasn't going to enter into a conversation about Rick. Not now, when I felt in imminent danger of criminal charges. 'It was very good of him, but I don't want to talk about it now.'

'OK. But don't be a fool, Lexy. Don't lose the sugar for the sand. Anyway, you know Cesare better than I do. You must have some idea of what he'll do now?'

I took a sip from my glass, enjoying the way the spirit grabbed at my breath before I replied.

'I'm not sure. Part of me says he'll sit tight and wait for us to make contact. The other says he'll go to the police and ask them to uphold his rights.'

'If he does, there'll be a lot of publicity. Sara's death, the money, a picturesque location –'

'– and a soap star,' I finished for her. 'They'll find us ten minutes after the papers hit the street or they show your picture on telly.'

Nella was shaking her head and fishing in her handbag. 'Rick wanted us to get legal advice before we came up here but there wasn't time.' She produced a folded sheet of paper. 'He rang a friend in London – a solicitor – and he recommended these people.'

The paper gave a string of names and a Glasgow address.

'One of us can go tomorrow,' Nella said. 'Now we ought to get some sleep.'

We left the door open between the rooms when we put out the lights. The children were still sleeping.

'Good night,' Nella called softly.

I lay for a moment, wanting to reciprocate but also wanting to say something I knew she wouldn't like.

'Have you considered that we might be wrong?'

Her answer was sharp and instant.

'We're *not* wrong, Lexy. Go to sleep!'

I turned on my side and tried to still the jumble of my thoughts but I couldn't sleep until I heard the front door shut softly and knew that Rick was there, a few feet away from me.

26

I woke early and lay still so as not to disturb anyone, but I was thinking furiously. We had got the children out of danger for the moment, but it could only be a temporary measure. I considered wild alternatives like spiriting them out of the country – but how long would that last? Between television and the internet it was almost impossible to disappear nowadays. And what would we live on if I had to leave the business behind? Nella could work and support us – just. But jobs in soaps were always precarious. Besides, Alex had an inheritance. We couldn't just kiss Ard-na-Shiel goodbye on his behalf. And what if we were wrong? That thought nagged at me.

I got out of bed and crossed to the window. Across Loch Lomond I could see a yacht proud on the water and on the opposite shore a fairy-tale castle. In an opposite lodge, a woman was eating breakfast on her balcony, lifting her face to the sun in between bites of toast. There was a road map on the coffee table. I leafed through it till I found the relevant page and searched for the castle. I turned away. Picturesque as it was, I was not in the mood for fairy tales. Except...

I closed my eyes and remembered last night. The wet bank, slipping and sliding and then Rick's hand on my arm: strong, safe. As though I was coming home. I felt a sudden flood of something engulf me, warm and sweet and satisfying. But was it love? Or was it gratitude?

When at last I heard Nella whisper *Are you awake?* it came as a relief.

'Yes,' I said and padded across the floor to her bed.

She lifted her duvet. 'Get in,' she said. 'It's cold and we need to talk.'

Somehow it was comforting to feel the warmth of her bed as I lay on my back, watching the early morning light dapple the textured ceiling.

'I've been thinking,' Nella said. I contented myself with a grunt, anxious to hear what she had to say. 'We can't keep on running, Lexy. At the moment, all the weight of the law is on *his* side.' Even now she couldn't bring herself to use Cesare's name. 'That's what we've got to change, we've got to get the law on our side – and quickly, before he catches up with the children.'

'How long d'you think we've got?'

There was a pause before she replied. 'A week perhaps. If Rick took them off with him – no one will be looking for children with a man; he's the right age to be a father. If he takes them to some holiday place –'

'– and if Alex was willing to keep quiet,' I interrupted. 'He's not entirely convinced, Mum. He likes Cesare. You haven't really seen Cesare with the children since Sara died. If you had, you'd understand.'

Nella raised herself up in bed. She was shivering a little at the cold but her voice was determined. 'Leave him to me. You find a solicitor – talk to Rick. He was going to sound his people out about it. There's that man in Glasgow. Find the right man – or woman – to present our case. I'll see to the children.'

Two hours later I was stepping out of a cab in a street of tall, terraced houses and Rick was paying off the driver. He guided me up the stone steps to an imposing door covered in brass nameplates.

'Harry says he's the best in Scotland. It was Harry's children I borrowed to set up the scam. He says this man's a fighter. Tell him everything. I'll wait for you in the anteroom.'

For a moment I wanted to ask him to come in with me, but only for a moment. I still felt uneasy in his presence. We had a lot of fences to mend before I could be as relaxed with him as I had been in the old days. And I still had to analyze my feelings towards him.

'Thanks,' I said and watched him subside into a leather chair as I followed a secretary through yet another imposing door.

The solicitor was small – no more than five-foot-four, with unframed specs covering eyes that twinkled but were too shrewd to be warm.

'Do sit down,' he said. 'Coffee's on the way. But start now – at the beginning. I've been told the bare bones, but begin at the beginning and assume I know nothing.'

'Well,' I said, my mind suddenly blank. 'I suppose it began the day my sister, Sara, fell in love.'

I wanted to say 'the day I fell in love' but I had no right to air my own feelings. This was Sara's business and I must act only on her behalf.

So I talked through the account of Sara's marriage to Jamie, omitting any mention of my own part in it, his death and her remarriage, her depression and the tragedy of her end. All that was relatively easy because it was fact. When I got into the realms of conjecture and doubt, it was more difficult. At last, though, it was done and I sat feeling almost foolish at my tale of the snorkel and the boat and a doting stepfather trying to amuse his children. How could I expect this man to believe me?

I wasn't cheered when he blew out his breath and pursed his lips. 'On the face of it, he's impregnable, He's the legal guardian and he hasn't laid a finger on them. You, on the other hand, have stolen – *stolen* – the kids and broken the law.' I felt my heart sink until he spoke again. 'But,' he said. 'If I'd been in your shoes I'd've done the same thing.' He held up his hand. 'And please don't tell me where you or the children are. As an officer of the court I'd have to give that address if asked.'

He blew air again and fiddled with a pencil. 'You can't go to the police with your theories; they'd laugh in your face. And even if they brought a prosecution, the most you could hope for would be a "not proven".' He smiled. 'That's a weird thing you'll only find in Scotland. It says "we hae oor doots", but once it's in there, there can't be another trial. He'd be away free and clear and you'd never be able to get at him again. He could take the children God knows where on the money that's sloshing around this case; they could have the accident you envisage – in Florida, say. There'd be an investigation there, during which he'd no doubt fool everyone and he'd be the grieving stepfather who happens to own one of the largest estates in Scotland.'

'So you believe me, then?'

He nodded. 'Oh yes. I believe you. It's how we convince anyone else that troubles me.'

When he ushered me back to the anteroom, we had agreed to wait and see.

'If you can give the investigation time, this Mr Gray may come up with something. In my experience good people don't suddenly turn bad. If we dig into Giulini's background we'll find something else. In the meantime, there's still the adjourned inquest. The police have not closed the case, and we can demand further forensics if we have to. They'll still have all the samples. Now, off you go and take care of those kids and I'll try and keep the law off your back.'

27

Next day the sun shone as though it were making up for the rain of the day before. We dressed the children in the clothes their stand-ins had left behind and went walking. The grounds between the lodges were landscaped, with pools here and there. Each lodge had a balcony, and on some of them people sat sprawled in garden chairs, eyes closed against the sun. No one paid any attention as we moved through the lodges towards the loch.

'See?' Rick said as we reached the water's edge. 'Everyone thinks we've been here for days. If something hits the papers, it won't seem applicable at all to us.'

I nodded, but I was far from sanguine. Somewhere, perhaps even a mile away, Cesare would be planning his next move. What would it be? How could I decide what he would do when I couldn't make up my mind as to whether he was saint or sinner? But, the sun was warm on my face, the air was still and there was no sound except the lap of water and the occasional honk of a goose overhead. I closed my eyes and tried to relax. When I opened them Rick was regarding me anxiously.

'Alright?' he asked. I nodded but I was feeling far from alright. All morning I had detected tension in Alex. Now it burst forth.

'Where are we going?' he demanded suddenly. 'I want to go home!' I saw Fiona's mouth opening to agree but before she could speak I moved in. 'I need to talk to you,' I said shepherding Alex away from the others. 'Sit down,' I said, as I lowered myself to the grass. After a moment he sat but he did it grudgingly. I put out a hand and touched his hand and to my relief he didn't flinch. There was a look of his father about him now and I felt a lump in my throat.

'Look,' I said. 'I need you to help me, so I'm going to be absolutely honest with you. After that, it's up to you. If you want to go straight back to Ard-na-Shiel, I'll take you, but please listen to me first.'

There was a long moment and then he spoke. 'Go on, then.'

I took a deep breath and launched into my plea.

'When your mother died there was something odd, something that didn't tie up. You knew that, didn't you?'

'She was unhappy,' he said reluctantly.

'She was unhappy and she was ill. She grew very fat, she was confused; she wasn't the person she had always been.'

'That was because my daddy died.'

'Yes. That was the start of the trouble. But then she went to Italy and met Cesare and for a while she was happy again, wasn't she?' He nodded and I ploughed on. 'They found some pills in her room – pills that would have made her the way she was. She was a doctor, Alex. She'd never have taken those pills herself because she'd have known they were harmful.'

His brow furrowed. 'So someone gave them to her?'

'I don't know. Someone might have.'

Should I tell him about the money and the snorkel? Should I even mention Cesare? Before I could decide he spoke.

'You don't think Cesare would hurt her? You like him – he made you laugh. I saw him. I saw *you*.' His voice rose as he spoke. He was accusing me now and there were tears of rage in his eyes.

'Yes, I do like him – I like him a lot. But I have to be sure, Alex. For your sake, and especially for Fiona and Imogen. You're quite a big boy now, but Imogen is just a baby. I have to make sure that what happened to Mummy was an accident. Once I do, I promise you, I'll take you back to Ard-na-Shiel – it's where you belong. But for now, please, I need you to help me.'

For a long moment I thought he was going to refuse, and then he said, 'How long will it take?'

'A few days. A week – a week at most.'

'And then we go home?'

'And then we go home,' I said, suddenly wishing with all my heart that that's how it would be: a clean bill for Cesare and a return to Ard-na-Shiel. We walked along the edge of the loch then, the girls running ahead, Alex following behind.

'What did you say to him?' Rick asked.

I shook my head. 'What *could* I say? I told him I had reasons to be afraid for the girls – and for him, but especially for Fiona and Imogen.' Fiona looked more like Sara every day, but she did not have Sara's quiet determination. Imogen was more confident. 'I said we'd soon know if I was right or not and once we did he could go back to Ard-na-Shiel.'

Rick grinned admiringly. 'Not bad – but it will only hold him for so long. He's a feisty little lad and he likes his stepfather – his father, as he's legally adopted.' He paused and turned towards me. 'You don't suppose…?'

It was my turn to smile now. 'That we could be wrong? Of course we could. In a way, I hope we are. But what if we're not?'

We walked on in silence for a moment, and then Rick spoke again. 'I think you have to talk to your mother. I'll take the kids into Glasgow. We'll go to a McDonald's and a movie. There's sure to be a Disney on somewhere. You talk to Nella and plan the next move.'

'Is Glasgow safe?' I sounded as scared as I felt, but he gave my arm a consoling pat.

'Probably as safe as anywhere. And we'll be in darkness most of the time.' He walked on then to round up the children, leaving me feeling quite strange. We had been lovers once – lately, although it seemed a lifetime away. And now he was patting my arm as though I were a maiden aunt. And somehow I didn't like that. The sun was glinting on his fair head and he looked lithe and slim in his sweater and jeans. But this was no time for analyzing my emotions. Instead, I hurried on ahead to tell Nella the plan. Ten minutes later we closed the car doors and watched it glide off.

'Come on,' Nella said as the tail-lights disappeared. 'Let's find somewhere to eat.'

'Well?' she asked, when we were seated in the hotel's roomy restaurant. 'Who's going to beard the lion in his den? We can't wait forever for him to make a move. We need to give him a push.'

I didn't smile. How could I, when all I could remember were the tense little faces as Rick drove the children away?

'I'll do it,' I said at last. 'But what exactly am I going to say?'

We were onto our pudding before a plan emerged. Tonight I would telephone Cesare and admit to taking the children.

'Find out if he's notified the police,' Nella said. 'For all we know there could be wanted posters out by now.'

Ever since we had got the children away from Ard-na-Shiel, rendering them safe in her eyes, my mother had been half-joking. She was grinning now, but I couldn't feel any sense of relief. In fact, my unease was increasing. With every second that passed, the evidence against Cesare seemed more flimsy, our actions in kidnapping the children more reprehensible.

'And if he has gone to the police? What then?'

Suddenly Nella was deadly serious. 'Then we'll know he means business,' she said.

'Or that he's justifiably annoyed because we're wrong about him?' I offered.

Nella shook her head sorrowfully. 'Oh, Lexy – are you the most naïve young woman in Britain or is he the cleverest of schemers ever? One of those is true.'

I gave up then and went back to picking half-heartedly at my excellent crème brûlée.

28

The following morning I sat behind the wheel of a hired Ford Mondeo and moved over the bleakness of Rannoch Moor.

I had agonized over whether I should ring in advance and decided against it. As the car rattled over the bridge at Ballachulish, a tiny hope sprang up in my head: that Cesare would not be there, that I need not face him and could turn the car round and speed back to Glasgow safely.

But he was there, standing in the gloom of the great hall for all the world as though he had been expecting me. His eyes flickered to the empty doorway behind me.

'Where are the children?'

No *Hello Lexy.* Not even *Where the hell have you been?*

I tried to keep my voice steady as I walked towards him.

'They're safe. I'm not going to tell you where.'

I was past him now and heading for the morning room, the place that had always seemed the least intimidating room in the house.

Once inside I crossed to the window and then turned to face him. There was sun streaming through the window and when he moved into its radiance I saw that there were lines of fatigue on his face and dark shadows beneath his eyes. Once again I felt a surge of sympathy for him, a need to move towards him, to feel his arms go around me, to feel safe once more.

'We have to talk,' I said to stop myself doing anything so foolish.

'Talk then. Explain, Lexy. Tell me why you left this house like a thief – no: not *like* a thief, *as* a thief. You took my children, Lexy. And they are *my* children: legally and morally. In your heart you know that. Now, tell me why you did it and then tell me when you're going to bring them back. And ...' His voice almost broke. 'And where are they?' What have you told them? The little one will be confused…'

'They're OK. They're with –' I was about to say 'with Rick' when I bit back the words '– with my mother.'

His 'Hah!' was loud and theatrical. 'Your *mother?* The saintly Nella! I might have known she'd be part of this, Why do you listen to her, *cara*?' He was moving towards me, hands out-stretched, and I felt rooted to the spot. 'You know she's always hated me, Lexy. From the beginning…'

He was close to me now, one hand reaching up to touch my cheek, the other encircling my waist. I wanted to move but it was beyond me. 'Oh, Lexy, Lexy…' His breath was warm on my brow and as I felt my legs give way his arm tightened until I was held against his body. 'Does she think the children have anything to fear from me? You know that isn't true. I could have gone to the police, I could have had you brought back here, but I didn't. I *trusted* you, Lexy. I knew you would come to me. Oh, Lexy. Little Lexy.'

I looked up into his eyes, the dark pupils clouded now with tears. 'Please,' he said. 'You know what's between us. You've always known – from the beginning. I couldn't say it. Sara needed me. But in my heart I knew it was *you*, Lexy. And now it can be, *serenissima.* We can be together and you will be a mother to the children. I don't want any of this.' His hand took in the room and the sunlit expanse beyond the window. 'This is for Alex. You and I, we will have our own place.'

I closed my eyes as his mouth came down on mine, warm and sweet, his tongue flickering lightly against my lips until they parted and gave entry.

We stayed like that for a long time while thoughts chased through my head. How would I convince Nella and would the children take to me? I opened my eyes after a while and began to withdraw but his mouth sought mine even more fiercely. I turned my head slightly in an effort to break free and at once he let me go.

'I'm sorry,' I said, but I was not sure why I was apologizing.

'No!' He lifted a hand. 'No. It should be me who apologizes. That was foolishness. I'll get you a drink and we'll talk.'

We carried our glasses through to the morning room and sat facing one another in the deep armchairs. 'Now,' he said. 'Tell me why you took the children away.'

I put down my glass, noticing the tremor in my hand as I did so. 'Because I think you might have murdered Sara. Or, at least contributed to her death.' I was proud that my voice didn't shake.

His reply was equally measured. 'Why do you think that? Why, after four happy years, would I ruin everything? You must have some evidence to accuse me.'

'The steroids.' I sounded almost triumphant as I flung the words at him. 'Sara would *never* have touched steroids. She was a doctor, she knew their effects unless they were properly managed.'

'Oh, Lexy, Lexy. I so much wanted you not to know all this.'

He was on his feet now, moving towards the door to the hall. He vanished for a second and I heard him call out. When he turned back into the room, the woman Belsy was behind him. He came back to his seat. She hesitated, just inside the room.

'Belsy,' he said. 'Will you tell my sister-in-law your true occupation?'

She turned to me. 'I'm a psychiatric nurse. Twenty years in Edinburgh hospitals, two years at Barlinnie Prison.'

Cesare was nodding agreement. I said nothing but my mind raced.

'Now tell us why you came here.'

'To look after your wife.' It was Belsy who looked puzzled now, as though she was wondering why he was asking what he already knew.

'Why?' Cesare said.

She hesitated but only for a moment. 'Because she was behaving oddly – substance abuse mostly. You were worried for your wife. And for the children.'

Cesare was looking at me. 'So, Lexy, if I had wanted to murder my wife, would I have involved a witness to move into my home? A witness who was qualified, who would know what I was doing? Does that not defy belief?'

My mouth was dry and I licked my lips. 'You looked after Sara?'

Belsy was nodding. 'After a fashion. She thought I was a servant – a mother's help. I couldn't dog her footsteps; I did what I could. In the end, though, she had the tablets. We hunted and sometimes we found them, but she always had more.'

'Was she suicidal?'

The woman's eyes narrowed. 'Maybe. Hard to say. I think she just over-balanced and fell. She was often unsteady like that.'

It was time to play my trump card. 'What about your sister?' I said. 'Mary Logan?'

The woman looked back at me impassively. 'I don't have a sister. I did once but her name was Sadie. She died in Ardgour a long time ago.'

I turned to Cesare. 'But they told me her sister was the woman in Glasgow – the woman at the fire.'

He shook his head. 'They lied, Lexy. Or they got it wrong.'

I turned back to Belsy. 'What was your maiden name?'

'McKay,' she said, without a second's hesitation. 'I was born Isabel McKay and I married Willie Leckie. I'm no Logan and anyone who says I am has got it wrong.'

'Have you heard enough?' Cesare sounded angry now.

I nodded. 'Yes.' I turned to Belsy. 'Thank you.'

She shrugged. 'It's nothing. Would you like some coffee now?'

'Yes, thank you,' I said, and she left the room.

I must have closed my eyes for suddenly his arms were around me and I sank into them. When I opened my eyes Cesare had moved his head back and was regarding me quizzically.

'That's better,' he said. 'That's how it should be between us.'

And his eyes were kind. Kind and soft and utterly, utterly honest! I knew then that he was innocent and I felt ashamed.

'Yes,' I said. 'That's how it should be between us.'

I put up my hand to touch his cheek. He caught it and turned it, so that he could press his lips into my palm. I smiled.

'Now I've got to convince Nella. It won't be easy but I'll do it. The children are dying to come back.'

We laughed then, throwing back his head. 'Oh, Lexy. We will be so happy, the five of us.' I kissed him then, opening my mouth to his tongue, feeling again the clutching at my breath that had told me I was in love. I felt tears of joy prick my eyes as he murmured in my ear, words soft and lilting in that wonderful accent. I laid my cheek against the lapel of his jacket and felt happiness flood over me at the sound of his voice.

'Oh *cara, cara,*' he said. 'How very much I love you, little sister.'

And then I saw his eyes. They were reflected in the mirror above the mantel and back to the mirror on a stand that stood on the sideboard. Sara had put it there to catch the light from the window and illuminate a dark corner. It was a few feet away from me and in it I could see the back of my own head, Cesare's shoulder showing above. And I could see his face. His cold, immobile face as his lips parroted words of passion. But it was his eyes that held me.

Eyes hard as stones gazing into some unknown distance.

The cold eyes of a murderer.

Belsy came back with the coffee then, setting it on the side table, allowing me to move away and pull myself together. How I got through the ritual of the coffee-drinking, I will never know, but I did. And with each sip my resolve hardened. I must get out of Ard-na-Shiel, and to do that I would have to lie. There was no one to turn to. Belsy was his creature. I could see it now in the way she looked at him, just as the woman in the Italian villa had looked at him. Both of them spellbound as I had been.

'Well,' I said at last, setting down my cup. 'I'm going to hurry now. The sooner the children are back, the better.'

We walked together across the hall and out into the sunlight. As I felt it light upon my face I quelled the impulse to run. Mustn't spoil things now.

'So,' he said, when we reached the car. 'How long will it take you to get back here? Where are the children?'

'In Edinburgh,' I said. If I said Glasgow he might offer to come with me. 'They're with friends of Nella's. I'll go there now.'

I looked at my watch. 'We can be back here by bedtime.'

'Should I come with you, Lexy? In case there's trouble?'

I had to bite my tongue not to sound too anxious. 'No. Better for me just to spirit them away. It'll be alright.'

I reached up then and kissed him on the mouth, a Judas kiss if ever there was one, but necessary. And then I was in the car and gunning the engine and gravel was spitting under the wheels as I headed towards the drive and safety.

I saw him in the rearview mirror, lifting his hand in salute, smiling. Always smiling.

'Fool,' I said aloud, but I was upbraiding myself, not him.

I had to keep brushing tears from my eyes in order to see the road, but they were tears of rage. So many things were racing through my mind. How could I have been so wrong? Why had I not believed my mother? What would we do about Cesare Giulini and how would we get him out of Ard-na-Shiel? Where could we take the children in the meantime? If necessary, to the other side of the world, because now I knew he *would* harm them, given the chance. Knew, too, that although I had never seriously contemplated having children of my own, I now loved my sister's children with all my heart.

There were tears of humiliation, too. What a fool I'd been all along! Where Nella had known, had seen through him, I had gone on hoping, wanting him to be – to be – *what?* To be Jamie! To be the subject of the adolescent crush that I had transferred from one man who was worthy of it to one who was not!

'Fool,' I said again and pressed down on the accelerator.

29

This wasn't the time for self-flagellation, it was the time for clear thought. As I crossed the moor, I glanced continually into the rearview mirror. I thought Cesare had believed me, but he was a master of deception. What if he hadn't? If my bluff had only been a match for his? Once or twice I saw the sun glint on something – a windscreen, perhaps – but if it was a vehicle from Ard-na-Shiel, it was keeping well behind. Once I reached civilization I slowed and then I could see that it was a small car and either blue or grey – certainly not a car I had ever seen Cesare drive. Perhaps it was some innocent driver on his way down from Fort William. Only one way to find out. I turned into the next petrol station and took my time buying petrol and a newspaper. I glanced at the road as often as I could but the car could have passed while I was paying. If it was not Cesare or someone working for him, it would be well ahead of me now.

I moved back onto the road and recommenced my journey. I had travelled about a mile when I glimpsed the blue car behind me. So, I was being followed. That meant I couldn't turn onto the A-82 at Crianlarich and show that my destination was Glasgow. I drove on through Crianlarich and then through Lochearnhead and Callander. The signs showed Doune and Dunblane ahead. There was an antiques centre at Doune, just off the road, and if I remembered correctly some sharp bends just before it. I put my foot down to widen the distance between me and the blue car and managed to lose it for a few minutes. As the Antiques Centre sign came up, I swung the wheel hard left and entered its access road. A few seconds later I was safe in its car park and outside the car, looking back at the road. Relief washed over me as the blue car sped past. Now it would never know that I would turn right for Glasgow instead of keeping on for Edinburgh, but I would have to wait for a while in case they realized I had eluded them and doubled back.

Ordinarily I would have adored an hour in the Antiques Centre. Case after case of gems: Doulton, Copeland, Minton, Spode... the names tripped through my mind like water normally, but today it was hard to concentrate on them. I gazed at gold and silver, fingered fabrics, came alive slightly at the sight of a Jumeau with the original clothes and then slipped away to the coffee shop. I ordered coffee and carrot cake and settled in a window, all the while half-expecting to see a small blue car nose into the car park but after half an hour there was no sign. I rose to my feet, paid my bill and took to the road again, but not before I had studied the map and found a way across country. The sooner I was off the main road, the better.

It was a relief when I reached the turn-off to Gargunnock and could take the A-811 for Glasgow.

As I drove I kept seeing Cesare's face, mouth inflexible, eyes like flint, reflected in the mirror. I could see it all now. He had tried to drive Sara to suicide, putting steroids in her food, destroying her beauty, probably plying her with drink. But she had found out, or at least suspected. So she had made that call to me and sealed her fate. He had to act before I got to Ard-na-Shiel. So he had killed her, or engineered her death in some way. And then he had driven away from the house, hidden in Glencoe for all I knew, and let me drive past him with McGregor. Easy then to turn up knowing he had an alibi ready to be used at the optimum moment – the moment when he had a gullible fool like me to 'uncover' it.

By the time I had skirted Glasgow on the north and reached Loch Lomond I was tired in mind and body, but Cameron House was almost in sight. I had missed the children. And Rick. It came as quite a shock, but I had missed him. I thought of the evening ahead and the quiet drink we could have and that thought was pleasing.

The lodge was strangely quiet and I felt panic rise. The living room was empty and so was the adjoining room. I called out.

'Ma, where are they?'

She appeared from the kitchen.

'They're OK. Calm down, darling. They've gone to get ice-cream.' I was opening my mouth to scream at her when she added. 'Rick's with them. So is Bob. And they're OK.' She moved to the drawers where the brandy stood and poured out a large dram.

I waved the glass away. 'We've got to get them back, now! Where are they? How could you let them out of here...?'

'Be quiet!' Her words rang out as she planted the glass in front of me. 'Now drink that and get your breath back. The kids are fine and I've got news for you. But I'm going to leave it to Bob to tell you.'

'Tell me now,' I said but she shook her head.

'I promised Bob he could do it. One thing I can tell you though. Isabel Logan was a pharmacist's assistant before she entered the Prison Service.'

'So that's how she knew about drugs?'

Again she nodded. 'Yes. But that's not important now. Not now there's this other thing.'

If Bob Gray and Rick hadn't appeared at the door just then I think I might have exploded. Nella ushered the children to the other room and closed the door.

'Tell her,' she said. 'Tell her before she does herself an injury.'

I subsided onto a chair and raised the glass to my lips. The whisky was pungent and brought tears to my eyes but I downed it anyway.

'Well,' Bob said. 'To put it simply, we've got our friend on toast.' He reached into his pocket and produced a folded paper. 'This' he said,' is a certified copy of a marriage between Cesare Michael Giulini and Luisa Maria Avolio, dated...' he paused for effect, '...August 12, 1989.'

They were both looking at me expectantly and I knew that what he had said was important.

'So he was married before,' I said slowly.

'Not *before*, Lexy darling.' Nella's voice was triumphant. 'Not before. *Then*. And if he was *already* married, you silly girl...'

'...he wasn't married to Sara,' I said slowly.

'Give that girl a prize,' Bob said. 'He was *never* married, therefore he has no right to anything under the terms of Sara's will, which specifically states 'my husband' and he inherits nothing in the event of the children's deaths. Which means he's no threat to them because there's no profit in it for him.'

'What about the adoption?' I said. 'Won't that still stand?'

'No.' Nella and Bob spoke together. 'We've checked that. Everything he said to procure the adoption was false. No judge in the land would declare it valid. Nor, I think, would he go to court.'

'So we have nothing to fear,' Nella continued. 'I still hope we can get him for the undoubted murder of my daughter, but even if we can't, we'll see him in hell before he gets anything else.'

'What about his wife?' But even as I asked I knew the answer. I had sensed it that day in the darkness of the villa in the Via Furnese. 'She was older than he was, wasn't she?'

Bob nodded. 'She was a widow with a small fortune – or what amounted to a fortune to a boy from Ruspoli. He married her and they moved to Rome. He was never faithful, but she held on: no divorce for a good Catholic. She even went to work as a house-keeper to support his lifestyle. She died two years ago,' again he paused for added drama, 'while he was on holiday in Italy. It was put down as an accident, but that would bear examination if we needed more ammunition. All we have to do now is show him this and tell him to scarper.'

'So that's why he didn't go to the police,' I said slowly. 'He couldn't afford the publicity.'

And then Nella's arms were round me and we were both crying with relief until the door opened and three small faces looked through.

'Come here,' I said, and held out my arms.

30

After the children had gone to bed, we talked.

'So Belsy was part of it,' I said, remembering the lovesick look on that otherwise Bastille face.

Bob nodded. 'How they teamed up, we'll never know but they did. She's his right-hand woman. She moved in a few months before Sara died. Why, we don't know. But if she didn't assist him, why was she so conspicuously absent during the inquest?'

Rick had been silent up to now. Suddenly he rose to his feet and looked at his watch. 'You must be hungry, Lexy. We could go over to the hotel. The food is good there.'

I was so tired I would have said no, but Nella was in like a flash and before I knew it she was ushering us out of the door.

'Go and celebrate,' she called after us.

We both laughed, but I could sense that Rick was not in the mood for celebration and neither was I. There was still too much uncharted water ahead.

One thing was sure, though: never again would I be swayed by Cesare Giulini. I knew him now for what he was. And other things were becoming clear. I glanced sideways at Rick. He was handsome, now, no longer a boy as he had been that New Year's Eve of 1991. I felt a sudden rush of tenderness for him and basked in the way he blagged us a table in the crowded restaurant and navigated his way through the wine list.

We ate osso bucco and drank a fine Merlot as the sky darkened and more lights sprang up on the opposite shore, and then he ordered coffee and asked for the bill. I hadn't expected the meal to end so soon, but it suited me. Tonight, when the lodge was asleep,

I would come to him and tell him what a fool I'd been. I made polite conversation as we poured coffee and then the waiter laid the tab discreetly on the table. Rick smiled his thanks, but left it lying there. Instead, he reached for my hand.

Three months ago I would have panicked at such an intimate gesture in a public place. Now it was welcome. If he asked me to marry him – though who could blame him if he didn't ask again after two refusals? – I would ask for time to think. I knew now that something was happening inside me: ice was melting. It was a strange feeling but not unwelcome.

Before he could speak, though, guilt overwhelmed me. How convenient that I was falling in love with the man who had bankrolled the rescue operation. A sense of shame overcame me. Rick deserved better than that.

'Rick,' I said, leaving my hand under his. 'I want to say thank you. Nella told me about you paying for the lodge – and everything else, for all I know. And you've taken time off to come here… We couldn't have done it without you.'

He squeezed my hand. 'Think nothing of it, Lexy. Take it as a parting gift.'

He must have seen the shock I felt written on my face. 'I'm leaving tonight. As you said, I took time off. And we were never going to get anywhere, were we? I have to be in London tomorrow. We start a European tour next month.' He smiled now. 'Don't look so woebegone. I'll write.' He was rising to his feet, laying notes on the bill. 'Do you mind if I leave you to finish your coffee? There's a car picking me up at ten.'

In all the ups and downs of my life, I had tried to keep my dignity. Only once had it deserted me, that moment in the barn when I had expressed my love for Jamie – my foolish, schoolgirl love. Now, though, I had never needed dignity more. I stood up and reached to kiss his cheek.

'Off you go. We'll talk – I'll write. And I *meant* that thank-you.'

He gripped my arms for a moment, looking into my upturned face. 'See you, Lexy. One of these New Year's Eves in Trafalgar Square?'

I nodded. 'Second lion on the right. It's a date.'

I went on smiling, knowing he would turn at the door. He lifted a hand in a last salute and I smiled ever more brightly. Only when he was gone could I sit down and let the tears rain unchecked down my burning cheeks.

EPILOGUE
December 1999

It is winter now. Snow caps Creag Ghorm and the peaks that ring Ballachulish. Alex sits beside me in the passenger seat, his face intent, the urn containing his mother's ashes on his knee. It is a macabre burden, but he carries it bravely, as befits the master of Ard-na-Shiel. Behind me in the back seat the girls sit either side of their grandmother, their childish chatter stilled today, for we have a mission. I drive across the bridge, feeling the familiar rumble, and turn in at the churchyard where Jamie has waited for his love for four long years. I hold Fiona's hand, Nella walks with Imogen, Alex leads as befits the man of the family. A soft wind rustles the winter grass, the pink aubrietia is in hiding until summer comes.

The wind catches at Alex's hair and he wipes a strand from his eyes with an impatient hand. He has a job to do.

We stand, the five of us, as the ashes of the good sister drift down onto the hard earth of her husband's grave. And I remember the girl whose warm bed comforted my childhood and the woman I loved too little until it was too late.

That is a habit of mine, leaving things until it is too late.

But I know now that she was proud of me and fond enough to chart my progress in the album I will treasure all my life. I have paid my debt to Sara now. Her children are safe and so is she, reunited with Jamie, who was never mine, except for one golden moment when a heron swooped and bees buzzed in the heather. Cesare Giulini is gone from Ard-na-Shiel, a free man still, but destined for destruction, I do believe.

The ashes lie powdery white on the dark earth. Soon winter rain will wash them down into the soil, nearer to her true love.

Alex is looking to me now, seeking reassurance. I nod and mouth 'Well done.' He doesn't want a fuss in front of the girls, or so he vowed last night in his almost grown-up way.

Goodbye, sweet Sara, I say but only inside my head.

'It's cold.' Nella is turning for the car. 'It'll soon be Christmas.'

I smile and nod and my heart lifts. After Christmas comes New Year – a special New Year this time. A new millennium, the year 2000. Trafalgar Square will see a crowd gone mad with excitement.

And I will be there, too, waiting by the second lion on the right.

Also available from Little Books:
Denise Robertson's
The Beloved People trilogy

In the Durham mining village of Belgate, the legacy of World War I has far-reaching consequences for rich and poor, socialist and aristocrat, Jew and gentile alike.

Howard Brenton, heir to the colliery, back from the trenches with a social conscience, but robbed of the confidence to implement it...
Diana, his beautiful, aristocratic wife, afraid of her dour new world and fatally drawn to the gaiety of jazz-age London...
Miner Frank Maguire and his bitter wife Anne, fired by union fervour as they struggle to survive the slump...
Esther Gulliver, to whom kindly Emmanuel Lansky shows new roads to prosperity beyond the pit...

Linked by place, chance and time, the people of Belgate grapple with the personal and general costs of war, coal and childbirth. And in the mid-1930s, they face together a new and terrifying crisis in Europe.

The story continues in
Strength for the Morning and *Towards Jerusalem.*

'An intelligent, evocative saga...written with a strong historical sense and a fine eye for authenticity, this is big-hearted stuff in the best style'
Sunday Telegraph